ACCLAIM FOR DANIEL KALLA'S NOVELS

"*Rage Therapy* is both an engrossing exploration of a savage crime and a powerful study of obsession, violence, and guilt. Dan Kalla's expert storytelling propels us through a maze of mirrors to a shattering conclusion. A great read!"

—Michael Prescott, *New York Times* bestselling author of *Dangerous Games*

"Michael Crichton ought to be looking over his shoulder. He has some serious competition in Kalla."

—*The Chronicle-Herald*

"*Resistance* will take you on a roller-coaster ride you'll never forget. The science is fascinating, and the suspense nail-biting. Watch out, Robin Cook. A new master of the medical thriller has arrived."

—Gayle Lynds, *New York Times* bestselling author of *The Last Spymaster*

"Daniel Kalla expertly weaves real science and medicine into a fast-paced, nightmarish thriller—a thriller all the more frightening because it could really happen."

—Tess Gerritsen, *New York Times* bestselling author of *Body Double,* on *Pandemic*

"*Pandemic* is a totally compelling novel, one of those rare thrillers that lays out a scenario that is not only possible, but terrifyingly probable."

—Douglas Preston, *New York Times* bestselling author of *The Codex*

"*Pandemic* is very much in the Michael Crichton school of cutting-edge, scientifically rooted thrillers. *Pandemic* is an absorbing, compulsive thriller, the sort of book you could stay up too late reading. A solid thriller."

—*Vancouver Sun*

"Kalla's ripped-from-the-headlines plot and confident command of both language and medicine make this sobering book a pleasure." —*Publishers Weekly* on *Pandemic*

Forge Books by Daniel Kalla

Pandemic
Rage Therapy
Resistance
Blood Lies*

*Forthcoming

RAGE THERAPY

DANIEL KALLA

A TOM DOHERTY ASSOCIATES BOOK
NEW YORK

This is a work of fiction. All of the characters, organizations, and events portrayed in this novel are either products of the author's imagination or are used fictitiously.

RAGE THERAPY

Copyright © 2006 by Daniel Kalla

All rights reserved, including the right to reproduce this book, or portions thereof, in any form.

A Forge Book
Published by Tom Doherty Associates, LLC
175 Fifth Avenue
New York, NY 10010

www.tor-forge.com

Forge® is a registered trademark of Tom Doherty Associates, LLC.

ISBN-13: 978-0-765-35083-1
ISBN-10: 0-765-35083-1

First Edition: October 2006
First Mass Market Edition: May 2007

Printed in the United States of America

0 9 8 7 6 5 4 3 2 1

For my wonderful girls . . .
Chelsea, Ashley, and Cheryl

ACKNOWLEDGMENTS

I wouldn't have a book in which to write my acknowledgments if not for my friends and family who have supported me from the outset of this novel-writing long shot. There are too many people to list, but I have to mention a few by name, including Duncan Miller, Geoff Lyster, Lisa and Rob King, Dave Allard, Dee Dee and Kirk Hollohan, Brooke Wade, Alec and Theresa Walton, Alisa Weyman, and Michael McKinley.

My deepest thanks go to Kit Schindell, a freelance editor and friend, who combs all my manuscripts chapter by chapter and draft by draft, ensuring I get the absolute most out of the stories. I also want to acknowledge Beverly Martin (of Agentresearch.com) and Sandra E. Haven for their editorial feedback.

Thanks to Susan Crawford for bringing this manuscript to Tor Books, a publisher that consistently exceeds my expectations. I can't imagine more involved and supportive publishers than Tom Doherty and Linda Quinton. I also want to acknowledge Tom Espenchied for his guidance, Seth Lerner for his cover designs, John Morrone for his copyediting brilliance, and Paul Stevens for keeping it all together. And of course, a very special thanks goes to my awesome editor, Natalia Aponte—a wonderful collaborator, champion, and friend.

Finally, unlike the protagonists in this novel, I am blessed with a stable and wonderful family who are always there for me. My brothers, Tony and Tim, and of course Mom and

Dad have been huge influences on my life. And my two amazing daughters, Chelsea and Ashley, and my wife, Cheryl, remind me there is something even more important in life than writing.

RAGE THERAPY

1

WHY PSYCHIATRY?"

I've heard the same question posed in different forms by friends, family, and even complete strangers. As often as not, implicit in their tone is the insinuation that something must be a little off-kilter in my own head for me to have wound up as a psychiatrist. I used to shrug off the suggestion with varying degrees of politeness. But standing under the shower's lukewarm spray, I realized I wasn't sure anymore. My psychological closets were full to the point of bursting. And the same was true of more than a few of my colleagues.

The ringing phone jolted me from my introspection. I considered ignoring it but then it occurred to me that I'd been in the shower for more than half an hour. Even my obsessive-compulsive patients would have to concede that by now I was clean. So I stepped out of the stall and slid out of the bathroom.

I reached the phone on its fifth ring—one too late. I waited until the voicemail light flashed on my phone and then I played back the message. "Doc, it's Dev," said Homicide Sergeant Ethan Devonshire in his unmistakable low-pitched Southern drawl. "Not the best way to tell you this, but Stanley Kolberg was found dead in his office. He was shot in the neck, and uh . . ." He left the word-picture unfinished. "Anyway, we're at the scene now. We could use your input. Can you call me on my cell as soon as you get this?" He paused. "Sorry."

Still damp, I sat on the edge of my bed, forgetting my towel. Conflicting thoughts and emotions swam in my head, but I forced myself to focus on the prospect of joining Dev at Stanley's office—an office I'd once shared with the victim. It made no sense for me to become professionally involved in his murder investigation. But call it shock, or maybe just morbid curiosity, I wanted to go to the crime scene. I needed to see what fate worse than a bullet to the neck had befallen Stanley and stopped Dev's description in mid-sentence.

I rose from the bed and wandered over to my dresser. When I reached for the top drawer, the photo on top caught my eye. I picked up the five-by-seven frame. Stanley had taken the action shot of Loren and me on the thirty-foot sailboat. Life jackets on, we had struggled to keep straight faces and look nautical, but we ended up looking just goofy. And happy. I looked from the photograph to the mirror in front of me. Still no gray hairs, and the lines had deepened only slightly at the corners of my mouth and eyes. But the mirror didn't tell the whole story. I felt as if I'd aged a lifetime in the five years since Stanley had snapped the photo. If Lor were still alive, I doubt she would have aged a day in the interim. Then again, maybe I wouldn't have either. God, I missed her.

After positioning the frame back in its spot, I threw on a pair of khaki trousers and a shirt that dampened on contact, not necessarily from the shower, and headed out the door to my garage. I climbed into my car and said my little prayer. It worked. The engine of the silver 1988 Honda Accord coughed a few times, sputtered, and finally lapsed into its familiar unhealthy rumble. Tomorrow I'm going to replace this piece of crap, I promised myself. I'd made that promise so often it was becoming a mantra.

I pulled into the underground parking lot of my old office building, which still had no gate despite multiple complaints from the tenants. Using the key I hadn't bothered returning when I quit the practice, I let myself in through the basement door. More than a few drug addicts also had let themselves in through the same door with the aid of a crowbar. Medical buildings and their promised cache of drugs and syringes draw junkies like pollen attracts bees; thus the complaints.

Even before the elevator doors opened on to the third floor, I could hear the commotion emanating from Stanley's office. I walked out into the sterile, fluorescent-lit hallway, passing a dental office and two family practices. At the end of the corridor, a door was ajar. The two shingles on the door read: STANLEY KOLBERG, M.D. and CALVIN NICHOL, M.D. Beneath them the paint was faded in a shape and size matching the other two placards. That was where my own shingle, JOEL ASHMAN, M.D., used to hang.

I pushed the door open and walked into the waiting room where I saw the first of the "bunny men." Crime-scene investigators from Seattle's Medical Examiner's Office wear white overalls, gloves, and foot covers to all crime scenes, but it is their white hats, worn with goggles and sometimes earphones, that make them look like mutant rabbits.

I watched the bunny men scour the walls and floors, using their infrared and violet-blues, and God-knows-what other equipment. To me, it looked like an Easter egg hunt gone awry. But I knew what the CSI guys were looking for—residues, fibers, and, most of all, a blood corpuscle or hair follicle or single sperm cell or any tantalizing scrap of DNA that under a microscope might divulge a social security number or zip code. They didn't acknowledge me, but I wasn't surprised; I'd long ago decided that the bunny men didn't have much time for bodies above room temperature.

Following the din, I rounded the corner and almost slammed into Dev coming the other way. Ethan Devonshire—"Dev" to everyone but his wife—was tall with broad shoul-

ders and a slight paunch. Below his unruly salt-and-pepper
hair, he had a round face with deep laugh lines, shallow acne
scars, and perpetually amused gray eyes. This evening, he'd
worn jeans with a collared pullover. As always, Dev had
erred on the casual side, but in his defense, it was after midnight.

His weathered face broke into a sympathetic smile. "Sorry
about your friend."

I nodded my thanks. "Can I see him?"

Dev reached over and patted me on the shoulder. I turned
toward Stanley's office and took another step down the hallway. "But Doc"—Dev's voice stopped me—"It's kind of
grisly. Sure you want to see it?"

With a nod, I began to approach Stanley's interview room
at the end of the hallway, stopping only when I reached the
wide-open door.

I had walked onto worse crime scenes, but I froze in the
doorway. This time, the victim wasn't a stranger.

The sheer volume of blood astonished me. No surface was
spared, but the floor bore the brunt. Near the center of the
room, the green carpet had blackened in a ring encircling
Stanley Kolberg's barely recognizable corpse.

Stanley lay in a heap in front of his desk. Of all the dis-
torted anatomy, his arms were the most jarring sight.
Twisted above his head and obviously fractured at the wrist,
his right hand appeared to have hold of its own forearm.
Though not as deformed, his left arm shot out unnaturally
above his head, hand turned over, as if trying to pat down the
carpet with its bloated fingers.

I took in the other details with growing nausea. Stanley's
face was a battered pulp. With all the tissue that oozed down
from his forehead, I couldn't tell whether his eyes were
open. His nose deviated badly to the right, and his lips were
swollen to the width of bananas. Crusted blood matted his
hair and stuck to his beard.

In one of those bizarre reflex-associations, I wondered
again why so many of my male colleagues wore those
Freud-like beards. It was Stanley—no one ever shortened it

to Stan—who'd once explained: "All other physicians have uniforms. OR scrubs, white coats, stethoscopes, and what have you. Helps sell the whole shtick to the public. But what do we psychiatrists have? Nothing. So we grow beards like Sigmund's." Then he smiled and winked conspiratorially. "Besides, most of us shrinks are a wee bit fucked in the head, no?" Stanley was as academic as they came, but when he wanted to emphasize a point, he'd slip into a folksy idiom and pepper it with expletives.

An excited voice pulled me back to the moment. "You get a load of that, Joel?"

I looked over to my right to see the chief crime-scene investigator, Nate Schiff, now standing beside me. Schiff was one worked-up bunny. He jabbed a finger at the hemorrhagic wall inside the room. "Check out the wall!"

I glanced at the red streak that arched across the wall like the band of a rainbow.

"A real pumper," Schiff exhaled. "Only one thing gives you a spurt like that. An arterial bleed. And a big one, to boot!" He whistled appreciatively. Schiff wasn't morbid the way some people who work around the dead were, but he had a scientist's appreciation for the mechanics of his study, which happened to be murder scenes.

I viewed Stanley, but I couldn't spot a wound through the layers of blood and tissue. Reading the uncertainty on my face, Schiff brought two fingers up to his own neck as if checking his pulse. "The carotid. The second-biggest artery in the body, after the aorta." Having been through medical school this wasn't exactly news to me, but I didn't interrupt Schiff; he was on a roll. "A fresh-cut carotid will spray close to ten feet. Drain a gallon or two in less than a minute. Like slicing open a garden hose!" He pursed his lips and made an unnecessary whooshing noise.

Schiff stepped into the interview room. I took a breath and followed him. Avoiding the dark patches on the carpet, we kept moving until we reached the victim's feet. From up close Stanley looked less like roadkill and more like the man I knew, which made the whole tableau that much more disturbing. To distract myself, I concentrated on forensic details. "Only one shot?"

"Only one that hit him." Schiff shrugged. "But our guy fired another. The stray up in the wall." He pointed at a small crater in the drywall above the door behind us. "Don't have a clue what that was all about. No one's that bad a shot from in so close."

"Stanley was standing when he was shot?"

"You can see exactly how he went down . . ." Schiff swept a hand over the room, looking more like an interior decorator pitching colors than a CSI technician describing an execution. "The victim is standing right in front of his desk. *Bam!*" He fired an imaginary shot from his fingertip. "He takes it off the side of his neck, reels, and spins to his left. Now blood's spurting out at a mean pressure of 120 mm of mercury. Just follow the spray. See how the blood trails down the wall, over the chair, and onto the carpet?" Schiff pantomimed Stanley's collapse. "The victim's dropping as he spins."

"And the other injuries? Obviously, they're not just from his fall."

"Not unless he fell from an airplane." Schiff chuckled. Then he cleared his throat and looked away, remembering, I assumed, that the deceased and I were friends. "I figure once he's on the ground, our perp gives him a real nasty working over."

"With what?"

"Dunno. Something blunt. A pipe? Maybe heavier. Not a pistol-whipping." He shrugged. "The pathologist should be able to fill in the rest."

"Was he beaten before or after he died?"

"Can't tell. Autopsy should help there, too."

Schiff shifted from foot to foot. I could see he was getting antsy. There was more to find in this gold mine of physical evidence, and he probably didn't want to miss a strike chatting with me. I asked him for a moment alone. And with a quick nod, he was gone.

I stood and stared at the remains of the man who had in-

fluenced my life more than almost any other. A man who had
come to remind me so much of my father that at times I had
confused the two. I saw past the mutilation and visualized
Stanley's youthful face—not handsome, but distinguished—
with bushy eyebrows, hazel-brown eyes, long nose, and a
beard that was darker than his uniformly gray hair. His face
commanded respect, but could still convey sympathy, understanding, and trust. Especially trust. Many, many people
over the years had willingly put their lives in those hands
that now lay mangled above his head.

A familiar voice broke the silence. "Doc?"

I looked over to see that Dev had joined me. Beside him
stood a woman almost his height but lacking any trace of his
paunch. Her tawny blond hair was clipped back away from
her face. With a strong chin, her face was on the narrow side,
but her milk-and-honey complexion and scattering of freckles set off her high cheekbones and intense green eyes. The
soft lines etched in her forehead and at the edges of her lips
suggested she was more experienced and older than the
twenty-something rookie she first appeared to be. She
glanced at me with a brief nod before turning her impassive
gaze back to the victim.

Dev regarded me with uncharacteristic somberness. "You
okay?"

"Could be worse." I cleared my throat and shrugged,
fighting off the torrent of emotions. "It could have been me."

Dev chuckled softly, but I thought I caught a disapproving
glance from his colleague.

As if to get out of Stanley's earshot we stepped out of the
room and talked in the hallway, but the door remained open,
leaving a clear view of the body. "Dr. Ashman, meet my new
partner, Detective Claire Shepherd." Dev pointed from me
to her. "Claire's just joined Homicide."

I stretched my hand out to her. "It's Joel."

"Nice to meet you, Joel." Claire met my hand with a firm
handshake, but maybe because of my earlier remark, she
didn't reciprocate my smile.

"Doc consults for Homicide," Dev explained in a Southern twang that more than twenty-five years of living in the Pacific Northwest hadn't masked. "Does our psychological profiling. Once in a while, he's useful."

"Stop gushing, Dev. You're embarrassing me."

Dev's smile faded. "Joel and the victim were friends," he said to Claire. "They used to share a practice."

Claire frowned and her green eyes widened sympathetically. "Oh, Joel, that's awful."

"Yeah," I said, breaking off eye contact.

"Hate to drag you down here so late." Dev cleared his throat. "I thought you might give us an early lead on the investigation."

"I was up anyway," I said noncommittally.

The businesslike squint creasing Dev's forehead told me that we'd just moved beyond condolences. "Doc, what's your take on this?" He pointed at the carnage in the room.

I tried to focus—the crime scene is the chassis on which all psychological profiles are built—but the mix of feelings and memories clouded my assessment. All I could muster was: "It doesn't look like the work of someone who stumbled across Stanley while pulling a break-and-enter."

"No shit," Dev grunted.

"So how did he get in?" I asked, stalling.

"Smashed the glass by the entrance," Dev said. "Wasn't even the good stuff. This building has no alarm. Security around here is a joke."

"You don't know the half of it." I told them about the overly accessible garage, and the trouble we'd had with previous break-ins. Then I got back to his initial question. "The killer shot Stanley in the neck, and then went to the trouble of beating him badly enough to kill him twice over . . ."

Claire nodded without taking her eyes off the cadaver. "Overkill."

"Exactly," I said. "Pure rage! And I don't think we're talking about a jealous spouse or cheated business associate. It's even more irrational than that."

Dev nodded. "You're talking about one of his nut-job patients, aren't you?"

I wasn't in the mood to take issue with Dev's politically incorrect choice of terms. "You've got to consider his patients. Stanley worked with all comers."

Claire cocked her head. "How so?"

"Nowadays, most psychiatrists sub-specialize. Private practice, geriatrics, the institutionalized, forensic psychiatry, and so on. Not Stanley, he did it all. The man is—he was—a giant in the psychiatric community."

"Nobody jumps to mind, huh, Doc?" Dev asked.

I hesitated.

Dev picked up on my indecision. "Doc?"

I needed more time to sort it out in my head, so I said, "Divorced for years. No children. Did well, financially. And for the most part, he was well liked."

Eyes narrowed, Claire viewed me quizzically. " 'For the most part?' "

"His colleagues respected him," I said. "His patients could be another story."

"Oh?" Dev chewed his lip. "Why's that?"

"Stanley was interested in anger management. In fact, he was a pioneer in the field."

Dev thumbed at Stanley's pummeled corpse. "I think it's possible our killer has anger-management issues," he said dryly.

"And Stanley used to consult at Western State Hospital." I turned to Claire to explain. "That's where they keep violent offenders with psychiatric diagnoses. The so-called forensic psych patients."

Claire nodded politely, but it struck me that she would've known about Western State. I mentally kicked myself for coming across as condescending, and then wondered why I cared how I came across to her on this of all nights. "I used to work with those forensic patients, too," I said. "Believe me, you wouldn't want some of them bearing a grudge against you."

"We ought to find out if any of them have been released lately," Dev said.

Claire pointed at the violent tangle of Stanley's arms.

"Joel, what about his hands and wrists?" she said. "What's the significance of that?"

"Sometimes you see bizarre positioning like that with ritual murders." I shrugged. "But the rest of the scene doesn't fit with ritual homicide."

Staring at Stanley's fractured wrists and crushed fingers, we lapsed into a brief silence. "I hope our perp left an easy trail," Dev finally sighed. "I can tell you already, we're looking at a long suspect list."

I gazed at the splatter on the wall that traced the path of Stanley's final tumble.

"You two were close, huh?" Dev rested his hand on my shoulder again.

Without taking my eyes off the wall, I nodded. "Over the years, we shared an office, a partnership, and a close friendship."

What I hadn't figured out how to tell them, yet, was that we'd once shared a patient. Technically, she was Stanley's patient first. Then she became mine. And remained so, up until the moment she plunged off the Aurora Bridge.

I first laid eyes on Angela Connor a year, almost to the day, before Stanley's murder. The night I met her, I was working my regular on-call shift at Swedish Hospital's Emergency Psychiatric Unit.

Watching the security guard unlock the door to Angela's quiet room, I wondered what awaited me on the other side. More often than not, people locked inside quiet rooms (desolate little spaces, designed to safely hold patients who were at risk to themselves or others) are anything but quiet. But when the guard opened the heavy door, I found Angela sitting silently on the mattress atop the bench built into the wall with her knees drawn and a blanket wrapped around her from the neck down. She didn't look at me as I approached. Even when I sat down at her feet at the edge of the bench, she stared straight ahead and rocked gently, as if still alone.

"Angela?"

No reply.

"Angela, I'm Dr. Ashman."

Still nothing.

"I'm a psychiatrist."

She grunted a laugh, but showed no sign of acknowledging me.

One of the wonderfully simple rules of the psychiatric interview is: If you have nothing useful to say, keep your mouth shut. I took advantage of the silence and studied my new patient, while she continued to ignore me.

Angela's short hair stood in disarray on her head. Her tired face bore no makeup, and her lips were cracked and bloody. In spite of her unkempt appearance, I could see she had striking features: high cheekbones, upturned nose, full mouth, blue-gray eyes, and short, jet-black hair. From looking at her chart, I knew that she was twenty-five, but if I hadn't seen it, I would have guessed younger.

After a couple of silent minutes, Angela finally blinked. "When can I leave?" she asked in a voice that was hoarse from having had the endotracheal tube of a ventilator recently pass through her vocal cords.

"Angela, do you understand what it means to be held here for evaluation?" I asked.

She shrugged. "Doesn't mean I have to talk to you."

True. According to state law, we can involuntarily hold anyone for seventy-two hours who we deem a potential danger to themselves or others. In that time, we can restrain, drug, force-feed, or even subject them to electroconvulsive therapy, but we can't force them to talk.

"Tell me, Angela, why amitriptyline? You're not even prescribed that."

Another shrug.

"Why not just swallow your prescription's worth of Fluquil?"

"Have you ever seen anyone die of a Fluquil overdose?" she asked.

"No."

She bundled the blanket tighter around her.

"But you're not dead," I pointed out.

"Not this time," she said. *"They told me I came close."*

"Very close," I agreed. If not for an astute ER physician, a ventilator, and an intravenous drip of sodium bicarbonate and potassium, no question, she would have died. But aside from a deep burn on her upper back—attributed to passing out too close to an electric baseboard heater—she'd survived her overdose physically unscathed.

"Do you plan to take another crack at it?" I asked.

Angela dropped her head into the blanket and sighed.

"What would you try the next time?"

"A gun? A rope? Carbon monoxide? What does it matter?"

"As you pointed out, some methods aren't that successful."

"I don't make two mistakes in a row," she said without looking up.

"What other mistakes have you made?"

"What a typical shrink's question!" She shook her head. Then, for the first time in fifteen minutes, she lifted her face to me, and her eyes challenged mine. *"If you have to know, my last big mistake was talking to one of you."*

Mentally filing the provocative comment to address later, when and if I could establish trust, I changed subjects. *"Angela, where did you grow up?"* Interview rule number two: When in doubt, go for the childhood.

"Here we go." She groaned and broke off the eye contact. *"Let me make this easy for you. I grew up here in town, in an upper-middle-class, stable family. Daddy was a successful lawyer, Mom a housewife. Two siblings—an older sister and a younger brother. All in all, I was a happy, well-loved little girl."* She paused, then added, as if as an afterthought, *"Okay, Dad was fucking me from eleven on, which didn't help, but hey, no one's got the perfect childhood. Right?"*

Accusations of incest don't shock me anymore, but I don't ever remember one being couched in the same context. I managed to keep the surprise off my face, sensing that no reaction was my best approach.

"High school was a breeze," she continued, as if she'd been describing a tediously routine upbringing. "No eating disorder. No drug or alcohol issues. Never was date-raped or anything. I went to college back east, Queens College, on a scholarship. Needed a break from the old man, you understand." Again, she looked up and challenged with her eyes. "Graduated summa cum laude. With my marks and Daddy's connections, I could've gone to law school anywhere, but I chose not to."

"How come?"

She dropped her eyes back to the blanket. "You're thinking it was because I didn't want to validate Daddy by following in his footsteps, right?"

"You don't know what I'm thinking."

She ran a hand through her short hair. "Chances are, you're thinking what a great fuck I would be."

This time I couldn't hide the surprise. "Where did that come from?"

"It's my life story. Men always want me. Truth be told, it's a blessing most of the time."

"What happened after college?" I asked, grabbing for a semblance of rapport.

Ignoring my question, she broke into a half-smile. "I don't mind you thinking about me like that. You're very cute in that intellectual way." Then the smile disappeared, and she added in a smaller voice: "Just don't hurt me, okay? I couldn't deal with that again."

With warning bells blaring inside my head, I rose from the bench. "Angela, I think it's best if I find you a female psychiatrist."

She said nothing until I reached the door. "I don't want another shrink."

"The fact is, Angela, you have to talk to someone."

"I want to talk to you . . . please, Dr. Ashman."

There was nothing special in the words, but something in her voice—a glimmer of vulnerability that I hadn't heard up to that point—struck me. I felt a sudden pang of sympathy for her. Or maybe, subconsciously I'd already noticed the

*glaring similarities between Angela and a girl from my
childhood. Whatever the reason, I turned and walked back to
her bed. "You've got to understand that my concerns for you
are strictly on a professional level." I met her stare. "Am I
clear?"*

"Crystal." She nodded. "No more nasty talk."

"Okay, after college . . ."

*"Oh, God." She rubbed her face in her hands. "Odd jobs.
A couple of short-term relationships. One with a girl. But
much as I like the concept of lesbianism, I'm just not wired
that way . . ."*

And so it went. Salvo. And countersalvo. I left the one-
hour interview frustrated and exhausted, and not much en-
lightened for my effort. By the time I reached the back desk,
Angela's old chart awaited me. She had only two previous
psychiatric admissions; her most recent was a year earlier
for a month-long stay at University Hospital. The faxed records reiterated what Angela had told me, but the University
team had never found anyone to corroborate her incest story.
Her discharge diagnosis read: "Major depression with suicidal ideation and probable BPD." I sighed when I read the
initials that stood for borderline personality disorder. Exem-
plified by patients with unstable relationships, frequent suicide gestures, and hopeless responses to therapy, that
three-letter acronym has the power to send a chill up a psychiatrist's spine. Mine, anyway.

Mulling over the interview as I scribbled notes, I realized
Angela wasn't a typical suicidal patient. Putting aside the
psychotic or the merely attention-seeking, people seen immediately following a genuine suicide attempt act remarkably
similar. Most are either regretful about the failure of their
attempt or indifferent to it. The depressed are easy to spot,
because their mood is contagious; after five minutes with
them, you begin to feel like stepping in front of a train.

But Angela exhibited neither the despair nor the indifference typical of the depressed. Even at the time of the interview, I had the feeling she was assessing me—deliberately

baiting me and then judging my reactions—as much as I was her. I didn't have a handle on Angela, and that troubled me.

Much about Angela troubled me. As frank as she had been for a first interview, I knew I was just scratching the surface. But already I was convinced that Angela was a tortured soul. And it wasn't merely my professional opinion. From the moment I met her, Angela reminded me of Suzie, the girl who had inadvertently cut short my childhood.

I fought off a chill. And I wrote off the visceral sense of unease as simply the remnant of a sad memory.

I was so wrong.

2

THE MORNING AFTER Stanley Kolberg's death, I was up and running, literally, before dawn. I clocked ten miles before the sun rose over the Cascade Mountains and warmed me as I reached the homestretch. The ache in my right knee reminded me I wasn't supposed to be jogging. After twenty marathons, my prematurely arthritic knee was facing a growing threat from the orthopedic surgeon's hammer and saw, but I couldn't stop. Running was my drug of choice. The greater the stress, the more I ran. The year after Loren died, I jogged enough to wear out three pairs of shoes.

I was shaving at the sink when I heard the anchor on the early-morning KOMO news lead with a story about Stanley Kolberg's murder. Soon as it broke, my phone rang. And rang. And rang. I stopped counting at fifteen colleagues. I was known as Stanley's protégé, and since he had no family to speak of, they phoned me on the pretense of expressing their condolences. What they wanted were the gory details. Most were curious. A few scared. I think my ex-business partner, Dr. Calvin Nichol, fell into the latter group.

"Joel," Nichol said in his clipped tone. "Have you heard about Stanley?"

"I saw him on the carpet, Cal," I said.

"Of course," he said distantly. "You work for the Seattle Police Department."

"Sort of." In fact, I was a consultant for the SPD, paid (or, sometimes, unpaid) on a case-by-case basis. But rather than elaborate to Nichol, I just sipped my coffee.

"Stanley was shot, right?" Nichol asked.

"For starters."

"What does that mean?!"

"Nothing," I said, softening the blow. "It's just that there was a lot of blood. Very messy."

"Have they arrested anyone?"

"He's been dead less than twelve hours, Cal." I was tempted to add that the killer didn't leave his wallet at the scene, but I thought better of it.

"I was hoping someone might have seen something," Nichol said tonelessly.

"You weren't in the building, were you?"

"Of course not!" he spat, before calming. "It had to be one of his patients."

"Kind of early to assume that."

"Come on, Joel," Nichol said. "Those criminals from Western State Hospital, and the others with rage disorders? It was a recipe for disaster. I warned him as much, but he wouldn't listen."

"When did Stanley ever back down from anything?"

"Maybe at the very end. Then again, maybe not." He sighed so heavily that my phone's earpiece whistled. "Poor Stanley. Mark my words, when they find the man, it will turn out to be one of his patients."

"*If* they find him," I said to myself once I'd already hung up.

I headed out to my garage. The old Honda choked a few times before revving tenuously. I pulled out into the lane.

As I drove to Harborview Hospital (home to King County's Medical Center where all official autopsies are performed) I remembered a conversation with Stanley concerning the anger-management patients Nichol had spoken of. We were sitting in Stanley's office; actually, Stanley was sitting and I was standing because what would have been my chair was lying in pieces on the floor. One of his patients had gone a bit too primal during therapy and had used the chair to express his dissatisfaction with his boss, his wife, the world at large, and more specifically, the floor. And it wasn't the first time that Stanley's office had taken the brunt of a berserk patient. Not even close.

"Doesn't it worry you?" I asked Stanley.

"Joel, you should play golf," he said, apropos of nothing.

"Golf?"

"It's a lot like psychotherapy. And life, for that matter. In golf the improvement is never linear. Your game worsens—in spite of the practice and teaching—before it improves. So it is with therapy, no? Regressions and setbacks are par for the course."

"But what if one of your patient's 'regressions' sets you back out the window?"

Stanley laughed. "Won't happen." His grin disappeared. "Or if it does, then I'm not nearly as good as I think I am."

As I walked down the cold beige corridor and through the main doors of Harborview's morgue, I discounted Stanley's remark. He *was* as good as he thought he was. Better. Stanley was a genius, but he'd made some very wrong choices along the way.

Sergeant Devonshire and Detective Shepherd met me in the morgue's intake room, a gray and somber space that was the dead's first stop on their way to the dissecting tables. Dev's shirt had a collar this morning, but his jeans were almost worn through at the knees. Claire wore a businesslike blazer and skirt but she jazzed it up with a funky mauve blouse and a pair of black pumps, guaranteed to draw attention to her well-defined legs. When we huddled in the center of the cold room, Claire showed a glimpse of a smile as we exchanged greetings.

"Any developments?" I asked.

"CSI puts the time of death between ten and eleven," Dev said. "The cleaning lady who found him—a Portuguese woman, who I'm not sure is ever gonna be right again—got there just after eleven. Didn't see squat." Dev tilted his head from side to side, working out a kink in his neck. "The bunny men recovered both slugs— .38 caliber. Not much else to find."

"But we found a witness," Claire cut in. "An elderly man at a bus stop half a block up the street claims he saw the break-in shortly after eleven. The entryway wasn't lit and our fellow's vision isn't twenty-twenty, so he couldn't give much of a description. Medium height and build. Dark clothes—maybe a tracksuit—and a baseball cap."

"Big help," Dev grumbled. "We already checked. Eminem's got an alibi."

"But here's the catch." Claire raised a finger and offered me her first lasting smile in my presence. "The perp didn't actually enter the building."

"He just broke the window, opened the door, and took off?" I asked.

"According to our witness."

"Doc, what's that all about?" Dev asked.

I had the feeling he already knew the answer. "Two possibilities," I said. "One, he wanted to wait and see if anybody responded to the broken window before entering."

Claire shook her head. "No, the man sat at the bus stop for a good thirty minutes. The guy didn't come back."

"Or, two," I said, "he staged the 'break-in' on his way out of the building."

Dev turned to Claire and said, "See?" by way of explaining that I wasn't as stupid as I looked. Then to me: "No question. Our perp must've already had access to the building."

"You could break into that building with a sturdy twig," I said.

Dev flashed a look back to Claire, as if to say he'd spoken too soon about me. "Doc, why break in one way, and then make it look like you broke in another?"

"Fair enough," I said, mentally wiping the egg off my face. "But I think it was pretty clear from the scene that Stanley knew his assailant."

"There's a difference." Dev wouldn't let it go. "Not only did he know his killer, but either he trusted the guy enough to let him in, or the guy already had a key."

"Either way, our assailant didn't want us knowing about his connection to the victim." Claire was all smiles now.

I was saved from the tandem offensive by an unlikely hero, when Dr. Mitch Greene burst into the room. That was how Mitch entered any room. I'd known him for ten years, and in that time, against the odds, he had grown messier, fatter, and even ruder. And I liked him even more.

"Ash-Man!" Greene greeted me with the nickname he alone used.

"You look good, Mitch," I said, pointing to his protruding scrub top, below which some skin hung out from under the hem. "You working out?"

When Greene stopped laughing, he asked, "You got a steady date, yet?"

I held up a hand to preempt his tired joke. "And no, I don't want yours. Poor Trudy has enough to deal with."

"Loving me is a full-time job, you know?" Greene grinned and patted his large belly. "Hey, how long has it been since Loren?"

"Three years," I said.

"Three years? Wow. Lovely woman, Loren. Shame. A damn shame." Greene shook his head and sighed. "But, Ash-Man, it's time to get yourself back out there." He let out another belly laugh. "Believe me, you're not getting any prettier." Then he turned his attention to Dev. "You neither! How are you, you Arkie son of a bitch?"

Dev hailed from Alabama, not Arkansas, and the pathologist knew it, too. Ignoring the taunt, Dev pointed from Greene to Claire. "Meet my new partner, Claire Shepherd."

"Mitch Greene." He stuck out his meaty paw and pumped her hand enthusiastically.

Claire looked as if she didn't know how to react to the

larger-than-life pathologist, but she smiled politely. "Plea-sure, Dr. Greene."

"Mitch, damn it! I'm only Dr. Greene to my patients." Then he chuckled again. "And if they're talking to me, I got problems."

Without another word, Greene spun and walked back through the doorway from which he'd emerged. We scut-tled after. Greene's morgue assistant passed us each a yel-low gown, gloves, a cap, and cloth booties that we struggled into as we entered the brightly lit, white-tiled dis-secting lab where Greene performed the city's forensic au-topsies.

"So Ash-Man, still playing cops and robbers, huh?" Greene asked, slipping on his gown and gloves.

"Well, I'm too bright to play pathologist."

Greene chuckled. "Plus you don't got the stomach for it. Remember last time?"

It was hard to forget the last autopsy I'd witnessed. Even at the time, I had no idea why I went. Guilt? Closure? Or, maybe, just plain disbelief. Whatever the reason, I wouldn't recommend witnessing an autopsy on someone dredged out of the water after twenty-four hours of submersion. Espe-cially if the victim has fallen 150 feet off a bridge before hit-ting the water. Halfway through the postmortem, Greene and his assistant had to catch me and drag me to a chair. And what had I learned? She died on impact. And that after 100 feet, it doesn't matter too much whether you hit water or concrete. I could have saved myself the embarrassment; I al-ready knew both facts. But in the end, I suppose I went to say good-bye to Angela.

"Stanley Kolberg!" Greene roared, jerking me out of my reminiscences. "Can you believe it? Someone went and killed a legend." He paused to sigh heavily. "Then again, who's more likely to get knocked off than a shrink?"

"According to the stats, patients are more likely to murder their plastic surgeon than their therapist," I pointed out.

"Figures. People!" Greene grunted dismissively, as if he wasn't a member of the species. "Of course, they'd be more willing to kill someone for fucking with their face than fucking with their mind."

"Hey, Socrates." Dev pointed to the stretchers in the big open room. "Any chance of you performing an autopsy today?"

"Keep that tone up and it might be on you." Greene let out what could only be described as a guffaw. Then he turned to his assistant. "Okay, Helen, let's get this show on the road."

We congregated around the draped body that lay on a steel gurney in the center of the room. The assistant wheeled a long silver tray on a stand to the head of the bed while Greene pushed a bucket over to the stretcher with his foot. Before pulling the sheet off the corpse, Greene turned to Claire. "Here's a bucket, and there are chairs in the corner. No shame in it, Claire, if you need either." He thumbed to me with a chuckle. "Even happens to some of our alleged M.D.s."

Claire shook her head. "I'll be fine, Mitch."

Greene yanked the sheet off the gurney, exposing Stanley's bloody corpse. Apart from the position of the limbs—now at his sides—little had changed in his disturbing appearance. But now that he was completely naked, the extent of the beating could be seen along his chest and abdomen, and most of all, his groin. The assailant had paid special attention to the genitals, smashing them so they were unrecognizable. I shot a quick glance over to the others. Claire's expression remained steadfast. I thought Dev paled a little, but he, too, maintained a poker face.

Beyond the mutilation, I was shocked by how old he looked. I'd always thought of Stanley, with his bone-straight posture and bounding stride, as youthful. But as I stared at the loose skin that hung from his skinny frame and his spindly legs, I realized he had the physique of the sixty-three-year-old he was.

Greene stood back from the table with his arms crossed and head tilted, staring at the remains like a sculptor might assess a block of marble. "No question. He's dead all right." There was no laugh this time.

Greene began to move, circling the body at least three times before finally stopping at Stanley's side. He extended his gloved hand and pointed at the welts on the arms. "Helen, pass me the ruler, would'ya?"

Greene measured the width of the contusions. "Three centimeters." He nodded. "Heavy, smooth metal." He brushed a finger along the course of a bruise. "A pipe, or maybe a crowbar. But notice how little actual bruising there is. Just the weapon's mark."

"Meaning?" Dev asked.

"The beating was laid down after he was already dead," Greene said matter-of-factly. "No pumping heart to produce the expected bruises." He reached for Stanley's right wrist. He flipped the hand back and forth, but instead of moving at the wrist joint, the appendage levered at its new fulcrum a couple of inches above the wrist. As Greene extended Stanley's hand the sharp ends of the radius and ulna protruded through the skin on the undersurface of the forearm.

I glanced at the cops. Dev lost more color. Unfazed, Claire leaned closer for a better look.

"The wrist is pretty bruised," Dev pointed out. "Think it was broken before death?"

"Nah," Greene grunted. "The blood is from the radius's marrow. That would leak out with or without a heartbeat."

"Was it broken with the pipe?" Claire asked.

Greene shook his head. He reached for a rolled towel on the tray and dropped it on the floor. "This is his arm, okay?" Greene stepped on one end of the towel, bent over, and grabbed the other end with both hands. *"Craaack!"* he mimicked the sound effect, as he jerked on the end of the towel.

Dev snapped his fingers. "Take a pretty strong guy to pull that off, huh?"

"Don't hang your hat on that, Columbo." Greene straightened up with surprisingly little effort. "I bet his bones are pretty osteoporotic. They'd probably snap like a couple of dry branches." He turned back to the cadaver. After measuring some of the other bruises, he used the ruler to push the smashed penis out of the way, revealing a scrotum the size of a softball. "Don't need to open it to tell you the testicles are ruptured. And yeah, it happened postmortem, too. Talk about hitting below the belt . . ."

Greene reached back to the tray and grabbed a pair of forceps and a probe, then stepped to the head of the table. He brought the forceps to the left side of Stanley's neck and delicately explored the disrupted skin. After a moment, he turned to his assistant and said, "Smallish caliber bullet—maybe .38?—penetrated the sternocleidomastoid, then transected the left common carotid artery, before exiting through the trapezius."

The medical examiner moved his tools up to Stanley's face. He picked off much of the dried blood with the forceps. With a gloved hand he lifted Stanley's head off the table and examined the back of the skull. "No headshots," he commented to his assistant, before guiding the head back to the gurney. He took one more slow turn around the body. He crossed his arms again, nodded his satisfaction, and then turned to us. "Time to look inside."

Positioning himself by Stanley's waist, Greene reached for the large scalpel on the tray. Then, with surprising grace, he began to disembowel my former partner.

I doubt many people forget the first autopsy they witness, but I haven't forgotten any of the ones I've seen. As I watched Greene make the massive Y-incisions across the chest and belly (causing the usual mess of bowels to spill out) and then systematically remove the abdominal organs, the lungs, and finally the heart, I felt the same heebie-jeebies as ever. If I ever needed a reminder of my own mortality, autopsies were just the ticket—from ashes to ashes, with a quick stop at the butcher's along the way.

After Greene and Helen had weighed and separately packaged Stanley's organs, he spoke to us while standing beside the dull metal sink. "I still need to look at the cross-sections of the brain, but I'm going to stick my neck out and say this: Stanley Kolberg didn't die of natural causes."

"So much for my theory," Dev deadpanned.

Greene chuckled, scrubbing his soapy hands roughly and

speaking over the noise of the running tap. "A few other tidbits off the cuff. One, I don't think your guy is a very good shot."

"Why?" Claire asked.

"From the size of the office, we know he was shot from no more than fifteen feet away. I bet the guy was aiming for head or chest. Instead, the bullet grazes the neck, nicks the artery, and by dumb luck happens to be fatal."

Dev leaned against the wall by the sink. "What else?"

Greene switched off the tap with the knee-level lever and then turned to me. "For what it's worth, I don't think old Stanley felt any of the bodywork laid on him." He read the doubt on my face. "Apart from the fact there are no defensive injuries, you cut a major artery like the carotid, and death is measured in seconds, not minutes." He reached for a few paper towels from the dispenser in front of him. "So if I was a detective, I'd ask myself—aside from why am I in this dead-end job"—he laughed heartily—"why do all this? Why execute someone with a bullet to the neck from close range and *then* beat the holy crap out of the corpse?"

A fair question. One that the Seattle PD would be expecting me as their psychological profiler to answer. But without betraying the trust of a patient or legally exposing myself, I still hadn't figured out how to tell Dev and Claire about a very relevant and very private aspect of Stanley's life.

Without responding to Greene, I stared down at the soapy suds in the sink, again remembering Angela Connor's autopsy. Watching the foamy water circle the drain, it struck me that in the time I'd known Angela her life had followed a similar course.

A year earlier, by the end of her first week in the hospital, Angela Connor had pushed the staff's patience to the wall. Two veteran nurses told me they were ready to strangle her. A remarkable fact, considering the sorts of patients they dealt with daily.

I think it was the potential that Angela showed—the charm-

ing, articulate flashes—that made her other side so hard to swallow. But then again, I didn't have to put up with all the bullshit—the temper tantrums, screaming matches, and hurtful comments—for twelve-hour stretches, like the nurses did.

At our first case conference concerning Angela, I tried to explain her behavior to the ward's social worker. "Most people who suffer a major depression withdraw into themselves. You know, the so-called 'flat affect' or lack of responsiveness? But others react unusually. Their depression manifests itself as anger, belligerence, and mood instability. It's called an 'agitated depression.' I think that's what Angela suffers from."

After considering my diagnosis for a few seconds, the social worker shook her head and asked with utter sincerity, "Isn't it possible that she's just a complete bitch?"

The same thought had crossed my mind. But at the time, I hadn't yet appreciated the degree of Angela's depression. Nor the reasons behind it.

Justifications aside, our first week together was, at best, rocky. When I visited Angela on the second day of her stay, all I got out of her were yesses and nos. The next day it was only monosyllabic grunts. That didn't concern me as much as her lack of personal hygiene. She smelled musty; her hair was a pointy mess; dried saliva and tears were caked on her face. Day four was more of the same. By day five, Angela refused to talk.

On the sixth day of her internment, I interviewed Angela's mother, Sally Connor. Though lighter in complexion, she shared her daughter's sharp features and blue eyes. And she was younger than I'd expected. I doubted Sally was a day over forty-five.

In the family interview room on the ward, Sally sat with eyes glued to the floor and hands folded tightly in her lap. I had the feeling she would have preferred to dissolve into the furniture than discuss her daughter's psychiatric issues. After fifteen futile minutes, I finally asked, "Mrs. Connor, why do you think Angela is here?"

Sally sighed. "Because of the pills."

"She very nearly succeeded in committing suicide," I said.

"You do stupid things when you're young," she said softly.

I shook my head. "This wasn't some impulsive act or cry for help, Mrs. Connor."

Sally sniffled. "Ever since her teen years, Angela has been very dramatic."

"Listen, Mrs. Connor," I said, deliberately putting an edge into my tone. "Your daughter really meant to kill herself."

She shuffled in her seat before finally looking up at me with tentative eyes. "Angela will be okay if she comes back home to stay with me for a while." She swallowed. "I am sure of it."

Eventually I gave up. Sally was convinced that if we only stopped talking about her daughter's problems, they would go away like rolling up a car window on a bad smell from outside. And I couldn't penetrate the many layers of her denial. In fact, Sally's penchant for avoidance reminded me of my own mother.

I have trouble picturing Mom—at least, as the whole person, before the early-onset Alzheimer's ravaged her brain— but whenever I flip through the old family albums, I'm reminded how pretty she was. In spite of her earthy clothes and the uncomfortable way she eyed the camera, there is no denying her beauty. Tall and thin, with a dark, flawless complexion, and brooding brown eyes, Tobi Ashman had the looks to be a model, though my guess is that modeling would have been several notches below drug mule on her list of ideal jobs.

Mom just wasn't comfortable in her own skin. Maybe that was why she committed herself so singularly to her academic ambitions within the college's political science department. And emotionally, Mom was ill-equipped to deal with a child. All the usual childhood crises—a beating at the hands of the class bully, an unrequited crush, and other moments of juvenile angst—were promptly referred to Dad. By the time I turned nine, I knew better than to even bother raising them with her. Still, I always felt close to her. Though I couldn't have articulated it at the time, I saw through her

*confident, intellectual air—something that struck others as
aloofness—and recognized the inner frailty. From a very
young age, I felt the need to protect Mom.*

But I didn't sense any protectiveness from Angela Connor's older sister, Ellen, when I tracked her down to Bangor,
Maine, following my interview with their mother. From our
brief phone conversation, I had the impression that the dis-
tance suited Ellen fine. "My sister has been a problem since
she was a teen. Unlike our little brother, Tommy, I can't afford to sacrifice my life trying to sort out hers," she said,
abruptly ending our conversation.

After hanging up, I headed to Angela's room and braced
for another struggle. But I noticed the change the moment I
walked through the door and found her sitting by the barred
window, pen in hand, scribbling in a pocket-sized notebook.
When she looked up at me, she nodded ever so slightly in
recognition. Even more encouraging, I could see she'd at-
tended to her appearance. Granted, she still wore the standard hospital-issue pajamas, but her short hair was combed
back and her face clean. Though not classically beautiful,
her almost androgynous features and intense blue-gray eyes
were striking. I realized she probably wasn't exaggerating
the effect she claimed to have on men.

"Am I interrupting?" I asked.

"Just writing notes for my lawyer."

"Lawyer?"

"For my lawsuit against you and the hospital. Unlawful
confinement, mental cruelty, that kinda stuff."

With Angela's laissez-faire delivery, it took me a moment
to realize she was joking. "Fair enough." I grinned. "But I
think the nurses are planning to countersue. Something
about spending a shift with you and ending up with post
traumatic stress disorder."

"They should see me when I'm not on my best behavior."

I had to laugh. "Today a better day?" I asked.

She shrugged and closed the notebook.

"What are you writing?" I pointed to the pastel-lined, textured sleeve of her book.

"A journal . . . kind of." Then she added self-consciously, "Another shrink told me it might help."

"Does it?"

"No."

"It's a good idea," I said. "Great way to vent."

She shot me a wary glance. "I'm not going to show it to you. Ever."

"I wouldn't ask to see it, Angela. Ever."

She nodded and her expression lightened. "How much longer, Dr. Ashman?"

"A couple of more weeks. At least."

She accepted the verdict with one of her signature shrugs. "There's no hurry. The Aurora Bridge will still be there when I get out."

I stared at her for a long while. "You ever hear about the boy who cried 'wolf'?"

"Fuck you," she snapped then turned her head to the wall.

As I stood there considering the wisdom of having provoked her, Angela surprised me with a revelation that came out of left field. "I still love him."

"Who?"

"Daddy. How weird is that? The pervert was screwing me from sixth grade on, but I loved him right to the end."

I didn't reply.

"But it wasn't easy for Dad," Angela continued. "I don't think he and Mom got it on much after my little brother was born. Mom drinks a lot. What she can't sweep under the carpet, she likes to drown in a bottle." She sighed. "Besides, I wasn't the easiest teenager."

I bit my tongue. If what she'd told me about her father having molested her was true, it was inconceivable that her teen years could have been easy.

"Dad would have done anything to keep us together. . . ." Her head was still turned from me, but I saw her wipe her shoulder against her eyes, trying to hide the tears.

A gentle knock at the door broke the silence. "Must be Tommy," she said without looking up. "Could you ask him if he'd give me a minute?"

The moment I saw Tommy, I knew I was looking at Angela's little brother. The resemblance was uncanny—they could've passed for twins—but he carried himself with gravity beyond his years. If I hadn't known better, I would've assumed Tommy the older of the two. "Dr. Ashman?" He extended his hand.

"Tommy, right?" I nodded and met his handshake. "Angela needs a minute, which works out fine. Maybe we could talk in my office?"

As soon as he sat down, Tommy said, "I'm worried this time."

" 'This time'? Has she attempted suicide before?"

He shook his head. "She's been down this road, but never this bad."

"What's different?"

"Just look at her! She's not even washing herself." A neon sign could've replaced the message on his face. What kind of fucking therapist are you? Open your eyes!

"Depression can change a person, Tommy."

"But the change in her is night and day. I haven't seen a flicker of the old Angela in weeks. It's like she's given up."

"Tell me about the old Angela," I said.

"Nothing like what you see now. Smart. Funny. Upbeat. Believe it or not, she's got a real spark." He sighed, and I saw frown lines that I would have expected in someone at least ten years older. "She has a good heart, but she's always bringing home strays."

"You mean men?" I clarified.

"Yeah." Tommy grunted.

"She likes to rescue them, huh?"

"Exactly. Even when they're nothing but trouble. Especially then. She could have any guy she wants, but she always picks the losers. Drives me nuts."

"She gets hurt a lot," I said.

"A lot."

Tommy had insight into Angela that I hadn't sensed from her mom or sister. So I broached the subject I'd avoided with them. "Angela talks a lot about your dad."

"Yeah?" Tommy shifted slightly in his seat.

I leaned forward. "You know what she accuses him of, don't you?"

He dropped his gaze to the desk then nodded.

"Is it true, Tommy?"

"Dad used to say it was all in her imagination."

"Who did you believe?"

"Her, I guess." Tommy shrugged, and I could've been looking at Angela that moment. "But I was never sure." He looked back up at me. There was no mistaking his expression. "If I had been sure, I would've killed him."

3

THE MORNING AFTER Stanley Kolberg's autopsy, I couldn't get so much as a cough out of my old Honda, even in neutral. Loren had long ago figured out the car's then-latest quirk—the gearshift had to be in Neutral before the engine would catch. In Park, the thing sputtered and coughed like a coal miner who'd spent ten years too many underground. In a city with a skyrocketing auto-theft rate, it made my heap theft-proof. Of course, anyone who thought twice about stealing it needed professional help. The car was crying for a scrap heap, but I didn't have the heart to take that step; it still held too many memories of Lor.

When I called Dev to let him know that I had to wait for a taxi on the rainy morning, he offered to pick me up. But twenty minutes later, Claire Shepherd stood at my doorstep, a raincoat over her simple navy suit and her hair already damp from the brief jaunt from car to door. When our eyes met, her smile was less reluctant than before.

"Can I have a peek at it?" she asked, shaking the rain off.

Responding to my bewildered expression, she steered an

imaginary steering wheel and pretended to honk its horn. "Your car." She broke into another smile.

"Sure," I said, doing a poor job of hiding my surprise that she would know any more about car engines than I did. Which was absolutely nothing.

She rolled her eyes. "Don't paint us all with the same brush, Doctor." Then she thumbed toward the side of the house. "The garage this way?"

I nodded and followed her around the path to the single-car garage out back. Even with the door open, the dank space was so dark that I reached for the light switch. The single overhead light bulb came on just as Claire's hand emerged from her purse holding a pair of disposable gloves. "What?" she asked when she caught me gawking. "I never know when I'll need these at a crime scene."

She popped open the hood of the old Honda, while I stood by feeling slightly emasculated as I held her raincoat and purse. I watched as she leaned over the engine and tugged at what I assumed were spark plugs. "Where did you learn your way around cars?" I asked.

"From my dad," she said, appraising the engine. "He loves tinkering with them. He's the quintessential guy's guy." She laughed. "Irony is, he ended up with three daughters."

I chuckled. "Ah, 'cruel, cruel fate.' "

"Didn't faze Dad. He raised us like boys. Especially me. I'm the eldest." She pulled the dipstick out of the oil sump, studied it a moment, and then wiped it on an old towel. "We spent a lot of weekends under the hood of one or another of our old cars," she said smiling at the memory. "That is, until the game started."

I leaned in closer, still clueless as to what she was trying to do. "What game?"

"Didn't matter. Football, baseball, hockey, whatever. Except basketball. Dad hates basketball. Says it's a stupid game because nothing counts until the last five minutes." She laughed. "But I think it has more to do with the fact he's only five-nine. Shorter than Mom."

"Are you still a fan?"

"Go, Broncos, go," her chant echoed out from under the hood. "It's in the blood. I'm a fourth-generation Broncos fan."

After another minute or two of poking and prodding around the engine, Claire straightened up and pronounced: "Sorry, Joel. She's beyond my help. Maybe anybody's." She dropped the hood shut, pulled off her gloves, and dusted the talc off her hands.

I grinned. "Shall I call for a priest to administer last rites?"

"Not a bad idea." She chuckled. "I thought doctors got to drive nice cars."

"Now who's painting with the same brush?" I said, feigning indignation.

Claire smiled and bit her lip. "Fair enough."

We walked out of the garage toward the street. When we reached her car, I asked, "Where's Dev?"

"The captain wanted a briefing on the investigation. The press is making a big deal." As she pulled out of the parking space, she said: "Stanley Kolberg was an important guy, wasn't he?"

"It's the clerics and doctors thing."

She glanced at me. "The *what*?"

"Priests, rabbis, and doctors aren't supposed to get killed," I said. "The public, or maybe it's just the press, gets worked up whenever one does. But, yeah, Stanley was an important guy. In some senses, Stanley *was* psychiatry in Seattle."

"And you were his partner?"

"Up until six months ago."

Claire glanced at me. "So what happened?"

"I needed a break." My gaze dropped to my hands. "I kind of hit burnout. So, I quit the practice."

"Hmmm."

I intended to leave it there—at least until Dev was present—but for reasons unknown I felt compelled to explain. "A mutual patient claimed Stanley acted inappropriately with her."

Stopped at a red light, Claire turned to me with penetrating eyes. "Inappropriately?"

I shrugged. "She said that he took advantage of her sexually."

Claire didn't visibly respond to my disclosure. "Aren't those allegations common in your line of work?"

"Very." I fiddled with my seat belt. "But I had a reason to believe her."

The light turned green, and Claire looked back to the road. "Who is 'she'?" she asked evenly.

I shook my head. "Ethically . . . legally . . . I can't divulge patients' names, or even share the details of her allegations."

She nodded slowly. "But you left the practice because of what she told you?"

"Not only that. I had burned out. Besides that, our interests had diverged. I'd stopped working at Western State, where Stanley and I shared coverage of the forensic psych ward." I met her stare. "But there was no way I could've worked with him again. Not after what she told me."

Claire frowned, clearly less than satisfied with the explanation. I thought she might press the issue, but instead she asked: "Why did you leave Western State?"

"Forensic psych patients wear on you."

"Kind of a weird thing for a psychiatrist to say."

"It's true. Not the genuinely psychotic patients. I feel sorry for the rare schizophrenics who kill because they hear voices or think they're protecting themselves. Their condition is treatable." I exhaled heavily. "But the others, with their vague diagnoses like dissociative states—"

"What's that?"

"Dissociative state? An uncommon reaction to an overwhelming stress," I said. "Something snaps, and the patient goes into a kind of autopilot. He or she is functional, but not rational. Or legally accountable."

Claire glanced at me with a raised eyebrow.

"I know." I nodded. "Many psychiatrists are skeptical, too."

"And you?"

"Oh, I think it's a real entity. But in spite of what defense lawyers would have you believe, it's damn rare."

"So you're saying these forensic patients fake their mental illnesses?"

"Not exactly." I'd worn the tires bare on this particular subject, but I pushed ahead anyway. "Many are genuine sociopaths. That is, they lack the ability to form any kind of meaningful bond with others."

She shook her head. "Is that really a mental illness?"

"Probably, but I don't consider sociopaths as having diseased brains. They're often the clearest-thinking people I've met. To me, it's more like they're missing part or all of their soul. Regardless, there's no cure—if that's the right word—for the condition. You can't teach someone to feel."

"But it isn't a legal defense, either," Claire pointed out.

"True. But unlike your garden-variety criminals, most sociopaths are very clever. What's more, they're born con artists. They excel at fooling so-called experts like me into diagnosing them with all kinds of bogus psychiatric conditions."

She nodded pensively as she tapped the steering wheel with a thumb. "Sounds challenging."

"Exhausting is more like it. On top of everything, a lot of these guys act like Charles Manson. The in-your-face stares, threatening remarks, the crazy cackle. At first it's spooky, then it's just annoying." I shook my head. "Charlie Manson is to forensic psychiatry what Elvis is to Vegas."

Claire laughed and ran a hand over her ear, tucking a few stray strands of dark-blond hair behind it. I decided that even in profile, with her delicate straight nose and strong chin, she had a warm face. "And you?" I asked.

"Can't do Manson or Elvis. But I do a wicked Kate Hepburn." Her head trembled slightly as she launched into a perfect Hepburnesque stutter. " 'I still love you, you old fool.' "

Claire Shepherd was definitely growing on me. "Why the detective thing?" I asked.

"I'm a hundred percent pure-bred cop," she said with a trace of pride. "Mom, Dad, and both sisters, all on the job."

"Wow. You like it?"

"I love it," she said without hesitation.

"And before you found love in Homicide?"

She shot me a sidelong glance. "I found divorce in Denver."

"Oh?"

"I did the usual female cop thing," she said casually. "I married the job."

"He was your partner?"

"No." She cleared her throat. "But we worked together in Narcotics. My first detective's assignment."

"What happened?"

She reddened. "It didn't work out," she said softly.

I picked up on the evasiveness in her tone. If she were a patient, I would've pursued it, but instead I asked, "Then what?"

"I moved to Seattle for a fresh start," she said, her voice strong again. "I had to work the beat for a year until I got my detective's stripes again. I was in Vice for a while, and now Homicide."

I smiled. "Working your way up the criminal ladder."

"I guess. How about you?"

"I never met anybody in Narcotics."

She fired another skeptical glance. "Didn't Dr. Greene mention somebody? Loren?"

He did, damn him. "I was married once, too."

"Didn't work out?"

"Not as planned." I cleared my throat. "She died."

She glanced over to me, eyes wide and lips parted in surprise. "Joel, I'm sorry," she said gently.

"It was a long time ago." I attempted to come off sounding light, but as usual, the subject of Lor was a conversation killer.

We parked outside the SPD's building on Virginia just off Eighth Street, the center of an eclectic area of light business and industrial enterprises. We mounted the steps to the third floor and met Dev in his cramped office.

"If that car of yours was a horse, they'd shoot it," he said by way of greeting.

"I might shoot it, anyway." I sat on the edge of his desk, leaving Claire the only other chair in his office. "Listen, Dev . . . um . . . ," I stammered. "I don't know how relevant it is, but there's something I should tell you about Stanley Kolberg." I went on to give Dev the same vague explanation as I had Claire about my patient's sexual abuse allegations.

When I finished, Dev stared hard at me. "And that patient's name is?"

"You know I can't say." I held my palms up. "Patient-doctor confidentiality."

He accepted my refusal with a side-to-side crack of his neck and a heavy sigh. "When doctors start abusing their patients, there's usually more than one victim, true?"

"Usually," I said.

"But it's rare for abuse victims to strike back," Claire said with a hint of disappointment in her tone. "Let alone with the kind of violence we saw on Kolberg's floor."

Dev nodded absentmindedly. I'd worked with him long enough to recognize that his gut told him my disclosure was significant but like Claire he opted not to push me further on the subject.

"I've been thinking about Mitch's question," I said. "Namely, why would the killer beat up a corpse?"

"Whad'ya come up with?" Dev asked.

"What if he didn't mean to shoot Stanley?" I said. "At least, not right away. Let's say he went in to punish Stanley. He's got the mother-of-all-hates on and he's going to teach him a lesson. But when he gets into the office, he snaps. He's raging so out of control that he shoots Stanley before he even has a chance to lay into him. I'm not even sure he's a bad shot like Mitch suggested. I see him shaking with anger.

Maybe that's why one shot ended up in the ceiling and the other almost missed, too."

Dev and Claire shared a glance, but neither commented.

"And the damage to Stanley's arms and genitals?" I said.

"What about it?" Dev asked.

"If you're looking for symbolism, it's not so much sexual as emasculating. Think about it. The right hand and testicles—the embodiment of a man's power and potency."

Claire folded her arms across her chest. "Since when are murderers so poetic?"

"I'm just trying to earn my keep around here."

"We'll see." Dev rose from his seat. "C'mon. Let's go talk to our guests."

Our three guests were Stanley's most recent discharges from Western State Hospital. All three shared the distinction of having committed at least one murder. According to Dev, they were appearing "voluntarily," but in my experience, that was a vague term in his vocabulary.

Though Stanley had been their attending psychiatrist, I'd spent time with all three at some point, so we agreed it would be best if I watched from behind the interview room's two-way mirror. I took my seat in the dark observation room and stared through the glass into the interview room, with its permanently flickering fluorescent light, as Dev and Claire led in the first candidate, Wayne Hacking, who—considering the crime he'd committed—had an unfortunate last name.

Tall and slight, Hacking was pushing forty. He had a baby face, jovial blue eyes, and an easy smile. I knew he'd been a model patient at Western State—compliant, motivated, and no behavioral issues. Hard to correlate the patient I knew, and sort of liked, with the man the cops had found in his apartment standing over his girlfriend and her sister and repeatedly stabbing their very dead torsos. According to the arresting officers, although the walls dripped with blood and the gore pooled a half-inch deep on the linoleum floors, Hacking still slashed away at the two women. No motive, no attempt to escape the crime scene, and no remorse. At his trial, Stanley Kolberg argued on behalf of the defense that Hacking's was the classic dissociative crime. The jury agreed, returning with a verdict of not guilty by reason of insanity. The judge sent him to Western State for what amounted to a five-year term, or, as one of the more cynical nurses pointed out, two and a half years per sister.

I had a head-on view of the interview table. Claire and Dev sat to my left, Hacking to my right. His clean-cut appearance hadn't changed since his discharge. Neither had his disposition. A grin was welded onto his face as Claire launched into the interrogation. "You were a patient of Dr. Kolberg's for more than five years?" she asked over the crackling of the speaker in the observation room.

He nodded. "True."

"And after your discharge ten months ago, you remained under his care?"

"That's right."

"When did you last see him?" she asked.

"At my appointment last Friday."

"You never had any problems with Dr. Kolberg?"

Hacking glanced to either side then leaned forward as if divulging a secret. "A lot of people tell me that the jury wouldn't have believed me without Dr. Kolberg's testimony. He saved my life and helped me get well again."

Claire asked a series of questions about Hacking's relationship with Kolberg, but none of Hacking's answers shed much light. I thought I detected impatience in her tone when she finally asked, "Monday evening, where were you between nine o'clock and midnight?"

"At my girlfriend's."

Dev, leaning back in his chair, weighed in for the first time. "Your girlfriend," he drew out the syllables. "Does she know about your dating history? More importantly, does her sister?"

Hacking's smile flickered momentarily, but soon returned in full radiance. "We met during my trial."

I remembered his girlfriend. I'd seen her at the psychiatric hospital a few times. She visited, phoned, and wrote him at every chance. Her puppy-dog attentiveness and transparent lack of self-esteem bordered on a stereotype of the breed of women who fell for incarcerated violent offenders.

"And when we ask her, she'll tell us the two of you were together the whole evening, huh?" Dev said.

"I hope so." Hacking laughed.

"She'd probably swear that the two of you were taking a stroll on the moon, if that's what you wanted."

Hacking shrugged pleasantly. "We were in Yvonne's apartment."

"Wayne, do you know of anyone who wanted to harm Dr. Kolberg?" Claire asked.

Hacking stared up at the flickering light before answering. "He worked with some violent and unpredictable patients, you know?" he said, seemingly unaware of the irony of his comment. "I think you're on the right track by checking up on all his patients from Western State."

Claire thanked Hacking for his time and led him to the door.

Before the interviewee chair had a chance to cool, Nick Papadous was sitting across from the detectives. I remembered Papadous well. At the age of nineteen, after stopping his medications, he'd gone on a shooting rampage through his family home with his father's hunting rifle. Why his father kept a loaded rifle in the house when he knew his son suffered from violent delusions was beyond me, but Papadous was a lousy shot and in the end only his grandmother paid the ultimate price for the father's questionable judgment, when a bullet ricocheted off the fireplace and slammed into her head.

Of medium height, chubby and bald, Papadous had a propensity for hypervigilance and excessive sweating that made him look perpetually guilty. I knew he wasn't going to fare well in this interview.

After introductions, Claire asked, "You okay, Nick?"

"Fine. Why?" The sweat had already begun to bead on his forehead. He pointed a shaky finger at the mirror in front of me, and asked, "Someone watching me?"

"Not important, Nick," Dev said. "Tell us about Dr. Kolberg."

"He was my shrink in lockup. So what, okay?"

"Nick, did you still see Dr. Kolberg after you got out?" Claire asked.

"I got my own psychiatrist now. An Indian guy, Dr. Singh."

"Why not Kolberg?" Dev asked.

"That's who they gave me," Papadous said. "I never liked Dr. Kolberg, anyway."

"How come?"

He glanced over his shoulder. "He made me nervous, you know?"

It seemed to me a ladybug would make Papadous nervous. I wondered why he singled out Stanley. So did Dev. "I bet lots of people make you nervous, Nick. What was so special about Dr. Kolberg?"

"He said weird stuff. Always pushing me on how it felt when I killed Grandma. And I didn't even remember. I was really sick when I did it."

"Pissed you off, huh, Nick?" Dev asked.

"I guess."

"Made you want to even the score, right?" Dev said.

"No." Papadous's eyes widened with alarm. Sweat dripped from his face onto his shirt. "I'm taking my medicines now."

"Nick." Claire smiled, her stillness in stark contrast to Papadous's writhing. "Where were you the evening before last?"

Papadous's eyes darted around the room, but Claire's voice had a calming effect on him. "I'm staying at St. Martin de Porres. The shelter downtown. I was just watching TV or whatever."

"Someone can confirm that?" Claire asked.

"I guess so." He shook his head. "I didn't kill Dr. Kolberg. Okay?"

When Papadous stood to leave, Claire asked, "Who did kill him, Nick?"

"Maybe some other guy he pushed too far?"

Claire had barely finished thanking Papadous for coming in before he disappeared through the doorway. With a chuckle, she got up and led in the next guest.

Of the three, I was least familiar with the final interviewee, but I knew that Ron Weaver was an enigma even in terms of Western State's population. Weaver had been convicted of voluntary manslaughter. The incident had begun in a bar over the contested ownership of a pack of cigarettes and ended in a parking lot where Weaver bashed in another man's skull with a garden shovel. He was convicted of the lesser charge of manslaughter in large part because of Stanley's testimony regarding the newly established entity called "rage disorder." As part of the sentencing agreement, Weaver served his first three years in prison and his final three at the psychiatric hospital.

In his mid-forties, Weaver had thinning brown hair and a face so nondescript that he could've safely robbed a bank without a mask. Sitting still in his seat, he stared straight past the detectives as they fired question after question at him.

"You were still seeing Dr. Kolberg after your release?" Claire asked.

"It was a condition of my discharge," he said in a monotone.

"You didn't like him?"

"He was okay."

"But you didn't need a psychiatrist?" Dev said. "You were doing him a favor, huh?"

"I still had issues."

"Oh, that's right. You've got a bit of a temper." Dev folded his hands behind his head. "You haven't been doing any shoveling lately, have you?"

Weaver sat motionless.

"Did you ever lose your temper with Dr. Kolberg?" Dev asked.

"No."

"Never?" Dev raised an eyebrow. "Because we could ask his secretary if she remembers you losing it."

Weaver paused a moment. "Sometimes he encouraged me to."

"To have a temper tantrum?" Dev asked.

"He called it 'controlled venting.' No damage done."

"Ron, where were you Monday evening?" Claire asked.

"At home. In bed with a book."

"Were you alone?"

"Yes."

"This book wasn't covered in blood, was it?" Dev prodded.

"I didn't kill Dr. Kolberg."

"Of course not," Dev said. "You'd come right out and tell us if you did."

I wasn't sure if the detectives could tell, but from my vantage point, I saw Weaver's legs moving. He rubbed his feet together in agitation though his face remained impassive.

"How do we know you're not shoveling us something?" Dev asked.

Weaver's eye twitched. "I'd like to talk to a lawyer."

"Why?" Dev smiled insincerely. "I thought you didn't do anything, Ron."

"I want to talk to a lawyer." Weaver struggled to keep the emotion from his voice.

Dev's grin grew wider. And nastier. "Want me to ask him to bring in a pack of smokes and a shovel?"

Weaver rubbed the table in front of him with the palm of his hand. "I have nothing more to say without my lawyer," he hissed. He pulled his hand from the table and dropped it to his side. "Am I under arrest?" he asked, his voice again passionless. "Or may I go now?"

Dev glanced at Claire and then, without looking at Weaver, he said, "Don't go too far, huh, Ron?"

After Claire led Weaver out of the room, Dev turned to the mirror and held his palms up. "Perfect, Doc. I think all three of them did it."

As I waited for Claire and Dev, I reflected on the differences between a psychiatric and a criminal interview. Psychiatrists don't often pull the good cop–bad cop routine. And I think we tend to come off as a little more empathetic.

But in the end, we're after the same goal: the truth. I'm not sure whose approach is more effective. I hate to think how long it took me to get anywhere near the truth with Angela Connor.

Eleven months earlier, by the end of Angela's second week of hospitalization, our rapport had improved substantially. But I couldn't shake my suspicion that she was holding something back. Needing a second opinion, I turned to Stanley when we met for our weekly lunch.

After giving a summary of Angela's situation without naming her—even between each other, we protected patients' confidentiality—I said, "There's something lurking under the surface that I can't get to, which makes no sense. Within five minutes of meeting her, she launched into explicit details of her incestuous abuse. What could she be hiding that's so much worse?"

Stanley took a long sip of his water before answering. "It's in the eye of the beholder, isn't it?"

"What is?"

"I had a patient once," Stanley said, and then stopped to have a bite of salad. (He always ate salad for lunch, which helped to explain his skinniness.) "A sociopath. The most dangerous man I've ever met. Off the cuff, during our second interview, he mentioned that when he was twelve he killed his entire family—both parents and a younger brother. Rigged a fire when he knew they were asleep. He understood the constraints of patient-therapist confidentiality, and he was a minor at the time so he had little to fear by telling me, but it was the casualness of the confession . . ." He shook his head. "I don't know why he told me. Not to shock me. Not to boast. And certainly not to relieve his conscience! He didn't have one. Two years later, after I'd established as intimate a therapeutic relationship as one can have with a sociopath, he told me of an incident when his mother dressed him in girl's clothes. He was all of four at the time, but it still mortified him." Stanley wagged his fork at me. "He hung on to

*that secret as if it were the key to life itself. He threatened to
kill me if I ever shared his preschool cross-dressing experience, and yet he didn't seem to care if I told the world he'd
incinerated his family. Odd what does and doesn't matter to
people."*

I shook my head. "So how does that help me get through
to my patient?"

"She'll tell you when she's ready. They always do."

"Two more years, you figure?"

"Didn't I teach you anything, Joel?" Stanley chuckled.
"Patients are predictable. All you need is patience." Fork
still in hand, he cupped his palms together and then opened
them like an oyster. "Win her trust, and you'll gain access to
everything."

What I didn't know, and what he never mentioned, was
that I might not want that access.

Despite Angela's guardedness, she was making progress.
Most of her nurses, even those who'd entertained thoughts of
killing her, had warmed to her. As the antidepressants had a
chance to work, a less volatile, sweeter, and surprisingly
more needy personality emerged. She began to resemble the
person her brother had described.

On her fifteenth day of hospitalization, we met in the hospital's interview room. She had combed her short hair forward so that it stood off her head in uneven spears. I was
pleased to see that she'd worn street clothes—jeans and a
sweatshirt, as opposed to the hospital pajamas. Tough to tell
with her sweatshirt on, but I thought her jeans looked loose.

She plopped down in the chair across from my desk.
"When can I go home, Dr. Ashman?" she asked, crossing
her legs.

"You're not under evaluation anymore, Angela. I can't
stop you from leaving."

She looked down and smoothed her jeans over her knee.
"You think I'm ready to go?"

"Do you?"

"You shrinks!" She groaned and worked the creases in

her jeans above the knee more vigorously. "Are you required by law to answer every question with another?"

"Should I be?" I smiled.

"That's so lame, Dr. Ashman." But she laughed anyway. "I think I could do with another week or two." Uncertainty crept onto her face. "Does that sound right?"

I marveled at her ability to flip-flop between defiance and indecision. Maybe it was exaggerated by her depression, but I was beginning to recognize that paradox as part of her nature. "Why another week or two? You don't trust yourself?"

She smoothed the creases of her sweatshirt's baggy sleeves. "I'm not sure I'm ready to go back into the world yet, you know?"

I nodded. "Will you be ready in another week or two?"

She shrugged and looked away.

I took advantage of the lull that followed to ask, "Angela, how did it begin?"

With a sigh, she said, "How did what begin?"

She wasn't fooling me. I folded my arms and leaned back in my chair.

"Oh, that's mature!" Angela moaned, but after a moment, she began to talk. "When I was eleven, I went with Daddy on a business trip to Victoria, up in Canada. He promised to take me to their provincial museum." She dropped her eyes to the floor. "I was so excited, because we were staying at the Empress Hotel. Posh, you know? We had a room with a king-sized bed. And they brought up a rollaway cot." She cleared her throat. "No one used the cot that weekend. I don't even remember if I saw the fucking museum."

"Did you tell anyone what happened?"

Angela moved her head almost imperceptibly from side to side.

"How come?"

"I didn't think anyone would believe me."

"But it continued after Victoria?"

She nodded at her shoes. "Not that often. Daddy was

careful. We had our share of father-daughter trips . . . always built around some lame excuse about whatever landmark was worth seeing in the local community."

"Did your brother or sister ever go on those trips?"

"Not on the same ones, but he wasn't stupid. He'd take my brother and sister on other business trips. Not as much, though."

I didn't comment.

"I'm pretty sure he wasn't screwing them, if that's what you're thinking."

"How do you know?"

Her head still down, she sniffed a couple of times and ran a hand across her eyes. "He used to call me his 'special girl.' He'd say how Ellen was the smart one, and Tommy the strong one, but I was the beautiful one. The one with a special gift. How only I could help him." She wiped her eyes again, and said, in a near whisper, "Isn't that stupid? But it used to mean a lot. Made me feel okay about myself. Made everything else bearable."

I could feel my ire rising, but I kept my voice in check. "When did it stop?"

"Beginning of twelfth grade. I was seventeen."

"Why?"

"Guess Daddy was getting on." She shrugged. "Viagra wasn't around yet."

"It's important, Angela," I coaxed.

"I told Tommy that summer."

"Did he believe you?" I asked.

She shrugged again.

"But he spoke to your dad?"

She nodded.

"What did he say to him?"

"I don't know." Another shrug. "But it stopped after that."

"That was about nine years ago, right?" I asked.

"I guess."

"And your father died when?"

"Four years ago," she said quietly.

I frowned. "You were first hospitalized three years ago, right?"

"Around there." She sighed.

"And this is your third time in the hospital since?"

"Something like that." Her tone suggested she was losing patience.

"After the abuse stopped, you spent four years away at college, and then held down a job for a year. In that time, you never saw a therapist or took antidepressants?"

"So?" she snapped.

"I'm confused by the timing of your troubles."

"You're right." She eyed me defiantly. "Daddy molesting me had nothing to do with it. My real problems began after he died, when I met my first shrink."

"Oh?"

She glared, looking as if she were about to expand on her comment. But then she looked away. Her voice calmed. "You're making a big deal out of nothing."

"It never started again with your father before he died?"

"He never touched me again. Not even a kiss on the cheek."

"No one else?" I asked.

"Not anybody I didn't want touching me," she said with a forced laugh, but I thought I picked up on a familiar evasiveness in her tone and body language.

After Angela left, I sat in my office and stewed. My thoughts drifted to my own dad.

He wasn't the most reliable guy. I couldn't begin to remember all the places he left me waiting, but a few of my more familiar haunts, like the empty school foyer or the curb in front of the closed ice rink, are etched in my memory. At some point, his car would fly up to the curb. "Sorry, pal. I got detained," Dad would say, whether he was ten minutes or three hours late. Sometimes he didn't show up at all. He would disappear from my life for weeks on end. Sometimes it was a lecture or book tour. (A psychology professor, he wrote a series of modestly successful pop psychology books before *the genre mushroomed into a multibillion-dollar industry.) Other times Dad was gone without explanation. Even if he was home when I went to bed, chances were that if I woke up in the middle of the night and stole into my parents' bedroom, he'd be missing. Mom would wave away his absence. "Working late," she'd say. By the time I hit ten, I knew "working late" was a euphemism for something less wholesome, though I didn't know what.*

But like most people, I loved David Ashman. With his runner's physique, sympathetic eyes, and square youthful face, Dad was good-looking enough, but it was his charm that won people over time and again. He had the gift of making anyone with him feel like the only person alive. Women, especially, gravitated to him. For me, Dad's attention was like an addiction. The more he lavished on me, the more I wanted to win his approval. His interests were my interests— football, jogging, jazz, historical novels, and baseball. Especially baseball.

In spite of all that has passed, memories of warm summer-evening ball games and hot dogs with Dad are among the happiest of my childhood. Thirty years later, I remain an avid baseball fan long after my dogged devotion for Dad decayed into pure contempt.

4

EIGHT HOURS AFTER THE INTERVIEWS of Stanley's three forensic patients, I left my day job at the Cascade Mental Health Team and took a cab back to Homicide. I strode into Dev's office determined to disentangle myself from an investigation that I was already far too personally invested in. But the sight of Claire Shepherd's emerald green eyes and welcoming smile dented my resolve. I decided my resignation could wait a few minutes.

I sat down beside her in the wobbly folding chair that had been dragged in since my last visit. Across the desk, Dev sat back in his seat with arms folded behind his head. His blue polo shirt was even more crumpled and the bags under his eyes a little more prominent than they had been that morning. Unlike Dev, there was nothing stale in Claire's appearance. Either she was a whiz with the cosmetics, or she possessed natural, low-maintenance good looks. Too early to tell, but I hoped for the latter.

When Claire spun her chair toward me, I caught a hint of

a fragrance that seemed familiar, but I couldn't place it. I liked it. "Out car shopping?" she asked hopefully.

"No reason to," I said. "The shop's fixing up mine good as new."

Claire grinned. "I see a lot of walking in your future."

Dev interrupted the exchange with a stifled yawn. "Doc, we've been busy since you left."

"Productive?" I asked.

Claire nodded eagerly. "We followed up on this morning's interviews. We spoke to Yvonne Carpinelli, Hacking's girl-friend. She vouches for him on the evening of the murder."

"Yvonne would've covered for the iceberg the night it sank the *Titanic*," Dev scoffed, shaking his head. "I'm not ready to close the book on Hacking yet."

"And Nick Papadous's alibi looks tight," Claire said. "Lots of people saw him fretting and sweating around the St. Martin de Porres shelter on the night in question."

"Leaving only Ron Weaver without an alibi," I thought aloud.

"Yeah, Doc, what did you make of the Shoveler?"

"Even before you got him riled, I thought he came off as a little too controlled," I said. "Too detached. His whole de-meanor reminded me of a fresh coat of plaster covering some serious dry rot. I think he's still seething on the in-side."

Dev nodded. "Your old secretary had concerns, too."

Bonnie Hubbard, Stanley's sixtyish secretary, was liable to have taken his murder harder than anyone. The sweet spinster worshipped Stanley. She used to wear her unre-quited love for him around the office like one of her cardi-gans. "Bonnie discussed patients by name?" I asked, troubled by the implication.

Claire nodded. "She gave us the last month's appointment books along with a list of Kolberg's anger-management group. All of fifteen names, including Weaver's. Who, by the way, she puts among the most volatile."

I grimaced. "That's privileged information," I said.

Claire eyed me intently. With her smile gone, I caught a

glimpse of the same toughness I'd seen at our initial encounter. "Bonnie gave us those names willingly. No coercion. Besides, as Kolberg was murdered in his own office, we have reasonable cause to suspect one of his patients. Legally, those records become part of the criminal investigation. And so by rights, they're ours."

The surprise must have registered on my face, because Dev laughed. "Didn't know she had a master's in criminology, huh?"

Claire reached over and touched me above the wrist. Save for our initial handshake, it was our first physical contact, and I was acutely aware of her soft warm fingers on my arm. "Bonnie's devastated, Joel." Her tone mellowed. "She just wants to see the killer caught. And she trusts us to be discreet."

It wasn't Bonnie's trust to give, but I understood her intention.

Dev stretched in his seat. "By the way, Doc, Bonnie didn't exactly buy the idea that Kolberg was molesting his patients."

"No, she wouldn't."

"I'll say." Dev cracked his knuckles. "It put her right over the top. We might as well have told her that Mother Teresa used to fondle the orphans and lepers."

I sighed. Dev could play the caricature of a hard-nosed cop so well that at times I would buy into it. But there was more to him than he liked to let on. I'd seen his other side: the dedicated husband, father of five boys, and football coach for the kids in one of the city's most underprivileged neighborhoods. Underneath the narrow-minded persona he often assumed, he was smart and well read with two night school college degrees to prove it. But today he was all streetwise cop. "Yeah, old Bonnie thought Kolberg was the hot dog and the bun, but she didn't have much good to say about Calvin Nichol." He clicked his tongue. "What's the deal with that guy?"

"What 'deal'?" I asked.

Claire held out a palm. "Joel, did you know Calvin had left the practice?"

I shook my head. "Really? Stanley was like a god to Cal."

"How the mighty have fallen," Dev grumbled.

"Meaning?"

"According to Bonnie," Claire said, "before Nichol left, there were at least two big blowouts between him and Kolberg."

I blew out my lips. "I'm not sure I've ever heard either of them raise their voice."

"Full-on screaming matches, Doc."

"About what?"

"Bonnie didn't know," Claire said. "But she said Kolberg looked worried after their last fight and that worried her because—"

"Stanley never looked worried." I finished her sentence. Stanley was ice incarnate.

"How do you get on with Nichol?" Dev asked.

"Cal was a good business partner, but we're not close."

"We're gonna go see him in a couple of minutes," Dev said. "Why don't you come along?"

I shook my head. "I think that would be too weird."

"He asked for you," Dev said. "Specifically."

This evening was full of surprises. "Why?"

"Maybe he trusts you, Joel," Claire offered.

Maybe. But I had my doubts. Before I could reply, a booming voice and roar of laughter interrupted us. I looked over to see Mitch Greene barge into the room. Free of his OR scrubs, he wore a rumpled gray suit, the jacket straining at the seams, and a tie that didn't reach his belt. "You all still here?" he asked. "If I made what you make, I'd be gone by four thirty." He guffawed. "Hell, I'd be gone by noon."

"Yeah," Dev said. "And if I made what you make, I'd buy a suit that fit."

"Thanks. I got oodles of respect for your taste in clothing." Greene thumbed at Dev's wrinkled and faded polo shirt. "Enough chitchat. I brought you something."

Greene dropped his briefcase on the floor. Grunting, he rummaged around until he pulled out a file folder holding a stack of enlarged photos. "After I got you out of my hair at the morgue, I went back and had a closer look at the victim's surface anatomy." He tossed down the first photograph.

We crowded around Dev's desk to study the photo of Stanley's chest. Greene dropped another snapshot on top of it—a close-up of one of his nipples surrounded by sparse hair. On its undersurface were two distinct puncture marks.

"Recognize these?" Greene tapped the skin lesions with a sausage-like finger.

Claire's jaw fell open slightly. "Kolberg pierced his nipple?"

"Both of them." Greene threw another close-up onto the pile. It showed similar holes on an area of skin I didn't readily identify.

But Dev did. "Kolberg pierced his pecker?!"

Greene nodded. "Right below the glans, or tip, of the penis."

"No!" Claire's expression lay somewhere between laughter and disgust.

Greene dropped one more photo on the desk—a picture of a man's back. "Without another morgue assistant, I couldn't log-roll the patient until after you left." The skin showed none of the weapon marks seen on his chest; instead, a series of vertical scrapes and cuts scabbed Stanley's back and buttocks.

"Oh my God!" Claire said. "Was he whipped?"

"Show me a man who isn't." Greene howled. "Sharp eye, Claire. The striations are from a good old cat-o'-nine-tails." He flicked his wrist and made a whipping noise like something out of a B Western. "But wounds preceded death by a good three to seven days."

Dev sat upright in his chair. "Put it together for us, Mitch."

Greene flipped through the photos. "These piercings, we see them in the bondage and sadomasochism crowd. You run little bars or hoops through the skin and then hook chains to them. So your life partner—or someone you're paying by the hour—can drag you around the room in a loving frolic. After, instead of a cuddle, he or she can beat the crap out of you." He chortled. "The scars don't lie. Old Stanley was seriously into S and M." Greene eyed me with a sad shake of his head. "Ash-Man, I knew you shrinks were some of the stragglers in the human race, but to find this on a renowned sixty-three-year-old physician surprised even me. And believe me, I don't get surprised often."

The rest of us sat silently as Greene showed us the mounting photographic evidence backing his theory. I stared at the photos, but my mind was miles and years away.

After Greene departed, Dev turned to me. "How about you, Doc? You surprised?"

"No," I admitted.

Dev tapped the photo of Stanley's raw back. "Your patient told you about this sadism stuff?"

I hesitated. "Yes," I finally said.

Claire turned to me, her eyes clouding with suspicion. "What did you do about it?"

"Wasn't much I could do," I said softly. "All I had was her word that she had participated, consensually, in his twisted sexual antics."

"Which is still illegal," Claire said sharply. "You didn't report him?"

"I wanted to." I shrugged helplessly. "But my patient wasn't willing to step forward. Even if she had, it would've ended up her word against his." I looked from one to the other. "Who would you believe? A psych patient or one of the most respected physicians in the city?"

Claire folded her arms across her chest. "Joel, I thought you said she had proof."

"Only a burn on her back. It was enough for me, but it wouldn't have convinced anyone who didn't know her." I paused. "And she wrote some journal entries, but that didn't support anything more than her word."

"Do you still have copies of her writing, Doc?" Dev asked.

I shook my head. "Even if I did . . ."

"You couldn't show us." To my surprise, Dev accepted my

defiance with a nod. "But if your patient was telling the truth about Kolberg, then there must have been others, right?"

I nodded.

"And one of them might have already complained." Claire snapped her fingers excitedly. "Joel, where would someone lodge that kind of complaint?"

"The Washington State Department of Health."

"We'll be visiting there tomorrow," Dev said.

"Might be a waste of a trip." I shrugged. "Unless Stanley was officially censured—and I'd have heard if he was— those records are confidential. The department won't disclose a list of unsubstantiated complaints."

Dev rose to his feet. "We'll just see about that." He grinned confidently.

I followed Claire and Dev out of the office and down to the street, but I didn't move when they began to load into Claire's car. Dev straightened up and looked at me. "You coming?"

"I think it's time for me to bow out."

"Your life too tangled up with the victim's?" Claire asked with an understanding smile.

I nodded, thinking how I might really miss her.

"Doc, I can live without your company." Dev leaned his elbows against the hood of the car. "But you know the players. This is your world. That's a huge plus for us."

Claire's half-grin didn't hide the ultimatum in her eyes: *Time to piss or get off the pot.* I wavered a moment and then, ignoring my inner voice, I opened the back door and slid into the seat.

A short drive later and we were in Belltown, a reclaimed former manufacturing district now considered one of Seattle's hottest neighborhoods for childless professionals. Claire parked in front of Nichol's modern condominium complex. Calvin Nichol's building was one of those cold steel-and-glass jobs that were so popular in the area.

Nichol buzzed us up and met us at the door of his seventeenth-floor, three-bedroom unit. In his early fifties, lean and very tall—at least six-four—he had a thatch of graying hair along with a meticulously cropped mustache and beard. Again, it struck me that his far-set, indecipherable gray eyes suited his mostly expressionless and unreadable face.

Occasionally, I'm surprised by people's homes; they contradict everything the therapist in me expects to find based on their personality. But Nichol's home was exactly as I'd imagined. Austerely furnished with matching Craftsmen oak pieces, sleek cloth sofas, and several abstract lithographs, I would have had no qualms about eating off the hardwood floors. I wondered how many times a day Nichol vacuumed. My obsessive-compulsive meter was reading high.

After introductions, Nichol led us into the living room where we sat in front of a gas fireplace in a circle formed by high-back chairs. He offered us mineral water—I suspected he couldn't bear the thought of anything else spilling on his furniture—but we declined.

Claire led the interview. "Dr. Nichol, you didn't know anyone, particularly patients, who might've wanted to harm Dr. Kolberg?"

"I'm sure Joel has told you about the . . ." Nichol looked to the ceiling for guidance. "The more challenging patients Stanley worked with."

Dev nodded. "We're looking for names."

"We weren't in the habit of sharing names with each other, but I might recognize the most disruptive ones."

Dev nodded. "How about a description?"

Nichol described two of Stanley's anger-management patients "whose tirades stood out over the others'." The second one sounded like he could have been anyone, which meant he must have been the Shoveler.

"How about Wayne Hacking or Nick Papadous?" Dev asked.

Nichol shook his head. "Again, I didn't know his patients by name."

"Okay," Dev said. "And the big fights? What were they all about?"

I'd seen Dev surprise witnesses before with the tactic of firing an accusation out of left field, but it was a bust with Nichol. "You mean between Stanley and me?" His eyes remained as opaque as ever.

"Bonnie told us you were leaving," Claire said.

Nichol turned to me. "I'd had enough."

"Of?" I asked.

Nichol took a deep breath. "For ten years we talked about his so-called special-needs patients. And each year more ex-convicts showed up in our office. And then his anger-management groups sprang up. Remember how our clients felt, Joel?" He turned to the detectives. "They had to share the waiting room with Stanley's patients or listen to the temper tantrums through the walls. Many of my clients have anxiety disorders. Imagine how they felt in that milieu." He shook his head. "I was starting to lose my practice. I felt unsafe walking to my car after dark. I decided to leave. And I told Stanley so."

"In no uncertain terms," Claire said.

Nichol stroked his beard the way Stanley used to. "He didn't like what I had to say, and the whole thing escalated into a shouting match."

"That's it?" Dev said skeptically. "A brawl over the kinds of patients filling the waiting room?"

"You have to understand, it was a big problem." Nichol sighed. "I feel sick about it now. An awful way to end a twenty-five-year friendship."

"I can think of worse," Dev said.

Nichol must have picked up on the less than subtle accusation, but he didn't rise to the bait. Instead, he lapsed into silence.

"Joel." Dev turned to me. "Do you want to tell Dr. Nichol about the autopsy findings?" He left it to me to raise the most awkward subject.

Nichol eyed me curiously. "What findings?"

"Cal, on autopsy Mitch Greene uncovered a few surprises about Stanley's . . . uh . . . lifestyle," I said.

Nichol raised an eyebrow.

"He had body piercings." I cleared my throat. "And cuts from a whip. The whole thing suggested Stanley was into S and M."

"Sadomasochism?" I thought Nichol might choke on the word. "Stanley?!" He shook his head. "I wasn't aware of Stanley dating since Olivia and he divorced. I assumed he had no romantic life. But this . . ."

The interview didn't go far after the disclosure. We left my flustered ex-partner in his chair and headed back to Claire's car.

No one spoke until we had loaded back into her car. Then Dev looked over his shoulder at me. "Whad'ya think?"

"It's true what he said about Stanley's violent patients." I shrugged. "It always bugged Cal more than me."

Claire nodded. "But?"

"As Cal said, it had been an issue for ten years. Why did it flare up in two fights and his sudden exodus?"

"Maybe Nichol really had had enough?" Claire suggested.

"Yeah, maybe," I said half-heartedly.

Claire dropped me off at my house just before 9 P.M. While walking from the car, she called out after me, "If you need a ride tomorrow, give me a call. I don't live far."

I thought I heard Dev add a remark, but when I looked over my shoulder Claire's window was already rolled up. She drove off with a quick wave.

When I opened my front door, Nelson lifted his head from where he lay in front of the staircase. That was as much of a greeting as I was going to get. My male retriever-shepherd cross was old, possibly thirteen. He was already getting on when Lor chose him at the King County Humane Society seven years earlier. Since Loren died, Nelson and I tolerated one another's company like an old married couple who never much liked each other even before the kids moved out. In Nelson's defense, I wasn't much of a dog person. In my defense, Nelson wasn't much of a people dog. But he did love Lor. He used to follow her around the house like her shadow. Then again, she was easy to love.

"Come on, Nelson," I said, reaching for his leash in the front closet. "Time to work those arthritic hips."

Nelson stood up with more enthusiasm than he usually showed for his walk. But instead of meeting me at the front door, he trotted to the back window. He began to bark and even tried to jump up on the window ledge so he could peer into the yard. Nelson rarely barked, especially with as much alarm in his voice. I hurried over to the kitchen and turned on the backyard light. I squinted out the window, but I couldn't see anything in the weak light.

I was about to write it off to Nelson's aged imagination when three bangs, each louder than the previous, came from out back. I knew the sound well. My warped back gate wouldn't close unless it was slammed shut, usually three or four times. I rushed over to the back door and stepped outside. I could see that the gate was closed and whoever was in the yard had already gone.

I had a quick look around the house and checked the basement. All the doors were locked and there was no evidence of anyone having gained access to the house. Who would want to break into my house? I wondered. It didn't look like much from the street. Probably just neighborhood kids, I decided.

I leashed Nelson up and headed out the front door. We'd walked only a few steps along the sidewalk when the flash of headlights from behind lit up the stop sign ahead of us. I squinted over my shoulder but couldn't see past the glare of the car's high beams. The car crawled to a halt right behind us and revved its engine once menacingly.

We stood motionless. Nelson whined at the blinding light. My mouth went dry and the hair on my neck stood on end.

Then the sound of a car approaching from the block ahead of us broke the stalemate.

Suddenly, the idling car gunned its engine, screeched its tires, and sped off. As it passed the lights of the oncoming vehicle, I made out the outline of a sole occupant in the big old sedan.

My stomach dropped. What the hell?

5

I GOT UP EARLY THE NEXT MORNING and headed out for a jog as light was just beginning to break over the city. Halfway through my run, I decided that the previous evening's deer-trapped-in-headlights experience had been at most an aborted breaking-and-entering but, more likely, a simple coincidence.

Returning home, I phoned my mechanic, who told me my car wasn't ready and probably never would be. "Why throw good money after bad?" he asked with frank but financially self-defeating honesty. But he couldn't appreciate the car's sentimental value. Fifteen years earlier, Loren and I pooled our student loans and scraped together enough to buy the used Honda. For four years, it got us to and from school. The summer after we married, we practically lived out of it as we crisscrossed the continent on its wheels. Nowadays I couldn't count on it to get me across town, but at the time that car covered over seven thousand miles without a hiccup. We ate, slept, and sometimes, with imaginative and limber positioning, made love inside it.

Rideless, I called Claire and caught her returning from a morning workout. She promised to pick me up in half an hour.

I showered, changed, and headed down the creaky staircase on my way to the kitchen. For three years, I'd intended to fix—or, more accurately, find someone to fix—those damn steps. I could have said the same for most of the house.

We'd bought the place as a fixer-upper. With Loren's design background, she saw so much potential in the early thirties Tudor design. I thought it was a bit of a dump, but I loved the location: a block from Green Lake. Within a minute of stepping out the front door, I could be jogging along the path that surrounds the lake and leads to the trail to the adjacent Woodland Park Zoo. For me, that was the house's main selling feature.

Partway through the planned renovations, we ran short on money. And Lor simply ran out of time. But not before she'd finished the kitchen and family-room area. Huge windows and a skylight bathed the rooms in light. Aside from sleep, I spent most of my time in the warm open space she'd created.

After her home pregnancy test finally revealed the elusive plus sign, Lor had launched into the project of converting our spare bedroom into a nursery. The walls of the powder blue room—now filled with boxes and other junk—are still decorated with the half-colored Pooh Bear and other Winnie the Pooh characters she stenciled on them. I once asked what would happen if our baby came out a girl. She laughed in her infectious way and said, "No. He's a boy. But on the outside chance I'm wrong, worst-case scenario, she grows up loving blue and Pooh." In retrospect, Lor had underestimated the worst-case scenario by a very long shot.

As promised, Claire arrived on time. Rather than honk from her car, she rapped on my front door. No clips today, but her hair was tied back in a ponytail. Together with her more prominent lipstick and eye shadow, it changed the accent on her face, making it more angular, more glamorous. Sexier, too. I would've invited her in, but the whole work-in-progress thing was getting harder to explain after three years.

Once seated in her car, she turned to me with a mischievous grin. "Amazing! Your car isn't roadworthy yet?"

"Any day now."

She looked away. "You know, my sister's friend works for one of the dealerships out in Bothell. He gets good deals on lease-returns. I could take you out there sometime, if you wanted. Or, you know . . . whatever."

I liked the awkwardness of her offer. "Would he look at a trade-in?" I deadpanned.

"Sure," she smiled. "I think if you played hardball, you might be able to get five, six, maybe even up to seven . . . dollars for yours."

I laughed. "Wow. That's three or four more than I bargained on."

We'd run out of lame jokes about my condemned car, and we fell into a clumsy silence, eventually broken by Claire. "Hey, yesterday I shared my life story, but you never told me how you ended up in psychiatry."

I shrugged. "I'm a pretty good listener."

"So I've noticed." She smiled. "Is that all it takes?"

"I'm not only talking about hearing the words," I said. "They can mislead. By listening, I mean absorbing the messenger with the message. If you do that, you can usually cut through the crap and get to the root of the issues."

"Hmmm." She sounded unconvinced.

"I didn't plan on psychiatry. After medical school, I went into an ER residency. Blood and guts were my future. But two years in, I realized that the psychiatric cases—the suicidal or manic or just plain crazy—stuck with me long after the traumas and cardiac cases faded from memory. One day, a year shy of finishing my residency, I went for lunch with the then-department head, Stanley Kolberg. I came back a psych resident."

She kept her eyes fixed on the road. "Do you like the job?" she asked.

"I used to love it." I turned to look out at the gray sky.

"This might sound corny, but I considered it a privilege to be allowed into my clients' personal spaces. I got a rush from helping them make a little sense of their world."

"What happened?"

"Loren died," I blurted.

I felt Claire's eyes on me, but she didn't comment.

"Right after she died, I lost myself in the job." I turned back to face her. "It helped me forget. But after a while, ironically, I suffered from too much empathy. I knew the abject loneliness of some of my patients. I dreaded seeing them." I cleared my throat. "I even had to dismiss one poor woman from my practice. She was a lovely person suffering from a pathological grief reaction. But I couldn't listen to her go on about her unrelenting heartache ten years after a drunk driver mowed down her husband." I swallowed again. "I couldn't imagine carrying the same pain for another nine years."

Claire reached over and touched my arm. "I'm sorry, Joel," she said softly.

"No. I should apologize. I didn't mean to lay all that on you." I laughed self-consciously. "You'd make a good therapist, you know? I don't usually pour my heart out to my drivers."

Claire gave my wrist a quick squeeze before withdrawing her fingers. "Sometimes it does help to talk."

Focusing my gaze on the offices and stores we drove past, I couldn't stave off the image of Loren's smiling face—the wild black curls, deep brown eyes, upturned nose, and adorable freckles. In my vivid memory, Lor always wore a smile, as she usually had in life. Three years after her death, the vision could reopen the wound like a knife.

Thankfully, Claire drew me back to the present. "Okay, we've figured out the psychiatry part but how did you get involved in the criminal profiling?"

"Like the rest of my career choices, Stanley led me into it."

"Did he do it?"

"No. But he knew there weren't any shrinks in the city doing profiling. So I went and did six months of training with the FBI."

"Glad you did?"

"I wouldn't be getting a free ride from you if I hadn't."

"No such thing as a free ride." She chuckled. "You didn't answer me."

"I enjoy it, in limited doses." I studied her pleasing profile. "You've got a master's in criminology, right? You must have some experience in the area."

"Not much." She ran a finger behind her ear, even though there were no stray hairs to comb back. "I used to be in Vice. No profiling to do there. It's all about money and sex."

"I think you've just described 99.99 percent of all crime."

"I suppose," Claire said distantly. "I thought the golden rule in profiling is that the criminal always leaves part of himself at the crime scene. True?"

"Most times. Why?"

"What did Kolberg's killer leave at the crime scene?"

"A lot. He knew Stanley. And he hated him almost more than you can imagine." I continued in a lighter vein. "Most people, especially cops, think psychological profiling is a load of crap. They might be right, too. I'm not sure I'm much more useful than some guy with tea leaves or a divining rod."

Claire shook her head. "I have a feeling you're going to lead us to his killer."

I wasn't so sure, but I was saved from commenting when Claire slowed to a stop in front of Seattle Police Department's headquarters.

Heading toward Homicide, we ran into Dev at the reception area. Wearing perhaps the last pair of stonewashed jeans in circulation, he viewed us with exaggerated disappointment. "Claire, the department frowns on detectives who moonlight as a taxi service. And, Doc, personally I frown on people who are too cheap to pay for a cab."

"I'm told there's no such thing as a free ride," I said, getting a smile out of Claire.

We followed Dev out to the elevator. "Doc, our lawyers say it'll be no problem getting a list of patient complaints from the Department of Health." He didn't disguise his I-told-you-so tone. "Tomorrow, at the latest."

Claire punched Dev playfully on the shoulder. "Where are you taking us, partner?"

"Busy, busy day," he said cheerfully. "We got to start in on Kolberg's anger-management patients. I'm itching to talk to the Shoveler again. Maybe even Wayne Hacking. Christ, I can't get over that guy's name!" He shook his head. "But let's not forget our Homicide 101. More times than not, you don't have to look further than the victim's ex."

Fifteen minutes later, we pulled into a parking spot in Seattle's densely populated Bellevue neighborhood. Stanley's ex-wife lived on the twenty-seventh floor of a newer high-rise that overlooked Lake Washington. Olivia Kolberg met us at the door of her condominium. Tall with gray hair and intelligent eyes, I would've put her in her mid-sixties, but she moved with youthful energy. Leading us into the living room, Olivia caught me eyeing the wedding picture on the mantel showing a very young and beardless Stanley. "I only had the one wedding, Dr. Ashman," she said. "It was a marvelous occasion. Please don't read too much into me hanging on to the photos."

I read far more into her defensive comment than the fact that she kept the photo. "It's just that I thought Stanley was born with a beard," I said.

Olivia glanced at the photo. "He was much better looking without it."

Once seated, Olivia turned to Dev. "As I told you earlier, Sergeant, I have seen very little of Stanley over the past years. I don't know how much help I'll be."

"When did you last see your ex-husband, Mrs. Kolberg?" Claire smiled deferentially at the handsome older woman.

"Six months ago," Olivia said. "Maybe more. We didn't keep much in contact after our divorce."

"How come?"

"No children to force the issue." Olivia shrugged. "We drifted apart, as people do."

"When did you get divorced?" Dev asked, twirling his own wedding band with his left thumb.

"Sixteen years ago." Olivia shook her head. "Amazing. We were only married for twenty, but it feels like most of my life."

After fifteen minutes of questions it became clear that Olivia Kolberg knew the Stanley of his youth, not the man who lay mutilated on his office floor. Again, it fell to me to raise the awkward subject of Stanley's sexuality. I led in with the same "lifestyle" line I had used on Cal Nichol. I was surprised by the utter lack of surprise on Olivia's face. "Mrs. Kolberg, I'm not telling you anything new, am I?"

Olivia shook her head very slightly.

"He was always into S and M?" I asked.

"I didn't know at the beginning." She let out a wry chuckle. "I was sexually naïve when we wed. A virgin. At first, he was such a tender lover."

Though accustomed to probing into people's sex lives professionally, I felt embarrassed here, as if I'd accidentally walked in on someone undressing.

"The late sixties and early seventies," she sighed, remembering. "People went from never mentioning sex to talking about precious little else. We'd been married close to ten years when Stanley introduced the concept of 'experimenting.'" She made quotation marks in the air with her fingers. "It began harmlessly. Handcuffs, soft shackles, and so on. Stanley liked to be tied up. I must confess I went along. In a way, it revitalized our relationship."

"You don't have to—"

But Olivia had already launched into her confession. Maybe for the first time ever. Once those floodgates open, they are often impossible to close. "Before long, he had to be tied or bound . . . just to perform. And then the spanking began. It escalated from there. After a while, he needed to hurt, or be hurt, to reach any kind of arousal. It was a sickness, Dr. Ashman." Her voice cracked. "I couldn't go along with it any longer. I just couldn't."

"So you left?" I asked.

"Not right away." She shook her head. "It wouldn't do for a rising star like Stanley to have his marriage fail. Instead, we lived separate lives. Stanley did, anyway."

Claire nodded sympathetically. "That must have been hard, Mrs. Kolberg."

"Hard doesn't begin to describe it, dear." Olivia smiled sadly. "To begin with, there's the loneliness, the loss of intimacy, after years of partnership. And how Stanley changed. Not so anyone else would notice, mind you, but it was black and white to me." She dabbed at her eyes with the back of her hand and sniffed.

"What made you finally leave?" Claire asked.

She rubbed her eyes. "One day I walked into the bathroom and found Stanley perched on the side of the bathtub, trying to apply ointment to his back. Blood was caked all over. Looked as if a tiger had used it for a scratching post. Stanley turned to me with a crazed grin and asked, 'Honey, could you rub this on for me?'" She shuddered. "I moved out that afternoon."

Dev asked, "You didn't know where he used to go—"

"No. I never knew the who, what, where, or how of it. And especially not the why." She paused. "Though I suppose it had to do with his mother. She raised Stanley and his two brothers alone after her husband walked out. And he left with good reason. She was a tyrant of a woman. She took out her anger at her husband—men in general—on the boys. She used to beat them relentlessly. Stanley told me it was the only time he felt any real attention from her." She shook her head. "Regardless, Stanley had a real sickness."

We thanked Olivia and headed for the car. Once inside, Dev said, "And to think, my wife gives me a hard time for leaving the toilet seat up."

Claire shook her head angrily. "That's not even funny, Dev. What her husband did."

"So he got his rocks off by getting the bejesus beaten out of him?" Dev said defensively. "Doesn't mean he deserved to die how he did."

"Did you hear me say otherwise?" Claire snapped, sounding ready for a fight.

But Dev showed little appetite. "Know what? If Kolberg was so into the S and M scene, he might have known Dirty Serge."

Claire nodded. "That's true."

"Who?" I said.

"Sergei Pushtin, AKA 'Dirty Serge,'" Dev said. "He's one of the last surviving members of the old Russian gang." He shook his head. "The guy's unkillable. He's been shot at least two or three times, but he's got more lives than a cat."

"I knew Serge in Vice." Claire nodded. "Been a pimp forever. Specializes in domination-and-submission. He's got a stable of Eastern European girls who are terrified of him. That's why he always walks. My old partner calls him the Teflon Balkan."

Until I started to meet these people through Dev and company, I wouldn't have believed gangsters with such ridiculous nicknames existed. Not only did they exist, as best as I could tell, they thrived in Seattle's seedy underbelly.

After a quick phone call to the parole office, we ended up outside of Sergei Pushtin's condo complex on the east side of Queen Anne Hill. "How do you know he's home?" I asked, as the intercom rang unanswered.

"You kidding me, Doc?" Dev checked his watch. "It's 10 A.M. and we're outside a pimp's pad. That's like showing up at anyone else's house at three on a weekday morning."

Sure enough, after five more rings a scratchy voice spat out, "What?"

"Dirty Serge, how the hell are you?" Dev asked pleasantly.

"Fuck off," Pushtin said in a heavy Russian accent.

"Serge, you wouldn't say that to a police officer, would'ya?"

"Police?" Pushtin said. "Call my lawyer . . . and then fuck off." The line went dead.

Dev rang through three more times before Pushtin answered again. "Listen, you piece of shit," Dev snarled into the intercom. "It's Sergeant Devonshire here. Homicide, remember? You and I have unfinished business. Let us up. Now!"

We rode the elevator to the twenty-second floor where

Pushtin met us at his door in a heavy, black bathrobe. He was a hulking man, as tall as Calvin Nichol, but three times as muscular and without any discernible neck. He had an oversized head with a mop of black hair, a jutting chin, and steely blue-gray eyes. No wonder he couldn't be killed, I thought. If I were the Grim Reaper showing up at his door, I would've apologized for bothering him and moved on down the hall. But neither Dev nor Claire appeared in the least intimidated by Pushtin's physical presence. Without invitation, they barged past him into his condo.

The apartment had huge bay windows with one of the best views I'd ever seen of Lake Union and the Cascade Mountains beyond. The decor was another story. The heavy wrought-iron and leather furnishings must've cost an arm and a leg, but together with the gaudy rugs and paintings, they struck me as oppressive. Dev, too. "I feel like I'm in a Kafka nightmare," he said, revealing a glimpse of his well-hidden literary side. "Spend some of your dirty money on a decorator, for Christ's sake."

Pushtin stood close enough for me to smell his stale garlicky breath. "What you wake me up for?"

"Help me close a file. Whydya kill Petey?" Dev looked over his shoulder at us. "Petey White was another pimp. Serge beat him to death last year."

He folded his tree-trunk arms across his chest. "I didn't touch him."

Dev slapped his forehead. "That's right. Petey fell on a bat . . . sixty or seventy times."

Pushtin sighed, unimpressed. "You didn't come here to hassle Sergei about Petey." The word sounded like 'pity,' and confused me for a moment. "You got nothing. Why are you here, Sherlock?"

"I missed you, Serge. I don't know, maybe it's your witty repartee, your understated sense of design, your delicate smile . . ." Dev covered his face in mock embarrassment. "Hell, I think I might be falling in love."

"Funny man, Sherlock." Pushtin sneered. "Where I come from, funny men don't live as long."

Dev's eyes widened and his nostrils flared. "Did you just threaten me? Did you, you steroid-pumped piece of dog shit?!" Dev stepped toward him and grabbed for the lapel on Pushtin's bathrobe. I'd never seen him as inflamed. Then again, I was never certain with Dev; the whole routine might have been part of his "bad cop" act.

Pushtin didn't respond right away. But I imagine it was as close to acquiescence as the man came, when he said, "Okay. I was just saying, Sherlock."

Letting go of Pushtin's lapel, Dev calmed dramatically. In zoological terms, the posturing had ended without a fight; the alpha male had established dominance.

Claire spoke up. "We want to talk to you about someone else, Serge."

"Ah, the pretty Lady Sherlock. I remember you." He leered at her. Suddenly, *I* wanted to grab the bear by the lapel and give him a shake.

"Really? I found you so easy to forget." Claire blew him off beautifully. She reached into her jacket pocket and pulled out a recent photo of Stanley. She held it up for him. "This guy a client?"

Pushtin didn't even look at it. "Sure. Why not?" He flashed his ugly Adonis grin at her. "After I tell you everything, then we call his wife, no?"

Dev nodded at me. "See, Doc, he's as protective as you are. Touching, really, how well he guards pimp-john confidentiality."

"You want Sergei to starve?" Pushtin said with classic Russian pathos. "If I start talking about clients, I go out of business in a big hurry."

"Oh, Serge, you're making my heart bleed. To think how hard you had to work to scrape all this together"—Dev pointed around the luxurious condo—"off the bruised backs of those underage girls."

The corner of Pushtin's lip curled, but he held his tongue.

Dev plopped down into one of the overstuffed chairs. "I'll make you a bet."

Pushtin's eyes narrowed in suspicion.

"By the time Narcotics gets here, I'm guessing I'll have found a few ounces of coke that you carelessly left on one of your countertops."

Pushtin glared at him. "You plan to frame Sergei?"

"And then we're going to pick up your stable of girls," Claire joined in. "Run the social security and immigration papers on all of them. You should have them back just in time for the Second Coming."

Pushtin shook his head and grunted, "Show me the picture."

Claire held up the picture in her hand. He glanced at it. "I know him."

"How?"

"We go to the same bridge club." Pushtin let out a roar of laughter. "Sergei can be a funny man, too. No, Sherlock?"

"A big old laugh riot." Dev tapped the photo impatiently. "How do you know him?"

"I get him a girl from time to time. Not so much last couple of years." Pushtin shrugged his massive shoulders. "But lots before."

"And?" Claire demanded.

"He pays cash," Pushtin grunted. "Girls come back. No problem. End of story."

"No it isn't!" Claire jabbed a finger at him. "What does he *like*?"

"He likes what all men like." Pushtin eyed her lasciviously. "Most ladies, too. No? He likes it rough."

He made the word "rough" sound filthy. I felt another surge of anger toward the oversized pimp.

"You don't know any ladies, Pushtin," Claire snapped. "You only know scared, coked-out little girls." She raised a hand, and, for a moment, I thought she might take a swing. But she just wagged her finger at him. "Be more specific!"

"He likes to be tied up . . . and beaten a little. Sometimes, he likes to do the beating. But he pays good. No problem."

"Really? That's not what he told us," Dev bluffed.

Pushtin's thick eyebrows furrowed. "What did he say?"

"He said it got ugly between you two."

After a long moment, Pushtin said: "Everything is okay now."

"What was the flare-up about?" Claire barked.

"He burned one of Sergei's girls," Pushtin said. "Okay, my girls know he likes to hit. No problem. One girl, he tied her up and burned with a candle."

"What happened to her?" Claire asked.

"She had infection. She went to hospital," he said with all the concern of a lamppost.

"When?"

"Eight . . . nine months ago, maybe."

"And you and he had a chat afterwards, right?" Dev asked.

"Sure. We have a chat." Pushtin nodded. "He makes it up to me."

"He paid you off?"

"No! He paid for lost time and hospital bills. Same like damage to a rental car."

"You son of—" Claire started, but Dev stopped her with a gentle hand on her shoulder.

"And if he ever did it again?" Dev asked.

Pushtin flashed a crocodile smile. "I tell him, one mistake with Sergei you pay damages. Next mistake . . . money doesn't help you."

"I guess he didn't believe you," Dev said.

Pushtin's forehead wrinkled again. "What do you mean?"

"He was beaten to death a couple of days ago," Claire said. "Just like Petey White."

"Or maybe he just fell on the pipe sixty or seventy times, then accidentally shot himself in the neck." Dev held up his hands helplessly. "Freak accidents, go figure."

"No, no, no." Pushtin shook his head and his dark bangs flapped back and forth. "Petey White got what was coming to him. This guy . . ." Pushtin pointed a meaty finger at the photo of Stanley in Claire's hand. "Who knows?"

After leaving Pushtin's place, I parted company with Claire and Dev. They had to go debrief Homicide's captain, who was keeping close tabs on their progress because of the media interest in the story. I headed home in a cab.

Just as I stuck the key in the front door, a car's horn drew my attention. I watched Calvin Nichol wriggle out of the driver's seat of his compact BMW parked across the street. My lanky colleague looked as comfortable in his luxury sports car as most clowns did in their undersized circus car, but I knew better than to point that out to him. Self-deprecation wasn't his strongest suit.

I waited at the door as he loped across the street and up the walkway to meet me.

Reaching me at the door, he asked, "Joel, can we talk a moment?"

"You want to come in?"

"No." He rubbed his close-trimmed beard between his thumb and index finger.

"What's going on?"

"I wanted to, um, tell you something," he said, refusing to meet my eyes.

I wasn't used to seeing Nichol so jittery. I felt sudden impatience with him. "What is it?"

"Look," he said quietly, still working his beard feverishly. "The investigation into Stanley's murder . . ."

"What about it?"

He glanced around. His voice dropped to a near whisper. "I think you'd do best to drop out of it."

"Why's that?" I raised my voice, as if to compensate for his.

"It's not . . ." He floundered for the right word. "Safe."

"What the hell does that mean, Cal?" I roared. "Are you threatening me?"

"No! God, no." He shook his head vehemently. "I'm just trying to warn you."

"How are you involved in all this?" I asked, struggling to sound calmer.

He sighed. "I can't explain it. Not right now. You wouldn't understand. But for your own good, you should just leave it alone."

"For my own good, huh?" I said. "And what about your good?"

"Forget it," he said, and spun away from me. "I'm sorry I even came." With that, he rushed down the path with giraffe-like strides.

"Cal!" I yelled after him.

Nichol didn't stop until he reached his car. "Just forget it, Joel." He opened the door, wedged himself into the driver's seat, and sped off.

So this was what had become of our former partnership? Stanley dead and Nichol uttering veiled threats. It had all been so different before I met Angela.

Ten and a half months earlier, by the fifth week of Angela's hospital stay, I had begun to look forward to our daily visits. I convinced myself that I was motivated by the challenge she presented, the improvement she'd already shown, and her potential for more. But in my job, I've come to realize just how spectacularly well people can pull the wool over even their own eyes. Truth was, I liked Angela. And more and more, she had come to remind me of Suzie Malloy—the girl who inadvertently shattered my childhood.

Between Mom's academic ambitions and Dad's womanizing, both kept long hours away from home when I was a kid. For child care, they relied heavily on a series of students from out of town, who lived a semester or two in our basement apartment and paid for their board in time spent babysitting me. And I didn't make it easy. I longed for a brother or sister. I was quick to foist the role upon those unsuspecting freshmen, becoming a relentless tagalong the moment they entered my life. I must have seen ten or twelve of them pass through our house, but only the last one stands out. Suzie Malloy.

A precocious student, Suzie had skipped two grades and was only fifteen when she showed up at our doorstep as a first-year college student. But through my twelve-year-old eyes, she was worldliness personified. From the moment I saw her long golden hair, hazel eyes, button nose, and toothy smile, I was awestruck by Suzanne Malloy.

If I held up a photo of the teenage Suzie beside a more recent picture of Angela, I would be hard pressed to point out a resemblance. Angela had dark Audrey Hepburn–like features whereas Suzie had California Girl good looks. But looks weren't the issue; it was the tragic parallel in their lives that made them so comparable.

But I wasn't in a particularly reminiscent mood when, one week after Angela's discharge, I was woken by her phone call at 2 A.M. "You know what time it is?" I said groggily into the receiver.

"I'm sorry, Dr. Ashman. It's—"

"Can't this wait?"

When she didn't reply, I said, "Angela?"

"I don't think I'm going to be able to make my appointment today."

"Angela, you insisted on Friday afternoon," I said.

"I don't think I can make it."

"We're not going to have your session over the phone at two in the morning."

"Who said I wanted that?"

"I'll see you this afternoon. Or not. I'm going back to sleep now."

"Wait, Dr. Ashman." Her tone suddenly turned contrite. "Can't we meet somewhere else?"

"My office at four."

"Not there. Maybe we could talk over dinner someplace?" I could just picture her piercing eyes widening and her lips breaking into their most seductive half-smile, when she added, "My treat."

"The only place you and I will meet is my office. Period."

"You think I can't see it, huh?"

"Angela, have you been drinking?"

"Not a drop. I didn't smoke, shoot, or snort anything either," she huffed, but then reverted to her siren's voice. "C'mon, Dr. Ashman. I've seen the way you look at me. You can't deny the chemistry between us."

I rubbed my eyes. "Angela, remember our first interview? You agreed not to go down this road."

"That was before—"

"I don't care," I said firmly. "You gave me your word."

"I didn't realize how well you were going to understand me." Then she added softly, "And I didn't know how important you were going to become to me."

"If you mean that, you'll come to my office at the appropriate time and we can work through this." I hung up the phone. But it took me a while to get back to sleep. I kept expecting, maybe even hoping for, Angela to call back. She didn't.

Later that day, I was almost surprised when my receptionist Teri walked into my office and announced: "Joel, your four o'clock is here. She seems kind of nervous."

My partners didn't work Friday afternoons, so I found Angela sitting alone in the waiting room. Wearing a heavy jacket and a baseball cap pulled down over her head, she leaned forward in her chair while writing in her journal. When she looked up from her pastel notebook to see me standing above her, she practically jumped out of her seat. I'd never seen her so edgy. Without a word of greeting, she followed me down the hallway to my inner office. She didn't begin to calm down until I'd closed the door behind me.

"How are you?" I asked, attempting to reassure her with a smile.

"Okay." She took off her hat. "Um, about this morning . . . I'm sorry I called so early."

I nodded.

She appeared to relax a little more. She filled me in on her new roommate and an exciting lead she had on a job opening at an art gallery, which "fit perfectly" with her undergraduate major in art history. Her anxiousness aside, I was pleased to see how upbeat and hopeful she came across. But her mood darkened substantially when I told her that I wanted to speak to her previous psychiatrist.

Her eyes narrowed in suspicion. "Why?"

"The background information might be useful."

"I don't think it would."

"What's the downside, Angela?"

She crossed her arms over her chest. "I've been through lots of shrinks. I never really liked any of them. I can give you all the 'background' you need. I don't want you dragging them into this."

"I won't 'drag' them into anything. I simply want to hear their perspective."

"Whatever," she murmured. "But I don't remember their names."

We both knew that was a lie, but I changed topics. "Can we talk about your father?"

She uncrossed her arms and shrugged.

"You never told me how he died."

She only shrugged.

"How old was he?"

"Almost sixty." She brushed her short hair forward with a hand. "In fact, he died the week before his sixtieth birthday."

"Sixty?" I said. "Your mom seems so young."

"He was thirty-seven and she barely eighteen and already pregnant with Ellen when they got married. Dad would tell people that Mom was twenty-three." She changed her mind about her hair and started to brush it back with the same hand. "Don't forget, Daddy liked them young."

Though he was a complete stranger and long dead, I'd developed a visceral hate for the man. I couldn't help but compare him to the father who had destroyed Suzie Malloy.

"His death made the news. About four years ago, remember? LAWYER DIES ON LOCAL SLOPES," Angela quoted.

I stared blankly at Angela. The headline didn't ring any bells. After a while, all the deaths at Seattle's nearby ski resorts blended in my memory.

"Daddy went snowboarding with my brother and a couple of his friends at Crystal Mountain." She shook her head. "There was a ton of snow that year. But the day they went up, the weather was terrible. All socked in. But Daddy insisted on following the nineteen-year-olds when they decided to do a couple of out-of-bounds runs. You know?"

I knew. Every year Cascade Search and Rescue spent thousands of dollars and long, cold nights in the dangerous, *unmarked terrain searching for marooned snowboarders who had been stupid enough to ignore the ropes and warning signs. Most of the time, they found them mildly hypothermic and scared shitless. Every so often, they found a corpse.*

"They figured he tried to hike out in the dense fog and got disoriented. That was when he fell into the gully."

"How did you react?" I asked.

"What do you think? He was my dad!" Her face creased into a grimace, and she might as well have added: You ass-hole!

"You weren't just any daughter, Angela."

"I told you. I loved Daddy, warts and all." She smoothed her hair forward, then back, and then mussed it in frustrated indecision. "The month after he died was probably when I sunk into my first depression."

After Angela left, I scratched a few notes in her chart, but I couldn't shake the sense that my profile was incomplete. Wondering if the psychiatrist who saw her through her first breakdown might shed some light on the situation, I flipped through her chart until I found a copy of the University Hospital discharge summary. Tucked inconspicuously at the bottom right corner of the page was the name of the attending physician—S. J. KOLBERG, M.D.

I felt a slight chill that I couldn't explain. I wondered why it mattered to me that Stanley had been one of Angela's previous psychiatrists. Nonetheless, the connection troubled me.

I tried to wait until our standing lunch date before raising the subject with Stanley, but I barely lasted to the next morning, a Saturday, before calling and arranging a rendezvous.

I met Stanley, an avid walker, at the northeast entrance to the Gasworks Park on a gray and record-setting cool July day. Situated in the midst of Seattle's urban sprawl on a small peninsula jutting into Lake Union, Gasworks Park is famous for its old gas manufacturing plant. Massive machinery stands vigil to the city's industrial past while framing to-day's skyline. And it holds a special place in my heart: I'd proposed to Loren on the same seawall bench where, two years earlier, we'd shared our first kiss.

Stanley wore a black nylon windbreaker, white jogging shoes, and jeans. I could never wrap my mind around the image of him in jeans and jogging shoes. To me, he looked as natural as a multi-tattooed defendant, wearing a suit and tie in court. A fiberglass cast poked out from the left sleeve of his windbreaker. That, along with a fading black eye, was the apparent remnant of his most recent seizure. As long as I'd known him, he'd worn the scars and bruises of adult-onset seizures that apparently no drug could control.

After arming ourselves with steaming coffees against the unseasonably cold breeze, we headed off for the eight kilometers that lay ahead.

"What did you get up to last night?" Stanley asked.

"Tried to finish a review article for the Journal of Psychiatry,*" I said.*

"On a Friday evening?"

"When else?"

"None of my business." Stanley sipped his coffee at full stride. "But far as I can tell, you spend most of your Friday and Saturday nights at home."

"Some of them."

"Hmmm."

"What?"

"Do you think Loren would've wanted that?" he asked.

"Wanted what?"

"For you to live the rest of your life alone," he said, as casually as if commenting on the weather.

I stopped. So did he. "How's that for the pot calling the kettle black?"

"Big difference, my boy," he chuckled. "I choose to be alone. Truth of the matter is, I'm as misanthropic as they come. Besides, I'm an old man. Who would want me? But you . . ." He waved his cast up and down me. "A handsome young man like yourself with not too grating a personality. You're a catch."

He started to move again and I followed after. "It's not like I've made some kind of posthumous vow of celibacy to Loren. It just hasn't ever happened with anyone else."

He pointed his cast at me. "But would you let it happen?"

I didn't answer.

"Tell me, Joel. If you had a client like yourself—a man who, more than two years after his wife passed away, still lived a solitary existence—what would you advise him?"

"Stanley, we don't advise clients," I said in mock outrage. "Our job is to facilitate them in making their own choices."

"I taught you well." Stanley laughed. "But what would you tell him?"

"I'd toe the company line and tell him: First and foremost, you have to live with yourself. No other person can be responsible for your happiness."

"True, but why is it that so many other people can be responsible for your misery?" he sighed. He turned to me with a sympathetic smile. "I do understand your reluctance, though. You really have had dreadful luck with women."

"Thanks!"

"You know what I mean," he said. "Loren, your mother, that girl from your adolescence . . ."

"Suzie."

He nodded. "When it comes to women, tragedy has been your shadow."

We walked in silence for several minutes. I stared out at the barges anchored near the edge of the horizon, and thought about the sailing trip Loren had planned on us taking after the birth of our little boy. She had talked about it often after learning she was finally pregnant. "Picture him in a cute little sailor's suit," she said, and then winked at me. "Maybe we could get you a matching one?" Who the hell am I kidding? I thought, shaking off the memory. Of course someone else can be responsible for your happiness.

"Joel, you still with me?" Stanley drew me out of my reminiscences.

"Just concentrating on my breathing. You keep a mean pace."

"For an old man," he added. Since his sixtieth birthday, he always referred to himself as an "old man," though I didn't know anyone else who thought of him that way.

"Stanley." I cleared my throat. "I'm, um . . . treating a former patient of yours." Broaching the subject of Angela felt more awkward than I'd expected.

"Oh?" Stanley turned his head to me without slowing his pace. "Who?"

"Angela Connor."

"Angela Connor," he said without any visible reaction. "How is she?"

"Okay . . . now." I hesitated. "She attempted suicide a couple of months ago."

Stanley shook his head. "I wish I could say that came as a surprise."

"It was her first attempt," I pointed out.

"I doubt it will be her last. Angela . . . what spark, what potential." He exhaled heavily. "But what an absolutely anguished psyche."

"That's Angela."

Stanley kept his eyes on me as we walked. "Did she discuss our therapy at all?"

"That's the thing, Stanley," I said. "She's extremely guarded about your relationship. Wouldn't even tell me that you were her previous psychiatrist." I asked.

"I'm not surprised. I completely failed her."

I stopped again. Stanley walked a few more steps then slowed to a halt. "What do you mean?" I asked.

"I was wrong," he said. "Exceedingly wrong about Angela. Right from the outset." Then he spun to face me and spoke what amounted to blasphemy to my ears. "I misdiagnosed her. And then I mismanaged her. She left my practice worse than how she came."

"Misdiagnosed her?"

"I overlooked the obvious." He tapped at the outside of his eye with his casted hand. "I thought, or maybe just wanted to think, she was suffering from an atypical depression."

"That's what she does suffer from—an agitated depression!" I said.

Stanley shook his head and sighed. "I remember those

first few months being relatively pleased with myself. I saw Angela emerge from that hostile, defensive shell. She practically blossomed in front of my eyes."

"But?"

"It was an act."

"Come on, Stanley!"

"You'll see," he predicted with calm certainty. "Angela's not depressed, she's personality disordered. A mixed bag, too. Part borderline, part histrionic, and part antisocial."

None of those were flattering diagnoses, especially the latter. "You're wrong, Stanley."

"Really?" he said. "Has she called you at home yet?"

I nodded.

"Has she made any . . . advances toward you?"

"Sort of." I shifted from foot to foot.

"Not exactly behavior typical of a depressed patient." Stanley rested his other, cast-free hand on my shoulder. "Unfortunately, Joel, I know where this is heading. Her behavior will grow more erratic. The phone calls will increase. And if you're anything like I was, she will draw you in deeper and deeper."

He dropped his hand to his waist. And we stood in the middle of the pathway for a while without exchanging a word. I bundled up my jacket as a gust of wind blew off the water.

"I can't speak for you," Stanley said quietly. "Maybe you're used to such attention from a beautiful young woman, but I wasn't. And so help me God, I developed . . . an emotional attachment for Angela. She was so manipulative. And so fucking seductive."

"Stanley, you didn't—"

"Of course not." He raised his hands in the air. "My point is, as an experienced and now ancient psychiatrist, I should've never let myself get so personally involved."

"Involved how?"

"Being at her beck and call. Taking her phone calls at any hour, and seeing her whenever and wherever she wanted to

meet. I even gave her money, for God's sake. How grossly un-professional was that!"

I was dumbfounded.

"As you know, Joel, borderline personalities don't appre-ciate limits of any kind," he continued in a more clinical tone. "Same story with Angela. Always blurring the bound-aries of her relationships and driving away the people she holds dear. Maybe I had the best chance of anyone to set up a stable relationship with clear-cut rules and boundaries—one she might have been able to model future relationships on." Then he added quietly, "But after a year or two, our re-lationship had grown so unstable that I thought it might kill one of us. In the end, I had to discharge her from my practice and cut off all contact."

The wind had picked up, and we both were shivering through our light jackets. We started to walk just to warm ourselves.

"What about her relationship with her father?" I asked.

Stanley sighed. "Of course, the alleged incest."

" 'Alleged'?"

"Did you ever find anyone to corroborate her story?"

"Her little brother, Tommy."

"Poor, poor Tommy." He sighed. "He reminds me of the painting in Oscar Wilde's The Picture of Dorian Gray. Tommy bears the weight of his sister's sins."

"You think she is lying about her father?" I asked.

"When it comes to Angela, I have no idea what to believe," he said. "Over time, she accused more and more people of sexually abusing her. I'm surprised she hasn't leveled that accusation at me." He eyed me with an unfamiliar expres-sion, somewhere between defensiveness and scorn. "Besides, her dad isn't around to defend himself, is he?"

"Meaning?"

"Did she tell you that she was with him the day he died?"

"She told me he was with Tommy," I said.

"Yes, but she was there, too."

"What are you suggesting, Stanley?"

Stanley shrugged. "A sixty-year-old who had just taken up snowboarding heads off into a treacherous, experts-only, out-of-bounds area with a group of twenty-year-olds in the middle of a blizzard . . ." He let the unfinished accusation hang in the cold air.

I didn't want to hear any more. I stuck my freezing hands in my pockets, put my head down, and trudged on without comment. We walked another mile while buried in our own thoughts. Finally, as we closed in on the parking lot, I asked, "If Angela truly is personality disordered and not depressed, why did you imply earlier that she'll make further suicide attempts?"

"Angela is the most self-destructive person I have met in over thirty years of practice." He turned to me with a sad smile. "My whole fucking life, for that matter."

6

THE DAY AFTER CAL NICHOL STOPPED BY to give me the cryptic warning, I opted to pass on Claire's offer to pick me up. Something was going on between us. I needed time to regain my perspective, and I knew another cozy morning ride wouldn't help.

Jogging through the crisp daybreak, I reflected on my nonexistent love life. Since I became a widower, a surprising number of women had asked me out. Maybe they felt sorry for me, but I don't think being a professional still on the young side of middle age hurt my prospects. And while I might not have inherited my father's charisma, I got his looks. At just over six feet, I have brown eyes, a square jaw, and thick black hair that curls when longer. I don't normally get too concerned with my appearance but whenever I'd asked Loren how I looked in something, she would usually qualify her candid opinion with the same tongue-in-cheek reassurance: "I promise, Joel. I'll let you know when you turn ugly."

After returning home and showering, I still had energy

left. I decided to forgo the cab and walk the two and a half miles to my breakfast meeting with Claire and Dev—a decision I regretted when, partway there, the Seattle sky burst open. I arrived at the greasy spoon—Dev's choice—carrying an extra couple pounds of moisture in my water-logged clothes.

After peeling off my coat, I sat down in the chair between the two detectives. While Dev had a good laugh at my soggy expense, Claire flagged down the waitress, who poured me a coffee.

"Doc, I was just bitching about the size of our suspect list—what with all of Kolberg's patients, not to mention every hooker, pimp, or pervert in town with a chip on their shoulder." He nodded at Claire. "But this one thinks it's fun."

Claire sighed. "Dev, what I said was that I think it's cool the way we're getting a handle on the victim and the players." Then she laughed. "Ah, screw it! It *is* fun."

Claire's wide-collared green blouse highlighted the glint in her similarly colored eyes. When those eyes met mine, I knew she had noticed me noticing. And from her half-smile and the color in her cheeks, I guessed that she didn't mind. Perfect, I thought, I'm in eighth grade all over again.

"Doc, what did you make of Dirty Serge?" Dev asked.

"Run-of-the-mill mobster sociopath."

"How so?" he said.

I ran a hand through my hair to stop the water from dripping into my eyes. "In psychological terms, his type has a distinct profile. They kill. All the time. And brutally. Take the way he bludgeoned Petey what's-his-name."

"But?" said Claire.

"It's not personal." I had a quick sip of the bitter coffee. "It's a job, like construction or insurance. If Serge beats someone to death, he's either meting out some kind of feudal punishment, or he's sending out a message to others. Just business. Who knows, maybe he's mentally going over his grocery list while crushing in Petey's skull? I wouldn't ex-

pect to see from him the kind of vindictive rage evident at
Stanley's crime scene."

Dev nodded. "I don't see Serge killing Kolberg either.
Your mumbo jumbo aside, I know his kind, too. Burn or no
burn to his girl, he doesn't kill the goose that lays the golden
eggs. Even if that goose set Serge's own mother on fire."

Claire reached to the floor and grabbed for her black
leather-bound notebook. She moved her coffee and un-
touched muffin out of the way, and spread the notebook
open on the table. She pointed to the photocopy of an appointment page. "Here's Kolberg's last day. Patients scheduled on the hour from one until eight o'clock."

"A typical day?" Dev asked me.

I nodded.

"A few familiar names." Claire ran her finger down the
list, stopping halfway to tap on W. HACKING. "Hacking was
scheduled for four."

"Hang on," Dev said. "Didn't Hacking tell us he last saw
Kolberg a few days before the murder?"

"See the 'N/S' beside his name?" Claire tapped the letters
with her finger. "No show." She moved her finger to the bottom of the page. "And how about this for a coincidence?
Brent McCabe was his last appointment."

Dev's blank stare suggested that the name was as lost on
him as it was on me.

"Remember?" Claire said. "Kolberg's secretary said Mc-
Cabe was one of his most volatile patients. The guy who
broke the office furniture."

The name didn't ring a bell, but I remembered McCabe's
handiwork—the chair smashed to pieces on the office floor.

"If he had the last appointment of the day . . ." Dev said,
drumming his fingers on the table. "He would've been done
at around nine o'clock, right?"

"Stanley always ran behind," I said. "Probably closer to
nine thirty."

"An hour before Kolberg's death," Dev said. "Give or take
an hour."

Claire's eyes widened. "McCabe could've hung around and continued their session at gunpoint until ten thirty."

Dev stopped drumming and pointed his index finger at us. "Or maybe McCabe goes out to his car. But instead of leaving, he sits and stews over all the terrible things Kolberg implied about him and his mother. He gets the pipe and gun out of his trunk, and then heads back upstairs for a rebuttal."

I interrupted their hypothesizing. "Why don't we meet McCabe before you give him his last cigarette and a blindfold?"

"Count on the shrink to suck the fun out of everything!" Dev grumbled.

With one phone call, we tracked down McCabe's work address. Standing in front of the glassed-in offices of Newbridge Accounting, Dev shook his head and said, "I still can't believe this Dr. Jekyll and Mr. Hyde is a goddamn CPA!"

The receptionist led us into Brent McCabe's spacious corner office, where the business cards on his desk informed us that he was a senior partner. McCabe breezed in wearing a dark gray suit and navy shirt. No tie. Apparently, even members of the world's most conservative profession were beginning to lose the "neck shackles," as Stanley, a habitual tie wearer (and coincidentally a shackle aficionado), had once referred to them. In his early forties, McCabe was undeniably handsome with salt-and-pepper hair worn short and fashionably messy, blue eyes, a strong jaw, and a welcoming smile. His smile disappeared as soon as Dev introduced me.

"A psychiatrist?" McCabe said with an edge. "What's going on?"

"You were a patient of Dr. Stanley Kolberg, right?" Dev asked.

McCabe's eyes narrowed to slits. "That's confidential."

"*Was* confidential," Dev corrected. "When someone killed Dr. Kolberg in his own office, it became our business."

McCabe hesitated, then walked around his desk and dropped into his leather chair. "Yes. I was a patient of Stanley's."

Something jarred about his use of the first name. Some therapists insist on patients calling them by their first name to create a less threatening and more intimate atmosphere. I think it's a load of crap, though some patients have taken to calling me by my first name. Never Stanley. He was always "Dr. Kolberg" to his patients.

"What does my therapy have to do with anything?" McCabe asked.

"You had an appointment with Dr. Kolberg the day he was murdered," Claire said.

"So?"

"You had a problem with the old temper, right?" Dev asked.

McCabe shot up from the desk. "You read my file?!"

"No, we didn't," Claire soothed. "We know about Dr. Kolberg's interest in anger management. You were identified as one of the more vocal patients in the practice."

McCabe eased back into his seat.

"Is that why you saw Stanley?" I asked.

"I saw your partner to save my marriage," he said, though none of us had mentioned my association with Stanley. "My wife gave me an ultimatum: Deal with my temper or leave. But it's not like I ever became physical with her or the kids."

"Course not," Dev said in a tone that contradicted his words.

McCabe fired him a scornful look, but didn't reply.

"Did the counseling help?" I asked.

"I'm still married," McCabe said with a noncommittal shrug.

"You don't sound very convinced."

"Look, I won't pretend to understand Stanley's technique. But my temper is under better control now. At least, my fuse is longer than it was."

"It's not the length of the fuse," Dev said. "It's the payload at the end that counts."

"What was so unusual about his technique?" I asked.

"All that 'controlled venting' stuff. He encouraged me to

lose my temper. In fact, he provoked me. Called it desensitizing, or something." McCabe exhaled. "It was weird."

"Did you like him?" Dev asked.

McCabe's face scrunched in confusion. "What do you mean?"

"Sorry. Vague question," Dev said dryly. "Did you or didn't you like the guy?"

McCabe didn't try to hide his sneer. "Where are you going with this?"

"You were Kolberg's last appointment," Claire said. "Ever."

"So?" McCabe rubbed his chin roughly.

"When did you leave the office?" Claire asked.

"Nine thirty . . . quarter to ten at the latest."

"So, you might have been the last person to see him alive."

"Except the guy who killed him!" McCabe snapped.

Dev stretched his arms behind his head. "We were thinking you might have mistook him for one of his chairs."

"I didn't kill him." McCabe looked as if he could've crushed a nickel between his teeth.

Then Claire surprised me with the kind of boldfaced lie I would've expected from Dev. "The cleaning lady told us she heard quite the quarrel coming from the office," she said.

The contempt left McCabe's face. He stared at his desk and spoke in a slow monotone. "I was fed up with his mind games. I told him I was through with it . . . and him."

"And how did he react?" I asked.

"He just kept provoking me," McCabe said. "He called me an unfit father and husband. Said people like me are nothing but cowards and bullies."

"Then what?" I nudged.

"I got up to leave," he told his desk. "Stanley blocked the doorway. He just stood in my face, taunting me with that sick gleam in his eyes."

When McCabe finally looked up, I offered my best therapist's tell-me-more face.

"I lost it, okay?" his voice rose. "I told him where he

could take his wacko therapy. But he just kept at me . . . and then he started to laugh."

I nodded. "Then what?"

"I punched him, okay? In the face and hard." He cleared his throat. "Stanley stumbled backward. I thought he was going to fall. I went over to see if he was okay. When he pulled his hands from his face, blood gushed from his lip. But he was laughing. He started right in on me again. Saying terrible things about my wife and kids."

"So you had to hit him again," Dev said.

"No!" McCabe cried. "I walked out the door. I never laid another hand on him."

"You went out to the car, got the pipe and gun . . ." Dev tried to put the words in his mouth.

"No. No. No." McCabe shook his head vehemently. "I was done. And I wasn't coming back." He looked at me. "Your partner had some serious problems."

"Why do you say that?" I asked.

"Whenever he'd get me really worked up—to the point where I couldn't control myself—he'd get this look on his face . . ." McCabe's words dissolved as he looked away from us.

"How can we confirm what you've told us, Mr. McCabe?" Claire asked.

"I've never fired a gun in my life," McCabe said. "Besides, why would I kill Stanley right after my own appointment? Who's that stupid?"

"You ever talked to an average killer before?" Dev scoffed. "Look. Maybe you didn't plan to. Heat of the moment, and all that."

"I didn't kill him." McCabe waved his hand in front of him. "Why don't you talk to the guy who pulled into the garage when I was leaving?"

"What guy?" Claire demanded.

"After I got out of there, I was pretty upset. I stopped in the lane to have a smoke. As I stood there, a car flew past me and pulled right into the underground garage."

"Can you describe it?"

"Too dark to get much of a look," McCabe said.

"Did you see the driver?" I asked.

"No. The engine sounded bad though, like it needed a new muffler. And I'll tell you this much, the driver was in a big hurry to get out of there."

Dev and Claire exchanged a glance and they rose to their feet. I followed suit. Claire handed McCabe a card, and then we headed out to the car.

The detectives dropped me off at the Cascade Mental Health Team's offices. I worked my way through my usual list of clients that afternoon—borderline-functioning schizophrenics with a few depressed and substance-abusing patients thrown in the mix—but I couldn't give the poor buggers my full attention; I was too preoccupied with the case.

Just before 5 P.M., I caught up with Claire and Dev in front of the drab cement building on Madison Street in the heart of Seattle's medical district, the so-called Pill Hill that is home to the Seattle branch of the State Department of Health. We were ushered into the office of the deputy secretary, where Dr. Charles Hollands rose to greet us. Thin and short, Hollands had perfectly combed silver hair, a pencil-thin mustache, and grave brown eyes. I thought his stern and humorless disposition was a perfect fit for his role as the chief disciplinarian for the state's licensed physicians.

We sat down facing Hollands's desk. "Dr. Ashman, for you and the detectives to review a file of unsubstantiated complaints like this . . ." He shook his head. "Frankly, it doesn't sit well with me."

"We understand," Claire answered for me. "But you read the court order?"

"Of course," Hollands said, reaching into a drawer and pulling out a thin manila folder. "We will cooperate fully. I just wanted to voice my personal concerns."

Hollands reversed the folder on his desk, so we could read the contents. "For a psychiatrist who practiced more than thirty years, Dr. Kolberg had a thin file," he said. "Of the three complaints registered against him, never once was he found at fault by the department."

"Can we go over them one complaint at a time?" Claire asked.

Hollands pulled out a few pages from the file. "We received the first one from a Mary Pierce in September of 1999." He passed us the letter. "Maybe you should read it yourselves."

We crowded around the desk and read the meticulously hand-printed, though rambling, four-page letter. Pierce went into excruciating detail about the issues—most of which she blamed on her poor relationship with her "physically abusive" father—that had led her to therapy. Then she catalogued a slew of charges against Stanley, ranging from a lack of empathy to verbal abuse. Like many complaint letters from psychiatric patients, it wasn't very convincing—until the final page. "The last straw," she wrote, "was when he forced me to relive experiences with my father. He said that in order to heal, we had to engage in role reversal, with me playing the part of my father." She went on to describe a specific incident. "Dr. Kolberg lay over his desk and made me spank him with a flat wooden paddle. He insisted I hit him hard, over and over again. When he finally stood up, I could tell he was aroused!" She vented her outrage in several sentences, before concluding: "It was degrading, disgusting, and grossly unprofessional. The Washington State Health Department must take immediate action. If you choose not to, I will pursue this with the police."

"What did the department do?" Claire asked.

"We investigated, of course. But you must understand that with respect to psychiatrists, we receive several letters a year with similarly outlandish allegations. The majority turn out to be unfounded." Hollands flipped through a few pages. "Unfortunately, three weeks after we received her letter, Ms. Pierce committed suicide. Her father found her hanging from a pipe in his basement."

Claire and Dev exchanged a glance, but Hollands didn't

seem to notice. He reached in the file for another letter and passed it to us. "This came to us just over five years ago from a Ms. Amarpreet Sohal."

Again, we hunched over the desk and read the one-page typewritten letter. Sohal was vague in her accusations. She wrote of "inappropriate behavior," but didn't cite examples. She concluded by suggesting that the department speak to other women in Stanley's practice.

Hollands consulted another sheet of paper. "We contacted Ms. Sohal in writing a week after receiving the complaint, but received no response. When we finally reached her by phone, she insisted she didn't want to pursue the matter. The file was closed at her request."

"Convenient." Dev sighed. "Who's next?"

Hollands reached for the last page in the file. "These are notes one of my assistants took from a phone call. It's not a formal complaint per se, but it is recent." He studied the paper. "About six weeks old." He paused. "And it's a little unusual."

"How so?" Claire asked.

"Because it came from the brother of one of Dr. Kolberg's patients."

Claire bit her lip. "Don't family members ever lodge complaints on behalf of relatives?"

"Often," Hollands said. "But this man called four months after his sister had jumped off the Aurora Bridge."

I felt my stomach knot even before Hollands said the name.

"Mr. Thomas Connor. He alleged that, prior to her suicide, his sister Angela had been abused by Dr. Kolberg." Hollands put the paper down. "We advised Mr. Connor of the need to contact us in writing before an investigation could be launched, but as of yet he hasn't done so." He paused, then added, "Which might be for the best. With the patient dead, it would have been very difficult to substantiate the charges. And now that Dr. Kolberg has died, I suppose it's a moot point."

We thanked Hollands for his help and left the building.

Standing under the still-threatening skies in the cool early evening, Dev viewed me intently. "Seems like Kolberg had a practice full of lemmings."

"Many of Stanley's patients were at high suicide risk." I shrugged. "It happens to even the best of psychiatrists."

"The best psychiatrists don't molest their patients," Claire grumbled.

"Speaking of"—Dev thumbed back at the office we'd just left—"Any of those complaints come from the woman who told you Kolberg was abusing her?"

"You know I can't say," I said.

Dev eyed me assuredly. "When it comes to your ex-partner, I think we're seeing just the tip of the iceberg. I bet plenty of people weren't heartbroken to see him go."

Without thinking, I found myself nodding in agreement. Suddenly, I was itching to get away from the building that housed all those allegations and the memories they brought. I wanted to go home and climb in the shower. I wanted to be alone. But Claire insisted on driving me. Noticing my withdrawn mood, Claire soon gave up on attempting to engage me in conversation and instead turned the music up louder on the radio.

At the curb across from my house, I climbed out of the car but Claire's voice stopped me. "Joel, I'm still kind of new to Seattle. I wondered if maybe sometime you wanted to show me one of those secret dining spots that only the locals know about."

I leaned down and rested my hands on the open window. "I'd love to, Claire." I forced a smile. "But now is not a great time for me. Especially, you know, while we're working together. How about some night after this case is closed?"

"Sure." She smiled closed-mouthed, but she wore the hurt like lipstick. She rolled up the window and drove off without another word.

You asshole! I chided myself. *Would you let it happen with anyone else?* Stanley's year-old question rang in my head. Looks aside, her intelligence, wit, empathy, and even the flashes of don't-shit-with-me toughness had made Claire ever more appealing to me. I hadn't experienced anything like this since Lor died. Though I couldn't deny the growing attraction, I had reasons to be wary of it, not the least of which was the "shadow of tragedy" (as Stanley had characterized it) that had clung to the women in my life.

Watching Claire drive away, I barely noticed the head-lights flicking on twenty feet in front of me. I stepped off the curb and started to cross the street to my house, but stopped when the same car gunned its engine and switched over to high beams. With a squeal of tires, the thing headed straight for me. I froze a moment in the blinding light and deafening roar, then lurched into action. I spun, bounded two strides, and dove back onto the grass. I rolled toward the sidewalk, just as the tires hopped the curb and tore through the wet grass a foot from my head.

From my back, I watched the car skid back onto the road and scream down the street. I stared at its shrinking tail-lights, too stunned to get up and off the sidewalk. I wondered if it would turn and come back for me, but its wail died down and the taillights faded into the darkness.

From the dull hammering in my ears, I recognized it as the same car that had framed Nelson and me in its headlights forty-eight hours earlier.

I lay beside the deep tread marks on my neighbor's lawn for what felt like days but was probably less than a minute. No one came out of the neighboring houses to check up on me, which I assumed meant the incident had gone unwitnessed. After rising and working the shake out of my knees, I studied the grooves in the grass that could just as easily have been gouged into my head.

I hobbled back to my house. For a hesitant moment, I felt an aftershock of fear in the dark entryway, until I realized that the approaching noise was simply Nelson's paw steps. Glad to see my old dog, I gave his back a good rub in wel-come. He had little time for the welcome. Instead, he led me to his bowl in the kitchen, knocking it around with his nose to remind me how empty it was.

After feeding Nelson, I dug around in my dusty liquor

cabinet until I found a bottle. I wasn't much of a drinker, but I figured etiquette dictated that I have a scotch after the experience. I poured a generous glass, while I contemplated calling Dev. With each refill, I swore I would make the phone call when the glass was empty. But by the time I downed my fifth glass, I wasn't sure I would make much sense to him.

My head swimming from the booze, my eyes drifted across the room to where my dog lay curled up in a ball on his bed. "Who, Nelson?" I slurred. "Who wants to take my head off?"

7

THE REST OF THE EVENING passed in a blur. After down-
ing half the bottle, I vaguely remember stumbling up to
bed. Rather than sleep, I tossed and turned throughout
the night, drifting in and out of a light scotch-induced semi-
consciousness.

My ringing phone yanked me out of one of those stupors.
"Hello," I murmured.

"That you, Doc?" Dev asked.

I glanced at the alarm clock, which read 7:32 A.M.
"What's up, Dev?"

"Doc, Fraud picked up a call last night. A suspect prescription."

"And?" I rubbed my eyes.

"Your friend, Stanley Kolberg, wrote it," he said matter-
of-factly.

I sat up in bed. "What was the prescription for?"

I could hear him fumbling through his notes. "Something
called M.O.S."

"That's oral morphine," I said.

"Any chance Kolberg wrote the prescription before he died?" Dev asked.

"Psychiatrists don't prescribe morphine."

"The guy who picked up the prescription, his name's Jay Baylor," he said. "According to the pharmacist, he looks like he might be a junkie. Ring any bells?"

"No."

"Happen to know where Kolberg kept his prescription pads?"

"Top drawer of his desk," I said, having had to borrow them a few times when my own supply ran out.

"Good thing Schiff is so anal," he said, referring to CSI officer Nathan Schiff. I heard Dev flip through more papers. "Schiff catalogs crime scenes like they're some kind of archeology digs. Here we go. 'Desk, top drawer: two ballpoint pens. Two notepads. Scotch tape. Letter paper.' Blah, blah, blah . . . Nope. Nothing about prescription pads."

"But they might have disappeared a month before CSI searched the scene," I said.

"Or a minute after Kolberg died," Dev pointed out.

"I guess," I said. "Have you picked up Jay Baylor yet?"

"Soon," Dev said. "When are you coming in?"

"When the pounding in my head stops," I said, trying to rub the hangover out of my aching temples.

He laughed. "Try living with five sons. The pounding never stops."

Shaking the last of my cobwebs away, I cleared my throat. "Dev, something weird happened outside my house last night. . . ." I went on to give him the rundown on how I was nearly run down.

He didn't say a word until I had finished. "We'll be there in thirty minutes!" The words sounded as if spoken through gritted teeth. Then the line clicked in my ear.

Twenty minutes later, Nate Schiff and his CSI team arrived. They clustered around the tire grooves in my neighbor's lawn, studying them with as much excitement as if the marks had been left by the landing of an alien spacecraft.

Several neighbors stood on their steps or peered through their windows, gawking at the bunny men with similar awe.

Dev and Claire showed up five minutes later. They had a quick look at the tread marks and then joined me where I stood taking in the warm spring sunshine from my front steps. There was nothing warm in the welcome I got from either of them.

"Why the hell didn't you call us last night?" were the first words out of Dev's mouth.

"I was in kind of a state of shock," I said sheepishly.

"Shock?"

"It all kind of hit home." I ran my hand down the rusty railing. "The first time that car came by, I didn't think too—"

"'First time'?!" Dev threw up his hands. "*What* first time?"

"Three nights ago. There was a car out front when I got home. He left after maybe five minutes. I didn't make too much of it at the time, but no question, it was the same car. Old seventies sedan. I can't tell you the color, but the engine's noise was unmistakable."

"Unbelievable!" Dev snapped. "What else should we know about?"

I took a big breath. "Cal Nichol dropped by two evenings ago."

By the time I'd finished recapping Nichol's visit, Dev stood perfectly still with shoulders at attention and arms by his side. His face was expressionless, his breathing slow. I'd never seen him as pissed.

"I cannot believe you withheld all this," he said, his Southern drawl more pronounced than usual. "Next time you decide to leave us in the dark, try to remember what your partner ended up looking like!"

"No proof last night's drive-by was related to Stanley's murder," I said, gripping the railing more tightly. "Anyway, the guy could've just as easily hopped out of his car and put a bullet in my head. Running me over, after giving me a twenty-foot running start, doesn't strike me as a high-percentage move."

Dev shook his head. "Maybe, like with Kolberg, the guy's temper got the best of him and he just couldn't wait to get at you."

"He wasn't trying to kill me," I said. "It was a warning."

"Warning you about what?" Dev growled.

"I don't know," I admitted.

Claire turned to me with a neutral expression, but her tone was frigid. "Maybe Nichol was punctuating his earlier threat?" she said.

"Cal?" I said. "I can't see that."

Claire's eyes narrowed. "Did Nichol tell you how he was involved in all this?"

I shook my head. "He was very agitated, though. Hypervigilant. Very unlike him. He's scared to death of something."

"Or someone," Claire said.

"We need to talk to Nichol. This time on our turf." Disappointment replaced the anger in Dev's tone. "When I work a case, I assume my own partners aren't holding out on me." He eyed me with a look that would've made a spoken threat redundant. "No more secrets, right, Joel?"

It was a statement, not a question, but I nodded anyway. I looked over to Claire, but she refused, understandably, to make eye contact. No question, eighth grade was repeating itself.

In the sullen silence of Claire's car, we headed out to see Amarpreet Sohal, the woman who had voluntarily withdrawn her allegation against Stanley. Sohal lived in a one-bedroom apartment near downtown in the International District, one of Seattle's predominantly Asian neighborhoods.

Sohal met us at her door in jeans and a loose sweater. Thirtyish and slim with delicate facial features, light brown skin, and huge brown eyes, she was very pretty in a china-doll way. "Call me Amy," she said in her accent-free English, leading us to the modestly furnished living- and dining-room area. We sat in the four chairs around her kitchen table.

"Amy, we wanted to talk to you about Dr. Kolberg," Claire said.

She fidgeted with a candleholder in her hand. "I'd rather not."

"It's important," Claire said.

"He's dead," Sohal said, without looking at us. "Why does it matter?"

"It still matters to us," Claire said gently. "We saw the letter you wrote to the Department of Health."

Sohal sat up in her chair and her eyes widened in alarm. "That was over five years ago. They told me the case was closed!"

"They keep those letters on file," Claire said. "Why were you seeing Dr. Kolberg?"

"I had panic attacks." Sohal tapped the candleholder softly against the edge of the table. "He diagnosed me with a generous anxiety disorder." She meant "generalized anxiety disorder," but I bit my tongue and stifled the smile.

With gentle coaxing, more ably than many therapists I'd seen, Claire teased out Sohal's story. Amy had grown up in Seattle as an only child in a traditional Sikh family. Her father was an authoritative alcoholic, unpredictable and violent when drunk, which, according to her, was most of the time. As she spoke, she kept her eyes fixed on the table and her voice wavered often. "I was a patient of Dr. Kolberg's for over a year. At first, he was amazing. He helped me get my confidence. Soon, I was having fewer panic attacks. But then, he, um, started to do things. . . ."

"What kind of things?" Claire asked.

"He told me I wasn't assertive enough because of my bullying father. And that I still lived in fear of him. He wanted us to do role-playing."

Sohal was taking us down a familiar path, but she danced around the specifics, saying only, "He wanted me to do things that I wasn't comfortable with."

Dev sighed. "He wanted you to spank him, didn't he, Amy?"

Sohal gaped at Dev as if he'd pulled a gun on her. "How did you know?"

Rather than offer any kind of smart-ass rejoinder, Dev smiled reassuringly. "Amy, you weren't alone. That sicko took advantage of many women."

Sohal dropped her head and spoke to the table. "I knew there had to be others."

"How long did it continue?" I asked, feeling the anger well up again.

Her head bobbed, and she began to sob softly. "I can't talk about it."

Claire laid her hand on Sohal's. "He's dead, Amy. He can't hurt you."

She looked up with a tear-streaked face. "After a while, he had me come to his apartment for our sessions. Everything was different there. He made me do things. Hit him and stuff. Always with a different bat or whip. Then he made me take my top off. Touch him . . ." She choked back a few more sobs. "He had me so confused. He said he loved me. He was doing it for me. To make me stronger. I know how it sounds, but at the time I didn't know what to believe."

The pounding veins in my head were no longer attributable to my hangover. "How did it end?"

Her voice steadied. "One day, I told him I wasn't going to do it anymore."

"What did he say?" I asked.

Sohal shook her head, still holding on to Claire's hand. "He said he wouldn't let me stop. If I tried to, he would tell my father everything I'd told him." Her eyes dropped in shame. "And all the sick stuff we had done together."

"So you wrote the letter?" I asked.

She shook her head. "I was terrified. I didn't know what to do. Then my cousin told me about the Department of Health. That's when I wrote them."

"Did you tell Kolberg?" Claire squeezed Sohal's hand supportively.

Sohal nodded. "I swore I'd tell them everything if he didn't stop."

"What did he do?"

"He said he was disappointed in me. Told me that we couldn't see each other anymore. Then . . ."

"Then what?" Claire asked.

"He told me that if I ever contacted the department again . . ." Sohal swallowed. "He said it would be very bad."

"What did that mean?" Claire asked.

Sohal shrugged and repositioned the candleholder. "I don't know, but it really scared me."

The rest of our questions brought no new insights, and Sohal was obviously too distraught to continue. We thanked her for her time and stood to leave. At the door, Claire said: "Amy, what we talked about today stays between us. You have our word." She passed Sohal a card. "If you think of anything else, or if you just want to talk, give me a call."

After we loaded back into the car, Claire looked over her shoulder and glared at me. "What kind of demented therapist preys on abused women? I'm not sure your ex-partner didn't get just what he deserved in the end."

I wasn't either.

During the drive back to SPD headquarters, Dev and Claire talked about mundane department politics, while I sat ignored in the backseat. That didn't bother me. They had every right to treat me like an outcast. Especially Claire. I'd hoped to find a private moment to speak to her, but no sooner had we arrived at Homicide, than I found myself behind the two-way mirror watching Claire and Dev lead in a scrawny man, who could've been anywhere from twenty to fifty. He had thinning, dirty-blond hair, a patchy beard, and an incomplete set of fuzzy yellow teeth.

I didn't recognize Jay Baylor, our prescription forger, but while working at the Emergency Psych Unit in Swedish Hospital, I'd met several intravenous drug users who could've passed for him on a passport photo. IVDUs—as they're known in my circles—don't usually have psychiatric diagnoses, except addiction, but it's mind-boggling how suicidal, homicidal, and generally fucked-up the pursuit of coke and heroin can turn a person.

Baylor exhibited the generalized skittishness of a heroin addict on the downslide of a high. He squirmed in his metal chair while Claire and Dev deliberately drew out the interview by shuffling papers and getting coffees, paying no attention to their guest.

Finally, Baylor piped up. "How did I end up in Homicide, anyway?"

Dev held up a piece of paper. "From your sheet here, it looks like you've been through everyone else: Vice, Theft, Fraud, Narcotics . . ."

"Hey, that's my life's work you're talking about," he said with a giggle.

"Mom must be proud, huh?" Dev grunted.

"Mom's dead," Baylor said. "But she might've been. I come from a long line of junkies and alcoholics."

Claire leaned forward in her chair. "You're a patient of Dr. Stanley Kolberg's. True?"

"Not exactly. He just sees me from time to time."

"And refills your prescription?" Claire asked.

"Sometimes. Yeah."

Claire tilted her head and smiled at Baylor. "What kind of doctor is Kolberg?"

"A damn good one!" Baylor chuckled as he repositioned himself and his chair.

"But is he a dentist? A chiropractor?" Dev asked. "A tree doctor?"

"Yeah, a tree doctor, I like that. I got this rash on my bark that I—"

"Answer the fucking question!"

Baylor jumped in his seat, but didn't shed his grin. "He's a family doctor, right?"

"Wrong, Jay," Claire said with deliberate condescension. "He's a psychiatrist."

"Oh, yeah." Baylor shrugged. "I'm getting my doctors

mixed up. I got so many problems. I'm like some ninety-year-old." He flashed his decaying teeth at the detectives. "I saw Dr. Kolberg for my, um, depression stuff."

"No, you didn't, Jay," Dev said.

Baylor held up a hand playfully. "Hold on there, sport—"

Dev's scowl cut him off. "We know you stole his prescription pad, and forged yourself a morphine script. So we're up to b and e, theft, and fraud. With your record, we're talking ten years minimum. Now let's talk murder. . . ."

The smile vacated Baylor's face. "I didn't kill anybody. And you know it." He raised his chin in a gesture of pathetic defiance. "And who saw me pull any of the other shit you just accused me of?"

Dev rose from his chair and walked around behind Baylor's seat. Baylor glanced from shoulder to shoulder. "You can't touch me," he said.

Dev just stood behind him without saying a word.

"We're Homicide detectives, Jay." Claire leaned close to Baylor. "We don't give a rat's ass about theft or fraud, you understand? But maybe we can help each other out."

"How's that?"

"When did you steal the prescription pad?" Claire asked.

"I didn't steal it."

Dev rested a hand on Baylor's shoulder, causing him to twitch in his seat. "Jay, let's save a little time. Tell the detective the truth. It'll make a nice change for you."

"I think he must've dropped it on the street—"

"Jay!" Dev barked, and Baylor jumped in his seat again. "We're saving time, remember?"

Baylor hesitated. "I found it in his desk drawer."

"Did you kill him?" Claire asked.

"No."

"But you were there, right? You saw him on the floor?"

Baylor nodded. "He was a fucking mess, all right?"

Dev removed his hands from Baylor's shoulders and returned to his seat. "Let's hear it, Jay."

"I was doing my usual route in the lane of his building, right?" Baylor said, referring to the Dumpster-diving for bottles and other valuables that alcoholics and IVDUs often pursue. "The back door of this building was open a crack. I could see light coming out. So, being the curious type, I check it out. I walk up a couple of flights of stairs and there's this office with a door wide open, right? So who wouldn't go in, okay?"

"And . . ."

"I follow the light down the hallway to this other room. And when I go in, the place is a mess. Blood everywhere. And the guy on the floor . . . Holy shit! I lost it. I grabbed the prescription pads and ran. I didn't even know what I was doing."

"You knew exactly what you were doing," Claire said.

"No. I was panicking, ma'am," Baylor pleaded, shuffling his feet so hard that he looked as if he were trying to run while seated.

"You walked around the blood without stepping a foot in it, and then you searched his desk for the prescription pads," Claire said. "Doesn't sound like panic to me."

"It wasn't like that!" Baylor was twitching wildly now.

"And how do we know Kolberg didn't put up a fight for his prescription pad?" Dev asked. "Maybe that's how he ended up on the floor."

"No fucking way, man! You're not pinning that on me."

"Not a bad idea, Jay." Dev grinned at the junkie. "This case has wasted enough of our time."

Baylor trembled to the point that his chair shook.

"Give us something, Jay," Claire said. "Maybe we can help you?"

Baylor scratched his head violently. "Okay. As I'm coming upstairs, I see this guy bolting out of Kolberg's office. He doesn't notice me."

"What guy?" Claire demanded.

"Tall bastard. Really tall."

Claire glanced at Dev then turned to Baylor. "How old?"

Baylor shrugged. "Fifty, maybe?"

"We need more, Jay," Claire said. "Fat or thin, hair color, clothes . . . that kind of stuff."

"Real tall and skinny. A beanpole. Wearing a nylon jacket and cords or something. Gloves, too. Looked like he's got money." His eyes darted wildly around the room. "He had short gray hair and a beard. Wore it like a fag, you know? Cut real short and even on his face, and none on his neck."

Baylor could be describing only one person. I'd never thought of Calvin Nichol as gay, but I understood what he meant. Nichol's detailed attention to personal grooming could fit the bill.

They led Baylor out of the interview room, and we reconvened in Dev's office. "Nichol won't know that we just punched a hole the size of Rhode Island through his story." He glanced at his watch. "Let's take what's left of the weekend off, and we'll pick him up first thing Monday morning."

Claire and I nodded in agreement. Breezing past me and out the door, she barely acknowledged my "good-bye," making it very clear that no offer of a ride home would be forthcoming. I took a taxi home.

Since Loren's death, most of my Saturday evenings were spent at home alone with a book or in front of the tube watching a ball game or a rented movie. But on this particular evening, I decided to make an exception. I changed into jeans and T-shirt and headed back out the door.

I got to the Railroad Club at nine o'clock. The ever-hip Seattle institution was already packed when I walked in. Its rundown, generic interior hadn't changed in the twenty years since I'd first seen it. I plopped myself down on a stool at the end of the crowded bar and nursed a beer, still smarting from the remnants of my hangover.

Tommy Connor stood off to the back corner of the stage, but he couldn't hide from the stage lights. He'd aged another few years in the weeks since I'd last seen him. Despite his taller frame and sparse beard, I'd forgotten how strongly he resembled his sister, especially around the eyes, and I felt a pang of sorrow at the sight of him. Six months after her death, I still missed Angela. And I supposed that was the reason I'd come.

Blues wasn't really my thing, but Tommy's band played

with enough of a rocking jazz flavor for me to enjoy it. For an amateur band, they were good. The instrumental play was flawless, rich and deep with the right mix of guitar chords and percussion, but to my ear the lead singer tried too hard to sell himself as a young John Lee Hooker.

Staring past the crowd with detached indifference, Tommy looked the consummate bass player. His playing was perfect, too. He knew how to add the right, desolate notes to all the love-gone-wrong and why-she-left-me tunes that the lead singer cranked out.

When their music turned more upbeat with a rousing version of "Soul Man," the small dance floor erupted. Had Lor been with me, she would've hauled me out. I was a reluctant dancer, but Lor never offered me a choice. When we first started dating, she would drag me anywhere she could find live music. Soon I was seeking out the best dance clubs in town. I loved how freely Lor moved on the dance floor, her body absorbing the music's rhythm. It was her release, similar to the way running was mine. She was a joy to watch. Admittedly, though, I had an ulterior motive—the sex we had was unparalleled after a night out dancing.

Tommy's band kept the dance floor busy for close to half an hour, but when they led into the first strings of John Lennon's "Yer Blue," the floor cleared. Listening to the singer wail the chorus of "I'm lonely, I want to die" over and over was enough for me. I stood up to go, but Tommy's mournful bass solo stopped me. Watching him gaze out at nothing while he played the sad riff, I wondered if the song reminded him, as it did me, of how much his sister had suffered in the end.

Ten months earlier—as if to live up to Stanley's prediction about her erratic tendencies—Angela was a no-show for her appointment that followed the cold walk in Gasworks Park. As days passed without hearing from her, I grappled with the urge to call but held out. Eight days and another missed appointment later, she resurfaced and, on Saturday morning at

2:30, a ringing phone wrenched me from a deep sleep. I recognized her cell phone number on my caller ID, but, pissed off and determined not to go down the road Stanley had laid out, I didn't answer.

Like one of those misguided, pre-programmed fax calls, my phone rang every five minutes for the next half hour. Finally, I grabbed for the receiver. "Angela, what is it?!" I snapped in lieu of a greeting.

"Dr. Ashman, I am so sorry to wake you. But it's important . . . I'm scared," she said with what sounded like very genuine distress. By that point, I was so confused by Angela that I wasn't sure I could tell a distress call from a crank call.

"What are you talking about?" I sighed, leaning back against my headboard.

"Can I come over? Please, it's—"

"Absolutely not," I cut in. "Listen, Angela. I'm going to hang up now. You can call my office Monday."

As I was putting down the receiver, I heard a tinny "Dr. Ashman, please!" from the earpiece. I shook the receiver in my hand and swore under my breath, then brought it back to my ear. "What?"

"Someone is following me."

Here we go. I rolled my eyes at Nelson, who lay half-asleep on the floor. Either Angela was pulling a borderline personality stunt, or she had slipped across the line into delusional. At three in the morning, I wasn't going to tackle either prospect.

"It's true." She rebutted my silence. "A weird-looking guy was waiting for me outside my apartment last Friday. Didn't even try to hide it. He just sat on the hood of his big old car, smiling in a creepy way. And when I got to your office, he was there outside the lobby, sitting in his car staring at me."

"Why would someone follow you, Angela?"

She hesitated. "I don't know."

"And how would he know about your appointments with me?"

Again, she was slow to answer. "Why would I make this up?"

"You tell me."

"I didn't, Dr. Ashman!" she said. "He was there. And I saw him a couple more times last weekend, but then he disappeared. Until yesterday, when I showed up for my appointment. Just as I'm crossing the street, I hear a loud engine, and his big old Cadillac or whatever the hell it is, pulls up. He even honked and waved. I freaked."

"Why didn't you call the police?" I asked.

"You think they'd believe me any more than you do?"

Agreed. "Why didn't you call me earlier?"

"I'm not sure," she mumbled. "I wanted to get far away from the guy."

"Let me get this straight. Someone, who knows our appointment times, is stalking you in a noisy and conspicuous old beater."

"I know how it sounds," she said. "But it's the truth."

My frustration got the better of me. "You sure you know what that is?"

Angela didn't comment right away. Eventually, she spoke in a chilly flat tone. "Thanks for your understanding. I'm sorry I wasted your time."

"Okay, Angela." Though she didn't reply, I could hear her breathing on the line. "Keep the phone by your bed. I'll meet you tomorrow morning. We can talk about it then." I hung up the phone, but I never did get back to sleep.

Angela was waiting outside of my building at 9 A.M. I was amazed by how fresh she looked after our curt middle-of-the-night phone call, while I must have looked like something the cat would have thought twice about dragging in. As we made our way to up to my office, she breezily updated me on her life of the past two weeks. I noted that she wasn't acting anything like a stalking victim. Once seated in my office, I pointed this out to her.

She grimaced. "Why would I make it up?"

Attention seeking? Manipulation? Just for the fuck of it? I kept the thoughts to myself. "I don't know, Angela."

"Dr. Ashman, maybe I overreacted." She looked at her feet. "I had no right to call you when I did. But my room-

mate's gone for the weekend. Tommy's out of town. You were the only person I could think of . . . who I trusted enough." She looked back up at me with steely eyes. *"I swear to God, I didn't make the guy up."*

"Next time, call as soon as he shows up."

Angela grinned her gratitude, but my next comment wiped the smile off her face. *"I spoke to Stanley Kolberg about you last week."*

She stiffened in her seat. *"I asked you not to."*

"I had to."

She looked away.

"Do you want to hear what he had to say?" I asked.

She shook her head slightly.

"He told me he failed you," I said. *"His exact words."*

She grunted.

"He's one of the most respected psychiatrists in this city. And he said he couldn't help you. Know why?"

"I don't care."

"He said your relationship had no definable psychotherapeutic boundaries."

She laughed again.

"Do you know what that means?"

Angela studied the floor without responding.

"It means that your relationship was inappropriate."

"Inappropriate, huh?"

"Phone calls at all hours, spontaneous get-togethers, no set limits on your time together." I shook my head. *"You can't have any kind of useful psychotherapy in that environment."*

"No, you can't," she agreed.

"I want to help you, Angela. But don't you see? We can't go down that same road."

"Believe me, Dr. Ashman, I don't make two mistakes like that in a row."

"What does that mean?"

She didn't move a muscle or speak a word.

I reached forward and touched her gently on the knee.

Her head snapped up. Her eyes were ablaze. "You want to know a little something about Dr. Stanley Kolberg?"

I nodded, taken aback by her sudden ferocity.

She shook her head and dropped her eyes back to the floor. "Forget it."

Over the ten weeks following our terse Saturday-morning session, Angela and I settled into a more consistent routine. She didn't miss any further appointments. The nocturnal phone calls stopped. And she never again mentioned her alleged stalker.

Happy with our progress, I attributed the breakthrough to Angela's newfound insight into her behavior. In psychotherapy, the old cliché about "half the problem is admitting you have a problem" often rings true; sometimes, it's 90 percent of the problem. When Angela accepted partial responsibility for her pattern of destructive relationships, a light switched on. Within three months, she had secured her "dream job" at the gallery and started dating a guy, who, by her own description, "broke the bad-boy mold wide open."

As her trust in me grew, the only wall I kept running into headfirst surrounded her relationship with Stanley. I never saw another flash of the raw emotion that came with the first mention of him, but every time I raised his name, she withdrew like a turtle into its shell.

I wasn't prepared to let it go so easily. One Friday, after she had recapped her week for me, I said, "Angela, let's talk about your father's death."

She frowned. "We've been through this."

"Dr. Kolberg gave me an account different from yours."

Her eyes narrowed. "What did he say?"

"He said you were on the mountain with your dad the day he died," I said.

"So?" She folded her arms across her chest.

"You told me he went with your brother and his friends."

"It doesn't change the way he died."

"It makes me wonder about some of the other details."

"Like what?" she huffed. "Maybe I made up the incest stuff?"

I didn't reply.

"You know what?" She shook her head angrily. "You don't get it."

"Give me some credit."

"How could you know?!" She uncrossed her arms and jabbed a finger at me. "How could you know anything about what it's like to have been abused that way?" On that note, she sprang to her feet and stomped out of my office.

I reached for her chart, but instead of writing notes, I sat with it open in front of me and reflected on what Angela didn't know about me. My own life had been directly touched by abuse. And, as often happened after seeing Angela, my thoughts drifted back to my childhood and Suzie Malloy.

Suzie's time at our house coincided with the waning months of my pre-puberty. With her feathered hair, tight jeans and tank tops, and tactile flirtatiousness, I definitely felt some stirrings, but without the raging pubescent levels of testosterone, my fantasies were sexually naïve. In spite of the developmental gulf between us—the difference between a mature child and a young adult—the two of us just clicked.

We used to hang out in her room listening to seventies LPs; Elton John, Fleetwood Mac, and Joni Mitchell were the favorites. Or we might hop a bus downtown to catch a matinee or wander the stores, especially bookstores. We wasted whole days in bookstores. Mainly, we talked. Suzie did most of the talking. I absorbed her thoughts and stories like a sponge.

Even accounting for my impressionable twelve-year-old mind, there was something special about Suzie. She never cared what others thought of her. If we bumped into her college pals when we were out on Friday night, she was happy to flaunt our close friendship, walking hand in hand with a boy whose voice hadn't even cracked. I saw how the others admired her. It was more than her quiet self-confidence; Suzie was one of those rare people who just had that elusive "it."

As easy as it was for me to forgo my seventh-grade buddies for her, I was surprised by how little interest she showed in the college guys who were always calling or dropping by the house. *They're all such boys!* she dismissed them with a sigh. When she saw the obvious hurt on my face, she leaned forward and pecked me softly on the lips. *You're more mature than any of them,* she explained, while I reeled from her conciliatory kiss.

Then, one day, in a musty row in Shelley's Bookstore downtown, Suzie lowered the boom on our perfect relationship. She announced that she had a new boyfriend. I was crushed. *Was he one of the guys from her school?* I demanded. No, he was older. More mature. A teacher. I couldn't believe it. A teacher!

As bitterly jealous as I was of her "teacher" (which was how we always referred to him), he never got in the way of our time together. I came to accept his presence in Suzie's life with grudging fatalism. At first, Suzie was uncharacteristically coy about him, as if she were the one—not the dirty old teacher—who had something to be ashamed of. With time, she opened up. She confided "the little snag" in her otherwise perfect romance. He was married. A temporary state, she assured. He was just waiting for the right moment to leave—after Christmas or the wife's milestone birthday or whatever other lame stalling tactic he'd dreamed up. Even at twelve, I smelled a rat when Suzie refused to. *He's stringing you along,* I warned. But she just laughed off the suggestion.

My feelings aside, the change in Suzie alarmed me. The fling had reached epic proportions in her fifteen-year-old eyes. In the months that passed, her ebullient self-confidence eroded. As her doubts grew, I saw more and more despair hiding behind her sunny disposition. Once, in the popcorn line of a movie theater, she turned to me and said in a calm and quiet voice—the kind that I would later learn is the most dangerous tone for a suicidal patient—"My life would be meaningless without him."

A month later, Suzie shuffled into my room and collapsed on my bed. I knew her teacher had dumped her. She cried *away most of the day while we listened to every done-me-wrong song that the seventies had to offer. After a couple of weeks of mourning, I saw flashes of the old Suzie. We began to venture downtown again, visiting the familiar book and record stores. She had me convinced that her breakup was behind her, that she herself was relieved it was finally over.*

Maybe I should've paid more attention to the little signs: her newfound fixation on discussing our place in the "big picture" or the fact that she never ate much anymore. But at the time, I knew nothing about depression or pathological grief reactions. One year shy of my teens, what the hell did I know about teenage angst?

Less than twelve hours after Suzie had kissed me for a second and final time and bewildered me with a teary-eyed "I'm sorry," Mom woke me at 6 A.M. to give me the news.

Poor Mom. She had trouble dealing with the most mundane of emotional events. And there she was, stammering at the foot of my bed, trying to explain how my best friend had died instantly on impact after jumping off the roof of the student union building.

I was drawn out of these disturbing memories when Angela walked quietly back into my office. She sat in the chair across from my desk. Without making eye contact, she looked straight ahead and spoke in a soft voice. "I was snowboarding that day."

For a moment, I was confused, but then I remembered. "The day your father died?"

She nodded. "I was the one who suggested that he come with us." She held up a hand. "Only because I knew he had gotten into boarding."

I sat still in my seat.

"It was a terrible day. Piss-poor visibility and bad winds. Which would've been fine for Tommy, me, and our friends. We were good boarders. But Daddy was just starting . . ."

Angela looked down and brushed at nothing on the leg of her jeans. "He insisted. He always had to keep up, you know? Daddy couldn't accept that he was getting on. When the rest of us decided to go for the powder out-of-bounds,

Daddy had no choice. His pride wouldn't let him stay behind."

There comes a point when any experienced therapist knows it's time to just shut up. Entirely. Not even to prompt a patient with an "and?" or a "so?" or an encouraging nod of the head. I understood that whatever Angela was about to say, she had to tell me at her own pace. When she stopped to scrub at her pant leg, I sat there with every intention of appearing like a bump on a log.

"The run we chose would've been a challenge in good visibility, but for an unfamiliar new boarder to cut a narrow path through trees and fog so thick you could grab a handful . . . A couple of Tommy's friends warned Dad that conditions weren't right for a new boarder. One of them offered to guide him back to the main trails. When Daddy looked at me, I could see he was scared, but I shrugged as if the others were making a big deal out of nothing. He waffled, then let out a fake laugh and said, 'I'm not sixty yet, kids.'

"Dad and I were the last ones down the slope. He pushed off down the trail, and I followed after. I didn't see him fall, but I heard the crash and his cry. I stopped, and sidestepped my way down the run. I saw his board's tracks veering off from the others, and the chewed-up snow at the edge of the gully.

"I pushed over to the edge, and looked down. We had just passed below the fog line, so I could see into the base. It must have been a forty-foot drop, and there were rocks and stumps all around. I didn't even see him at first. Then his blue ski suit caught my eye. He lay in a pile at the base. His legs were all twisted and his arms held above his head. Even his head looked out of position. I thought he was dead."

Angela looked up at me with bloodshot eyes. "As I was about to turn and go after the others, I saw something move. He started to wriggle on the ground. The way he writhed, I knew he must have been in pain. I'm not sure whether he saw me, but he waved his arms like a guy from a shipwreck trying to hail a passing plane. I just kept staring at him. Then I *turned and boarded hard as I could after the others. About a thousand feet later, I caught up with them on the trail.*

" 'What happened?' someone asked . . ." Angela stopped for a moment, staring in my direction, but beyond me. "I said, 'Daddy stopped at the ledge above. He didn't feel comfortable. Decided to get back to the main run. He was going to follow the trail back to the flags, and he wanted us to go on ahead.' "

Hard as I tried, I doubt my face hid the surprise.

"Dr. Ashman, it was like I was watching myself tell them. As if I had no say in the matter. I don't even know where it came from. It just came."

I nodded.

"You understand? I killed my father."

"Sounds to me like he made his own choice."

She shook her head. "I led him to that run. And then I let him die there, instead of getting help."

"He made his own choices," I repeated. More than the ski run, I was thinking of how he brought along his eleven-year-old daughter on a business trip for the sole purpose of molesting her.

"Dr. Kolberg called it 'passive homicide,' " Angela murmured.

"Fuck Dr. Kolberg!" I said, surprising myself with my vehemence.

"I already did."

8

T HE BUZZ HIT ME as soon as I stepped into Dev's office Monday morning. Like a couple of bloodhounds hot on a scent, Claire and Dev were clearly charged by the Calvin Nichol lead.

"Doc! Glad you made it." Dev grinned. "I was worried we were going to have to scrape you off the grille of some old sedan." And I knew my holding out on him had been forgiven, if not forgotten.

"Hello," Claire said. The coolness from our last interaction was gone, but there was something impersonal in her welcome. I could've just as easily been the guy on his way to replace the little white pucks in the men's urinals.

"Our buddy, Jay Baylor, identified Nichol for us," Dev informed.

"From a lineup?" I asked.

"No," Dev said. "From Nichol's hospital ID photo."

I had a mental image of Baylor withdrawing from heroin so badly that if asked, he'd have identified the guy on the grassy knoll the day Kennedy was shot. Dev read the skepticism on my face. "Baylor picked Nichol out of ten photos. None of them were women or horses or whatever. All bearded guys."

I sat in my designated metal chair. It creaked loudly as it scraped against the floor. "Are you going to pick Cal up?" I asked.

Dev shook his head. "We're gonna start with a search warrant."

I frowned. "Before you even question him?"

"People do a lot of spring cleaning when you give them a heads-up on a search warrant," he said, making me feel foolish for asking. "By the way, CSI got back to me about the car that nearly knocked your block off."

"What did they find?"

"They got a good set of treads from your neighbor's lawn, but they're as good as useless unless we find a car to match to them."

Dev's desk phone rang. He grabbed for the receiver, listened a moment, and then said, "Okay, we're coming." In one motion, he dropped it into its cradle and stood from his chair. "We should have the search warrant for Nichol's place by noon. Meantime, we got another interview."

"With whom?" I asked.

"Tommy Connor. The guy whose sister dove off the Aurora Bridge."

I fought to keep the surprise from my face.

Dev stretched his arms wide apart and yawned. "Of course, it might be a waste of time now that we're on to old Cal."

"Tommy is coming here?" I asked.

Dev nodded. Claire viewed me quizzically, picking up on my discomfort. I looked from one to the other and realized I was cornered. But at least part of my dilemma had been resolved for me. I had no choice now but to tell them. I shook my head. "I can't participate in this interview. Tommy's sister Angela was my patient."

Claire's eyes went wide in recognition. "Wait a minute!"

She pointed a finger at me. "Was Angela the patient who told you Kolberg had abused her?"

I nodded.

Claire grimaced. "And after she committed suicide, you still didn't turn Kolberg in?"

"No, but I encouraged Tommy to."

Claire held out her hands, palms up. "You told Tommy about his sister's accusations but you couldn't tell the authorities?"

"Tommy already knew."

She dropped her hands, but I still saw accusation in her eyes. "How?" she asked.

I shook my head. "Why don't you ask him?"

"Give it up, Claire." Dev sighed heavily as he lumbered for the door. "You're flogging a dead horse. Let's just go ask the brother."

At the door, Dev turned to me. "Do your *ethics*," he said with a trace of disdain, "allow you to watch from behind the mirror?"

"I'm not sure either of you understand how tightly I'm bound by the patient-therapist confidentiality covenant."

"I'm not sure either," Dev said. Claire studied me impassively.

I shrugged. "It's up to you two whether I watch or not. But I can't give you any feedback."

"Who cares about your feedback?" Dev grunted a chuckle. "I just like an audience."

I assumed my post behind the two-way mirror as Claire and Dev led Tommy Connor in. In jeans and a T-shirt, he sat between the two detectives. Resting his hands on the table, his face was cast in the same faraway expression as it had been at the Railway Club two evenings earlier. While Tommy was the epitome of calm, I was anything but.

Claire asked the first question. "Tommy, you reported Dr. Kolberg to the Health Department for sexually abusing your sister, right?"

Tommy nodded.

"Why did you wait until after she died?"

"I didn't know until a couple months ago."

"Oh?" Dev weighed in. "Did she tell you at a séance?"

Tommy stared at Dev for a moment, but I was relieved to see that he didn't rise to the bait. "Angela kept a journal. I only found it a few months after her . . ."

Dev leaned back in his chair. "How come you never wrote the complaint letter the Health Department asked you to?"

Tommy looked down into his lap. "It's complicated."

"Complicated how?"

Tommy rubbed at the stubble on his chin for a moment. "When I got through the rest of her journals, I realized that Angela claimed a lot of people had molested her."

"Like who?" Dev asked.

"Our dad, for example. I wasn't sure what to believe."

Dev nodded. "Not your sister, apparently." But again, Tommy ignored the provocation. "So you had no further beef with Kolberg then?"

Tommy could have just nodded and walked away, but he didn't. "Whether or not Kolberg abused Angela, he was a shitty psychiatrist," he said. "She got worse under his care. And one way or another, he helped her over the ledge of that bridge."

Claire leaned forward. "Doesn't sound like you're sorry about what happened to him?"

I held my breath, hoping Tommy would let it rest. But I knew he wouldn't.

"Not in the least," Tommy said.

"How about Dr. Ashman?" Claire asked. I gripped my chair in surprise.

"What about him?" Tommy shrugged.

"He saw your sister after Kolberg," she said. "Don't you blame him, too?"

Tommy shook his head. "Angela had nothing but good to say about Dr. Ashman. He almost saved her life."

The phrase hit me like a slap. I wanted to bang on the mirror and yell, "No, I didn't!" Instead, I hung my head and listened with mounting worry.

"Where were you last Monday at around ten P.M., Tommy?" Claire asked.

I knew from when Angela was still alive that Tommy's band jammed on Mondays. He guarded those evenings like a black bear protects her young. Except, apparently, for the Monday that mattered the most. "I was at home, working," he said.

"Alone?" Dev's smile exuded skepticism.

"I'm a Web designer. I usually work from home. And I happen to live alone."

Claire leaned forward in her seat. "When was the last time you saw Dr. Kolberg?"

"Never," Tommy said flatly.

Claire shook her head. "You *never* met Dr. Kolberg?"

"No."

Claire and Dev traded a brief glance. I knew Tommy's answer had surprised them both. It seemed to suck the wind out of their sails and the interview soon petered out.

"Don't go too far," Dev advised Tommy, ending the interview. "We might need to talk to you again."

Tommy shrugged and walked out without another word.

After Tommy left, I joined the detectives in Dev's office. "Sounds like Tommy boy had an outstanding issue or two with Kolberg," Dev said.

"Families often blame the therapist after the suicide of a loved one. It's understandable."

Claire looked at me, her head tilted. "Funny. He doesn't seem at all unhappy with the care you provided."

I broke off our eye contact. "People don't always assign blame fairly."

"I suppose," she said. "You don't happen to know what kind of car Tommy drives?"

I looked back up at her. "Not a big seventies sedan, if that's what you're getting at. I promise you Tommy wasn't the person trying to run me down."

She nodded. "Unless he's a damn good actor, he thinks pretty highly of you."

"But not Kolberg," Dev said.

"Not Kolberg," Claire echoed.

Dev's phone rang again. He picked up the receiver, listened a moment, and put it down with a smile. "Our search warrant just got signed."

He got up and headed off to assemble the search team, leaving Claire and me alone for the first time in three days. We walked down to her car in silence. I climbed into the backseat.

I cleared my throat. "Claire, about your dinner idea the other day . . ."

"Forget it. It was stupid." She spoke hurriedly to the windshield. "You would've thought after my divorce I'd have learned not to mix work and play."

"No, Claire. See, there's this dog who lives with me."

She glanced at me in the rearview mirror with a hint of a grin. "That's a strange way of saying you own a dog."

"I sort of got stuck with him. Anyway, Nelson's an old fellow, but I like to take him down to the lake on nice evenings to give both of us and our rickety old bones—"

"Yeah, right," Claire scoffed, good-naturedly. "How old are you, Joel?"

"Forty. But that's 280 in dog years," I said. "I know you live in the area. I thought you might want to join us one night. There would be a coffee in it for you."

Claire looked over her shoulder and flashed the nicest smile I'd seen in days, but it was gone as quick as it came. "Joel, you had a good point about us working together. Maybe we should wait and see."

As Dev opened the door and climbed into the passenger seat, I decided that my situation wasn't like eighth grade at all. I was smoother back then.

Claire drove us to Nichol's glass-and-steel apartment tower. Two bunny men, Nate Schiff and another CSI guy, joined us out front. Five minutes later, a skittish property manager led all of us up to Nichol's condo. He read carefully through the search warrant before unlocking the deadbolt, opening the door, and scurrying off.

Inside, I stuck with Claire and Dev while the bunny men

headed for the bedrooms. We spent a few minutes nosing around the pristine kitchen and living room, searching cupboards and drawers but finding only more of the same anal-retentive touches, like a fruit bowl filled with perfect lemons and rows of red wines organized by dates and regions.

We walked down the corridor to the bedrooms. The first room had been converted into a home office. The other bunny man, whose name I never caught, was looking at Nichol's computer. We walked past the second bedroom and into the master. Someone, maybe even Dev, once told me that when it comes to searches, 95 percent of the payload is in the suspect's bedroom. In this case, however, I had my doubts. With matching teak bed, bureau, and nightstand, it reminded me of a high-end hotel room. I wouldn't have been surprised to see the bed cover folded down and a wrapped chocolate on the pillow.

Without much regard for Nichol's neatness and order, Dev rifled through the nightstand while Schiff rummaged under the mattress and beneath the box spring. I followed Claire into the huge walk-in closet. Suits and shirts hung from racks, sorted meticulously by color, weight, and season, like something the autistic character in *Rain Man* might do. Against the far wall, Claire knelt in front of a built-in dresser, working purposefully. She pulled out the bottom drawer then patted a hand around in the space where the drawer had lain. She yanked out a panel, then fished inside and removed a black plastic bag.

"Maybe Nichol is human after all." She reached in the bag and extracted three videotapes along with a stack of magazines. After flipping through one of the magazines, she shook her head and sighed. "Then again, I might've spoken too soon."

I peered over her shoulder. She was leafing through a hardcore rag called *Domi Dearest*. The photos showed leather-clad female dominatrixes hovering over naked men and/or women, most of whom were bound and hooded. Claire shoved the magazines back in the bag and rose to her feet. "What the hell is wrong with these psychiatrists? All this S and M crap."

"I'm no expert," I said, pointing to the bag in her hand. "Technically speaking, those are about bondage and submission, not S and M."

Claire shot me a who-gives-a-fuck look as she elbowed by me and reentered the bedroom. "Guys," she called to Dev and Schiff. "I think we better have a look at these videos."

We sat in front of the living room TV while Schiff loaded the first tape, entitled *After-School Detention,* into the VCR. We fast-forwarded through a continuous stream of women in various leather get-ups dominating and degrading other people in a cheap classroom mock-up. The surgically enhanced "actresses," many of them looking stoned, barked out pointless obscenities at their "slaves" and forced them into various humiliating acts. Eventually they lapsed into graphic, ugly sex that sometimes culminated with them urinating or defecating on the slaves. The second tape was more of the same.

Pornography doesn't normally offend me. Through my work, I've had access to the private lives of enough people to know that the multibillion-dollar porn industry is supported by more than a few dirty old men. And I've come to appreciate that you can never predict what goes on behind people's bedroom doors. I don't normally judge people for engaging in any type of sexuality involving two or more consenting adults. But the thought of a fellow psychiatrist getting off on the degradation and contempt depicted in those bondage videos struck me as depressing.

Schiff loaded in the last videotape. From the shaky camera work and the lack of credits, I knew immediately it was homemade. I didn't recognize the setting, but in spite of the leather hood covering his face, there was no mistaking the naked lanky "slave" who rolled around on the hardwood floor with his hands duct-taped behind his back.

A girl stood above Calvin Nichol, holding a riding crop in her hand and wearing nothing but a figure-eight leather-studded belt, matching leather cap, and pair of black stiletto pumps that must have had eight-inch heels. She might've been twenty, tops, and was thin to the point of emaciated.

Her innocent pixyish face didn't fit the pierced and tattooed bony frame below it, as if a special effects computer had superimposed the two. She strutted around the fallen Nichol, but her movements were robotic as if she'd done the same routine a thousand times before, which she probably had.

"Kiss my feet," she barked in a high-pitched Eastern European accent.

Nichol obliged, his long tongue stabbing through the hood and lapping at her shoes. After a few minutes of this bootlicking, the girl jerked her foot away. She stood over Nichol, before raising a foot and resting the sharp heel in the small of his back. Then she leaned forward and jabbed her riding crop into the base of his neck.

"That's it. That's it! Ride him!" came the off-camera command. "Like he's a wild fucking stallion!"

The voice was unmistakable, though the tone and phrasing were alien to me. "That's Stanley's voice!" I said, attracting brief looks from the others. Soon all eyes turned back to the spectacle on the TV.

With his arms still tied behind his back, Nichol pushed himself up onto his knees though his chest still touched the ground. He looked as if he were trying to perform some mutant prayer. The woman sat on Nichol's bound hands. She started to bounce up and down, rubbing her crotch against his hands.

"Use your bloody arm as a rein!" Stanley again commanded from off-screen.

"A what?" the girl squeaked.

There was a brief gray storm on the TV then the picture reappeared with the woman bouncing on Nichol's back, her right arm wrapped tightly around Nichol's neck. She continued to slam her vulva against his hands, while wearing a forced grimace of "pleasure" that was bad acting even by porn standards.

"He's being very naughty," Stanley's voiceover said. "He needs to be disciplined."

"Not hard," Nichol pleaded through his mask. "I don't like to be hurt."

The woman reached behind her and started to spank Nichol's bony paper-white ass with her riding crop. After spanking for a while, the woman dismounted Nichol. She rolled him onto his back and squatted over his head. He licked at her wildly, while she looked to fight the boredom off her face. After a few minutes, she stood up straighter. She peed on Nichol, who rolled underneath like a farmer feeling rain for the first time in months. Then the screen reverted to its gray storm.

Claire turned to me, her lips threatening to curl into a sneer. "So Stanley Kolberg was calling out the off-screen direction, huh?"

"No question," I said.

Schiff ejected the tape from the VCR and placed it back in the bag with the others. At that moment the door flew open and Calvin Nichol barged into the room. He stopped in the middle of the room and locked his hands on his hips. "What's going on, Sergeant Devonshire?" he said to Dev, though he glared at me.

Dev pulled the crumpled search warrant out of his pocket and handed it to him.

Nichol didn't even look. "What grounds do you have to search my home?"

"We have an eyewitness who places you at the murder scene," Claire said.

"That's ridiculous, because—" Nichol stopped in midsentence when he caught sight of the black bag dangling from Schiff's hand. His arms dropped to his sides, and his gaze fell to the floor.

"How'd you like to come and answer some questions, Dr. Nichol?" Dev asked.

"Am I under arrest?" Nichol asked quietly.

"If you cooperate, we might be able to avoid that."

"I'd like to speak with an attorney, please," he said.

"Lawyers just complicate things," Dev said in a collegial tone.

"I'd very much like to speak to an attorney," Nichol repeated shakily, then walked into his home office and closed the door behind him.

Maybe I'd been watching too many late-night movies, but I half-expected to hear a gunshot come from the other room. When none was forthcoming, I can't deny that part of me was disappointed.

Filing out the door, I thought about my ex-partners. I'd always found Stanley and Calvin's close friendship inexplicable. Aside from their practice of psychiatry, which they approached from opposite ends of the professional spectrum, I didn't know of a single shared interest between them. That is, not until Angela Connor first told me about what I had just witnessed on Nichol's TV.

Seven months earlier, the day after Angela's disclosures about her involvement in her father's death and her sexual relationship with Stanley, I was still unsure what to make of it.

But as Stanley hailed me over to the table he was occupying in the corner of the restaurant, the emotions stirred with each step closer to him.

He launched into his usual chitchat, but my uneasy mood didn't escape his eye for long. "Joel, what's going on?" he asked amiably as a waitress brought me a cup of coffee.

"It's Angela Connor."

"Oh." He nodded sympathetically. "How is Angela?"

"Better."

"And that's bothering you?"

"No." I reached for my coffee. "Something she told me is."

"Which is?"

"About you and her," I sighed.

"What did she say?" He arched an eyebrow.

I struggled for the words. "That the two of you had . . . inappropriate relations."

" 'Inappropriate relations'? What is this, 1907?" Stanley chuckled and took a long sip of coffee. "She told you we fucked, did she?"

"Did you?"

Stanley held his cup to his lips and eyed me for a moment before speaking. *"No, as a matter of fact, we didn't."*

I nodded noncommittally.

"Ah, but you don't believe me, Joel," he said. From his relaxed tone, we could've just as easily been discussing the lunch specials.

"The way she told me made it very convincing."

He rubbed his beard thoughtfully. *"How so?"*

"We had reached one of those intense . . . breakthrough moments," I said. *"We weren't even discussing you. Angela just blurted it out. She had no reason to lie."*

Stanley's jaw dropped. *"You don't honestly believe Angela needs a reason to lie?"*

"I don't know what to believe," I said with a sigh. *"But I know I have to find out."*

He reached over and patted me on the arm. *"Joel, if the situation were reversed, I'm sure I would do the same."*

I could have done without his empathy. It made me even more uncomfortable than if he'd reacted with the defensiveness I'd expected. *"It wasn't just the accusation. For months, she dropped hints that something was going on between you two."*

"Hints," Stanley echoed, as we waited for our waitress to refill our coffee cups. Once she'd left, he said, *"I remember Angela as being a bit more direct than that."*

"How so?"

"With me, she used to fling her closet doors wide open and flaunt her dirty laundry. She willingly disclosed all of it: the incestuous abuse, her promiscuous lifestyle, and even the murky circumstances of her father's death. No hinting about it." I nodded, realizing he made an irrefutable point. *"So why, with our supposed affair, does she dance around the topic like it's that much worse than anything else?"*

"I don't know," I said.

Stanley put his cup down. *"She's manipulating you, Joel."*

"So you say."

"Did you ever wonder why Angela would stick with you in light of our alleged history if she knew—and believe me she did—that you were my partner?"

"Why don't you tell me, Stanley?" I said, frustrated by his condescending tone.

"It's what Angela does. It's her modus operandi, playing people off of one another. Look at the job she did with her dad and her brother."

"Let me see if I've got this straight," I said sarcastically. *"Angela came within a couple of heartbeats of killing herself and then spent five months in therapy just to pit two psychiatrists against each other?"*

"Of course not." Stanley stroked his beard with the back of his hand. *"Angela's more complex than that. And I'm not even suggesting she consciously plotted any of it. But nonetheless, it's how she works."* He pulled his hand away from his beard to list the damning nouns with his fingers. *"Manipulation, seduction, deceit, attack-and-retreat . . . those are Angela's coping mechanisms. She doesn't have a clue what trust and loyalty are. Not even love,"* Stanley sighed. *"She tries to keep people close by muddling with their heads and continually throwing them off balance."*

"Why?"

"The attention, Joel! It's classic borderline-personality behavior. I imagine nothing would please her more than to know we're having this conversation about her now."

I stared into my coffee, digesting his argument. *"I've seen a different side to Angela."*

Concern creased his face. *"Joel, are you sure you've maintained your objectivity?"*

"You mean have I fallen for her?"

"Exactly," he said, and then held his palms up in disclaimer. *"I did, Joel. Hook, line, and sinker. Didn't sleep with her, mind you. But I definitely fell prey to her wiles."*

"I'm not in love with her, Stanley," I said.

"But?" He knew he was on to something.

"She reminds me of someone I used to know. That's all."

He bit his lip, suppressing a smile. "Another victim?"

"Kind of." But "victim" was exactly how I thought of Suzie Malloy. "Anyway, when Angela told me about the two of you—more how she told me, actually—I took it as the truth."

"The truth? Angela??" Stanley sighed. "Let me tell you something that is proven fact. It might help to put your mind at ease." He broke off our eye contact. "I'm impotent."

I didn't respond.

"For over fifteen years," Stanley said in an even tone, though his face reddened and he avoided my eyes. "Surely, at some point, you must have wondered why I hadn't dated since my divorce?"

"I guess."

"It's because the old drawbridge doesn't rise anymore." Stanley forced a self-conscious smile. "There. I've made it easy for you. You don't have to choose my word over Angela's, or vice versa. You can just ask my urologist."

We filled in the rest of the lunch with small talk, most of which came from Stanley. Nothing in his demeanor suggested that he was offended by my accusation. Stanley was nothing if not persuasive. In the time before our entrées had arrived, he'd successfully overturned my mental image of him to the point that I felt foolish for having even raised the subject.

I was anxious to discuss the issue with Angela, but the following Friday she didn't show for her appointment. Fifty minutes into her scheduled time, she phoned to cancel.

"Where are you?" I demanded.

"Dr. Ashman, I can't make it today. I'm sorry."

Something in her tone stopped me from asking why she was calling after the fact to cancel. "Look, Dr. Ashman, I said a lot of stuff off the cuff last session." She swallowed. "I've got a pretty active—sometimes overactive— imagination. I wouldn't want other people to think—"

"Angela, what we talk about is confidential," I reassured.

"I know. It's just that . . ." She struggled to find the words.

"I don't even know why I said anything. Maybe I wanted to shock you or whatever. Anyway, it wasn't true."

"Okay." I tried to be soothing. This wasn't my first time hearing a patient backpedal after a particularly intimate or difficult disclosure. "So you made it all up?"

"Yes," she said quietly.

I couldn't resist asking, "Why would you want me to think you were involved with his death?"

" 'Death'?" she repeated, sounding confused, then after a moment added: "Oh, no, not that. The stuff about Daddy was pretty much true. It's what I said about Dr. Kolberg."

"Oh," I said, gathering my bearings. "You mean, you didn't sleep with him?"

"No."

"Why did you tell me you had?"

"I don't know." She cleared her throat. "After all that stuff about Daddy, I don't know. I felt kind of raw and . . ." She sighed. "Nothing happened between Stanley and me."

"Okay." I hadn't remembered her calling him by his first name before, but I let it slide. "Then why didn't you want me to know he was your previous psychiatrist?"

"I was really sick back then. Some of the weird things I did and said . . ." She exhaled. "I shouldn't have said what I said about Stanley, okay?"

"Okay." I didn't see the value in pushing the point over the phone. "Angela, can you come on Monday? We can talk through some of this."

She didn't answer.

"Angela?"

"Dr. Ashman, I want to take a break," she said quietly.

"From our therapy?"

"Yeah. It's been so intense." She quickly added, "You've been great. And I'm doing way better. Except for the odd lie"—she giggled nervously—"but I'm kind of overwhelmed."

"All right," I said.

After a pause, she said uncertainly, "So, I'll give you a call in a month or so?"

"You know where I am."

She waited for me to say more. When I didn't, she said, *"Thanks for understanding. And for . . . everything."*

"Take care of yourself, Angela."

My heart sank as I hung up the phone. I knew my response had confused her, but I'd been down this road before. Experience dictated that I'd hear from her very soon.

Experience was wrong.

Four weeks after I'd last spoken to Angela, her brother Tommy dropped by my office unexpectedly on a Friday afternoon. With a haggard frown, he sank into the chair across from me. *"Dr. Ashman, it's started, again."*

"What has?" I asked, knowing the answer but hoping I was wrong.

"The whole cycle," he sighed. *"She dumped her boyfriend, quit her job, and then last week her roommate kicked her out."*

"Where is she staying?"

"With me. When she's there. Some nights she's just gone. Others, she's up all night listening to music." Tommy mussed his hair the same way Angela did when frustrated. *"She's not herself."*

"Meaning?"

"She's withdrawn, same as before, but . . ." He wound a couple of strands of hair around his finger. *"She's really edgy. Like she's scared."*

After Tommy left, I dialed Angela's cell number, but she didn't answer. I left two messages, but by the time I drove home I still hadn't heard back from her. So I plopped down in front of the TV with a pizza and a beer, and glumly watched the Rockets thrash my Sonics.

Nelson's anemic bark awoke me around 2 A.M. I dragged myself out of bed, threw on a pair of sweatpants, and headed downstairs. Angela, makeup running and hair dripping wet, stood at my doorstep. *"Come in,"* I said.

Reeking of rum, she breezed past me. I followed her into the family room. She pulled off her soaked, light-cotton jacket and dropped it on one of my leather couches. Her wet

T-shirt was pulled up, revealing a flat abdomen with an Aztec sun tattooed around her belly button that came as news to me. Her near-transparent white top failed to hide much of her bra-less breasts and nipples. She glanced down at her see-through shirt, but didn't bother pulling it down or covering herself up. Instead, she flopped on the couch and stretched her feet until they rested on the armrest.

"How come you didn't return my phone calls?" I asked.

"What do you call this?" She held an arm up in the air and made a regal circling gesture with her hand, implying her presence was at my request.

"Come on. Let's get you dried off, and home in a taxi. We can meet at my office in the morning."

"I'm here." She smiled widely at me. There was no mistaking her expression. "Why don't you crack a bottle of wine, and we can chat now."

I grabbed the throw-blanket hanging from the chair beside me, and started toward her with it outstretched. "That's not how we operate. Remember?"

She shot off the couch and met me in the middle of the room. She grabbed the blanket out of my hand and tossed it back onto the chair where I'd found it. When she locked her blue-gray eyes on me, she was standing so close that I could feel her warm breath on my cheek. "Why don't we stop pretending?"

"Angela—"

"Shhh." She brought a finger to my lips. "I'm not your client anymore," she cooed. "I fired you last month. Remember?"

I pulled her finger gently from my lips. "Angela, you're drunk."

"So?" She took a firmer hold of my hand, brought it to her lips, and then kissed it sensually. I stood motionless as she kissed each finger individually. Still kissing, she leaned forward and pressed her chest against my loose T-shirt. My shirt went damp from the wet skin and fabric, and by the time I felt her nipples press into my chest, I was aroused.

She inched her face to mine and planted a warm, breathy

kiss on my lips. I didn't reciprocate, but I didn't stop her from landing more quick, teasing kisses. Then she put her lips against mine, and I felt her tongue slide between my lips.

The reality hit me like a mallet. I jerked my head away from hers and grabbed her roughly by the shoulders. "Stop it!"

My forceful rebuff didn't discourage her. She smiled provocatively. "What's the matter, Joel? Don't you think I can feel how excited you are?" She ran a hand along the leg and up the crotch of my sweats.

I stepped back and held her at bay with my hands. "Angela, this won't happen."

"Why?" she breathed, and I caught another strong whiff of rum. "Can't you stop being a fucking analyst for two minutes? Just enjoy the moment."

I started to guide her toward the door. "You have to go now."

She let me lead her a few steps and then turned and asked in a small hurt voice, "What's wrong with me?"

"We have a professional relationship. For me to cross that line"—I sighed—"is unconscionable."

"Your partner had no problem crossing that line."

I dropped my hands from her shoulders, concerned I might otherwise shake her. "What's that supposed to mean?!"

"It means he had no problems fucking me," she said. "Well, I wouldn't actually call it fucking. What he did was . . ." She didn't finish the accusation, lending it even more weight.

"Here we go again." I threw my hands in the air. "He did. He didn't. He did. . . . What the hell do you expect me to believe?"

Angela didn't answer. She walked into the family room, grabbed the blanket off the top of the chair, and wrapped it around her shoulders on her way back to the couch. When she spoke again, her voice was crisp and clear, as if the alcohol had instantly cleared from her system. Or maybe she had never been as drunk as she was acting.

"When I first went to Stanley, I guess I was depressed," she said. "I don't know. But the guilt around Daddy's death was eating me up. At first, I was scared to tell him what happened, but he got it out of me soon enough. Shit, after a couple of months there was nothing I wouldn't have told him. And he helped me. God, did he help me!" She shot me a glance that suggested I might have come up short by comparison. "He had me feeling better about myself than I had since my eleventh birthday." She repositioned her blanket before continuing. "One day, he said it would be easier if we met at his place for our sessions. He wasn't fooling me, but I didn't care. I knew he had a thing for me. Besides, I'd always found him cute in a Sean Connery way." She stared into my eyes. "I had no problem with the idea of screwing him. I owed him that much."

"But?" I whispered.

"Your friend didn't have old-fashioned screwing in mind," she said. "I've always been pretty open-minded sexually, but what he was into . . ." She shuddered under the blanket. "He tried to sell it as some kind of bullshit unconventional therapy for dealing with abuse. As if!"

"Tried to sell what?"

"At first, it was pretty harmless," she grunted. "He liked to be tied up and slapped a bit. We'd do other stuff, too, but Stanley kind of struggled in the hardness department."

Hearing for the very first time that my sixty-plus-year-old partner, who I'd always thought of as asexual, was into bondage and masochism was surreal. She might as well have told me that he breathed underwater.

"It got worse," she said. "He had all these whips and shit." She shook her head and her voice cracked. "He wanted me to beat him. To really hit him. To cut him with the whips until he bled. It was gross."

"But you went along with it, of course," I scoffed.

"You think I wanted to?"

"You owed him that much, huh?"

"Are you out of your fucking mind?" Angela wrinkled her

face in disgust. "I might've felt obliged to give him a blowjob or two. But not that! Don't you get it? I had no choice. He was blackmailing me."

This was too much. "About what? Your father's death?"

Angela nodded slowly. "He said he'd turn me in for killing my dad." She huddled the blanket tighter around her neck.

I laughed in disbelief but that didn't discourage her. "Getting beaten wasn't enough for Stanley anymore," she said. "He wanted to hurt me. After a while I stopped caring about his threats. I told him I'd take my chances with a judge. But he knew me too well. He said he'd turn Tommy in, too." Angela stopped to wipe her face with a blanketed arm. "Even if they couldn't prove anything, the charge would've killed Tommy. I couldn't let that happen to my little brother."

Just when I thought her accusations couldn't get any more outlandish, she proved me wrong. "Then Stanley started to bring along that freaky sidekick of his, Calvin Nichol." She rocked under the blanket on the couch. "At least Nichol didn't like pain. Humiliation was his bag. He got off on being verbally abused. And he liked me to . . . oh, it's too gross to talk about." She wiped her eyes again. "I just shut down. Like with Daddy, I pretended it wasn't me. Like I was watching it happen to someone else. But one day . . ." She faltered, and it took her a few seconds to find her voice again. "He had me chained to the wall. I had a gag in my mouth, and I was blindfolded. I hung there, just waiting. The bastard loves to draw it out. Usually, the anticipation was worse than the pain, but not this time. I caught a whiff of burning wax. Then I felt pain just before I smelled burning flesh. My flesh. It was the worst pain I'd ever felt. And I couldn't even scream without choking on that fucking gag. That's when I decided I'd had enough of your partner."

She cleared her throat and steadied her voice again. "I had an old prescription of amitriptyline. I swallowed the whole bottle, but just my luck"—she grunted a humorless chuckle—"Stanley comes by my place and finds me. He called nine-one-one. And you know the rest."

The rest of what? I wanted to scream. "Have you seen him since?"

"Only once. At first, he left me alone. But later—I guess when he found out I was seeing you—he sent that freaky guy in the big old car to wait for me. I got the message: Stay away from you. But I thought, fuck him! I wasn't going to let him intimidate me again. Then about a month ago, he came by my place. Told me if I didn't stop seeing you, Tommy was in deep shit. Showed me a letter he had written for the DA. It was no bluff." She rebundled the blanket around her. "That's why I had to drop out of therapy and pretend none of it happened."

I sat perfectly still, in stark contrast to the turmoil raging inside.

"What is it?" Angela shifted in her chair.

I couldn't keep the anger from my voice. "I'm supposed to believe that my partner and good friend not only had sex with you, but he tortured and threatened you?" My words stoked my fury. "Then he brought another respected psychiatrist into his twisted games, blackmailed you, and eventually drove you to attempt suicide?!"

"That's what happened."

"A one-night stand . . . an affair . . . but this!" I folded my arms across my chest. "No way."

"Look!" She reached for the hem of her shirt and started to lift. Before I could stop her, she'd raised it up and spun her back to me. In the center, just over her spine where bra clips might sit, was a red, ragged, raised four-inch scar from a poorly healed burn. "Here's your best friend's brand," she hissed.

"What does that prove?"

She dropped her shirt down and hopped off the couch. "Why don't you get your head out of your ass. Maybe you'll see Stanley Kolberg for what he is."

I jumped up from my chair. "For twelve years I've worked with Stanley. In that time, I've never heard so much as a rumor about him. Now I'm supposed to believe he's the Marquis de Sade! How could I not have an inkling about a secret like that?"

"It's not his secret to keep," Angela snapped. "He's a slippery son of a bitch who tricks victims like me into carrying all the shame."

"Victims like me"—it sounded like the battle cry of the borderline personality. My anger dissipated, replaced by disappointment. Maybe Stanley was right about Angela. Maybe this was her way of dealing with the people in her life— uttering lies and accusations to pit friend against friend.

"What?" Angela demanded.

"That's how you really see yourself, Angela, isn't it? A victim, your whole life long."

"Not anymore," she spat. She grabbed her still wet jacket off the couch and strode for the door.

I followed after. "Where are you going?"

"Fuck you," she said with her back to me.

I caught her at the front door. She tried to open it, but I put my hand out to stop the door. "Let me at least call you a cab."

"I don't need your help anymore, Dr. Ashman."

"What are you going to do, Angela?"

She turned to me, her face consumed by contempt. "Just wait and see." With that, she yanked the door open and stormed out into the dark wet morning.

9

THE DAY AFTER WE SEARCHED Nichol's condo, I jogged the six miles to pick up my resuscitated Honda at the garage on Sixty-fourth Street. When I turned the key in the ignition, I got nothing more than an unhealthy sputtering. Then I remembered to slip the gearshift into Neutral, and the engine purred like a cat—granted, a very old and asthmatic cat.

I spent the rest of my day catching up with my real job, attempting to put out fires at the Cascade Mental Health Team offices. I had no time to spend on the Kolberg investigation. As soon as I got home, I fed Nelson, leashed him up, and headed straight out for Green Lake.

Stepping onto the lake's pathway, I spotted Claire walking toward us from across the parking lot. She wore her tawny-blond hair down, barely reaching the neck of her light green sweater. I'd never seen her in jeans, which aside from showing off her long legs, allowed me to appreciate her graceful athletic stride.

"Who's this?" she asked with a smile, closing the gap.

"Nelson."

"Hey, Nelson." She leaned over and scratched behind his ears.

I was surprised that Nelson's tail flickered a few times. "That's as warm a welcome as I've seen him give in a long while," I said.

"That's how I like my men." Claire laughed, giving the dog a good pat. "Reserved."

I thought I glimpsed redness in her cheeks when she stood up again. "Shall we walk?" I suggested.

She nodded.

"Thanks for joining me tonight," I said, clearing my throat and feeling silly for the banal comment. But her warm smile made me feel more at ease.

We started down the gravel lakeside trail. Claire gazed out across the water toward an island covered with small trees. "I should've moved here sooner." She closed her eyes and inhaled a big breath of the damp evening breeze.

"I thought you were a mountain girl, through and through."

"Was." She sighed a laugh. "I grew up in Denver. I loved it. And yes, even the winters. I thought the Rockies were unbeatable. Then I got a taste of the waters out here."

I grinned. "So you moved because of the nicer backdrop?"

"Partly." Claire pushed up the sleeves of her sweater. Her more casual look complemented her more relaxed "away from the office" demeanor. "Mainly, I was trying to keep ahead of my past."

"Your husband?"

She kept her eyes fixed on the lake. "Him, the force, all of it."

I hesitated, trying to avoid sounding like a therapist, but curiosity got the best of me. "How long were you married?"

"Long enough," she sighed. "Two years or so."

I shrugged helplessly. "Nosiness, it's a professional hazard."

"Not at all." She smiled. "It's just a little uncomfortable to talk about."

"I know the feeling." I'd become expert on avoiding the subject of my own past. Odd, I supposed, for a guy who spends his workdays trying to make sense of other people's histories.

We walked awhile farther without talking. We were so close that our shoulders nearly touched and I noticed her fragrance. Lilac, I decided, enjoying our physical proximity despite the silence.

Claire stared at the gravel path. "We were pretty happy," she said so quietly that I barely heard it.

I nodded.

"Not perfect, but pretty happy," she said. "Compatible, you know? We both loved travel, sports, and the outdoors. Dale's even a diehard Broncos fan."

"I won't hold that against him."

"We were trying to squeeze as much in as possible before having the kids we both wanted." She stopped to face the water, but her gaze drifted beyond the horizon. "Money was tight. Two junior detectives' salaries don't go that far in Denver. But just before we married, our luck turned. Dale told me how a couple of stock tips paid off. When we came back from our honeymoon in Hawaii, we had new ski stuff, a new SUV, and other toys I didn't think we could afford."

Claire knelt down and picked up a handful of rocks. She skipped one along the water. "I began to get wind of rumors at work suggesting we might be on the take." She threw another rock straight into the water. "But Dale denied it. He told me all the money came from a stock market windfall. But the seed was planted, you know? I searched our home, but I couldn't find anything on paper to explain our new wealth. When I confronted him, he became extremely defensive. Then he just took off. I didn't hear from him for two days. I was worried he might have done something stupid." She hurled another rock into the water. "When he finally came back, he was calm, resigned even. He told me the truth."

I waited. Even Nelson's head was tilted, as if he was hanging on Claire's revelation.

"Dale admitted he'd made a little extra money 'looking the other way,' as he put it," she sighed. "He said it was no big deal. Just pot. One or two of the local 'grow ops' had paid him to back off."

I shook my head. "What did you do?"

Claire let the rest of the rocks fall from her hand and then began to walk. "My identity was totally wrapped up in the force. It was my family." She shook her head. "Then I find out that my husband is a dirty cop. It would've killed Dad to think I was involved."

I wanted to reach out and squeeze her hand but instead I mustered a smile. "Oh, Claire."

"Mmmm." She bit her lip. "It got worse. After I moved out, Internal Affairs approached me. They wanted to know what I knew." We walked a few silent steps farther. "They wanted me to choose between my husband and my career," she said. "But it was more than just a career, it was my whole belief system . . . my family." She turned to me with plaintive eyes. "Don't know if I would've talked or not, but Dale took the decision out of my hands. . . ." She paused, remembering. "He struck a deal. I was cleared of all suspicion." She paused. "Except, of course, in my colleagues' eyes."

"So you came here for a fresh start?"

She shrugged. "There was no going back for Dale and me. He knew it, too. I guess it just wasn't meant to be."

I stopped. "You honestly believe people are meant for each other?"

"Absolutely." She faced me with a look of determination. "Don't you?"

I stared into her intelligent green eyes. "Meant for each other? No. But I do think that, every once in a while, the right two people stumble upon each other."

"Like you and your wife?" she asked, tucking her hair back behind her ears.

I broke off our eye contact and nodded.

"Nosiness." Claire smiled. "A professional hazard."

I chuckled and tugged on the lead to pull Nelson away from the grass he was sniffing at a bit too intently.

"What was she like?" Claire asked.

"That's not fair," I said. "You know how memory distorts people."

She took a step closer and brushed her hand over mine. "I'd really like to know."

"She wasn't perfect," I said. "Lor could be a slob. I mean a real slob. Imagine, an architect and designer whose bedroom looked like a war zone. And, man, could she be competitive. When we played tennis, if she thought I made a close line call, look out! She'd go up one side of me and come down the other."

Claire laughed. "I like the sound of her already."

"The thing was, Lor loved life. Everything was a new opportunity to her. And she cared so much about people. Off the tennis court, anyway. Standing at a bus stop, Lor could get the life story out of a complete stranger. Because she showed such genuine interest, people knew they could trust her. She was that rare type who made others feel better about themselves." I cleared my throat. "No wonder everyone loved her."

I flushed with embarrassment. "I knew I'd end up canonizing her once I started, but like I said earlier, she wasn't perfect. Every few months, Lor fell into these black moods. She'd sit at home. Wouldn't eat. Barely said a word. No one could get through to her. Including me. Then, just as quick as it came, the mood would disappear like a fog burning off."

"I don't know," Claire said. "She still sounds pretty close to perfect."

"A lot closer than I am," I blurted out, then looked away and started to move again. Claire had gotten far more out of me than I'd intended to say.

Recognizing my embarrassment, Claire flashed a disarming smile and changed the subject. "Something I've been wondering. Why did his patients put such blind trust in Kolberg?"

"You mean like Amy Sohal?" I asked.

"And that girl who hanged herself. And Tommy Connor's sister. And God knows how many others."

"You've never been in therapy, have you?"

She shook her head.

"A patient of mine once described it as 'the ultimate nakedness,'" I said. "Imagine sharing your most private thoughts and shameful secrets with a stranger. Most people don't tell that kind of stuff to their own family."

"I'd think it might be easier with a stranger."

"Maybe. But consider the level of trust these people give to their therapists. On top of which, many patients have inadequate coping skills and very low self-esteem."

We slowed to let Nelson sniff a bush, which he did, leaf by leaf. "I see your point," Claire said. "So the psychiatrist becomes like a god to his patient?"

I nodded. "In some cases. But it's more like a parent-child dynamic, where the client turns blindly to the doctor for direction and advice." I tugged on the leash to get Nelson moving again. "Often patients misinterpret these feelings of trust and intimacy for romance."

Claire elbowed me gently. "Must be a real nightmare having all those women falling for their handsome doctor."

"Sometimes it's a powder keg."

"Yeah, I guess we've seen that side, too," she said. "There's probably not much some patients wouldn't do for their therapist."

"Not to sound melodramatic, but with the right patient and the wrong psychiatrist, it's tough to imagine anything they wouldn't do."

Nelson decided he'd gone far enough. He promptly dropped to his belly and lay on the grass. I knew from experience it would now take a tow truck to pull him from the spot. "Looks like we'll be here for a while," I told Claire.

Claire sat cross-legged on the dry grass beside Nelson and began to rub his back, but he was already asleep. Still rubbing, she looked up at me. "You and Stanley were partners for a long time?"

"Almost eight years." I sat down beside her.

Then she asked the question that I'd been expecting for days. "How could you not have known earlier?"

"I look like an idiot, huh?"

"Look at me and my ex-husband. People in glass houses and all . . ." She laid a hand on my shoulder. "But you seem so observant."

"Did I deliberately overlook something?" I asked myself as much as her.

Claire eyed me without judgment. I appreciated that. And I liked the way her hand felt on my shoulder, especially when she let it run down my arm to rest on my wrist.

"In my work, I've met child molesters who'd convinced parents to let them baby-sit their kids," I said. "They were great actors. But Stanley was one better. I don't think I missed anything obvious. It wasn't until Angela told me how he manipulated and abused her. Even then, I refused to believe her at first."

"You didn't want to believe her?" Claire nodded.

I nodded back. "After Lor died, I hit rock bottom and went straight through. Stanley helped dig me out."

Staring at my sleeping dog, Claire pulled her hand from my wrist and asked: "Do you honestly think Cal Nichol killed Kolberg?" Her face was skeptical.

"Maybe not," I said. "I don't know."

Claire stood, brushing the sand off my pant legs. "We should head back."

After raising Nelson from the ranks of the near-dead, we meandered—at the dog's insistence—back the way we came. When we reached the parking lot and the point of good-byes, the ambiguousness of our walk led to an awkward moment, which was broken by Claire. She bent down and gave Nelson a good scratch behind the ears. "Thanks for the walk, old feller." She stood up, leaned forward, and brushed her lips against mine. "You, too, old feller." She turned and hurried off in the opposite direction.

"Where's *my* scratch?" I called after her, feeling a slight glow from her fleeting kiss.

She laughed and, without turning, waved her hand above her head.

As I walked Nelson home, I relived the intimate little moments of our walk, experiencing a warm rush I hadn't known in a long time. Once home, I checked the windows and doors. In the past, I hardly ever locked the deadbolts, but seeing those tires roll by my head had given me a whole new perspective on home security. Just as I finished battening down my hatches, the phone rang.

"Joel? It's Calvin. I'm glad I caught you. I apologize for calling so late, but—"

"Cal, I'm not sure you should be calling at all!"

"It's very important," Nichol said in a hushed tone.

"Cal . . ."

"I have information regarding Stanley's murder."

I didn't respond.

"You don't honestly think I killed Stanley?" Nichol implored.

I let another cold moment pass. "Why did you run from the crime scene?" I asked.

"I was set up!" His voice cracked.

"C'mon, Cal," I snapped. "You sound like every forensic patient I've ever met."

"Stanley—or whoever killed him—paged me. I've still got the text message. I can show it to you." I heard him groping around for his pager. "It says: 'Meet me at the office. Urgent. Stanley.'"

"I can page myself and show you the same message," I sighed. "It doesn't prove anything."

"This whole situation is a mess. As you've discovered"— I heard him gulp—"I'm not entirely blameless."

"Your point?"

"I did not kill Stanley," he said softly.

"What about the fights Bonnie overheard?" I said dubiously.

"I told you. His violent patients had started—"

"Bullshit!"

"All right, Joel. Stanley got me mixed up in a difficult situation. My fault, I accept that. But he wanted me to be part of something I couldn't do." He paused. "His involvement explains why he was murdered."

My heart sped up. "Tell me."

"It's complicated," Nichol said. "And messy. It will take some explaining. Can we meet someplace in about half an hour? I have something to show you."

"Where?"

"How about the office?" Nichol asked.

"Okay." The destination seemed strangely appropriate. "Give me an hour."

"Just you and me." His voice was ragged. "No one else, okay?"

"I thought your information was for the police."

"You should hear it first. Alone. You'll understand."

"Right. Last time you showed up to 'warn' me, the very next day I almost got run over!"

"One hour," Nichol said. "It will all make sense."

As I headed to the meeting in my rejuvenated car—which drove no better now than before I dumped the two grand into it—I fretted over how angry Claire and Dev would be when they learned I'd left them out of the loop again. I was tempted to call and run it by them, but something in Nichol's message prevented me.

I pulled into the office building's underground garage, which looked as insecure as ever, and parked between Nichol's wine-colored BMW and an old motorcycle in the otherwise empty lot.

The remnant of yellow crime-scene tape still stuck to the door casing of the third-floor office. I stuck my key in the deadbolt, but from how easily it turned, I knew it wasn't locked. I pushed the door open and stepped into the lit waiting room. A few areas in the room were taped off; I wondered if the bunny men had noticed traces of DNA lying around, but I couldn't see much. I walked around the corner and down the hallway to Stanley's office. Curiosity got the better of me, and I poked my head inside. Sure enough, chalk dashes outlined the spot where Stanley had fallen.

Even in chalk, the awkward position of his body looked bizarre, as if a cartoonist had gotten the anatomy wrong. But the chalk was right; Stanley's anatomy had ended up wrong.

I walked five yards farther to Nichol's corner office. "Cal?" I knocked on the door. Nothing. I tried again, but got no response. Reaching for the door's handle and turning, I knew something was very wrong.

Nichol lay in the middle of the room face up with his head flopped back and eyes shut. Blood dripped from the corner of his gaping mouth. His arms sprawled on either side. His hips and long legs, bent at the knees, were rotated toward the door. I didn't need Mitch Greene's help to know that Nichol had been stabbed in the chest and abdomen. I saw the slash marks on his green shirt, which had turned mostly brown from blood.

"Cal?" I asked, moving to him. About two feet away, my foot sank in the bloody carpet and made a sloshing noise like I'd stepped in a shallow mud puddle. I stared at the motionless Nichol, convinced he was dead.

Kneeling closer, I caught a slight hissing sound. I wasn't sure if the noise came from his lips or the holes in his chest, until I noticed the blood bubbling in his mouth and saw his neck muscles contract in a respiratory effort. I reached with two fingers to search for a neck pulse. As soon as I touched his cool skin, my fingers turned sticky as if dipped in glue. I slid them up and down the side of his neck, before finding a faint, rapid beat.

I was so focused on locating the pulse that it took a while for me to notice that his eyes had opened and were looking in my direction. "Cal!" I said.

His eyelids fluttered and more bubbles formed in the blood between his lips, but I couldn't hear anything. I leaned closer and listened again, picking up only a few raspy breaths and grunts that sounded about as clear as words spoken under water.

I grabbed his frigid left hand in mine. "Squeeze my hand, Cal!" After a moment, I felt a flicker—like a leaf falling in my palm—and I knew that he was still conscious. "I'm going to get help."

I groped in my pocket for my cell phone. When I held it up to dial, I saw the NO RECEPTION message on the phone's screen and cursed myself for not having a carrier with better cell coverage. I rose to my knees and scanned Nichol's desk but couldn't see his phone. I spun, sliding on the slick carpet, and ran out down the hallway and into the receptionist's area. I raced over and grabbed for the desk phone. Using my blood-encrusted right index finger, I fumbled for the digits on the keypad.

I had just punched in the "nine" and the first "one" when the receiver flew out of my hand and my head was yanked violently to the right. I felt pain in my mouth and tasted the rough leather of a glove.

"You should've left well enough alone, Dr. Ashman," a man's voice whispered.

The warm breath hit my ear at the same moment as a knife dug into my throat below my Adam's apple.

"Time to join your partners." Another whisper.

Certain I was about to die, I was surprised by my sudden serene calm. I heard a loud *whoosh* that, for a moment, I assumed was the sound of my throat being ripped open but then realized came from the main door of the office suite bursting open. Without premeditation, and surprising even myself, I took advantage of the distraction and slammed my right elbow into my attacker's midsection. He gasped. I felt a sudden sting at my neck as I twisted violently to free myself from his arm. I whipped my head and upper body around to face the masked assailant.

He had stumbled back a few steps where he stood hunched over and grasping the belly of his dark sweatshirt. But before I could strike back, he straightened up. "Bad move, doctor . . ." He coughed through his black ski mask. He waved the massive blade at me.

I backpedaled three steps and bumped up against the wall. As he moved toward me, I raised my arms to protect my head and face. I felt searing pain as the knife slashed across my right arm. I dropped my hands long enough to see a glint in his eyes. He raised the knife again, and I flexed my arms back to my face, blocking my vision and bracing for another blow.

Before it came, a voice shouted, "What you do?!" in a thick accent.

I dropped my arms to see my attacker spin and lunge for the janitor standing behind him. But the stout little man reacted with surprising speed. He darted to the left and avoided the knife's arc. He recovered his footing and bravely faced the man. In his hand, the janitor held the sponge end of his heavy metal mop, wielding it like a lance.

"What you do?!" the janitor screamed again. "You stop!"

The masked man hesitated. For a few long moments, everyone was still. Then the attacker glanced over his shoulder at me. Just as I expected to see his blade come for me, he spun and ran for the doorway where the janitor stood. The janitor dove out of the way as the knifeman bolted past him, turned the corner, and headed for the door. He bounced off the cleaning cart blocking the doorway. Yelping in pain, he squeezed by the cart and out the door.

Stunned and bleeding from my arm, I stood and watched the janitor climb to his feet.

"You call police!" he screamed, startling me into action.

I grabbed the dangling receiver, and punched in 911. A calm female voice answered on the other end of the line.

"Someone's been stabbed. Send an ambulance!"

After confirming the address, she said, "I'm dispatching the emergency response now. Please hold." Within seconds, she was back on the line. "Is the assailant still there?"

"No . . . I don't think so."

"Is anyone else injured?" she asked.

"I've got a cut, but I'm okay."

"Is the victim breathing?"

"He was a few minutes ago." I realized no one had checked on Nichol. "Call Sergeant Devonshire, Homicide.

He'll understand. I'm going to check on the victim." I hung up and turned to the janitor.

"Thank you," I said, feeling light-headed as I wobbled toward him. "You saved my life."

The janitor backed up, shaking his head for me to come no closer as he frantically pointed to my right arm. I looked down and I understood. Blood was pumping from my wrist like a sprinkler, splattering the walls and floor. Just as I grabbed for the arterial gusher with my other hand, my legs abruptly abandoned me.

10

A STRANGE METALLIC TASTE filled my mouth. My throat stung. I remembered being wheeled out of the brightly lit operating room. Surgery. I would have had an endotracheal tube stuck down my windpipe during the operation; thus the sore throat. The wheels in my head weren't turning quickly but, I realized with considerable relief, at least they were turning.

I raised my head off the pillow and looked at the sling enveloping my right arm that, strangely, didn't hurt. As I laid my head back, I caught movement out of the corner of my eye. I turned my head to see Claire and Dev sitting in the bedside chairs. It might have been the sedative lingering in my system, but Claire looked particularly gorgeous with her hair tied back, even though she wore the same green sweater from our previous evening's walk.

She stood up and took hold of my hand in hers. "Hey." She smiled at me. "How are you feeling?"

"Kind of stoned." My words came out all slurred. "How's Cal?"

"Still dead," Dev snapped from where he sat with arms folded across his chest. The color of his crumpled black polo shirt matched the deep bags under his eyes. And, apparently, his mood. "Remember?"

But I didn't. The anesthetic had wiped out the memory of everything since my collapse on the office's floor. "He didn't make it?" I asked through parched lips.

"No." Dev sighed. "And if it weren't for one heroic little Portuguese janitor, you'd be down in the cold room with him."

"José." I tried to rise in my bed but the IV tubing clotheslined me back to the mattress. I readjusted the tubing and sat up. "Is he all right?"

"Yeah. But between his wife finding Kolberg's body and him stumbling onto what looked like the set of a slasher film, I think they'll be looking for a new building to clean. One with a little less blood and a lot fewer shrinks." In spite of his wisecracks, there wasn't much levity in Dev's expression. "Why the hell did you go there without us?"

"Cal insisted." I shrugged my sling. "I didn't think he'd stick around unless I showed up alone."

Dev glared at me. "You think we're not capable of keeping a low profile?"

"I didn't think it through." I sighed.

"It never crossed your mind that he might be setting you up?" Dev grunted.

It hadn't. "If that was a setup, then he took one big hit for his team," I said.

"So?" Dev said. "His partner double-crossed him."

"Someone might've followed Nichol," Claire said. "We don't know that it was a setup."

"Either way, there's someone out there looking to make you an organ donor." Dev jabbed a finger in my direction. "After you get released, you're not staying in your own home. Understand?"

The drugs in my system had made me unusually agreeable. I just nodded.

Claire squeezed my hand. "You're sure you didn't recognize the guy, Joel?"

"Not through his mask. He was average height and wore a bulky sweatshirt, so I'm not even sure of his build." I stopped to clear my aching throat. "I was more focused on the meat cleaver in his hand."

"Which hand was the knife in?" Claire asked.

"Right . . . I think. Yeah, right."

"Perfect," Dev groaned. "We've narrowed it down to right-handed people. Possibly."

Claire reached for the pitcher of ice water on the table at the end of the bed and passed a cup of it to me. "What about his voice?"

I drank a big gulp of the water and promptly choked on it. After I stopped coughing, I shook my head and croaked, "He only spoke in a whisper."

"What did he say?"

"Something like 'You should've left well enough alone.' "

"What the hell does that mean?" Dev asked.

"Don't know." I took a smaller sip of water, which I managed to keep out of my lungs. "No leads at the scene?"

Dev rolled his eyes.

"No witnesses except the janitor. The bunny men weren't much help, either." Claire frowned. "No forced entry and the outer doors were all locked. Either Nichol let the guy in or he already had a key. Same as Kolberg's murder."

"How did you get in?" Dev asked.

I took another sip. "I never turned in my old office key."

"Hmmm," Dev grumbled, and then checked his watch. "Captain must be waiting." He pointed at me. "Joel, I don't want you going anywhere alone, is that understood?"

I nodded.

"Dev, I'll catch up in a minute," Claire said.

He looked from her to me but didn't comment. I appreciated him for that. After the door closed, I said, "I don't even know what kind of surgery I had."

"The surgeon told me the knife cut a big vessel, the ulnar artery," Claire said uncertainly. "You lost a lot of blood and took plenty of stitches, but you'll be fine."

I pointed at Claire's sweater. "You stayed the night, huh?"

She flushed slightly. "By the time we got done at the crime scene . . . it was just easier than coming and going."

I reached for her hand again. Our fingers intertwined. "I was so sure I was going to die in that office."

She squeezed tighter. "Terrifying, huh?"

I shook my head. "That's the weird part. I wasn't scared." I paused. "But I didn't feel ready to go either."

Claire cocked her head. "And that surprises you?"

"My life hasn't exactly gone according to plan lately." I adjusted my arm in the sling. "I kind of thought that with Lor gone, when my time came . . ."

Claire squeezed my hand.

"But for the first time in ages, I am ready to get on with life again." Embarrassed, I looked away. "Listen to this crap. It's the drugs. They're making me channel some kind of self-help guru."

Claire gently turned my head back to her and planted a long kiss on my lips. "I'm a sucker for helpless guys."

I felt a drug-enhanced glow. "Especially if they're reserved and helpless." I laughed.

From outside the room came Dev's gravelly voice. "Claire, you want me to tell the captain you didn't have time for him today?"

After she left, I dozed off. I awoke to find a nurse standing at my bedside and adjusting my dressing. She told me I would be staying in the hospital for the next two days. I told her she would have an empty room within half an hour. After signing the "discharged against medical advice" form, I went straight home, but I kept the cab waiting out front, changed, and headed for Harborview Hospital.

I walked through the hospital, still feeling some post-operation wooziness, and down the stairs toward the morgue. I found Dev and Claire in the morgue's intake room. Before they had a chance to lay into me, Mitch Greene burst into the room in full autopsy getup. "Another day, another dead psychiatrist," he roared. He pointed at my arm. "Almost a two-for-one special! Jesus H., Ash-Man, you all right?"

"Yeah. Fine."

Greene shook his big head. "I think you boys are giving the plastic surgeons a run for their money in terms of pissing patients off." He turned to Claire with a big grin. "Ah, the lovely Detective Shepherd. Still stuck with Mutt and Jeff, I see." He thumbed at Dev and me.

"You want to do this today?" Dev asked with a slight grin.

"What's the big hurry?" Greene said. "Apart from mosquitoes, I thought the one thing you people from Arkansas had plenty of was time."

"Arkansas." Dev rolled his eyes. "You need an atlas, Mitch."

"Arkansas, Alabama, Arizona . . . what's the difference? They're all too hot and crawling with people who talk funny." Mitch whirled around with such commotion that I expected to feel a breeze blow off him. "C'mon. I got plenty to show you."

We followed Greene into the dissecting suites. After Claire helped tie my yellow gown over my sling, the four of us formed a circle around the center gurney on which Nichol's naked cadaver lay. His face fixed in an expression as impassive as in life, Nichol's glassy eyes stared at the ceiling. His chest and abdomen were splayed wide open, leaving just a fleshy shell from where the organs had been harvested.

Greene grabbed a large scalpel off the tray beside the body. He flicked it up and down, indicating Nichol's body. "Notice the lack of mutilation." He tapped his chest with the palm of his other hand. "Excluding, of course, the handiwork of yours truly. I guess Nichol wasn't quite as kinky as Kolberg."

"Don't bet on that, Mitch," Claire said.

Greene shook his head. "Figures. Shrinks . . ." He looked over his shoulder, and bellowed at the morgue assistant in the corner. "Helen! Bring me the heart."

While waiting for Helen to accommodate his macabre request, Greene pointed out various features of Nichol's hollowed-out corpse. I noticed that Dev struggled to keep the sway out of his legs, but Claire held firm.

"Check out Nichol's arms." Greene lifted the right arm up by the wrist, holding it as if dangling a rope. Twisting it back and forth, he showed us both sides. "Not so much as a scrape."

Claire nodded. "No defensive wounds."

"Exactly!" Greene lowered the arm back to the gurney. "He was stabbed three times in the chest and upper abdomen. I'd expect to see more of what Ash-Man has on his arms."

"So he never saw the knife coming," Dev said.

"Not only that, he allowed his assailant to get very close without even raising his arms," Greene said. "Unless he was too damn lazy to commit hari-kari himself, he definitely wasn't expecting our boy to knife him."

Head down and eyes glued to the floor as usual, Helen approached and held out a kidney-shaped basin for Greene. He reached a gloved paw inside and pulled out the shiny muscled-red heart. He turned it over and held it upright facing us. "This is how the heart sits in the chest, with the right ventricle facing out and the left ventricle—the main pump—tucked behind." He used the scalpel in his other hand to point to a ragged gash near the base of the muscle. "See this? Bull's-eye. Dead center of the ventricle." He moved the blade up to the top of the heart, where a smaller cut lay. "This one just nicked the atrium. Might not have done the job. But the other slash went right through the spleen, and that probably would've finished him off, too. All in all, three pretty deadly swings."

"So even if the paramedics had been called sooner . . . ," I said.

Greene pointed the scalpel at me. "Don't sweat it, Ash-Man. If Nichol was already in the OR when our boy stabbed him like that . . ." He slashed through the air three times with his scalpel. "He'd still be down here with me today."

Greene dropped the heart back into the basin. "Any moron can kill with a gun. Just hit your target and the bullet's bound to ricochet around until it tears through something vital. But a knife?" He crossed his big arms and shook his head. "You've got to know what you're doing, or be just plain lucky. Now granted, our boy was using a one-and-a-half-inch wide, twelve-inch long, serrated blade—the bazooka of hunting knives—but still . . ."

"Is that a common weapon?" I asked.

"As common as herpes at a frat house," Greene chortled.

"Still." Claire thumbed at Nichol's corpse. "Quite a difference from the way Kolberg was killed."

"Yup." Greene nodded. "Nichol was taken down with the precision of a surgeon, but Kolberg was batted around like a piñata that just wouldn't crack."

Claire tilted her head. "Should we be looking for two different perps?"

"Your job, not mine." Greene tore off his gloves and tossed them into the garbage. "But I'll tell you this. If it was the same guy, he must've been drinking decaf yesterday."

After parting ways with Greene, we congregated in the parking lot by Claire's car. "Why did you leave the hospital?" Dev asked.

"It's just a cut," I said.

Dev shook his head and sighed. "Let's stop by your place and pick up your suitcase. You're going to crash with Elaine, me, and the boys for a while. I hope you like noise."

About a year earlier, Elaine and Dev had had me over for dinner. It was my first time meeting their five sons, whose ages ranged from eight to fifteen. Sweet kids. And Dev was great with them. But their small house struck me as overpopulated. "You can have the twins' room," Dev said, referring to the two youngest. "We'll stick them in with Rick. Course only one of them will come out alive, but that's fine. More room in the van."

"You could stay at my place," Claire offered. Then she hurried to add, "I've got a fully furnished extra bedroom I keep for when my parents, or one of my sisters, come to town."

Dev looked from Claire to me, struggling to keep the grin off his face.

"You sure?" I asked.

"Just don't expect food with the lodgings." She grinned. "The only time I go into my kitchen is to get the Chinese leftovers out of the fridge."

"Settled," Dev said. "Doc, we'll need you to stick with us today. If we come across our guy, maybe you'll recognize him from his movement or voice or whatever. Okay?"

I nodded.

Claire pulled out of the parking lot then turned to Dev. "What does your gut tell you?" she asked. "Are we looking at two different killers?"

Dev studied the traffic outside his window before answering. "On the face of it, the MOs are different. Gun versus knife. Execution versus mutilation. And so on. But think about it. Two psychiatrists, each sharing a kinky hush-hush sex life, killed in the same office by someone with access to the building. And neither of 'em saw it coming. That has to be the key! Kolberg and Nichol both trusted the killer." He shook his head slowly. "It's the same guy."

"I agree. Nichol always felt wrong for Kolberg's murder," Claire said pensively. She glanced over her shoulder. "How about you, Joel?"

"Don't know about the killer," I said. "But the motives were different."

"Why?"

"Nichol's murder was a cold, calculated affair. The polar opposite of the slaughterhouse Stanley's office became."

"So?" Dev said.

"What happened to Kolberg was an angry, hateful payback. But Nichol's death was all business. It served some kind of purpose."

"To shut him up, maybe," Claire said.

"That makes sense," Dev said.

"None of this makes sense," I said, thinking of all the blood spilled in my former office over the past weeks. However, when it came to senselessness, my ex-partners' deaths couldn't hold a candle to Angela's.

* * *

Six months earlier, in the sleepless hours following my heated 3 A.M. exchange with Angela, the shock faded and was replaced by doubt.

At first, I balked at the idea that Stanley could be involved in the kind of bizarre sexual abuse Angela had charged. But the more I mulled it over, the more the pieces began to fit: the timing of Angela's first breakdown, her distrust of psychiatrists, and even Stanley's injuries from unwitnessed "seizures." But what bothered me most was her comment about Stanley's impotence. How could she have known?

A familiar sense of betrayal mushroomed inside me. Was the man who had been like a second father to me capable of hiding such a secret? Then again, why not? My birth father had done pretty much the same.

What had begun in me as loneliness during the months following Suzie Malloy's suicide, festered into something worse—pervasive guilt for not having seen it coming or doing more to stop her. Then, in the midst of this period of self-recrimination, Dad moved out. There were whispers among the neighbors about other women. But there were always those rumors; most were true. Even as a teen I was aware of my father's womanizing. I'd overheard my parents fight over the issue. I remember my mother saying, "David, I know you're sleeping with half the grad students on campus, but can you please try not to flaunt it at the faculty parties?" Dad hadn't even bothered to plead innocence.

Since that was the extent of Mom's indignation, I couldn't understand why an affair would force Dad out of the house. And not only did he leave home, he left the state, taking a job teaching at a college outside San Francisco.

It was never the same between Dad and me after that. From the ages of twelve to fifteen, I only saw him sporadically. I spent the first July after the separation with him in Sausalito. I was supposed to go back the following summer, but his book tour disrupted our plans. And by the summer after, there was too much concern about Mom to leave her alone for that long.

Mom had become more than just an "absentminded pro-

fessor." Her academic output dried up, and her students—
who used to love her classes—complained that her lectures
were jumbled and sometimes nonsensical. One day, her department head called and asked Mom to take a leave of absence "until things got sorted out." We moved into
Grandma's house, purportedly so Mom could help look after
her own mother. In fact, the opposite was true; unbeknownst
to Mom, at forty-five she had already been diagnosed with
early-onset Alzheimer's.

One day during the move, I was boxing up mounds of paper that Mom, a packrat, had stockpiled. I was emptying out
her nightstand, when several envelopes fell out on the floor.
Picking them up, the handwriting on one caught my eye. I
unfolded the letter inside.

Dear Mrs. Ashman,
    I can't tell you how sorry I am for the troubles I've
caused. You have been nothing but kind. And in return,
I tried to steal your husband and break up your
wonderful family. You had every right to kick me out
today.
    You have to know that I didn't want to fall in love
with David. I couldn't help myself. For what it's worth,
he never loved me. Only you. I think I was kind of like
his midlife crisis.
    Please don't tell Joel anything about us. Not for my
sake, but for his. His dad is so important to him and I
can't stand the thought of wrecking that. He doesn't
deserve to have his life screwed up by my selfishness.
    I am so very, very, very sorry . . .
    Yours, Suzanne Malloy

It was so obvious! Dad was Suzie's special "teacher" all
along. But until I read the letter, the realization had never
crossed my mind. She wasn't a twenty-something grad student, a grown woman like his others. She was just a fifteen-
year-old kid; the same age I was when I read the letter.
I knew about sexual abuse, too. My high school had been

rocked earlier that year by the scandal of a counselor who knocked up a ninth-grade student. The counselor was facing criminal charges for sexual abuse of a minor. My father should have faced the same, I thought. No, worse—he should be up for murder charges. He broke Suzie's heart. He shamed her. And he sent her off the top of that building as sure as if he'd picked her up and tossed her off.

After reading the letter, I cut off all contact with Dad. He soon stopped trying to contact me. He must have known that I had uncovered his ugly secret. My guess is he'd always known I would, and that was why things had changed between us. Or maybe the guilt of knowing he was responsible for her suicide had gotten to him. I doubt it, though. In my experience, guilt is not a big issue for sexual predators.

Angela's drunken middle-of-the-night intrusion brought all those lousy teen memories to life. Soon, her words began to feel just as damning as the ones Suzie had written years before.

I called Angela several times the following day, but she never answered. I left two messages at her brother's place, but it wasn't until the next morning that he phoned back. "Angela's gone," were the first two words out of Tommy's mouth.

"Since when?"

"Yesterday afternoon."

"Hold on," I said. "So she did come home yesterday morning?"

"At about four A.M.," he said. My relief at hearing that she'd returned home after our run-in was short-lived. "She slept a few hours. When she got up, she made a phone call and then left around noon. I haven't heard from her since."

"She disappears for days sometimes, doesn't she?"

"Not like this," Tommy said. "She didn't take any of her stuff."

"Have you checked with anyone else?"

"I called her friends. Even her ex-boyfriend. No one has seen her."

"Did you check her room?"

"Of course," Tommy snapped. "She's not there."

I hesitated. "I mean, did she leave anything behind?"

"Like what?" I could tell from his tone that he knew where I was heading.

"A note."

"No. Nothing like that." Then he said quietly, "The last time—when she took those pills—she didn't leave a note either."

"I'll make some phone calls. Hospitals and so on." I couldn't bring myself to be more specific, though he probably knew I meant the morgue. Then, with as much credibility as I could muster, I added, "I'm sure she'll turn up soon."

She did.

The next morning I was shaving over the sink while listening to the 7 A.M. newscast. At the end of the headline news items, the anchor told of "an unidentified woman in her twenties" who'd washed up on a rocky beach at Gasworks Park after a presumed jump off the Aurora Bridge. As soon as I heard the anchor's words, I nicked my chin with the razor. I knew.

I found the phone and called Mitch Greene. "Mitch, I think I might know your jumper. . . ."

Half an hour later, Greene met me in the changing rooms outside the morgue's dissecting room. He threw a big arm around my neck by way of a greeting. "You okay?"

"Yeah." I shrugged. "Thanks, Mitch."

He grabbed two yellow gowns hanging from the wall and handed one to me. As we changed, Greene said: "The preliminary blood work came back on the girl."

"And?" I asked, slipping my arm into a nylon sleeve.

"Alcohol level was forty-six millimoles per liter. That's a good half-bottle of tequila right there. And she had high levels of benzodiazepines in her system, too."

"I once wrote Angela a prescription for a few oxazepams to help with sleep."

"With those blood levels, she must've taken five or six pills at once. Besides, it was Valium we found in her blood." As we stepped into the dissecting room, Greene sighed. "Then again, the drugs were the least of her problems."

It must have been a slow night in Seattle. There was only one cadaver lying covered on the center gurney. Two lab techs circled the gurney, preparing trays, buckets, and weigh scales. As we moved closer, I prayed I'd gotten it wrong.

But as soon as Greene reached down and peeled the sheet off her, the last shred of my hope was dashed. Not that I recognized her immediately. The right side of her face had been smashed, almost beyond recognition. Large cuts and abrasions covered most of her face, and the grayish-white skin had started to slough off. But her eyelids were open. Those piercing blue eyes staring lifelessly back at me were unmistakable.

Greene looked over his shoulder at me. "Your patient?"

I nodded.

He peeled off the rest of the sheet. And for the second time in three days, I saw the Aztec sun tattooed around her belly button. The damage to her body matched her face, with far more bruising on the right side, though both sides were covered in scratches, welts, and multiple small cuts that I couldn't identify.

Greene stood back a couple of feet from the gurney with his arms crossed and resting on his belly. After a while, he said, "She hit the water right side down. Good thing, too."

"Why's that?"

"The way she landed—on her head and chest like that—would've killed her on impact, or very soon after. At the very least, she would've been knocked out. Some poor bastards land feet first and then last long enough to drown." He tilted his head from side to side. "Tough to be certain, but she probably had at least a day of submersion."

An unwelcome mental image of Angela bobbing in the cold, choppy water came to mind.

"The water at this time of year isn't a bad preservative. Good salt content, nice and cold." Greene pointed to the area on her face where the skin was starting to peel. "That skin sloughing means decomposition has started. At salt-water temperatures of fifty to sixty degrees, we're looking at

a minimum of a couple of days before you'd see that. So she must've had a couple hours on shore to ripen before being found at . . ." He turned to his assistant. *"Helen, what time did they find her?"*

"Six this morning," she replied.

"Okay." Greene nodded. *"Now we're getting somewhere. In the water twenty-four hours . . . she washes up two to three hours before being found . . ."* He mumbled the calculations aloud. *"It's a damn busy bridge. Unless she jumped in the wee hours, someone would've spotted her for sure. So we're looking at yesterday morning, somewhere around three or four. Which makes sense; Sunday morning's the quietest time for the Aurora Bridge."*

"How do you know she didn't jump this morning, and wash ashore right away?"

"Your girl was in the water for at least twelve hours."

"You said the water was a good preservative. So how would you know?"

"Cold salt water's a good preservative, but sea life isn't." Greene pointed to the little cuts and divots on her body. *"The fishies were nibbling."*

"Christ!" I muttered under my breath, as my legs buckled and my body swayed.

When I began to crumple, Greene caught me by the armpits just as I was about to hit the floor. With the help of an assistant, he dragged me to the chair in the corner of the room.

As I hunched over with my head between my legs, Greene knelt in front of me checking my pulse. *"So this is what one of these feels like,"* he joked. *"Pretty strong and regular. I don't think you'll need one of my gurneys for a while."*

The lightheadedness cleared. *"Go back to work, Mitch. I'll be fine."*

Greene remained in his crouch, frowning, with his big gray eyes still showing concern. *"You sure?"*

"Absolutely." But I wasn't as convinced as I made out.

I called my office and cancelled my week's schedule. I

needed breathing space to figure out what went wrong. Throughout my whole career I had dreaded facing my first patient-suicide, but I never expected it to hurt like this.

I kept picturing it in my mind. The chilly morning breeze. Angela resting her feet on the bridge's railing. The lights illuminating a glimpse or two of black water. I wondered if, in that moment before she let go of her grip and stepped one foot toward the dark abyss, she felt fear, regret, relief, or maybe nothing at all? Did she think of her father, or Stanley, or—worst of all—me?

It was Suzie's death all over again. But this time, the guilt was better founded. I was trained to recognize the signs. I should have stopped Angela. And this time, the man responsible was still a part of my life.

Her funeral was held four days later. Without referring to any notes, Tommy spoke Angela's eulogy in a quiet steady voice, maintaining his composure throughout. The same couldn't be said of the attendees in the small but crowded church.

Tommy caught up with me in the church's vestibule. His resemblance to Angela was so strong—even their postures were alike—that his presence brought a fresh wave of melancholy.

"Thank you, Dr. Ashman." He held out his hand.

"For what?"

"You tried."

I dropped my head. "I wonder."

"What else could you have done?"

"She came over Saturday morning, a day before . . ." I said quietly. "She was a mess. I should have never let her go."

Tommy's eyes narrowed in sudden suspicion. "What was she doing at your place?"

"She just showed up at two A.M. Drunk and upset."

He eyed me with the same penetrating stare his sister used to level. "What was she upset about?"

"A lot of things." I hesitated, but only for a moment. "Especially Stanley Kolberg."

"Why Kolberg?"

"She claimed he'd sexually abused her."

Tommy's face blanched. "Everything went wrong after she started to see that son of a bitch," he growled. "So what happened at your place?"

I looked away. "I told her I didn't believe her. That's why she left."

His lip curled into a venomous sneer. "You thought she was lying about Kolberg?"

"No . . . I don't know," I said. "You've got to understand, he's been a close friend for a long time. I didn't want to believe her."

"Fucking shrinks!" He spun on his heels, and walked back into the church's nave.

"I believe her now," I said, but Tommy was already gone.

After the funeral, I took an indefinite leave from my office, with the hope of putting Angela's death out of mind. Instead, I thought of little else.

Two weeks after she was buried, I was in the family room trying to lose myself in one of those lawyer-against-the-world novels, when the doorbell rang. I would have ignored it, except Nelson wouldn't stop barking.

Stanley, wearing a suit and tie, stood on the other side. "Hi, Joel," he said, offering his most empathetic smile.

I said nothing.

"Caught you at a bad time?" he asked.

I merely shrugged.

"May I come in?"

He followed me into the family room and sat on the same couch where Angela had lain a few weeks earlier. He appraised me with a shake of his head. "You look like shit."

"I haven't shaved." But he was right. Stained T-shirt, uncombed hair, scruffy beard grown out of neglect. I'd lost five pounds that I didn't really have to lose.

Stanley was unfazed by my iciness. "She was your first, huh?"

"First what?"

"Suicide in your practice."

"Yes."

"I'm very sorry, Joel." He nodded. "It's brutal. Especially in light of your childhood experience. Suzie, was it?"

Stanley never forgot a detail. But I wasn't about to discuss the parallels between Suzie and Angela with him of all people. So I kept silent.

He smiled again, his face offering all the sympathy in the world. "I've got some bad news for you. There are going to be others."

"You figure?"

He nodded. "And the worst part? It doesn't get any easier."

"I'd think it would be worse if it did get easier."

"It's the nature of the beast. Look at our patients. We're the bomb squad for the human mind. Regardless of how careful you are, a few are still going to blow up in your face."

"That's a strange analogy."

"Some of our patients are time bombs."

"Like Angela?" I asked, staring at him directly.

He met my gaze. "Exactly."

"She didn't blow up in your face, though, did she?"

Stanley stiffened. "You've lost me, Joel."

"She didn't kill herself while under your care."

His shoulders relaxed. He smiled sadly. "Coincidence, Joel. She very easily could have. As I think I already told you, in the end I didn't help her at all."

"Neither did I."

"We tried, though, didn't we?"

I stepped away from the kitchen counter. "What exactly did you try, Stanley?"

He eyed me, warily. "The Ps—psychotherapy, psychoanalysis, pharmaceuticals."

"You might've missed an S and an M."

"What?" he frowned.

"Sadomasochism. Whipping and beating. Was that what you meant by 'trying'?"

" 'Beating'?" Stanley shook his head in apparent bewilderment.

"Pain, Stanley. The ultimate pleasure." I stabbed a finger at him. "Angela told me about your little kink."

"Oh, we're going to have this conversation, again." Stanley sighed. "I don't know how else to convince you. I'm impotent."

"Impotent or nonsexual? There's a difference."

"Not to me." Stanley chuckled in a show of patient understanding. "Why do you insist on taking Angela's word over mine?"

"I saw it, Stanley."

"Oh, of course. In her eyes, right?" he asked with a hint of mockery.

"On her fucking back!" I snapped.

"What?"

"I saw the scar." I walked a couple of feet closer to him. "Where you burned her with a flame as part of . . ." I threw my hands up. "God only knows."

Stanley nodded forgivingly. "Joel, I know how upset you are—"

"You want to beat and be beaten? Fine. With another screwed-up consenting adult, it's your business." I shook my finger at him again. "But you were her psychiatrist. Her counselor. Her doctor, for Christ's sake! And not only did you sexually exploit her, you blackmailed and threatened her." With each accusation, I took a step closer. "You crossed the line so far you couldn't even see it behind you."

Stanley sat motionless. "I appreciate your mourning and your guilt, but it's affecting your judgment. Otherwise, you wouldn't throw away ten years of friendship like this."

"No, Stanley!" I shook my head wildly. "Problem is that I let ten years of friendship stand in the way of the truth. And as a fucking result, Angela is dead."

Stanley reached out to touch me on my wrist, but I yanked my arm away.

I hovered above him for a few seconds. Neither of us spoke. Finally, Stanley said, "So you alone stand as judge and jury. My word doesn't mean anything. And yet you don't have a speck of proof."

"I was at the autopsy," I said. "I saw where the water smashed her face like a brick, and the spots where the fishes started to eat her."

"What does that prove?" he asked quietly.

"How could you have done that to her, Stanley? Your own patient!"

"How can I justify what I didn't do?" Stanley eyed me so sincerely that a week earlier I might've flinched. "Angela must have fixated on me as the root of her problems. I don't know why else she would've concocted a story as strange as this."

"No way! My eyes are scratched from having the wool pulled over them so often. Not this time."

"But Angela Connor—borderline personality and compulsive liar—speaks God's truth, huh?"

"She wasn't lying about you."

He jumped to his feet so quickly that I was caught off guard. "That silly little bitch lied about everything," he cried, his face less than a foot from mine.

"That's some respect for a patient."

"What respect does she deserve?!" he sneered. "Her whole fucking life, she was a suicide looking for a bridge. To pass the time, the little whore got off on ruining others' lives—her father, her brother, her boyfriends, on and on. Now, even in death, she's after mine."

I clenched my fists. "You sent her off that bridge. And now you're blaming her for it. What kind of twisted bastard are you?"

Rage danced in his eyes. "I'm not responsible for her death. Which is a hell of a lot more than I can say for you."

"What does that mean?" I shouted.

"Open your fucking eyes! She shows up at your home in the middle of the night, desperate for help. You're the very last person she feels she can turn to. But do you console her? Do you validate her? No, you kick her out into the cold night." He grunted a malicious laugh. "That's a death sentence."

I hadn't punched anyone since third grade, but I cocked

my right arm back and punched Stanley so hard in the face that my hand ached on contact.

Stanley staggered a step back and grabbed for his face, covering it with the palm of his hand. Blood gushed between his fingers. He made a grunting, chortling noise. At first, I thought he might be choking, but then I realized he was laughing. "What a disappointment you've turned out to be," he sputtered through his bloody hand. "First, you forfeit any chance of happiness after your wife dies. Now, you throw your career away over some pathetic, inadequate soul."

"Get out of my house," I said quietly.

11

AFTER LEAVING NICHOL'S AUTOPSY, it took me a while to shake the mental image of his gutted remains. As the remnants of the anesthetic cleared, the realization sunk in that I could have been lying on the gurney beside Nichol—my organs carefully weighed and packaged in little baggies.

"What do you think?" Dev asked from the backseat of Claire's car, having deferred the passenger seat to me in view of my injury.

"Sorry, Dev," I said, "I wasn't listening."

"Like I don't get enough of that at home." Dev sighed. "What I asked was, could you picture the Shoveler, Hacking, or McCabe behind the ski mask?"

"They're all the right height," I said. "It would help if I could see each of them holding a knife."

"Oh, sure!" Claire snorted.

"But it would help."

Dev tapped the back of my headrest. "The defense lawyers are gonna love this idea."

I lifted my right arm, but the sudden jolt of pain served to remind me not to point with that hand. "Think about it. The guy has tried to kill me at least once, right?"

"So?"

"He must think I know more than I do," I pointed out. "We could use that."

"You want us to dangle you as bait?" Dev asked.

"I don't know about *want,* but it might draw him out."

I caught the profile of Claire's concerned frown and then looked over my shoulder at Dev. Eyes narrowed and forehead creased, he appeared to be considering the idea. "How would our boy know where to find you?" he asked.

"I could just go home."

"Then what?" Dev held up his palms. "He might never come. Or he might wait a month or two until things cool down."

"What if I provoked him?" I said.

Dev grimaced. "Provoked who?"

"Everyone we've come across so far. I could phone each of them and tell them I know something. Ask for a meeting."

"Doc, are you at all familiar with the term 'entrapment'?" He whistled. "I don't think so."

"Me neither," Claire said without taking her eyes off the road. "Nichol's body is barely cool. We don't need desperate measures yet."

Claire headed past the turnoff to SPD headquarters and continued on to Pioneer Square. She drove along the cobbled streets of the touristy district (the site of Seattle's origins in the late nineteenth century) and then turned toward the city's seedier streets. She parked in front of one of the many rundown hotels lining Jackson Street.

In my capacity with the Cascade Mental Health Team, I'd been in most of these hotels at some point. Populated by drug abusers, alcoholics, and chronic psychiatric patients, these flophouses rented rooms by the month or week. Sometimes by the hour. In my eyes, they stood as bleak testimony to human shortcoming.

We climbed out of the car and walked by a grubby bearded man who sat against the front of the hotel, teetering from side to side and threatening to collapse onto the empty wine bottle beside him. As we passed, he held up a tattered baseball cap with a shaky hand. Claire and I dug in our pockets and came up with a couple of quarters between us, while Dev pulled two slips of paper from his wallet and dropped them in the hat. The old drunk looked down at the papers in confusion, but I knew what they were. As long as I'd known him, Dev carried McDonald's gift certificates to pass out to panhandlers.

Claire pulled open the steel door of the Hotel Astoria. We followed her inside. The natural brightness of the afternoon died when the door closed behind us. In the dimness, the stench of fried chicken and cigarettes assaulted our senses. Behind the desk, an emaciated, fortyish-looking man slumped back in a wooden chair. His eyes were at half-mast, and he stared blankly at a soap opera on an old TV mounted above the desk. "We're looking for Ron Weaver," Claire told the acne-scarred man.

Without bothering to ask who we were or even glance in our direction, he thumbed at the staircase. "Room twenty-four. Second floor," he grunted.

With each step up the staircase, the smell grew stronger. Dev looked over his shoulder and wrinkled his nose. "Anybody else feel like they're being smothered with a two-pack-a-day roasted chicken?"

Once on the second floor, we walked five or six doors down the hallway before reaching the door with "24" labeled beside it. Claire knocked. Nothing. As she reached to rap again, the door opened a crack and Ron Weaver stuck his forgettable face through the gap. "What is it?"

"We'd love to chat," Dev said cheerfully.

"I told you I wouldn't talk anymore without my lawyer present—"

Dev shoved the door wide open. "We got another fresh corpse. Either you talk to us here or we take you back to our turf and do it there. Course, then you won't be a priority for us, and you might rot in lockup for a couple of days till *we* feel like talking."

Weaver digested the threat and then turned and plodded back into his suite, leaving the door open for us to follow.

I was struck by how clean Weaver's pad was compared to other rooms I'd seen in similar hotels. But even in the pigsties that some of the drug users called home, I'd noticed pictures hanging on walls or books on the table or some personal touch. Weaver's room had none.

Weaver stood in the center of the room with his wet hair combed across his head and his thin arms hanging at his side. Though I'd watched him from behind the two-way mirror of the Homicide interview room, he hadn't laid eyes on me since his discharge from Western State. However, he seemed less than sentimental about our reunion. "What's Dr. Ashman doing here?" he asked the detectives as if they'd brought over an unwanted cat.

"He's helping us draw a psychological profile of the perpetrator," Claire said.

Dev pointed a finger at Weaver's head and made a circular gesture. "And guess who his drawing ended up looking an awful lot like?"

Weaver remained impassive. "You said someone died."

"Calvin Nichol," Claire said. "You know him?"

"Dr. Kolberg's partner," Weaver said emotionlessly.

"He used to be before someone filleted him," Dev said pleasantly. "Where were you yesterday evening around ten?"

"Here."

"Can anyone confirm that?" Claire asked.

"My neighbor."

"Oh, I see." Dev took an exaggerated glance around the depressingly austere room. "You were entertaining? You had the neighbors in for tea and biscuits?"

Weaver shook his head. "The junkie broke in here last night and threatened me with a dirty needle," he droned. "Said he'd give me AIDS if I didn't give him money."

Claire's eyes narrowed. "And what did you do?"

"Told him to leave."

"Did he?"

Weaver showed a rare glimpse of a smile. "Eventually."

"Would he be at home now?" Claire asked.

"Probably still at the hospital."

Dev rubbed his eyes and sighed. "You didn't take a shovel to him, did you?"

"It's all in the police report," Weaver said.

With Weaver's minimal cooperation, we pieced together the story of how he beat the stuffing out of his neighbor with a frying pan after the man allegedly accosted him at "needle-point." Having run out of questions, we prepared to leave.

On the way to the door, I stopped and turned back to Weaver. "Why would a guy who doesn't touch drugs or al-cohol live in this shooting gallery?"

Weaver eyed me with a flicker of resentment before his face turned back to stone. "I'm a convicted murderer and mental patient. Where else am I supposed to live?"

As we headed downstairs, Dev turned to me. "Shovels . . . frying pans . . . this guy's pretty resourceful. You sure he wasn't the guy behind the ski mask?"

"Not certain, but I don't think so. My spider sense wasn't tingling back there." I chuckled, trying to breathe through my mouth and avoid the hallway's nauseating stench.

Once we'd loaded into Claire's car, Dev pulled his cell phone out of his jacket and dialed a number. After a few grunts and a couple of sarcastic "greats," he stuck it back in his coat pocket. "Weaver's alibi holds up. Couple of patrol guys were called to a disturbance at his place just after ten P.M. He wouldn't have had time to kill Nichol and get back to pull that off."

"So we scratch Weaver off the list?" Claire said.

"Yeah, but use a pencil," he sighed. "That guy . . ."

Claire pulled into the parking lot of a convenience store on the upper end of Main Street on a block composed of flea-bitten bars and boarded-up buildings that wasn't much of an upgrade from Weaver's neighborhood.

A weak bell tinkled as we stepped into the store. At the sound, the man behind the counter in the pressed green uniform shirt faced us with a smile. Wayne Hacking's youthful face beamed, matching the light shining off his brow. "Hello, Dr. Ashman. What happened to your arm?"

I shrugged. "Minor injury."

Dev walked up to the counter. "Wayne, you didn't dust off the old Ginsu knife yesterday, huh?"

"Excuse me?" Hacking's forehead wrinkled in confusion.

"You remember." Dev feigned a sales pitch. "It dices, it slices, it cuts through the human heart like it's a ripe tomato."

Hacking held up his palms. "You're losing me, Sergeant."

Claire joined Dev at the counter. "Calvin Nichol was stabbed to death last night."

"Ohhhh," Hacking said as if the world suddenly made sense again. He looked beyond the detectives to me. "I'm sorry to hear that, Dr. Ashman."

I nodded noncommittally.

"You knew Dr. Nichol?" Claire asked.

"Only to say hello to." Hacking reached down and straightened a few of the gum packages in the countertop display. "I'd met him a few times at Dr. Kolberg's—and Dr. Ashman's—office."

"You were never his patient?" Claire asked.

Hacking shook his head. "Just Dr. Kolberg's. In fact, I'm looking for a new psychiatrist." Again, he looked past the detectives to me. "You're not taking new patients, are you, Dr. Ashman?"

"I'm out of private practice."

Hacking smiled sympathetically. "Seems to be a dangerous business these days."

Dev leaned forward and rested his elbows on the counter. "Where were you last night, Wayne?"

"With Yvonne," he said.

"I should've known." Dev clicked his tongue. "You're always with your girlfriends when people are being killed. Like the evening Kolberg died." He snapped his fingers. "Or that other time you were with your last girlfriend and her sister, the night they were butchered . . . by you."

Hacking was immune to Dev's antagonism. "We went to a movie last night. An Iranian film. *Dawn's Glory.*"

"Where and when?" Dev said, rising from the counter.

"The Wormwood's late show. From nine thirty to about midnight."

"And someone—other than your girlfriend—can verify that?" Claire asked.

Hacking nodded. "The theater was pretty empty, but I'm sure the ticket guy will remember me. We joked about how *Dawn's Glory* might break the *Lord of the Rings* box office records."

"A couple of real cards," Dev grumbled.

The bell chimed again as the front door opened. Two teenage boys in baseball caps and blue-tinted sunglasses walked in carrying skateboards. Hacking's eyes glommed onto them as they ambled up and down the store's aisles. "Hey, boys!" he called out to them. "Soon as I'm done with these police officers, I'll be able to help you." Then he turned back to us. "Detectives, if there's nothing else, I have to mind the store . . ." He nodded to the kids. "If you know what I mean."

The detectives headed for the door, but I stood my ground and asked, "Wayne, what kind of car do you drive?"

Hacking smiled so widely that I could almost see his wisdom teeth. "I'm green-friendly, Dr. Ashman. I don't own a car. I barely ride my bike."

As I turned to join the others, Hacking called after me, "Take care of that arm, Dr. Ashman."

Once in the car, Claire said, "We better talk to Yvonne again."

Dev groaned. "And she'll tell us whatever Hacking instructs her to. No, we better talk to the guy at the theater." He reached forward from the backseat and tapped me on the shoulder. "How about Hacking? Wouldn't he look good in a ski mask?"

"There's something about him," I said. "But I don't know."

On the way back to Homicide, my post-operation exhaustion caught up with me, and I nodded off in the passenger seat. After we arrived, Claire insisted on showing me to the lounge in the back. To appease her, I lay down on the sofa bed, intending to nap for fifteen minutes. Four hours later, I woke up to find Dev's craggy face above me. "How you doing, sleeping beauty?" he asked.

I yawned and started a stretch, which I aborted abruptly when I felt the searing pain in my right arm. "Where's Claire?"

"Making calls." He turned and started for the lounge's door. "She wanted me to let you sleep, but I knew you'd want to come along."

I rose to my feet. "Where?"

"Clubbing." Dev walked away without elaborating.

I got up and followed him out through the department and down to Claire's car. As we drove through downtown, it occurred to me that I'd spent the better part of the ten days since Stanley's murder inside her car. Then again, I could think of worse places to be.

"While you were hibernating back there," Dev said, "we got some police work done."

"Like?" I asked.

"For starters, Brent McCabe, our temperamental CPA, left for Chicago two days ago. We know he didn't knife Nichol and you. And we spoke to Yvonne Carpinelli, Hacking's girl. Amazingly, she gave us the same story he did."

"Verbatim," Claire said. "Right down to the stupid joke about the movie setting box-office records."

Dev leaned forward and pointed. "There it is, up on your right, Claire."

I doubt Claire would've missed the place. Even though it was only dusk, the flashing lights and gaudy entryway were bound to catch her eye. She pulled up in front of the roped-off entrance to Club Russe. When we climbed out, a bulky, perfectly coiffed bouncer approached us waving his thick arms. "You can't park there!"

Dev nodded in the guy's direction and said loudly, "Get a load of this guy. Sure this isn't a gay bar?"

The bouncer headed straight for him. "Listen, buddy," he snarled. "You better get that car—"

Claire stepped between them and shoved her badge in the beefcake's face. "SPD. The car stays here. And you stay to watch it."

The bouncer's broad shoulders sagged, and he nodded deferentially. We strode past him and through the dark entrance into the club. Inside was just the kind of techno-pop décor that I'd expected to see. Everywhere I looked were neon lights, chrome fixtures, and cocktail waitresses in tight black bodysuits. The whole package came accompanied by the constant drone of a drum machine. I felt as if I'd stepped off a Seattle street straight into a nightclub in Berlin or Moscow.

Dev and I followed Claire across the empty flashing dance floor to the granite bar lining the far wall. She hailed one of the bartenders. He pointed to a flight of stairs beyond the end of the bar. With Claire in the lead, we mounted the red-carpeted staircase to the second floor. At the end of a short corridor, we reached two black leather-padded doors with a PRIVATE sign hanging across them.

Claire dropped the sign on the floor and pushed the doors open. Dev and I followed her inside. In the middle of the room—which looked like a smaller replica of the club downstairs, right down to the granite bar—Sergei Pushtin sat at a table between two barely clad platinum blondes. The girls drank Martinis while Pushtin tore into a huge steak and massive mound of mashed potatoes. In front of his plate was a three-quarters-full bottle of Stoly and a tumbler.

The girls might've been sisters, but neither looked like natural blondes. Their thick black eyebrows and swarthy facial features suggested an Eastern European heritage. Their natural hair color might've been debatable, but their age wasn't. "Dirty Serge, who you kidding?" Dev pointed from one girl to the other. "If these two had birth certificates signed by the Pope, I wouldn't believe they were old enough to be in here. Or anywhere near you."

Pushtin swallowed a mouthful of food before pointing a fork at Dev. "Sherlock, I thought I was finished with you," he said in his low-pitched Russian accent.

Crossing the floor toward Pushtin, Dev growled, "When you hear the dirt landing on top of your casket, then you'll be finished with me. Not until."

Pushtin turned to one of the girls and grumbled a few words in Russian. They rose together, collected their identical Louis Vuitton knock-off bags, and locked arms as they sashayed by us on their way to the door.

We stood in a row in front of the table. Pushtin put down his cutlery but didn't rise from his seat. "What now?" he sighed, and used his little finger to pick at a bit of broccoli stuck between his teeth.

"Kolberg's partner, Calvin Nichol, was killed last night," Claire said.

"And?"

"And where were you last night?" Claire asked. But ski mask or not, Pushtin was twice the size of my attacker. We knew he hadn't killed Nichol.

"I run a business." Pushtin pushed the plate away. "I was here last night. Lots of witnesses."

"So you sent one of your flunkies out to cut Nichol up," Dev said.

"Who is this Nichol?" Pushtin grimaced as if the name was causing him pain.

Claire reached into her bag and pulled out a stack of photos. She slapped a snapshot of Nichol down on the table in front of Pushtin. After a moment, she threw down two more. In the first Nichol was lying dead on his back at the crime scene; in the second he was on a morgue gurney with his abdomen splayed open. Pushtin reacted with no more shock than if she'd shown him a couple of postcards. "You already told Sergei. He's dead. So what?"

Claire swept the pictures off the table. "Did you know him?"

"He was client. Not many times. Always came with the other one."

"Kolberg?"

Pushtin nodded.

"And what was Nichol's thing?" Claire spat the last word.

"Domination and . . ." Pushtin snapped his fingers proudly. "Degradation."

"Meaning?"

Pushtin smiled lewdly at her. "He liked water sports and the other—how do you say?—body produce."

Claire didn't correct Pushtin. "He didn't hit the women?" she asked.

Pushtin shook his head, and reached for the tumbler of vodka in front of his plate. He drank it in one swig. "No hitting. Just pissing and crapping."

Claire tossed another picture on the table. It was a still captured from Nichol's home video of the girl who'd been "horseback" riding him. "Recognize her?"

Pushtin nodded. "Anya."

"She's one of your girls?" Dev cocked his head.

"Was, Sherlock, was."

Dev nodded. "You killed her?"

Pushtin laughed and pointed his glass at me. "Sherlock thinks I am Stalin. That I kill everyone, no?"

Dev snatched the bottle from his hand. "Don't tell me what I think! How come she doesn't work for you anymore?"

Pushtin shrugged. "After the infection, Anya wasn't the same. She wasn't bringing in business. Too scared. I had to let her go."

"Wait a minute." Claire held up a palm. "Is she the one you told us about last time? The one Kolberg burned with the candle?"

"Anya," Pushtin sighed. "She used to be one of my best."

Dev pointed at Pushtin. "So when Kolberg put her out of business with that flame, you lost a lot of money?"

"Lots of money, Sherlock."

"Ah, so that's why you killed Kolberg." Dev nodded. "And his buddy, too."

Pushtin rolled his eyes and shook his huge head. "Just like Stalin, again. No. I told you, Kolberg paid me for damages. It wasn't a problem."

"Well, aren't you just a benevolent bastard." Claire kneed the table, sending Pushtin's cutlery into his lap.

A fleeting sneer drifted across Pushtin's lips. Then he retrieved the silverware and straightened his place setting. "Those losers were good business for me," he said calmly. "Why would I kill them?"

"How do we find Anya?" Claire asked.

"Find her boyfriend, Nikolai Krutov. You find him, you find Anya," Pushtin said in his singsong accent. "And maybe you ask him about the infection. He's not such good businessman like me. Bad temper. Maybe he knows how the losers died."

After leaving Pushtin, we dropped Dev off at Homicide and headed for my place. I threw together—as well as one arm would let me throw together—an overnight bag. I leashed up Nelson and hurried back to Claire's car.

Her condo was only a few blocks away, just off Roosevelt Way. Claire's was a relatively new stucco building that, like many of the city's condo developments built in the late eighties and early nineties, had fallen prey to water leaks. Consequently, the building was encased in scaffolding for construction crews to work on replacing the damage and stopping the leaks. Once inside her fourth-floor apartment, I would never have guessed that her roomy two-bedroom pad was rotting behind its cheerfully painted walls.

The spare bedroom felt like someone's own home with colorful prints on the wall, an old pine dresser, and a red quilt decorated with yellow ducks stretching over the double bed. I sat on the bed and measured the mattress's firmness with my good hand, finding it nice and hard, just as I preferred.

Claire strode in holding a stack of bath and hand towels

that reached her chin. I laughed. "How long are you expecting me to stay?"

"Depends." She turned from me and organized the towels on top of the dresser. "How long will I be able to put up with you?"

"Not as long as those towels will last," I said, trying not to stare at her shapely rear view.

She turned around. "Everything all right?"

I smiled. "Everything's perfect."

"Okay, well . . ." She shifted from foot to foot.

I shuffled my butt up the mattress, deliberately leaving Claire a space open beside me.

Claire sat down. "So this is what it has come to?" She laughed nervously. "Takes an attempted murder to get a guy over to my place."

"I think you're fishing, but I'll bite." I reached over to touch her cheek with my good hand. "You're kind, smart, funny . . . and beautiful. Guys ought to be busting down your door."

She blushed. "Not for a female cop. Men are terrified of us. Except male cops. And when it comes to political correctness, they're only a couple thousand years behind the times."

"What about Dev?"

"Underneath his missing-link act, he's a good guy."

I put my hand on her warm neck and massaged it gently. "A real family man, too."

"Mmmm," she murmured appreciatively. "Goes to show, though. The good ones are all taken."

"Thanks!"

"No. Not you, I mean . . ." you know . . ." She wrapped her arm around my neck, and buried her head in my shoulder.

I found her awkward vulnerability endearing. And desperately sexy. I pulled her face to mine and kissed her softly. She leaned against me and kissed harder. Her tongue darted between my lips. Arousal tore through me. Our lips and tongues eagerly explored the other's. Then Claire slid a hand under my sling and started to unbutton my shirt.

Suddenly, unwelcome guilt broke what was otherwise the perfect moment. I gently pulled her hand away from my shirt.

Claire withdrew her lips from mine. She eyed me with a bewildered frown. "What's wrong?" she asked in a slightly hurt tone.

"Nothing." I touched her cheek.

"But?"

"I'm winged." I lifted up my sling. "And I'm rusty at this. Since Loren . . . I haven't . . ."

Claire pulled away further. "Look, if you're not ready—"

"It's not that." I grabbed her hand and pulled it to my chest. "I want to savor it. You know? Go slow."

Her lips broke into a faint smile. I leaned closer and kissed her again. She responded tentatively, but soon the enthusiasm of her kisses matched my own.

We sat on the bed kissing like school kids for a long time. Finally, I whispered, "I want you to fall asleep in my arms. Well, my *arm,* actually."

We lay down on the bed beside each other. Somehow, we managed to find a workable position. I spooned her on my left side with my good arm tucked underneath her waist and my splinted wrist resting relatively comfortably on her shoulder.

Perched like that, Claire soon drifted off. But I had more trouble finding sleep. I thought of her ex-husband and the mess he had dragged her into.

I winced at the memory, realizing I had no right to drag her into another.

12

I AWOKE IN THE DAYLIGHT-FLOODED BEDROOM. Claire was nowhere to be seen, but the welcome smell of coffee drifted into the room. I climbed out of bed. The sudden throb in my arm reminded me of the recent attempt on my life. I was itching to throw on my running shoes and jog off the nervous energy that the memory of the event generated. Frustrated, I realized the knife wound would keep me from running for the time being.

When I bent my wrist, I noticed I had more movement than I did the day before, so I pulled off the sling and headed for the kitchen. I stopped at the doorway to watch Claire leaning over the stove. Her dark blond hair spilled over the back of her oversized, pale blue terry cloth housecoat. I found it as sexy as any piece of lingerie I'd seen. I had a flashback to breakfasts with Lor when she wore nothing but one of my long-sleeved shirts; her sensual and full thighs—"my grandma's legs," she used to joke—surfacing below the shirt's hem. I loved that look.

I shook off the memory and stepped into the kitchen inhaling the aroma of eggs that joined the coffee in a pleasant duet of breakfast smells. Claire turned to face me. She hesitated before leaning forward and kissing me on the lips. "How'd you sleep?"

"I don't know if it was that duck-lined quilt or the elephant-sized tranquilizer I took, but either way, I slept like a lamb."

She laughed. "I think you squeezed a whole zoo into that sentence."

I pointed at the frying pan. "Hey, I thought you said you didn't cook."

"This? Just eggs. That's not cooking." She moved the frying pan over to the counter and deftly divided the eggs onto two waiting plates.

"I think I'm being conned," I said as I eagerly accepted the plate in my left hand and headed for the kitchen table.

Claire deposited a mug of coffee beside my plate and sat down across from me. "How's your arm today?"

"It's okay. But I'm dreading my shower."

"Have a bath," she said. "I've got a nice soaker tub that fits two comfortably." Then she flushed at the realization of how it sounded.

"Perfect." I smiled. "Maybe Nelson and I can get scrubbed up together. Speaking of . . ." I looked over my shoulder, but there was no sign of my old dog.

Claire pointed toward the floor. I poked my head under the table to see Nelson curled up in a ball across her feet.

I chuckled. "He always did like women better."

"Was he Loren's dog?"

"Very much so. He took her death hard. Didn't eat for weeks after."

"The two of you make a good pair, huh?"

"Yeah, right. Oil and water."

"But both in love with the same woman."

"We're flexible. We'll both lick the hand that feeds us."

Claire eyed me as if she might add something else. Instead, she glanced at her watch. "Hey, eat up. We're late."

I had a quick bath in Claire's soaker tub, thinking how

nice it would be to have her join me. I felt foolish when I had to solicit her help in buttoning my shirt, but the loss of autonomy was more than compensated for when she pressed her mint-flavored mouth against mine and slowly did my buttons up, from the top down. I'd been undressed erotically before, but no one had ever made dressing me such a turn-on. When she fastened the last button and broke off our embrace, I sighed. "You've got no idea how sorry I am that I didn't wear my button-fly jeans today."

She laughed. "Your loss."

We reached Dev's office just before 9 A.M. Dev rested his worn oxfords on his desk and leaned back in his chair reading a file. At the sight of us, he pulled a photo out of the file and sailed it across the desk. "Meet our hooker's boyfriend, Nicolai, AKA 'Nikki,' Krutov."

Claire held up the black-and-white mug shot, while I studied it over her shoulder. Krutov stared blankly at the camera with cropped hair, wide nose, and square jaw. He could have been eighteen or fifty; it was impossible to tell from the photo.

"He's twenty-nine," Dev grunted as if reading my mind. "To his credit, he's got a rap sheet that reads like he's twenty years older. I spoke to his parole officer." He leafed through the papers and then read from his notes. "Immigrated here at sixteen. Three convictions as a young offender—theft, assault, theft. Graduated to the adult courts at eighteen, grand theft auto, did six months. Tried at twenty-one for trafficking. Convicted of aggravated assault at twenty-five. Did two and a half years. Since then a couple of parole violations . . . blah, blah, blah . . ."

"What was the aggravated assault all about?" Claire asked.

"Glad you asked, Detective." Dev's pocked face broke into a cat-that-ate-the-canary grin. "Seems young Nikki shot another Russian boy in the leg."

Claire dropped her purse on the desk. "Oh?" she said.

"Nikki used a .38. Same caliber as the slug used to off Kolberg. But no big deal, that's a common size bullet."

Dev's grin grew wider. "Want to know the motive for the shooting?"

Claire rolled her finger in a get-on-with-it gesture.

Dev was clearly enjoying himself. "He was protecting the honor of his ex-girlfriend. Apparently the other Russian got a bit too physical with her." He pointed at the mug shot in Claire's hand. "Nikki went ballistic. Literally. Put a bullet in the guy's leg."

The smile spread from Dev to Claire. "If a beating merits a bullet to the leg, wonder what a disfiguring burn is worth?"

Dev jerked his feet off the desk and hopped up. "Let's go find out. I've got his address from his PO."

We followed Dev down to Claire's car. After a quick drive across town in the light midday traffic, we pulled into one of the many parking spots in front of Krutov's most recent known address, a nondescript concrete building just off Denny Way. A sign on the front door read O VACANCY, leaving me to wonder whether the building was full or desperate for tenants. There was an intercom beside the front door, but when Claire pulled at the wobbly latch, the door opened freely. We stepped inside and followed the main floor's corridor around a 90 degree turn. We stopped at Krutov's door. Before knocking, Claire reached into her jacket and unclipped her handgun. I felt a few butterflies in my stomach when I looked over and saw Dev do the same. Neither removed their guns from the holsters, but both laid their hands on the handles as Claire reached for the door and knocked three times.

A high-pitched female voice called from inside: "What do you want?"

From the squeaky accent, I recognized her as the girl in Nichol's homemade bondage video. We all shared a glance. Claire and Dev relaxed their grips on their guns.

"Anya?" Claire said.

"Who is it?" Anya demanded.

"We're detectives with the Seattle Police," Claire said.

"You have a warrant?" Anya asked.

"We don't need a warrant," Claire said. "We just want to ask you and Nikki some questions."

There was a long pause. "How do I know who you are?"

"We have identification," Claire said calmly. "Open your door with the chain on, and we'll show you."

"I don't know . . . ," Anya said.

After another long wait, Dev piped up. "This is bullshit," he grumbled, before speaking to the door. "Anya, it's Sergeant Devonshire. Step back from the door, I'm going to kick it in now."

The door opened a few inches, and somehow Anya managed to slip her body through the space. Her short hair was dyed so blond it was nearly white. In spite of her loose cotton long-sleeved T-shirt and sweats, it was clear she'd lost even more weight since her emaciated appearance in Nichol's video. The gauntness of her face stole most of its youth. The bones stood out so prominently that her face looked like an X-ray someone had touched up with skin color and a pair of chocolate-brown eyes.

"What do you want?" She put her skinny hands on her hips.

"Is Nikki home?" Claire asked.

"No."

"Where is he?"

Her steely eyes didn't flinch. "I don't know."

"We'd like to ask you some questions," Claire said.

Anya flounced defiantly.

"May we come inside?" Claire asked.

"Why you need to come inside?"

"Because we're the police, not Jehovah's Witnesses," Dev said, pushing the door open and walking past her into the apartment.

Anya hurried after him into the living room. Claire and I followed. The apartment was surprisingly homey inside, with comfortable-looking furniture, potpourri on the coffee table, and even a few pictures hanging on the walls, including a traditional Eastern Orthodox icon.

Inside, Anya's attitude did an about-face. After ensuring we were comfortably seated on her well-worn sofas, she walked over to the chair beside the corridor leading to the bedrooms. She perched herself on its arm, crossed her legs, and leaned a bony elbow against its backrest. "What do you want to know?"

"Stanley Kolberg," Dev said flatly.

She didn't respond.

"Serge Pushtin thought you might remember him," Dev said.

At the mention of Pushtin's name, her eyes narrowed. "I don't work for Sergei no more."

Claire nodded. "He told us he let you go."

Anya laughed bitterly. "For five grand, the son of a bitch 'let me go.'"

"Where did you come up with that kind of money?" Claire asked.

"I save money," she said proudly. "I don't inject every penny like the other stupid girls."

"Stanley Kolberg was the man who burned your back," Claire said.

A flicker of pain crossed her lips. She nodded impassively.

"We understand you had a serious infection after," I said.

She tilted her head from side to side, but said nothing.

"And you weren't able to work anymore," I pressed.

"I didn't want to do *that work* anymore," she snapped.

"You didn't go to the police," Claire said.

"It's a . . . how do you say . . . risk of the job."

Claire eyed her intently. "So you just let Kolberg get away with it, huh?"

Anya held up her palms and set her face in a stoic expression.

"What about Nikki?" Dev demanded. "He didn't mind Kolberg burning you?"

Anya shifted in her seat. "Nikki doesn't stick his nose in other people's business."

"Know what?" Dev grunted. "There's a guy limping around with a bullet in his leg who thinks different."

"What do you mean—" Anya started, but a loud crash stopped her in mid-sentence.

Dev and Claire leapt to their feet and grabbed for their guns. They rushed for the small hallway leading to the bedroom where the noise had come from, but Anya jumped in front of them. Looking like a human "T" with arms outspread from her twig-like body, she blocked their path. "No! Leave him," she cried. "He didn't do nothing!"

Claire grabbed Anya by the shoulders. Firmly, but not roughly, she pulled her out of the way. Anya didn't resist. Instead, she screamed at the bedroom door, *"Nikki!"*

Dev and Claire rushed to the door and positioned themselves on either side. I stood behind and gently pulled Anya farther back from the door and into the living room.

"Nikki, open the door," Claire said. "Now!"

"Nyet, Nikki!" Anya cried.

Claire shot her a glance that would've frozen hot lava and then barked at the door, "Now, Nikki!"

Nothing.

Dev pointed from his eyes to the door. Claire nodded her understanding. She moved to the side and trained her gun on the door's center, while Dev reached for the doorknob. He tried to twist it, but it didn't budge. He nodded once to Claire, stepped back, and kicked out his right foot, impacting heavily just above the level of the knob. There was a crackle of splintering wood. The door flew open.

Dev dove for cover against the far wall, while Claire held her aim into the room. He peeked around the doorframe and then, with gun extended, inched his way into the room. He disappeared from view. He called out, "Claire, the alley!"

I reached the room's doorway just in time to see Dev squeeze through the wide-open window. Without hesitation, Claire tucked her gun into her holster and followed him out. I put my damaged hand on the windowsill, but she turned back and said, "Stay here, Joel. Call for backup!" Then she disappeared out the window and into the alley beyond.

I found the phone lying off its cradle on the floor. I dialed 911 and explained our situation to the skeptical operator, trusting she would dispatch a few police cars if only to investigate the crackpot making the call.

After hanging up, I glanced around Anya's bedroom while she stood at the doorway watching. The sheets lay in a tussled ball on the bed. Cheap jewelry, some change, and three mismatched religious statuettes were scattered on top of the plywood dresser. The top two drawers stuck out below. A breeze blew in from the open window and scattered papers around the bedroom, making an even bigger mess. Beside the bed, a floor lamp had toppled over, which I figured must have accounted for the crash. From the deep grooves on the carpet, it appeared as if Krutov had moved the lamp and nightstand out of the way, presumably in a hurry to get at something. Then I noticed two baggies full of white powder lying on the floor where the nightstand had stood. I knelt down to study them, but I knew better than to touch them with bare hands.

Anya snorted in disgust and stomped back into the living room. I followed. I had no official reason for staying, but Anya didn't seem to care, so I sat down on the sofa to wait for the others while Anya paced the room. She picked a pack of cigarettes off the kitchen table and lit one at full stride. After several long puffs, she stopped and pointed the trembling butt at me. "What kind of cops are you?"

"Homicide," I said, not bothering to explain my tangential role.

"Homicide?" She grimaced. "What they want with Nikki?"

"Kolberg, the one who—"

"I know who he is," she snapped, starting in motion again.

"He was killed a couple of weeks ago," I said. "And then two days ago Calvin Nichol was murdered."

Anya appeared unfazed by the news.

"Nichol was in a video with you. Really tall guy . . . he licked your shoes." When she stared blankly at me, I added, "Kolberg was there, too, behind the camera. Remember?"

Slowly, recognition crept into her expression. "Oh, that tall freak. Who liked piss. I remember him. But *Kolberg*"— she hissed his name—"wasn't behind camera."

"No?"

"He was waiting his turn," she said. "The one with the

camera, he didn't want to fuck or anything. Just take pictures with that big stupid grin all the time." She shook her head and stared at me defiantly. "You know what? I'm glad that asshole Kolberg is dead. And the tall one . . . who cares?"

I met her stare. "Kolberg hurt you badly."

"Look at me!" she cried. "I lost fifteen pounds. I'm sick all the time now. I can't eat." She spun around and pulled up her T-shirt. In the middle of her back lay a thin, homogeneous pink rectangle about the size of a CD jewel case. The skin graft hadn't healed at its edges; instead, weeping sores and blisters marked the borders. It was the second time in six months that I had to view the consequences of Stanley's twisted penchant for candles and flame. Anya's burn was even more extensive than what I'd seen on Angela.

After giving me a longer view than I wanted or needed, Anya dropped her shirt and turned back to face me. "Why Nikki? How come you don't think I killed Kolberg?"

Before I could answer, Claire burst into the room. She shook her head. "He's gone."

A minute later, Dev staggered in. "You call for backup?" he panted at me.

I nodded.

Breathing easily, Claire said: "Anya, we need your help."

Anya shook her head.

Claire approached until her face was less than a foot from Anya's. "We will find Nikki. But if you help, Anya, he's a lot less likely to get hurt."

"No!" Anya spat. "He didn't do anything. I won't help you destroy him."

Without a word of explanation to Anya, the detectives headed back into the bedroom. Anya and I followed. Claire reached into her bag, produced three pairs of rubber gloves, and threw Dev and me a set each.

I walked around the fallen nightstand and picked up one of the powder-filled baggies. Dev took the bag from my hand. I half-expected him to stick a finger inside and lick the contents, but he held it up to the light. "Coke," he grunted.

Across the room, I saw Claire rifling through the dresser

drawers. She stuck her arm in the second drawer's slot as far as her shoulder. Fishing inside, she twisted her arm so aggressively that my wrist ached watching. When she pulled back her hand, pinched between her index finger and thumb, she dangled a gun by its trigger casing. A few strands of duct tape were still attached. "Taped behind the drawer. Looks like a .38."

Dev walked over and took the weapon out of her hand. He gave it a quick once-over then nodded. "Semiautomatic. Definitely .38." He smiled. "How's that for coincidence?"

"Don't most killers dump their guns after using them?" I asked.

"Not always," Claire said.

"But if he used that gun on Kolberg, why didn't he take it out the window with him?"

"Look around, Doc." Dev pointed at the disastrous shape of the room. "Nikki was in full-scale panic. I doubt he meant to knock over that lamp and leave two bags of coke at the scene, either."

Claire nodded. "Besides, ballistics can easily tell us if it's the same gun."

Before leaving, Dev marched back to the laundry hamper in the corner of the room. He pulled out a crumpled T-shirt and bagged it separately from the gun. Satisfied, he headed for the door.

By the time we reached the street, three patrol cars had converged in front. Dev spoke briefly to the uniformed policemen, showing them Krutov's mug shot and organizing an impromptu search of the area. But we didn't hang around, knowing the odds were slim that Krutov was still in the neighborhood.

We dedicated the rest of the day to tracking down Krutov's known contacts. By mid-evening we still hadn't found him, but Dev and Claire weren't discouraged. They had a prime suspect, which is all it takes to make a Homicide cop happy. Usually.

We arrived at Claire's place just after 8 P.M. Nelson met us at the door with a demanding bark. I hurried to the kitchen, found his food, and put a bowl out for him. When he'd finished, I leashed him up and took him to the park across the street.

When I returned, I found Claire sitting in the kitchen. She'd changed into a formfitting, sleeveless white shirt, which showed off her toned arms and trim torso. She'd also unclipped her hair, letting it fall back to her shoulders. She rubbed her hands together, smacked her lips, and grinned. "I'm going to be barking like Nelson if the food doesn't get here soon."

"What's on the menu?"

She lifted up a brochure she had left by the phone, but the name meant nothing to me. "Thai."

Soon enough, we downed our dinner along with a bottle of zinfandel. My one-handedness put me at a distinct disadvantage in fighting for the remnants of the pad thai noodles. When I held up my bandaged right arm like a wounded puppy, Claire was unmoved. "Survival of the fittest," she said with a laugh, stuffing the last bite of noodles in her mouth.

We moved into the living room. Snuggling on the living room sofa, we drained the last of the wine while listening to Miles Davis. She nestled her head under my good arm. When the CD ended, she studied me with an inviting smile. I couldn't help but kiss her.

As the heat intensified in our kisses, I moved my hand to her blouse and touched the thin fabric over her small but firm breasts, encouraged by the slight moan she sighed into my mouth. But the pangs of guilt intervened again. I dropped my hand from her chest and broke off the lip contact.

Claire sat up and viewed me with hurt exasperation. "Joel, I don't get it."

"I don't get it, myself. I just . . . I don't know."

"I can't imagine what it must have been like after Loren," she said quietly, reaching for my good hand. "But when will it be okay again?"

"Look, Claire. It's not that." I studied my bandages. "I have so much . . . history. I don't think it's fair to you . . ."

"I'm all grown up," she said. "I can make my own choices."

I stared hard at her. "There are things you don't know about me."

"Like?"

I wavered. I considered trying to explain how tragedy seemed to befall all the women who became part of my life, but I knew how ridiculous it would sound. Besides, this was only a part of my hesitance. "Things from my past," I said vaguely.

Claire pulled her hand from mine. "You weren't involved in your partners' sexual—"

"God, no!"

She nodded, and her expression softened. "There are things in my past, too."

I wondered if she meant the ex-husband or something else, but she didn't elaborate any more than I had. We sat together for several minutes buried in our own thoughts. Finally, Claire looked at me, her expression set. "It doesn't matter," she said.

"What doesn't?"

"Your past," she said. "I don't care about the Joel Ashman of three years ago. Or even three weeks ago, for that matter." She tilted her head and bit her lip. "I care about *this* Joel, right here, right now."

Staring into her bottomless green eyes, I felt my resistance drain.

I drew her face back to mine and kissed her lips and chin. Moving my head down her neck, I alternated licks and nibbles of the soft skin, tasting a hint of fragrance. She lay back against the sofa and moaned softly in response. I dropped my left hand to her waist and found the hem of her shirt. She held her arms up for me as I lifted the shirt over her head.

Mouths and hands in constant hungry contact, we struggled to undress each other. Clothes fell on and to the side of the couch. I climbed on top of Claire, our mouths locked and bodies intertwined. The ache in my wrist didn't even register. The tenderness dissolved into urgency. I was so desperate to be inside her. To rediscover a passion I had almost forgotten.

We stumbled back to her bedroom. After what felt like weeks, Claire finally collapsed on top of me, both of us dripping with sweat. Exhausted from the fervor and the release, I fell into a heavy sleep.

But it wasn't restful.

Angela Connor visited me in my dreams. And she brought along Stanley. I woke with a start. And I couldn't stop thinking about the day when I'd first read—in Angela's own words—what Stanley had subjected her to.

Hours after nearly breaking my hand on Stanley's face, the implications of what he'd told me finally sank in—Angela must have spoken to him after storming out of my house. How else could he have known that I had "kicked her out into the lonely night"?

Why had she turned to him, of all people? The question burned in my mind. And I couldn't stop speculating on what he might have told her.

I'd seen Stanley unmasked for the bastard he was, but I had no proof. Nor did I want to find any. I just wanted to wash my hands of him forever. Moreover, I began to appreciate that changing partners wouldn't solve my problems. Suicide or not, I'd lost my edge. Burned out. So a month after Angela's death, I closed my practice.

To make ends meet, I settled into work with the Cascade Mental Health Team, practicing crisis intervention and medication stabilization for the many chronic psychiatric patients who eked out an existence outside the confines of a hospital. The gray winter months passed by uneventfully with each day blending into the next, but Angela never strayed too far from my thoughts.

Then, four months after her death, I received an unexpected phone call. "Dr. Ashman, it's Tommy Connor," he said, his voice no warmer than it had been in the church's vestibule.

"Tommy, how are you?"

He ignored my question. "I found some stuff that might interest you."

"What sort of stuff?"

"You still believe Angela was lying about your partner?"

"Ex-partner," I stressed. *"Tommy, what's going on?"*

"Why don't you have a look at what I've found? It will explain everything."

"I just got home." I glanced at my watch, which read 6:15. *"I'm going to grab a bite of dinner, but I can be over in an hour."*

"Not tonight," he said. *"My band jams on Mondays. How about tomorrow night?"*

"Fine," I said. *"Tomorrow at eight."*

Tommy's condo was in the heart of Broadway—"the" neighborhood for the twenty-something singles to live in. Barefoot in jeans and a black mock turtleneck, Tommy met me at his door. Following him to the living room, I realized that whether he rented or owned, he must have been doing more than all right to have afforded the renovated three-bedroom, split-level apartment with its striking view of downtown.

"You want a drink or something?" he asked, kneeling in front of a stack of rolling papers and a pile of weed on the coffee table.

"No, thanks," I said, watching him roll a joint.

Finished rolling, he offered it to me. *"Want first honors?"* I shook my head.

"You don't mind, do you?" he asked, but he had the joint lit before I could reply. He took two puffs, then croaked, *"Believe it or not, this stuff is what keeps me sane these days."*

"What's threatening your sanity, Tommy?"

He coughed as he said, *"Psychiatrists. More specifically, your partners."*

"Ex-partners," I said, wondering how he knew to include Nichol in his wrath.

"Whatever." He stood up. *"I want to show you something."*

I followed Tommy upstairs to a spacious guest room that filled the entire upper floor. He walked to the far corner of the room where an old oak roll-top desk stood. *"Used to be my dad's,"* he grunted as he took another toke. *"Angela stayed here during her last days. I didn't touch a thing after she died until . . ."* Another toke and cough. *"A couple of* days ago, I decided it was time to clean out her stuff. When I went through the desk . . ." He slid back the curved cover that hid its contents. "I found these."

From the pastel textured sleeves, I recognized the journals on the desktop as hers.

He tapped the top volume. "The first one dates back to three years ago." He lifted it up and held it out for me. "Why don't you have a read-through? Real page-turners."

"I know Stanley Kolberg abused your sister," I said, but didn't reach for it.

He waved the book at me. "But don't you want to know the details?"

"She told me some."

His laugh turned into another cough. "Don't you owe it to her to know all of it?"

I stood motionless. Tommy dropped the diary back on the pile and started for the door. "You can let yourself out." With that, he was gone, leaving the pungent smell of pot hanging in his wake.

I sat at the desk. For a long time, I stared at the journals in front of me, remembering my promise to Angela that I would never read them.

But some promises were meant to be broken. I reached for the top volume.

Angela's journal read like an engrossing autobiography. None of it came as news to me, but each neatly printed word that laid out Angela's hurt and helplessness cut me a little more.

In the first volume, she wrote of the joy of finally finding someone who "understood her so completely" as Stanley. Her trust in him jumped off the pages, sounding like a schoolgirl's crush on a teacher. One entry read: "Thanks to Dr. K, I understand that I'm not to blame. Daddy took advantage of a defenseless child, and everything that followed—everything!—happened because of him. Not me!"

As the entries progressed, storm clouds rolled into Angela's writing, coinciding with Stanley's escalating abuse. From the start, she had seen through his attempts at passing *his perversion off as therapy. Her mistake seemed to lie in not recognizing how dangerous he was sooner.* "I whipped Stanley again today," *she wrote in one entry in the second volume.* "He makes me do it harder and longer each time. It's gross the way his skin bleeds. And all those scars on his back! I know he's been into it for a long time. He tells me to pretend I'm hitting Daddy. As if! He's getting his rocks off, whether I'm thinking about Dad or breakfast. Still, Stanley has helped me so much. I can deal with this. I've dealt with worse. And besides, aren't all geniuses eccentric?"

But her tolerance for Stanley's "eccentricity" faded as the spiral of abuse escalated. Soon, no longer was he "Dr. K" or "Stanley," just "He." "He's so fucked up. Twice now, He's brought that beanstalk of a partner over, so I can piss on him. And more and more, He wants to do the hurting. Today, He strapped me to the wall and whipped me until I thought I was going to pass out. It made the bastard come like a teenage boy. But what can I do? He holds 'my little secret' over me like it was one of his whips."

Then I got to the entry dated May 7. "He's bored with just hitting. Today, He seared my back with a candle. I didn't know pain like that existed. But my fucking skin is indestructible. It just keeps healing."

Below that paragraph, Angela's ink had switched from blue to black but there was no new date heading, only a space with a couple of stars. "Things never got this bad with Daddy. Even if I reported Him to someone, I'm sure He would talk his way out of it. There's too much at stake for Tommy. Funny. I'm not scared anymore. I've even stopped hating Him. He's just a pathetic, dirty old man. But I don't sleep anymore. I'm so tired. And I don't care. I really don't. I think it would be best for everyone if I just drifted off."

On second glance, I recognized the date of the entry. It was the same day I met Angela. The day she was admitted to Swedish Hospital for an antidepressant overdose.

I squirmed through the final volume, because it chronicled her therapy with me. I felt like a peeping Tom when I read: "After Him, I never imagined trusting a shrink again.

But Dr. A is different. He cares about me without wanting anything. How rare is that?!?" Even the passages that documented the improvements in her life were tough to read, because I knew they were akin to branches on a river temporarily holding back a raft as it drifted toward a waterfall.

I was relieved to reach the end of the volume and discover that it stopped six weeks short of her death. I dreaded the idea of reading her take on our run-in the day before she died. Still, the abrupt ending made no sense. Why had she stopped chronicling events during the last six weeks of her life, when she had so meticulously documented everything right up to the very day of her previous suicide attempt?

I stood from the desk and stretched my neck and back, which ached from hunching over for so long. Two hours had passed since Tommy left me with the books, and even the stale smell of marijuana had cleared from the attic. I left the journals where I'd found them and headed downstairs to the living room. "Tommy?" I called out, once I got there.

A door opened and Tommy stepped out in the hallway. "You read them, huh?"

I nodded.

"She didn't make it up about Kolberg, did she?"

"No."

"If you were me, what would you do?" he asked.

"I'd turn the son of a bitch in."

"To?"

"The Washington State Department of Health, for starters."

With hands tucked in his pockets, he shrugged. "And what would they do?"

"Investigate. And if they found enough evidence to substantiate the complaint, they'd ban him from practice and launch a criminal complaint."

"If," Tommy snorted.

"I'd testify in a heartbeat, Tommy. You've got the diaries.

And we both know there are bound to have been others. The case against him would be very strong."

When Tommy finally spoke, his voice was emotionless but definite. "Know what? I think I should just kill him."

13

"OH, DEV . . . HI," I heard Claire murmur in a husky morning voice so sexy that I forgave the phone for waking me. "The alarm must have been set wrong," she said, clearing her throat and, to my disappointment, freeing the frog from her voice.

When I rolled over, she was sitting up in the bed with the sheet pulled to her chest. Her hair was tussled and a few strands drifted over her eyes. I reached a hand to her adorable face, but she batted it away with a smile and brought a finger to her lips.

Listening to the receiver, her face flushed. "Yeah, I guess Joel must have slept in, too." She fired a warning glance in my direction that kept me from piping up. "Twenty minutes. Tops."

She sprang from the bed, but grabbed the top sheet and wrapped it around her in an effort of morning-after modesty. "We've been involved for less than twelve hours, and you're already getting me in trouble at work," she complained with a big grin.

"Don't blame me. You're the one who went and slept with the hired help."

We arrived at Dev's office at 9:30. Leaning back in his chair, he appraised us with a knowing nod but didn't speculate—not aloud, anyway—on the reasons for our lateness. "Anya's boyfriend Nikki is proving to be quite the slippery bastard," he said. "If you believe his Russian friends, they haven't seen him since their dodge-ball days on the streets of Moscow."

"Now what?" I asked.

"We should have ballistics on the gun we pulled from Krutov's dresser by the afternoon." Dev stretched in his chair. "Meantime, we put a bit more pressure on Krutov's friends. One of them is bound to cough Nikki up like a hairball."

"Krutov will turn up soon enough," Claire predicted. "For now, we ought to go talk to Bonnie Hubbard."

I frowned. "Why Bonnie?"

"She worked for both Kolberg and Nichol," Claire said. "She might know something about Krutov. We haven't spoken to her since Nichol died."

We pulled up to Bonnie Hubbard's bungalow in Newport Hills. The house was an anomaly on a street of much newer and bigger houses in a neighborhood where Bonnie's salary would have barely covered the property taxes. I vaguely recalled that she'd inherited the house from her parents. She maintained it meticulously with a spotless exterior and a perfectly groomed landscape.

Stanley's former secretary met us at her screen door. Plump and of average height, Bonnie had short gray hair she kept in a bob that hadn't been in style since Dorothy Hamill won a gold medal. She wore navy stretch pants with a light blue cardigan. In her mid-sixties, her fussy grandmotherly appearance hadn't changed an iota in the ten years I'd known her. She struck me as having a fixed physical age; one of those people who looks old at thirty and young at seventy because nothing in their dress, shape, posture, or attitude changes during the intervening years.

"Dr. Ashman!" Bonnie said with embarrassed delight. For the first time ever, she threw her arms around me and gave me a quick hug. "It's so good to see you."

"How are you doing, Bonnie?" I asked.

"I'm holding up." She smiled bravely. "It's so horrible what happened to Dr. Kolberg and Dr. Nichol. Such good men."

I nodded my condolences.

"Everything changed after you left, Dr. Ashman." Bonnie heaved a deep sigh. "Dr. Kolberg was never the same—" She stopped abruptly, as if betraying a friend's confidence.

We followed Bonnie into her living room, which I imagined would've made the cover of *Spinster's Home and Garden* if such a magazine existed. From the floral fabric sofas down to the abundant doilies and "collector's" ceramic plates, the room was all of a piece. She'd already laid out a selection of home-baked shortbread cookies. As soon as we entered the room, she poured the kettle in the pot to steep the tea.

Once our hands were occupied with tea and cookies, Claire began. "Does the name Nikolai or Nikki Krutov mean anything to you?"

"Krutov . . . Krutov . . . ," she mumbled, racking her memory. Finally, she shook her head.

Claire reached inside her notebook and withdrew an enlargement of Krutov's mug shot.

Bonnie's eyes widened. "Yes, I do remember him."

Claire put her notebook aside. "Where from?"

"He came in to see Dr. Kolberg one day."

"Why?"

"I don't know. But at first, I assumed he was a new patient I didn't know about." She smiled faintly. "Dr. Kolberg would do that to me all the time."

"Why'd you think he was a patient?" Dev asked.

"He had that manner about him." She squinted at the photo. "Like so many of Dr. Kolberg's patients."

I knew she was being diplomatic. "You mean royally pissed, right?"

Bonnie giggled. "A lot of them were like that. Volcanoes ready to erupt. The carpet in our waiting room was worn threadbare from their pacing."

"How did Dr. Kolberg react to Krutov?" Claire asked.

"'React'?" Bonnie shook her head, bewildered.

"Did he seem scared or nervous around the man?"

"No," Bonnie said. "They talked for a while and then Dr. Kolberg left with him."

"He left with Krutov?" I couldn't contain my surprise.

Bonnie nodded. "It was a Friday afternoon. Dr. Kolberg was done for the day."

"Bonnie, when was this?" I asked.

"Nine months ago. September fifteenth, to be exact."

"How do you remember the date?" I asked.

"Because Dr. Kolberg had a terrible seizure that evening. He ended up in the hospital." She looked at me as if I should have had the date burned in my memory, too. "He broke his arm and had those awful black eyes."

Claire and Dev exchanged a glance that Bonnie picked up on. "You don't think this man beat him up?" Bonnie pointed at Krutov's mug shot. "It wasn't unusual for Dr. Kolberg to have seizures. He'd have no warning that they were coming. Sometimes, he'd really hurt himself. Isn't that so, Dr. Ashman?"

No, I thought, the hurting was done by whoever was wielding the whip, bat, or fist used on Stanley—not some invented seizure disorder—but I just nodded sympathetically.

"You never saw Nikki Krutov again?" Claire asked.

She shook her head.

Dev put down his cup and folded his hands behind his head. "How about Wayne Hacking?"

"Oh, sure, Wayne," she said, her voice full of fondness for the man who had once butchered his previous girlfriend and her sister.

"Did Wayne have much contact with Nichol?" Dev asked.

"With Dr. Nichol?" Bonnie frowned. "Not that I'm aware of."

"No tension between them, huh?"

"Tension?" Bonnie laughed. "I can't imagine Wayne tense. Such an easygoing fellow. Despite his tragic childhood." She leaned forward to share her gossip in a near whisper. "When he was barely twelve, his entire family—both parents and a younger brother—all died in a house fire. Wayne spent the rest of his childhood in foster care."

"Yeah, fine," Dev said, sounding anything but moved by Hacking's plight. "How about the Shovel—" He quickly corrected himself. "Ron Weaver—did he and Dr. Nichol interact?"

Bonnie shook her head. "Mr. Weaver is such a private man. He never said so much as good morning to me. I doubt he shared a word with Dr. Nichol."

"Bonnie, can you think of anyone else who had a grudge against the doctors?"

Bonnie stared at the tea cozy in front of her. "Honestly, no one comes to mind. But Dr. Kolberg did see all those anger-management patients." She hinted at their dangerousness with an arched eyebrow. "But Dr. Nichol's patients were all so polite. I can't think of—" she stopped in mid-phrase. Her jaw fell slightly.

"What, Bonnie?" Claire asked.

"Dr. Ashman, remember that poor girl who took her own life, Angela Connor?"

"I remember," I snapped, hoping my frigid stare might discourage her.

"Her brother came to the office about two months ago." She shook her head. "He was most upset."

Claire turned to me. "Joel, I thought you'd already left the practice by then."

Bonnie waved her hand. "Not to see Dr. Ashman," she said. "He came looking for Dr. Kolberg. But I told him he wasn't there. When he saw Dr. Nichol, he stormed past me and into his office. So angry. I could hear him shouting from my desk."

"What was he shouting about?" Claire asked.

"Something to do with Angela. I didn't hear the details." Then she lowered her voice, and nodded understandingly. "It was only three or four months after his sister's suicide. After he left, I went to check on Dr. Nichol. He told me he was okay, but he was white as a ghost. Very shaken, I could see."

"Did Tommy Connor ever come back to see Kolberg?" Dev asked.

"Not that I know of, Sergeant."

We thanked Bonnie and headed for the door. She stopped me with a gentle tug at my sleeve. "I couldn't imagine a better boss, or a more wonderful man than Dr. Kolberg." Her teary eyes pleaded. "I so hope that you can find his killer."

I nodded and forced a smile, then hurried after the others.

Once inside Claire's car, Dev commented, "Sounds like Krutov laid an old-fashioned shit-kicking on Stanley back in September."

"Big deal," Claire said. "Kolberg probably enjoyed having his wrist broken."

"Remember what Stanley's wrist ended up looking like at the crime scene?" I said. "Think that's just a coincidence?"

Claire glanced over her shoulder at me. "Why would Krutov wait nine months to finish the job?"

"Maybe he's a born procrastinator," Dev said.

She shook her head. "It sounds like Tommy Connor had a major bone to pick with Nichol *and* Kolberg. I just don't buy his story anymore that he never met Kolberg."

"Before going down that road, let's talk to Nikki," Dev said.

"How do we find him?" Claire asked.

Dev just grinned confidently.

Twenty-five minutes later, we were back inside Pushtin's gaudy Queen Anne–style condo, facing an unshaven unhappy Dirty Serge. Wearing a black Armani bathrobe, he sat on one of his black leather couches cross-legged and arms folded. With his jet-black mop of hair and thick five o'clock shadow, he almost blended into the sofa. "What now, Sherlock?" he demanded.

"We need information." Dev's tone made it clear he was telling, not asking.

Pushtin heaved a martyr's sigh. "Still more information?"

"Where's Nikki Krutov?"

Pushtin stretched his tree-trunk arms. "How the fuck do I know?"

Dev stared at Pushtin. The threat in his silence was palpable.

Pushtin roughly scratched the back of his head. "Nikki does some work for the Dreznik brothers." He rolled his eyes. "Croats! Go wake *them* up."

"Where do we find them?" Claire asked.

"They have a warehouse on the south side." Pushtin eyed Claire with more indifference than usual, like a lion who had already gorged himself but might be interested again later. "Maybe Krutov and his Croat friends are there."

"Lots of warehouses down there," Dev said. "Which one would Krutov be in?"

"By the railroad tracks." Pushtin yawned. "You want Sergei to draw a map?"

"That's asking way too much of you." Dev stepped over to the couch, grabbed a lapel on Pushtin's bathrobe, and pulled. "Why don't you just take us there?"

Half an hour later, wearing a shiny track suit and still seething, Pushtin squeezed in beside me in the back of Claire's car. I had to keep my window down to ventilate the smell of his aftershave. Staring out his window, Pushtin grunted directions. Off Atlantic, we pulled up to a dilapidated warehouse, complete with boarded windows and graffiti-covered walls. Pushtin pointed at it and growled, "The Croats' castle."

We waited in the car until two police cars pulled up behind us. Claire and Dev climbed out to join the four uniformed cops and the dog handler. His massive German shepherd sat quietly by his side, on the street in front of the warehouse's door.

Faced with the prospect of being holed up in the back of the car with Pushtin and his nauseating cologne, I abandoned the agreed-on plan and hopped out of the car after the cops. At the sight of me, Claire shook her head angrily and pointed to the car.

"I'll be careful." I nodded at the dog. "I'll stick close to Cujo."

Claire eyed me icily and then turned her attention back to the metal door that Dev was banging on with the side of his fist. A minute passed before the door opened a crack. "What?" the voice from the crack asked.

Dev stuck his badge up to the gap. "Seattle Police."

"And?"

"And . . ." Dev waved the badge. "Open the fucking door, Dreznik!"

The door opened wider and out stepped a fat man in a double-breasted suit with big sweat stains around his shirt collar. Balding, Alex Dreznik had grown his hair long at the sides and tied it back in a ludicrous ponytail. "What you looking for?" he asked.

"Nikki Krutov," Dev said.

"Haven't seen him in long time," Dreznik said in a thick Slavic accent.

"I've seen your rap sheet, Dreznik. So you'll pardon me for assuming that you're full of shit." Dev walked by him and into the dingy warehouse with the rest of us in tow.

Inside the musty, open main floor, boxes and crates were piled high in some places and strewn haphazardly elsewhere. Two teenaged boys stood in the center of the room, packing newspaper-wrapped parcels into boxes. Hearing us approach, they dropped their packages and turned to us with jittery guilty stares.

The fat mobster tried to block our path, but Dev and Claire sidestepped him and headed for the boys. They separated allowing Claire to pass between them. She stopped at one of the boxes they had packed. Reaching inside, she withdrew a package. She unwrapped it slowly, like a much-anticipated birthday present, and held out its contents. "Look at how the factories are shipping new car stereos these days."

"Know what?" Dev scowled at Dreznik. "My stereo was ripped off a little while ago. Maybe I'll buy one off you. Hell, maybe I'll just buy my old one back from you."

"Couple of punks sell us those," Dreznik faltered. "We don't ask no questions—"

"Where's Nikki Krutov?!" Dev snapped.

"Okay, okay." Dreznik held both hands above his head. "Nikki is here this morning. But he left, maybe two hours."

Dev waved for the dog handler, who joined the gathering. Reaching in his bag, the handler pulled out the T-shirt Dev had confiscated from Krutov's apartment and held it up to the dog's snout. The shepherd buried his nose in it. As soon as the handler pulled it away, the dog leapt up to his hind legs and strained at his lead. Once untethered, the dog fired off like a rocket. He darted around the main floor of the warehouse before focusing on the far left corner of the room where empty crates were discarded.

Growling and whining, the dog squeezed his thick shoulders between the boxes. With his nose glued to the ground, he crawled over to the second to last crate piled against the wall. He sniffed and scratched it, barking fiercely. He jumped up and rested his front paws on top of the three-foot-high box, trying to pry off the lid with his paw and snout.

The handler snapped his fingers and said, "Down, Titan." In a heartbeat, the dog switched from rabid to docile, hopping off the lid and trotting over to sit by his master's side.

Dev walked up to the crate and yanked the lid off. "C'mon out, Nikki," he said in a voice so bored it sounded as if he spent his entire day pulling suspects out of cartons.

A pair of hands poked out, followed by a head and a neck. Two uniformed cops walked up and jerked the rest of Krutov out by his armpits.

We left Krutov for the patrolmen to bring in and headed back to Claire's car. Pushtin was nowhere to be seen. We drove back to SPD headquarters. As soon as we arrived at Homicide, the receptionist greeted Dev with an official-looking fax. He scanned through it and then looked up at Claire and me with a shake of his head. "The markings on the bullet used on Kolberg don't match the barrel of Krutov's .38."

"Maybe he changed guns," I suggested.

"Yeah, maybe," Dev said skeptically.

I assumed my position behind the two-way mirror and watched Claire and Dev lead Krutov into the interview room. Krutov was younger and better looking than his mug shot made him seem, but the photo had well captured his wary defiance. Flanked by the detectives, he sat perfectly still in his chair and kept his hands folded in front of him, appearing not the least bit intimidated by a process he probably had sat through a hundred times before.

"When was the last time you saw Stanley Kolberg?" Claire asked.

He shrugged. "Maybe eight months."

"Why did you see him?" Claire asked.

Krutov closed his eyes as if he might drift off. "Why do you think?"

"Listen, Nikki, we're in no mood for your shit," Claire said.

"To talk about how he burned Anya," he said.

"And what happened?"

"We talked."

Dev joined the fray. "Nikki, I understand where you're coming from on this one. What he did to Anya . . . If that was my girl, I would've killed him, too."

Krutov chuckled. "I didn't kill him."

"Not that day." Dev nodded. "You just smacked him around and broke his wrist. What I don't get is why you waited eight more months to kill him."

Krutov smiled, exposing chipped and yellowing teeth. "You got the wrong guy."

"Where were you the evening of Monday, May seventh, Nikki?" Claire demanded.

"I can't remember."

"Can you remember what you were doing two evenings ago?" Claire asked.

Krutov shook his head. "I want to see my lawyer."

"Nikki, you mention lawyers and suddenly we're talking reams of paperwork," Dev groaned. "And with each page, you can add a year or two to your sentence. Let's see." He listed with his fingers. "We got the drugs you left at your place. The stolen property at the warehouse. Resisting arrest—"

"I didn't resist arrest," Krutov snorted.

"You didn't exactly help us. And I think you took a swing at the police dog. So we'll throw in a cruelty-to-animals misdemeanor." Dev glanced at his hands. "Okay. What else? Customs fraud. Parole violation. Hell, we don't need the murder rap to—" Dev stopped in mid-sentence when the room's door opened.

Dev got up and walked to the doorway, where he spoke to a man for a moment, and then gestured for Claire to join him. They left the room without a word of explanation to Krutov.

Krutov tapped his fingers on the table, showing his first signs of alarm. He stood up and began to pace, stopping every so often to stare at the mirror. He must have known someone was behind the glass but all he would've seen was his own hardened face looking back at him.

After ten minutes, a heavyset uniformed cop walked into the room. "We're going back to your cell," he said.

"That's it?" Krutov frowned. "I'm done?"

"Guess so," the guard said, and pointed to the door.

I caught up with Claire and Dev in the hallway. "Well?"

"I just got a call from Narcotics," Dev said. "They've been watching Krutov and the Drezniks for the past month. The night Kolberg died, Krutov was downtown trying to unload some crack. No way he could have killed him."

Claire nodded as if she had expected as much all along. "Time to take a much closer look at Tommy Connor."

14

LIKE A HARBINGER OF BAD WEATHER, by early evening my lacerated right wrist ached worse than before. Sitting at Claire's kitchen table, I picked at a plate of Indian food without much interest.

Claire frowned. "What's wrong, Joel?"

I rolled a piece of chicken vindaloo around the plate with a fork. "I took a couple of painkillers for my arm. Now my appetite's gone."

"You seem a little off." She bit her lip and swallowed. "Nothing to do with . . . what happened between us last night?"

"Definitely not." I forced a smile. "It's everything else. Especially the sudden official interest in Tommy."

"Oh?"

"He's a decent guy," I said. "His family has been through enough."

"We don't have any proof he's involved, yet."

"You think he's our guy, don't you?"

"I don't know." She smiled sympathetically. "But it

doesn't matter much what I think. Time will tell." She viewed me tentatively. "You and I are okay, though, huh?"

"Yeah." This time my smile came naturally. I reached over and ran my fingers along her wrist and hand.

"I've eaten enough." She flashed her perfect teeth, then stood up and walked over to my side of the table. She leaned over and kissed me on the lips, sharing a faint taste of curry. "Did the painkillers take away your appetite for everything?"

I pulled her close and kissed her again. "I didn't take the whole bottle."

Laughing, she grabbed my good hand with both of hers and started to pull me up and toward her bedroom. "Come on."

I resisted her tugging. "The appetite is there, but my arm is really aching. Any chance of a rain check for tomorrow?"

"Sure." She let go of my hand. "I think I'll turn in now," she said with a trace of hurt in her voice. She pecked me on the cheek and then walked to her room, closing the door behind her.

I sat at the table reflecting on Claire's paradoxical nature—tough as nails in many respects but so vulnerable in her approach to our new relationship. I suspected that her insecurity had to be attributable, at least in part, to an ex-husband who had trapped her between both sides of the law. I had a sinking feeling that I might end up reopening the same wound.

Walking down the hallway, I hesitated in front of her bedroom door. In truth, my arm wasn't the issue. Now that my dormant sex drive had reawakened, I longed to climb back into her bed, but I knew this would further muddy the waters, so I kept walking.

Pushing open the door to the spare bedroom, the hinges whined loudly in response. Earlier, I'd volunteered to fix the creak but who was I kidding? I lived in a house whose stairs cried out with every step for the past four years, and I still hadn't done anything about it.

I climbed in bed and pulled the sheets and comforter tight around me. Alone, the bed felt cold and empty. For the next three hours I tossed and turned. My thoughts drifted from Claire to my wife. I wondered what Loren would've made of recent developments. Not as much as I had. Lor was one of the most forgiving people I had ever met.

At two in the morning, still wide awake, my thoughts were interrupted by a dim noise outside the window. It was so soft that I might not have noticed it if my hearing acuity hadn't been heightened by the room's utter blackness. I sat up and listened. It was definitely a shuffling noise, like the sound of window wipers in a gentle rain. At first I thought it might be a cat or a dog out on the scaffolding that besieged Claire's building, but I realized the sound was too plodding and heavy for an animal.

The spare bedroom's thick blinds were designed to keep out the eastern-exposure morning sunlight. They covered the windows to the point where I couldn't make out so much as a shadow through them. I concentrated, but from the loudening shuffle of feet, I couldn't differentiate the sound of kids fooling around on the scaffolding from that of an approaching killer.

The noise grew. My throat thickened. My heart slammed against my ribcage. Aware of the throb in my arm, this time I wasn't so quick to dismiss my fear as paranoia. I considered keeping my head down and waiting out the noise, when a bleak thought dawned on me: What if it were the knifeman outside, but instead of my room he crawled into Claire's?

I slid my feet over the side of the bed and slowly stood. Creeping to the door, I stopped suddenly when I realized the screaming hinges would wipe out any chance of slipping out of the room unnoticed to warn Claire. I tiptoed back to the window, held my ear inches from the glass, and listened. At first, I heard nothing. Then I detected a padding noise, softer than what I'd heard earlier, with the rhythm of rapid footsteps.

I gently pushed the Venetian blind aside until I had a sliver of a view out the window. A weak light reflecting off the commercial signs from the street lamps below dimly illuminated the scaffolding, but I couldn't see anyone. I pushed the shade further back and peered to either side. Still nothing. On my next attempt, I shoved the blind out of the way and stuck my nose to the window. No one.

I unlocked the window's latch and pushed, praying it was better oiled than the door hinges. It opened silently. I stuck my head out. I glanced to the right. Nothing. I looked to the left. A shadowy figure stood at the end of the scaffolding.

Then I saw the gun.

I jerked my head back into the room and dropped to my knees. I waited on all fours, slowed my breathing, and hoped the pounding in my chest didn't really sound as loud as the cymbals I heard in my ears.

I heard the rapid thumping of feet running along the planks toward my room. I jumped to my feet and dove over the bed, landing painfully on my right side. Lying on the ground, I desperately groped the surface of the nightstand with my left hand, feeling for anything solid. All I came up with was the clock radio. I grabbed it, brought it to my chest, and yanked the plug out of the wall. I lay on the floor, clutching the pathetic weapon and waiting for the inevitable.

When I heard the noise of someone climbing through my window, a surge of anger replaced my fear. Fuck it! I thought. This bastard is going to get a mouthful of clock radio before I die. I pushed myself up, ignoring the pain in my right hand, into a crouch. Ready to attack.

Steps approached the bed. My temples pounded.

Just as I tightened to pounce, the bedside lamp flicked on.

"Joel?" Claire stood wide-eyed on the other side of the bed, pointing her gun at me.

Still kneeling, I looked at the clock radio in my hand. Then I started to laugh.

Claire's hand fell to her side. The bewilderment on her lips gave way to a broad smile. "What were you planning to do? Stun me with a weather and traffic report?"

"I was hoping to repulse you with John Tesh music." I giggled, giddy with relief.

"I don't know why we find this so funny," Claire choked

out between laughs. "Someone was out there." She pointed her gun at the window.

Regaining my composure, I asked, "Did you see anyone?"

"No. But I heard him scuttling down the scaffolding as soon as I got out there."

"Was it *him*?"

Claire shrugged, but I think we both knew it was.

Claire tucked her gun into the waistband of her sweats. "We probably should get out of here."

I climbed to my feet and approached. "He's not coming back tonight." I pointed at her gun. I kept moving until our faces touched. I brought my lips to hers. "Thank you," I said.

"For what?" she looked away, shyly.

"Protecting me."

"Oh," she said, returning the smile. "Just doing my job."

I put my hand behind her neck and rubbed softly, then planted another long kiss on her lips. "Claire, I need you."

"Mmmm," she moaned. "I'm not sure that's in my job description."

"It is now," I said and pressed against her. Ignoring the hard metal digging into my lower abdomen, I pulled her toward the bed.

"Careful, cowboy," she said, pulling the gun from her waistband. "Could lead to a tragic mishap."

"The risk adds to the thrill," I murmured, still pulling.

She placed the gun on the nightstand just as I dragged her down to the bed on top of me. I left the undressing for her. Barely breaking off our embrace, she had us naked in no time. She was on top of me again. And as her lithe body arched above me, I felt a different, but equally welcome, wave of relief sweep over me.

Watching her sleep beside me, my earlier doubts dissipated. For the first time in three years, I didn't feel lonely. I wanted to be with Claire. The sudden happiness was like a reprieve. I forgot about the footsteps on the scaffolding, Claire's semiautomatic on the nightstand, and even the bloody mess at my old office.

I awoke the next morning to the smell of coffee and French toast. Rolling over in the bed, I noticed the gun was gone. In spite of only four hours of sleep, I didn't feel tired at all. Even my arm hurt less. The world was a sunny place.

Before getting out of bed, I grabbed for the bedside phone and called home to pick up my messages. There were several calls from concerned friends and colleagues as word of my stabbing got around. All the calls were welcome. Until the last one.

The second I heard his voice, my skies clouded over again. "Dr. Ashman, it's Dr. Charles Hollands from the Washington State Health Department. I was hoping you would call me at your earliest convenience."

Although I had a strong hunch as to why he was phoning, I decided to enjoy breakfast before returning his call. But it was no use; his message had stolen my appetite. After the meal, I made up my mind to ignore his message on the slim hope the medical bureaucrat would leave it at that.

Claire and I arrived at Dev's office shortly after 8 A.M. Dev listened to Claire describe our nocturnal prowler without interrupting. When she finished, he shook his head angrily and growled, "Why the hell don't I learn about these developments in real time?"

Claire folded her arms over her chest. "What would have been the point of waking you at three in the morning, Dev? The guy was long gone. Besides, we don't know it was connected."

"Oh, it was connected, all right," Dev said with finality, but the anger left his face. "I wonder how he knew where to find you." He rested his hands behind his head and broke into a slight grin. "Sounds like we better find new digs for you two. I don't want the department to end up on the hook for getting bloodstains out of your carpets and curtains."

Claire rolled her eyes. "Your concern is touching."

"Let's go ask Tommy what he was up to this morning," said Dev.

"Tommy wouldn't have done that," I said.

"Don't bet on it, Doc," Dev sighed. "One thing I've

learned on this job—you never know what people will do when pushed far enough."

"Not Tommy," I said flatly.

Claire laid a hand on my shoulder. "We still have to check."

The phone rang. Dev grabbed it. "Homicide, Devonshire." He listened a moment. "Yeah," he said with surprise. "He's right here." He held the phone out to me.

Feeling as bewildered as Dev looked, I reached for the phone. "Dr. Ashman, it's Charles Hollands with the State Health Department."

My stomach sank at hearing his voice. "Yes, Dr. Hollands. How can I help you?"

"Sorry to track you down but I couldn't reach you at home, Dr. Ashman," Hollands said. "As you are aware, I am not wholly comfortable with the extent to which the police department has delved into the Health Department's files."

"Very aware," I said, hoping it was the reason for his call.

But of course, it wasn't. "When I read about Dr. Nichol's death, I realized the detectives would insist on searching his records as well," Hollands continued. "After carefully weighing the pros and cons, I've decided to be proactive in releasing information I'm convinced the police are bound to discover anyway." He cleared his throat. "Information that might prove helpful to your investigation."

"What information?"

"Two months ago, we received a verbal complaint against Dr. Nichol by a patient's brother," Hollands said. "I told you about him when we last met. Thomas Connor. You might remember that he registered a similar complaint against Dr. Kolberg, his sister's psychiatrist. Mr. Connor alleged that both Dr. Kolberg and Dr. Nichol had molested his sister. But as with the complaint against Dr. Kolberg, Mr. Connor never followed up in writing on the complaint against Dr. Nichol."

Claire and Dev were both staring at me after I hung up the phone. "Tommy Connor filed a complaint against Nichol, too," I said matter-of-factly.

As soon as I'd finished recapping Hollands's call, Dev started for the door. "Now we've got enough for a judge."

The same team who'd searched Nichol's condominium reconvened in front of Tommy's. In jeans and a Hawaiian shirt, Tommy met us at his door with hands on hips. "What do you want?" he snapped.

"We have a search warrant," Claire said, holding up the official paper for him.

Tommy walked back into his condo without responding.

As the team scoured his spacious home, he sat with feet up on the couch, his body language alternating between disinterest and disdain. When one of the CSI techs held up the baggie of marijuana he'd found in the kitchen, Tommy snorted a laugh. He stopped laughing when Claire emerged from the spare room holding the stack of Angela's journals. "Those are private!" He jumped to his feet. "They have nothing to do with your investigation."

"They're your sister's diaries, right?"

"So?"

"They might help establish motive." Claire's master's degree in criminology resurfaced. "Legally, we're obliged to seize them."

Tommy looked down at his feet. "It's not right," he said quietly.

After the rest of the team left, Claire and I sat on the sofa across from Tommy while Dev filled out the leather chair between us. Tommy's piercing blue-gray eyes—Angela's eyes—assessed the detectives but ignored me.

"Dr. Nichol's secretary said you and Nichol had a screaming match a few months back," Claire said.

Tommy shrugged. "I was the only one screaming."

Claire nodded. "And how did Dr. Nichol respond?"

"He was scared shitless," he snorted.

"Because you threatened to kill him," Claire said evenly.

"No," he said. "Because I threatened to expose him for what he was."

"Ohhh," Claire said, as if she suddenly remembered. "Nichol molested your sister."

"He did worse than that," Tommy said very quietly.

"Where were you Tuesday evening, Tommy?"

"Here, working."

"Alone?"

Tommy nodded.

"Same as the night Kolberg died," Dev chimed in. "Isn't that so?"

"Like pretty much every evening," Tommy grunted. "I work out of my home."

"Just a coincidence, huh, Tommy?" Dev flashed a sly grin.

"Whatever."

I shifted uncomfortably in my seat. I could see from Tommy's mood that Dev's baiting was going to get to him.

"In my experience, coincidences are a lot like fishing stories," Dev said. "Everyone's got 'em, but few have the pictures to back 'em up."

I wanted to grab Tommy's attention with my eyes, but he wouldn't look. "I must be lying, right?" he said. "I've got no alibi for either murder. And a decent motive for both."

"Better than decent," Claire said.

"Yeah." Tommy nodded, still staring at Dev. "I'm glad they're dead."

Dev yawned. "That's good. You don't want to be second-guessing yourself now."

Tommy sprung to his feet. "Where's your proof? Do you have a witness? Did you find a scrap of evidence here?"

Dev chuckled. "Trick is, first you find your guy. The proof always follows."

"You think Angela was the first patient these assholes fucked with? Why don't you look for some other victim or family who got totally screwed over? Or better still, just let it go. They got exactly what they had coming to them."

"Did they?" Claire asked.

He turned to her fiercely. "Do you have any idea what Kolberg did to my sister?"

"Not really," she said in a tone that invited explanation.

Tommy hovered over the coffee table, shifting his angry eyes from Claire to Dev. "He tricked her into trusting him. Seduced her with empathy. Then he fucked with her mind before starting on her body. That wasn't good enough. He had to destroy her. And he brought his sick partner in to help." Tommy's face went beet red. He took a huge breath. "She didn't stand a chance. He drove her to suicide, twice." Then he shook his head vehemently. "No, not suicide. He killed her, sure as if he threw her off that bridge."

"Did Angela tell you about this abuse?" Claire asked.

"If she had, don't you think I would've stopped him?" Tommy's voice cracked. "I only read about it in her journal. After she was already gone."

"That was proof enough?" Dev yawned. "The writing of an unreliable psych patient?"

"It happened, you bastard!" Tommy kicked the coffee table. It teetered for a moment before dropping back into place.

Dev rolled his head from side to side, as if bored. "Okay, Tommy, I believe you. It happened. Kolberg and Nichol killed your sister. And you knew this months before either of them died, but you did nothing."

Tommy's lip trembled, but he said nothing.

"Some brother you are," Dev said with a slow shake of his head. "They violate her like she wasn't even human, and you let them get away with it. Scot-free."

Tommy's nostrils flared and his eyes went wider. "I reported them to the Health Department," he snarled.

Claire nodded. "But last time we met, you told us you didn't follow up on that complaint because you weren't sure whether or not to believe Angela."

Tommy fell back onto the couch with a sigh. "I always believed her."

"So why didn't you do anything about it?" Dev asked.

I held my breath, waiting for Tommy's answer. He just shrugged. "I don't know."

"I think you do, Tommy," Dev said. "What choice did you have? What would any decent brother do?" Suddenly, he was Tommy's ally.

Tommy stared at the floor.

"You were right earlier," Dev said. "Kolberg and Nichol

got what they deserved. Look." He adopted his best car salesman's I'm-going-to-cut-you-a-break-but-it-will-cost-me tone. "I want to tie this case up, but I'm not even sure who the real victims were. You spell out for me how it happened, and I'll talk to the district attorney. He's a friend. I'm thinking you may not need to do much, if any, time considering your mental state. Closest thing I can think of to justifiable homicide."

When Tommy looked up, his redness had dissipated. "I didn't kill them," he said firmly.

"Then why, Tommy?" Claire asked. "If all of what you said is true, explain to us why you didn't follow up on your complaints?"

Tommy glanced at me, his eyes uncertain. Then he turned back to Claire. "Am I under arrest?" he asked calmly.

"Not yet," Dev said. "Not yet."

Tommy stood up and walked past us to his front door and held it open. "Would you please leave now?"

A few moments later, standing in the warm breeze out on the street in front of the building, Dev turned to me. "Doc, you were pretty quiet back there."

I shook my head. "Wouldn't have been appropriate for me to get involved."

Dev nodded noncommittally. "Could you picture Tommy behind the ski mask?"

"No."

"He's the right height and build," Dev argued.

"Even with a mask, I would've recognized him."

"Know what, Doc? When it comes to Tommy, I think you've got blinders on."

Claire looked at me with a supportive nod. "Dev, we have to keep Tommy front and center. No question. But Tommy raised a good point. Probably there were other Angelas in Kolberg and Nichol's practices. Someone else might've had just as good a reason to want them dead. Maybe we should look for other victims."

Dev ran a hand through his unruly salt-and-pepper hair. "We're not the sexual assault team. We investigate homicide, not suicide. Right now, the only victims we're interested in are Kolberg and Nichol."

But to me Angela was far more of a victim than either of those two. Especially considering what I'd learned about her final hours.

A month after Tommy told me he thought he should kill Stanley, my ex-partner was still alive. And would be for another week. I never reported Tommy's threat to the police or warned Stanley, which I suppose could've made me an accessory to murder, but at the time I didn't care what happened to Stanley.

I was preoccupied with Angela's words. The incompleteness of the journals—those missing last six weeks—nagged at me to the point of obsession. I was desperate to better know her state of mind in the days leading up to her death. So I dropped by Tommy's on the weak premise of checking up on him. Standing in the living room, he confronted me. "Dr. Ashman, what's this really about?"

"You said some strong words last time."

"I haven't killed anyone . . . yet."

"You still plan to?"

Ignoring my question, he said, "I took your advice and called the State Health Department."

"What did they say?"

"I spoke to a nice lady. Very sweet. Full of empathy and support." He grunted a laugh. "Didn't believe a fucking word I said."

"Doesn't matter, Tommy. Once they receive the complaint, they have to investigate."

"She told me I have to write a letter first."

"Have you?"

"I'm thinking about it." After a moment, he added, "I went to see them."

"Who? Kolberg and Nichol?"

"Yeah," he said. "Kolberg wasn't there. Just Nichol."

"What did you say?"

"Not nearly enough." His face broke into a bitter grin. "But he got the message. And I am pretty sure he'll pass it on to Kolberg."

"Are you planning to go back to talk to Kolberg?"

"If I go back, it won't be to talk."

After a moment, I cleared my throat. *"I wanted to tell you that I was sorry."*

"For?"

"For telling Angela I didn't believe her."

"You know what gets me?" Tommy said without acknowledging the apology. *"My sister didn't care about herself. She put up with all of Kolberg's crap to protect me."*

"Why did Angela feel she had to protect you?"

He frowned. *"What do you mean?"*

"According to Angela, the day your dad died, you'd snowboarded ahead with your buddies. You would've had witnesses."

"I wasn't with my buddies," Tommy said matter-of-factly. *"I was with Angela. Standing on the edge of the overhang, watching Dad in the gorge below."*

I straightened in surprise. *"Oh?"*

"Look, we never planned to kill him, but I wasn't sorry when he fell into the gully."

"And Angela?"

"For a while, she kind of zoned out. Just kept staring at him. When she focused, she said we had to get help. She started to look for a way down to him."

"What stopped her?"

"Me." His piercing eyes bore into me. "I told her if she tried to go down there she was going to kill herself. And to leave him be. He was only getting what was coming to him."

"What did Angela do?"

"She freaked. Screaming that we couldn't leave him there to die. I had to shake her a couple of times before she calmed down. By the time we reached the bottom of the run, I thought we were on the same page. She didn't say a word when I told the others Dad had gone off to find a way back to the main runs."

I nodded, remembering how in her account Angela had removed her brother entirely from the scene, assuming for herself the role of both the instigator and the silent accomplice. The two of them had been so determined to protect each other. Tommy still was.

"The whole thing was my idea," he said without a trace of remorse. "Didn't stop Angela from blaming herself. The guilt ate her up. Led to her first big depression." He sighed. "Led her into Kolberg's clutches."

I stood from the couch. "Tommy, do you mind if I take another look at her diaries?"

"What are you looking for?"

"I'm not sure."

Tommy nodded without getting up. "They haven't moved."

In Angela's old room, I headed for the roll-top desk. I flipped through the journals again but put them back after a quick scan. They weren't going to help.

I stood up and wandered the room. I didn't expect to find anything, but I felt compelled to look. I searched the dresser drawers, but came up empty. I walked to the closet. Three or four jackets hung inside. The bulky silver nylon jacket was the one I'd seen Angela in most often. I pulled it off the hanger. It felt heavier than I expected. I ran a hand along the oversized front pockets, until I came up against something square and hard in the right pocket. I reached in and pulled out a pastel-sleeved book.

I took it to the desk and laid it beside the others. A perfect match. As soon as I saw the date of the first entry, I knew it followed, to the day, from where the previous one had ended. I knew I had just found the final volume of her diary.

The first two weeks' worth of passages were relatively uninformative. Angela wrote of the same lingering doubts that we'd discussed at the time in therapy. She wore her new lifestyle—the promising job and supportive boyfriend—as uneasily as a beggar might have worn a tux. The sense of unworthiness was classic for an abused patient experiencing a normal relationship. But overall, she came across as hope-

ful. Until I reached the entry from one month before her death. The day Stanley paid a surprise visit.

"He *showed up today out of the blue*," she wrote. "*Didn't say a word, just handed me a letter addressed to the District Attorney and told me to read. The first part went on about how his conscience wouldn't let him cover up what He knew about Daddy's murder. Then it gave these details—mostly bullshit—about how Tommy and I pushed Dad off the ledge. He told me if I didn't stop seeing Dr. A, He'd send the letter. I could see it in His black eyes. He was dead serious.*

"*This is tearing me up. Dr. A has helped me so much. But I've got no choice. It's not worth ruining Tommy's life over.*"

Reading on, I learned in painstaking detail how Angela's life had crumbled in the weeks after she'd dropped out of our therapy. She quit her job, dumped her boyfriend, and moved in with her brother. As the entries progressed, even her writing style changed, growing more bitter and hopeless as her depression reemerged in full bloom. Like a car skidding out of control on a mountainous highway, her trip over the ledge appeared to be inevitable.

In the last entry, written hours after I'd last seen her, she wrote, "*I fucked up this time. I got completely pissed last night. I meant to pick some guy up at the bar and use him to forget my life for a while, but no luck. No surprise. For some stupid reason, I got the cabby to drop me off at Dr. A's place.*

"*I was out of my mind. Soon as I got into his house, I tried to jump his bones. Of course, he stopped me. What did I expect? But I was so drunk and hurt that I snapped. I broke my promise to myself. Stupid bitch! I told Dr. A about Him. All of it!*

"*What was the point? I'd already sworn to Dr. A that it never happened. Why would he believe me now? Besides, he holds the asshole on some kind of pedestal. Still, I couldn't believe how Dr. A reacted. He dumped all over me. He even said that I've been 'a victim my whole life.' Like it was my fault! That got me so mad. I told him where he could go. I took off.*

"But I've been up all night thinking about what Dr. A said. I think he's right. I *have been a victim most of my life. I didn't ask to be, but I let it happen. But I've got news for Dr. A. No more!*

"I've been thinking about His blackmail letter, too. What am I so afraid of? In the end, it comes down to His word against Tommy's and mine. Maybe if they knew what a sick fuck He is, they wouldn't be so quick to believe Him. It's time to turn the tables on that prick. I'm going to write a letter of my own."

Her written characters lost some of their meticulous precision as her idea took flight in a fiery scrawl. "I'll tell all about the esteemed Dr. Kolberg and the whips and gags He uses on his own patients! Then I'll send it to the cops and the press and the medical association and whoever else I can think of." Angela's enthusiasm flew off the page. "Time for Him to know what fear feels like. To have His life and precious fucking career turned upside down. I want to be there, too. To stand at His door and have Him read the letter in front of me, so I can see the defeat in His vile face."

The last line read: "Got to go now. I've got a letter to write. A victim no more!" She had underlined the last sentence three times.

I read the passage over and over. Nothing about it fit with the mental state of someone intent on suicide. If she had written the letter she threatened to, it would've explained why she had contacted Stanley after storming out of my house. Maybe they met face to face when she delivered her letter. If so, did she really think Stanley would stand by and watch her upend his life and "precious fucking career"?

Footsteps on the stairs interrupted my wild theorizing. "Dr. Ashman, I've got to go now," Tommy said, walking into the room.

"I'm done anyway." I shut the journal and slipped it onto the pile with the others.

"Did you find what you were looking for?"

"I'm not sure." I stood from the desk and followed Tommy out of the room.

At the front door, I said, "Damn! I forgot my keys." I hurried up the stairs to Angela's room. I grabbed the top journal off the pile and slipped it under my jacket, tucking it into my pant waist.

When I returned, I said, "Tommy, I need you to promise me something."

"What?"

"I need a few weeks. Maybe a month. In the meantime, I don't want you to do anything about your sister. Understand?"

"Why?"

"I have to look into a few things. It could take a while."

He stared blankly at me, though he knew exactly what I was asking of him. He shrugged. "Guess a few weeks won't matter one way or the other."

I skulked out of Tommy's place with the final volume of Angela's diary tucked in my pants and headed home. Nelson met me at the door. I'd never given him much credit for being a sensitive dog, but he must've picked up on something in my mood, because he followed me into my main-floor study. As soon as I dropped into my chair, he lay down across my feet.

I spread the journal open on my desk and read the last passage over again, though I probably could've recited it from memory. I wasn't even certain why I'd sneaked the book away from Tommy's. So what if he had seen it? But I knew exactly what. If Tommy reached the same conclusion I had— and how could he not have?—I doubted Stanley would've lived to see morning.

From the moment I saw Angela lying on the morgue's gurney, I'd held Stanley accountable. By making her life unlivable, I believed he had figuratively pushed her over the railing of the bridge, in the same way my father had helped Suzie Malloy off the top of the student union building. But never had it dawned on me that Stanley's involvement could have been even more literal.

I closed the journal and stuck it inside the desk's top drawer, but I wasn't finished with it. Nowhere near. For the *first time since Angela's death, I felt respite from the crushing guilt. With the relief came a sense of purpose.*

Half an hour later, I sat in Bonnie Hubbard's throwback of a living room with a cup of piping hot tea in hand. I made up a weak cover story about how I was doing a paper comparing patients who were under psychiatric care with those who were not at the time of their suicides. Deliberately playing up my only case, Angela, I asked if she knew of any of Kolberg or Nichol's patients who had killed themselves while under their care.

Sweet gullible Bonnie never even questioned why I was asking her and not my ex-partners directly. She wasn't aware of any of Nichol's patient-suicides, but Stanley was a different story. "You have to understand, he works with much higher risk patients," she said. She gave me the names of three patients from the seventies and eighties. I wrote them down, but I'd decided to focus on more recent deaths.

"In 1996, there was Kerry-Lynn Smith." Bonnie blew out her cheeks. "Tragic. The poor soul died of an overdose the day before her twenty-second birthday."

"What kind of overdose?"

"Valium and an antidepressant of some kind. I think alcohol was a factor, too."

Valium and alcohol, I thought. *Just like Angela.* I kept my head buried in my notes and asked, "Anyone else?"

"In late 1993, Avery Buckams," she sighed. "A true gentleman. They found him in his garage with the car running on the anniversary of his wife's passing. He missed her so."

"Any others?" I asked, not even bothering to record his name.

"Just one," Bonnie said. "Mary Pierce committed suicide in the fall of 1999. She was thirty-one, I think." She glanced from side to side and then whispered, "Quite an odd duck, but really very sweet. The poor girl hung herself from a pipe in her father's basement."

"Anything else unusual about her suicide?"

"Unusual?" Bonnie shook her head. "Oh, wait a minute, Dr. Ashman. Of course, Mary wouldn't fit in your study. You *see, she had left Dr. Kolberg's practice about a month before her suicide."*

"Why?"

"She stomped out of her last session in quite a huff," Bonnie explained. "She called me the next day to say that she wouldn't be returning. I think Dr. Kolberg must have touched a raw nerve." She shook her head at the thought of Stanley's clinical prowess. "You know how good Dr. Kolberg is at getting to the root of the issue."

I knew exactly how good Stanley was at exposing raw nerves. What Bonnie didn't realize was how much pleasure he took from it.

15

WE STEPPED INTO DEV'S OFFICE just in time for him to reach his phone on the fourth ring. He listened a moment and then said, "We'll be right up." He dropped the receiver in the cradle and turned to Claire. "Captain wants to see us."

"Right now?" Claire asked.

Dev nodded. "He's got the press and the brass breathing down his neck, and the sharks need to be fed." He didn't specify whether he meant the press or his bosses.

"What are you going to feed them?" I asked.

"The usual line. That we're looking at a 'person of interest.'"

"Dev . . . ," I said.

"Don't sweat it, Doc. We won't release Tommy's name just yet." But his reassurance lacked conviction. We both knew how leaks sprang once the powers-that-be got involved.

At the door, Dev turned back to me. "We could be a while. You gonna wait here?"

I nodded. "Dev, you think I could have another look at Nichol's bondage video?"

"If you're that bored why don't you go down to Vice? They've confiscated way better porn than that."

"The Nichol tape will do."

"I'll see if I can find someone to set you up, but there might be a few hoops to jump through." There must have been several hoops, because well over an hour passed before I ended up in a small windowless room facing a TV and VCR on a trolley.

Watching Anya ride the leather-hooded Calvin Nichol like some kind of deviant mechanical bull was no easier to stomach the second time around. By the time the screen changed to snowy static, I hadn't spotted anything of note. I rewound it and watched it again but learned nothing. Frustrated, I stared at the dead screen and considered my options.

Ten minutes later, I still hadn't stumbled onto a viable plan, but I'd been oblivious to the still-running videotape, and had enough of the stuffy little room. Just as I lifted the remote to switch off the TV, the screen's snow suddenly gave way to a new shot of the same room where Nichol had been ridden. Except, now Stanley had joined Anya in the frame.

I dropped back in my seat, blown away by the sight of him. I'd heard about his fetish in sickening detail, but to see my former mentor in his getup—shirtless in black leather pants with a chain running from one nipple to the other across his sunken chest—gave me a chill.

Naked, Anya leaned against the wall with arms and legs spread apart. Aside from a small tattoo at the base of her neck, the skin on her back was flawless—a far cry from the festering scar she'd forced me to view. Her ankles were already fastened into the leather shackles. She held her wrists in similar wall-holders while Stanley reached above and fumbled with the straps.

"Cal, would you please lend a hand?" he called over his shoulder.

The lanky and now hoodless Nichol walked into the picture. With his height advantage, he had a much easier time reaching up and securing the straps on Anya.

"Remember," Anya hissed over her shoulder at Stanley, "you don't cut me, right?"

"Don't worry, dear," he said with a disarming smile. "I won't."

My stomach churned, wondering if I was about to witness the fateful burn. But my concern was unfounded. Stanley looked directly into the camera, and said, "You have changed the tapes, haven't you, Wayne?" And the screen went to snow again.

The brief scene so overwhelmed me that for a moment I didn't even realize I had found my answer. I rewound it a few seconds and listened again: "You have changed the tapes, haven't you, Wayne?"

Wayne! Just as Anya had told me, a third man had been behind the camera on the day of filming. She'd described him to me as wearing "a big stupid grin all the time"—as apt a description as I could think of for Wayne Hacking.

Buoyed by the discovery, I grabbed for the phone on the desk behind me and dialed the number from memory. The line rang twice before a cigarette-ravaged voice croaked, "Western State Hospital, Ward B."

"Micky?" I said. "It's Joel Ashman."

"Dr. Ashman!" rasped one of my favorite nurses. "How the hell are you?"

"Coping, Micky. And you?"

"Not coping at all," he coughed a laugh. "What can I do you for?"

"You remember Wayne Hacking?"

"Sure. Old happy-face."

"Do you remember who he roomed with?" I asked.

"Jeez, he had a few. Let's see. There was Wilkins, Weaver, Fong . . . Christ, there must've been others but I can't remember."

"That's plenty, Micky. Thanks." I hung up the phone, no doubt leaving Micky bewildered as to the point of my call. I doubted he would lose sleep over it; in a psychiatric hospital, the bizarre and nonsensical are the rule.

Just as I reached for the phone again, the door opened and a highly distraught Claire walked in. I rose to meet her. Without a word, she rushed over and threw her arms around me. After a long hug, I pulled back and cupped her face in my hands. The running eyeliner highlighted her bloodshot eyes. "What's wrong?" I asked.

"I just read Angela's journals."

I ran my hand across her forehead and kissed her on the cheek.

"What Kolberg put her through . . ."

"I know."

She grabbed the only other chair in the small room and set it facing mine. We sat down across from each other close enough that our knees touched. "I know you don't want to believe Tommy was involved, but if that monster Kolberg had done the same to one of my sisters . . ." She took a deep breath, then exhaled. "I would've taken matters in my own hands, too."

I said nothing.

"Wouldn't you?"

"I don't have a sister," I said quietly.

"What about your wife?" Then she stammered, "Oh, Joel, I'm sorry. I didn't mean . . ."

I reached for her hand and held it in mine. "It's okay. Claire, I do know a little about having your world turned upside down by abuse."

She squeezed my hand gently. "How?"

"When I was a kid there was a girl who lived with us . . ." I went on to tell Claire about Suzie Malloy, explaining my father's ugly role and the parallels I'd seen between Suzie and Angela's life and death.

Claire leaned forward and kissed me gently on the lips. "Joel, that's awful."

I shrugged. "What's awful is that this isn't even my worst experience with sexual abuse," I blurted.

Claire's eyes widened. "You were abused?"

"No." I hesitated. "Loren was."

Claire didn't say a word.

"In Lor's case, it was her uncle," I said hoarsely. "Not a real uncle. One of those family friends you end up calling 'uncle.' The kind you'd trust like they were blood."

Claire sat absolutely still.

"She was fourteen years old. Her parents had to leave town to see her mom's sister, who'd been injured in a car crash. Lor had no relatives in town, so they turned to this guy, who said he was happy to take care of her for the week." I tasted bile in the back of my throat and I stopped to swallow. "He took care of her all right. Got her drunk for the first time ever. And when she was practically unconscious, he raped her."

Claire closed her eyes and shuddered.

"Lor was so ashamed," I said. "Like any accomplished abuser, he made her feel responsible. She didn't tell a soul until she was in her thirties. She never even blamed the bastard. When he had drunk himself into an early grave, she even went to his funeral." I cleared my throat. "Lor didn't escape unscathed. I don't think she ever could trust again after that. Not fully. Not even me. And I'm sure her sporadic black moods had everything to do with him."

Aside from Stanley, I'd never told anyone about Lor's uncle. I hadn't planned on telling Claire either, but once I started I couldn't stop. "Loren had other damage, too. PID—pelvic inflammatory disease. Heard of that?"

Claire shook her head.

"The son of a bitch gave her chlamydia. It scarred up her insides—her fallopian tubes. That's why it took us five years to get pregnant. Wasn't until we ran into the fertility trouble that she even told me what had been done to her." I wiped away the tears that had begun to roll down my cheeks. "But pregnant Lor was. She was so happy. When she reached the thirteen-week mark—when it's supposed to be safe to share the news without worrying about a miscarriage—she headed for Bremerton to tell her parents in person."

I had to pause for a moment to get my voice to cooperate.

"But scarring from PID can be a bitch, you know? Sometimes the tubes close partially, allowing the egg to be fertilized but never letting it reach the uterus. It's called an ectopic pregnancy—a pregnancy outside the womb.

"Lor started to bleed on the ferry over to the Olympic Peninsula. She was standing at the railing talking to a stranger when she went pale. She staggered for a seat but didn't make it. She collapsed on the deck. . . ." My voice wavered. "The tube that housed the embryo had burst and she was hemorrhaging into her belly. I hear that her last words before losing consciousness were 'Tell Joel we're okay.' " I swallowed. "But they weren't. And there was nothing anyone aboard could do about it. By the time the ambulance got her to the hospital in Bremerton, Lor was dead."

Claire leaned forward and wrapped her arms around me. After a long hug, she broke off the embrace and wiped her eyes. But my eyes were dry. "I met the bastard a couple times. But he was long dead when I found out how he'd raped his adolescent niece." I looked past Claire. "Far as I'm concerned, he killed Lor and our baby. Christ!" I snorted. "The number of times I've wished he was still alive, just so I could take matters in my own hands. . . ."

"I can't imagine. Know what? I think Kolberg got what he deserved."

"Me, too."

"But I'm a Homicide cop," she said, sitting up straighter and running a hand through her hair. "Many of our victims are bad people. It's not my job to decide who had it coming. Only to find their killers."

"Tommy didn't kill Stanley Kolberg."

Claire looked at me with a sad smile. "Who could possibly have a better motive?"

"Don't know about motive, but I think I've found an even better suspect."

Claire cocked her head in surprise. "Who?"

"Let me get Dev. I have something to show both of you." I started to my feet.

Claire laid a hand on my shoulder and gently pushed me

back down. "I'll get him. I need to freshen up on the way." She chuckled. "After all, cops don't cry."

She leaned forward and brushed her lips against mine. "God, Joel, I'm so sorry about Loren." Then she rushed out of the room.

Five minutes later, Claire returned with Dev. We crowded together facing the TV and watched the previously over-looked "outtake" from Nichol's home video. Once the brief clip ended, Dev pointed at the screen. "And people were paying *these* sickos good money to set their heads straight?"

Claire's mouth hung open. "So Wayne Hacking was the guy behind the camera?"

I nodded.

"Doc, I know where you're going with this—" Dev tried to stretch but ended up almost knocking a manual off the bookshelf. "Hacking was another clown in Kolberg's freak circus. So what? It doesn't make Tommy Connor any less of a suspect."

I rewound the tape and froze the scene where Kolberg and Nichol stood in the same frame. "There were three of them in on this. Only one is still alive. Wayne Hacking. The guy who butchered his ex-girlfriend and her sister."

"What about his 'dissociative state'?" Claire asked.

"Bullshit! There's his expert witness with the nipple chain." I pointed at the image of the shirtless Stanley on the screen. "And another thing. Do you remember what Bonnie had to say about Hacking's family dying in a fire?"

"Yeah," Dev said.

"Stanley once told me about a patient of his who rigged an electrical fire. Killed his parents and little brother. He was twelve at the time, too. Stanley described him as 'the most dangerous psychopath' he'd ever met."

Dev frowned. "And he told you it was Hacking?"

"No, but what are the chances of Stanley having two patients who both incinerated their families at the age of twelve?"

Dev shook his head. "Hacking has an alibi for both murders and this"—he flicked a hand at the screen—"doesn't give us a motive for either."

Claire held out a palm to her partner. "Dev, you were the one who didn't trust Hacking's girlfriend when she covered for him."

Dev glanced from Claire to me. "I guess we can dig a bit more in Hacking's deep closet. But we're nowhere near done with Tommy Connor yet."

"Okay," I said, "but can we go see Ron Weaver again?"

"The Shoveler?" Dev frowned. "What's he got to do with Hacking?"

"They roomed together at Western State. He might know something."

An hour later, we'd survived the stench of the hotel's hallway and stood again in the middle of Weaver's austere apartment. Wearing the same black wool pants and dress shirt, he was as uncooperative as on our previous visit. After a few minutes, Claire lost her patience. "Give me a break, Ron! You lived with the guy for six months. You expect us to believe he never said boo to you?"

"We didn't live together," Weaver droned. "We were stuck in the same room. And Hacking talked all the time. I never listened much."

I'd had enough, too. "Look around, Ron. You live in a rat-infested shit-box."

Weaver stiffened.

"You were right the last time. You're a convicted murderer and mental case," I grunted. "What other place would have you?"

His gaze narrowed, but he still didn't say a word.

"In the heat of the moment, you hit a guy with a shovel. And look what happens." I listed the points with my finger. "First you do your time in jail and then you get stuck in a loony bin. And once you've more than paid your debt to society, you end up rotting here among the drunks and junkies."

The muscles in his neck tightened. "Your point?"

"Don't you get it, Ron?"

"Get what?" he said through clenched teeth.

I felt Dev and Claire's eyes on me, but I didn't take mine off Weaver. "You're a huge loser!" I spat.

"I don't have to listen to this!" he said, his voice rising several decibels.

"Sure you do," Dev chimed in. "He's a doctor. He's only making a diagnosis."

Weaver shifted from one foot to another, and he crossed and uncrossed his arms. I knew he was close to where I wanted him. "You live a life that a dog would turn his nose from," I said. "Now think about your ex-roommate."

Weaver's lip trembled. "What about him?"

"With premeditation, Hacking butchers two women. But does he do one second in jail? No. He gets five cushy years in the hospital. And, presto! He's out. Now he's got a good job, a pretty girlfriend, and a place people would actually want to live in. How does your life stack up in comparison?"

"You don't know the fucking half of it!" Weaver cried.

"And you do?" I challenged.

"What do you think?!" Weaver's hand fired out so quickly I thought he was going to hit me. But his shaky finger stopped a couple of inches shy of my face. "He made asses out of all of you!"

I stared down at his hand. "How did he do that, Ron?"

"The guy got away with every goddamn thing," Weaver said. "Of course, he knew what he was doing when he cut up those girls!"

"Why did he do it?" I demanded.

"They knew too much? Or maybe they knew about the others."

"What others?" I asked.

"Hitchhikers, hookers, whoever." Weaver's lips broke into an ugly smile. "Sounds to me like you're the ones who don't get it."

"Hacking killed before?" I asked.

Weaver chuckled, but the rage still sparked in his eyes.

"Don't you see? Don't you get it, Dr. Ashman?" he mocked. "Hacking likes to kill people."

"He told you this?"

"Why not?" he growled. "The guy was untouchable."

"Because of Kolberg?"

"Yeah, his buddy." His face contorted into a sneer. "Kolberg got Hacking off, but all he did for me was get me time in a prison *and* a nuthouse." He laughed bitterly. "Next time I'll take Hacking's advice."

"Which was?" Dev asked.

Weaver's furious eyes darted to me. "Always talk to one of you stupid shrinks before you go and kill someone!"

"You stay nearby home, Ron," Dev said. "We still might need a lot more out of you yet. You understand?"

Before Weaver could answer, Dev turned for the door. Claire and I silently followed him out. Back in the car, Claire looked over her shoulder and studied me with a look reserved for a lover who's surprised you in a disturbing way. Without a word, she turned back and started the engine.

"What do you think of Wayne Hacking now?" I asked Dev.

"What I always thought of him. One dangerous bastard. I never bought that Barney-like act of his. But we're no closer to connecting him to our murders."

We left the seediness of Weaver's neighborhood and drove east until we pulled up to a small house in a working-class neighborhood in the heart of Rainier Valley. The block was lined with cheaply constructed square houses that mirrored one another in their blandness.

We walked over the patchy brown grass and followed the path around the side of the house where the paint was peeling off in strips. We stopped at the door to the basement apartment and knocked. Hacking's girlfriend, Yvonne Carpinelli, met us with a nervous grin. I didn't understand why it felt so cramped in the two-bedroom apartment until I realized how low the ceiling was—with any kind of jump, my head would've been embedded in drywall.

Claire re-introduced me to Yvonne, but she needn't have

bothered. The girl remembered me from Hacking's Western State days. "Nice to see you again, Dr. Ashman."

We sat in mismatched vinyl chairs around the kitchen table. While Claire explained the purpose of our visit—misrepresenting it as "routine follow-up"—I studied Carpinelli. Chubby, she had an attractive face with large brown eyes, freckles, and curly black hair. I remembered her nervous energy from the hospital—she used to pace the hallways as tirelessly as most of the patients. Even sitting, she was in constant motion, fidgeting with her hands and crossing and uncrossing her knees.

"Can you tell us again where you were last Tuesday evening?" Claire asked.

"Wayne and I went to that Iranian film at the Wormwood."

"Which showing?" Claire asked.

"The late show, which I never do," she said. "I'm a morning person. Usually, I'm tucked in bed and asleep by nine o'clock. But Wayne had to work late. He really wanted to see it."

"Was it any good?" Dev asked.

"Not too bad." Carpinelli giggled. "Those subtitles are tough when you're tired. I nodded off now and again."

"Wayne sat through the whole movie?" Dev asked.

"Yes."

"Yvonne," I said, "you've been with Wayne since his trial?"

She nodded sheepishly. "That was when we started to write each other. We didn't meet in person until he was hospitalized."

"Oh, sure," I said pleasantly. "After Wayne had gotten away with murder?"

She shifted in her chair. "He was found not guilty on account of his . . . um . . . dissociative state."

"That's right." I nodded. "Dr. Kolberg helped him make up that defense."

"That's what Dr. Kolberg said Wayne had." Carpinelli glanced at the detectives for support, but Claire and Dev were watching me, not her.

"Dr. Kolberg was Wayne's friend, wasn't he?" I asked.

"He was Wayne's psychiatrist."

"Yes, but Wayne used to see Dr. Kolberg outside of his therapy, didn't he?"

"Every so often . . . I guess."

"More than every so often, right?" I said more firmly.

Carpinelli chewed her lip and nodded.

"The thing is, Yvonne, Dr. Kolberg is dead now," I said. "So Wayne won't be able to use that bogus psychiatric illness defense anymore."

"He's not on trial for anything," she said to the table.

"He will be soon, though," I said. "After all, he killed Drs. Kolberg and Nichol."

Her head shot up. "No. Wayne wouldn't do that!"

"Have you heard of the term 'accessory after the fact'?"

Eyes frantic, Carpinelli gaped at me.

"It means that if you help cover up a crime, you're held responsible for it," I explained. "Yvonne, you could face twenty-five years."

Recognition crept onto her scared face as tears welled in her eyes. "I didn't cover up anything. Wayne didn't do—"

I slammed my fist on the table. "Wayne didn't sit through the whole movie, did he?"

"Most of it," she said, starting to choke back the sobs.

"But he left the theater, *didn't he?*"

"Only to move the car and make a phone call," she said weakly. "That's all."

"When?"

"I don't know," she pleaded. "Soon after the movie started, I guess."

"How long was he gone?"

"Not long," she gulped. "Half an hour or so."

"Or maybe an hour."

"It didn't seem like that long," she whispered.

I glared at her. "And the night Kolberg died. You told the detectives you were with Wayne all evening."

"I was." She writhed in her seat and wiped away tears with the backs of her hands.

"What time did you go to bed?"

"Ten or eleven," Carpinelli squeaked. "I don't know."

"Come on, Yvonne!" I said. "You're not a night owl, remember?"

She looked desperately around the room for help but found none. "Nine, maybe."

"Wayne could've gone out after nine without you knowing."

"He wouldn't . . . I know he wouldn't." She covered her face with her hands and dissolved into tears.

Claire placed a hand on the girl's thick shoulder. "Listen, Yvonne, do you have somewhere you can go to for a while to get away from the city? If Wayne found out what you just told us, you could be in real danger. You have to believe me on this."

Her face still buried in her hands, she nodded. "I've got an aunt on Vashon Island. I guess I could go there for a while, but—"

"No buts." Claire cut her off. "Go, okay? And do not tell Wayne anything about our visit. Do you understand, Yvonne?"

"Okay," she croaked.

At the door, I was hit by an afterthought. "Yvonne, do you own a car?"

"It used to be my grandpa's," she said. "I don't drive it much."

"Can we see it?" Dev asked.

Less than a minute later, Dev was sitting in the driver's seat of the big black sedan. Even before he turned the ignition, I thought I recognized the '72 Chevy Malibu. But as soon as the engine roared to life, I knew beyond a doubt that the same car had nearly taken my head off.

16

A S WE LEFT CARPINELLI'S GARAGE, Nate Schiff and two other bunny men were still fussing over her black Malibu. Down on all fours, molding plaster to the front tire, they reminded me of the veterinarians I'd seen on the Discovery Channel applying a cast to a fallen elephant's leg. I didn't need a mold of the tires to know Wayne Hacking had almost killed me with the same car. But I knew my word wouldn't matter to the CSI guys; they only trusted things they could see under a microscope.

On the trip back to Homicide, I caught Claire looking me over in the rearview mirror with the same wariness she had shown following Weaver's interview. But Dev seemed to find my newfound aggressiveness entertaining. "Doc, you're on a roll." He chuckled. "How about we head over to Hacking's store? Maybe you can beat a confession out of him."

"So you do think he's our guy now?"

"Looks like he's your stalker, anyway. How far do you figure it is to the Wormwood Theater from your old office?"

"A mile or two, tops," I said.

Dev nodded. "At that time on a Tuesday evening—we're talking five minutes there, five back—he'd have plenty of time to kill Nichol, take a swipe at you, and still pick up a bag of movie popcorn in under an hour."

"Why don't we go pick him up?" Claire asked.

Dev looked over his shoulder, his expression unusually solemn. "Doc, can you tell us for certain that Hacking was the guy who stabbed you?"

"No, not for certain."

Dev blew out of his lips. "Apart from poking holes in his alibi, we haven't linked Hacking to the scene. And we still don't have motive."

Claire turned to Dev. "Time for another search warrant?"

I shook my head. "Hacking's a typical sociopath. Smart and careful. Don't think a search would do more than tip our hand."

Dev waved away my objection. "Yvonne's going to tell him all about our visit."

"Not if she leaves town today," I said.

"Don't count on that," Dev deadpanned. "She loved him when she thought he'd killed only two women. Wait till she hears his death toll might hit double digits."

Claire disagreed. "Yvonne's terrified. Trust me. She's going."

"Okay," Dev conceded. "We'll play it Doc's way and hold off on the warrant. Meantime, let's stick a tail on Hacking and see where it leads."

"Doubt that will help," I said. "The best predators like Hacking have a sixth sense for the out of the ordinary. If we're hunting him, he'll know it. He'll keep his head down forever, if necessary."

Dev looked over and arched an eyebrow at me. "I sense a serious 'but' coming."

"The question I can't shake is, Why me?" I said. "Why has Hacking been after me from the outset?"

Claire pointed at me in the mirror. "He thinks you know something," she said.

"That's what I think, too," I said. "Right from the start, he's seen me as a threat."

"And after the stabbing . . . ," Claire said.

"I'm an even bigger threat," I said. "Except no one's arrested him yet. Which tells him that I'm not certain."

Dev rubbed his eyes. "Doc, I know where this is going. . . ."

"All we have to do is give him a nudge," I said. "If I were to call him and let him somehow know that I know . . ."

"Here you go with the whole entrapment thing again." Dev shook his head. "Even if he came after you, it doesn't prove he murdered the others."

"Exactly," Claire said, but more out of protectiveness than reason, I thought. Or, at least, I hoped.

Back at Homicide, Dev went off to organize a surveillance team for Hacking while Claire arranged for a change of cars and an SPD "safe house" that in reality was simply a well-situated downtown hotel. The biggest hitch was finding a place that would accept Nelson as a guest.

As we were leaving for our new digs, Dev stopped us on our way to the elevator. "Just heard from Schiff," he said. "The tread marks pulled from your neighbor's lawn match the tires on Yvonne's Malibu."

"So let's go pick up Hacking," Claire said.

"On what grounds?"

"Attempted murder, for starters," she said.

"We can't place him inside Yvonne's car. But the noose is tightening." As the elevator doors were shutting, Dev added, "No chances with this guy, huh?"

After stopping off at Claire's and collecting our bags and Nelson, we dropped by my house so I could pick up some clean clothes. Claire had never been inside. Standing in the open family room and kitchen, she pointed around the room. "I love this space. So open and warm."

"Can't take credit for that," I said.

"Loren was a designer, right?"

"Yeah," I said, flipping through the pile of mail on the counter. "A good one, too."

She bit her lip. "I bet."

I sensed she had more to say. I put the envelopes down. "What is it?"

She looked away. "It's a good-sized house for one person."

"And a dog," I pointed out.

She smiled. "I guess Nelson needs his space. You ever think about moving?"

"I've thought about it. I'm too cheap and too lazy. Look how long I've dragged my feet on upgrading my car."

She smiled. "Maybe you're just sentimental?"

"All right, I give in, Claire." I laughed. "Even I can see the psychopathology here. Christ, my spare bedroom is still a three-quarters-finished nursery. All I need is an empty crib. I'm sure any therapist would tell me that I'm living among the dead."

Claire viewed me warmly. "What's so wrong with living in a place with a nice bright kitchen and happy memories?"

"Of course, that's the other way of looking at it." I smiled, realizing that I might be falling in love with Claire Shepherd.

"Hey, can I use your phone?" she asked. "I want to call Mom and Dad and let them know I won't be coming back to Denver this weekend."

I pointed down the hallway. "There's a phone in the study that'll give you privacy."

Claire walked off in search of the phone. After I'd sorted through my mail, I headed upstairs to pack a fresh bag of clothes. I rummaged through my drawers until I'd found enough shirts and underwear to last a couple of weeks. As always with my packing, the choices took longer than they needed to. I stopped in front of the snapshot of Lor and me on the boat. I felt a twinge in my chest but I resisted the urge to put the frame in the bag. Instead, I headed to the bedroom closet. I pushed the rack of shirts and pants aside to get at the wall-mounted safe.

The safe had come with the house. According to our real-estate agent, the previous owner had been so paranoid about her meager jewelry collection that she'd installed a unit that a bomb wouldn't scathe. I'd never met the woman, but Lor and I used to jokingly picture her as a little old lady wandering aimlessly around the rubble of a post-nuclear apocalypse wearing nothing but rags and perfectly preserved costume jewelry.

I dialed in the combination and felt the lock click. I pulled open the heavy door. I reached inside and pulled out the only remaining contents—a .38-caliber handgun and its loaded magazine. I clicked the magazine into the base of the handgun and weighed it in my hand. Barely a pound, it still made my injured wrist ache. I switched hands. Didn't feel any better. The sight of a gun in my hand brought back all kinds of unwelcome memories.

As I knelt down to pack it in my suitcase, Claire stepped into the room.

Her face was pale. "What the hell is that?" she asked.

"I've got a permit."

"So? What are you doing with a gun?"

"Through my work, I've met some scary individuals. I decided I'd sleep better knowing there was a gun in the house."

Claire's eyes narrowed. Her face creased into a grimace. "You're planning to bring it with us?"

"Claire, I've taken lessons at the range," I said, trying to convince myself as much as her. "I know how to use it."

She shook her head. "I've got a gun, too. One I'm *properly* trained to use. But the whole reason we're going to the hotel is so using it won't be an issue."

"Wasn't supposed to be an issue when I moved into your place, either." I met her stare. "But last night, lying on the ground with a clock radio in my hand, you have no idea how much I wished it was a gun."

"Remember?" She glared and pointed to her chest. "I was the one who came through the window. You might have ended up shooting me."

"I'd only use it as a very last resort," I said, realizing how lame it sounded.

"You've got the permit." She spun on her heels and stomped out of the room.

I threw the gun in my bag and followed after. We didn't exchange a word until we arrived at our "safe house," a three-star hotel situated near the financial district. Claire took care of the check-ins. I half-wondered if she was going to request separate rooms, but she didn't. Whether or not she still liked me, her job was to protect me.

When we got into the comfortable two-bedroom suite, Nelson wandered off to give it the once-over. Claire carried her bag into the larger bedroom. I watched from the hallway as she laid it on the king-sized bed. When I started for the second bedroom, Claire pointed to the room's dresser. "I'll take the top two drawers, you can have the bottom ones."

I grinned. "How about you get the first and third, and I'll take the second and fourth?"

Still poker-faced, she muttered, "Just remember which one you put your gun in."

After we unpacked, we ordered room service and ate dinner at the small kitchen table. The half-carafe of wine we shared went a long way to warming the chill that came with our first clash, but Claire remained subdued. After a few bites of her angel hair pasta, she put her fork down. "What do you plan to do once this is over, Joel?" she asked.

"I'm thinking about returning to private practice." I held up my bandaged hand. "But I should be able to squeeze a few more weeks of disability out of this." I cleared my throat. "That reminds me. I've been meaning to take a trip for a while. Nothing too exotic. Somewhere warm for a week or two. Hawaii or Mexico. Any interest in coming along?"

"I'm new to Homicide," she said, avoiding eye contact. "Not sure I could get the time off. Why don't we play it by ear?"

"Sounds good," I lied.

I was in bed before Claire. When she crawled under the covers and reached an arm behind my back, I was surprised to feel her naked body press against me. After her reaction to my handgun, I was amazed she was in the mood. I wasn't. But when she snuggled her warm body close to mine and planted a long kiss on my lips, the mood found me in a hurry.

Our sex was louder and more passionate than before, but tenderness was replaced by need. And after, as we lay panting under the thin sheet, Claire drew away slightly when I leaned in to hold her.

"I thought we were okay now," I said.

Claire must've seen the hurt in my eyes, because she stroked me gently on the cheek. "Sometimes I don't know what to make of you."

"Makes two of us."

She pulled her hand from my cheek. "Joel, I want to ask you something."

"Shoot."

"When did Angela first tell you that Kolberg had abused her?"

"About six months ago. The day before she died."

Claire showed no reaction.

"At first, I didn't believe her. At least, I wasn't willing to accept it. By the time I came around . . ." I swallowed. "It was too late."

"You didn't do anything about Kolberg?" Rather than accusatory, she sounded as if she were struggling to understand my inaction.

"I quit the practice. I cut off all ties with him."

Her eyes narrowed. Naked and with our bodies still touching, Claire wasn't my lover at that moment. She was a detective. "Why didn't you report him to anyone?"

I rolled on my back and stared at the ceiling. "After Lor died, Stanley pulled me back from the abyss. He was like a father to me. After what happened with my own dad, stumbling onto Stanley's little secret was like a big dump of salt in a still-fresh wound."

" 'Little secret,' " Claire murmured. "You make it sound as harmless as if he liked to dress up in garters and a bra."

"There was a monster inside of Stanley, too."

"Too?"

"Stanley was an extremely complex person. He wasn't simply some sociopath pretending to care. I'd seen him go the extra mile for his patients and friends as few others would. Stanley was the closest I've ever come to knowing a real-life Jekyll and Hyde."

"But you turned a blind eye to the Mr. Hyde part?"

I turned back to Claire. "My first order of business was trying to talk Tommy Connor out of killing him."

"Why?"

"Why did I have to talk Tommy out of it? Or why did I stop him?"

She shrugged. "Either."

"He read the same diary you did. He knew exactly what Stanley did to his sister."

"How did you stop Tommy?"

"I told him I needed time to look into Stanley," I said. "We both knew that there must've been patients before Angela. And probably since. Tommy gave me his word that he wouldn't do anything until I'd investigated more."

"Did you investigate?"

"I started," I said. "I even came across a couple of other patient-suicides who were probably abused by Stanley. But he was killed before I got much further."

"What were you going to do with the information?"

"I don't know. Take it to Dev, I guess."

Claire laid her hand on mine. "Joel, why didn't you tell us any of this?"

I squeezed her hand. "I thought it would make Tommy look even more guilty. I couldn't stomach the idea of him rotting in jail. Not after what happened to Angela."

Claire bit her lower lip and searched my eyes. She opened her mouth as if to continue the interrogation, but instead she simply said, "Good night, Joel." She kissed me on the cheek, then rolled away from me.

Tired as I was, sleep didn't come easily. When I finally drifted off, I dreamed I was at the pier walking Loren to the ferry. Most dreams of Lor brought a sense of melancholic happiness; thrilled as I was to be with her, part of me always knew I was dreaming. Not this time. With each step closer to the ship, I felt rising dread. We stopped in front of the gangplank and kissed good-bye. I stood on the pier and watched the ship set off. Several passengers, including Lor, lined the railings of the ship's stern and waved landward like passengers on a cruise ship. Then someone else caught my eye. Three passengers down from Lor, Wayne Hacking stood with his usual grin plastered on his face. When I looked closer at his waving hand, I saw that he was holding a hunting knife.

I woke up in a cold sweat.

I shot my hand out to switch on the lamp and almost knocked it over. Claire stirred and repositioned the comforter but didn't open her eyes. Giving up on sleep, I sat under a lamp in the chair by the dresser, not ten feet from the hotel safe in which I housed my gun, and stared at the same page of a paperback for hours without making it past the second paragraph. Every bump or knock in the hallway sent a jolt through me.

When Claire awoke, she climbed out of bed and pecked me on the lips. "Guess we had our first fight," she said with a self-conscious grin.

"If that was your idea of a fight, I could be the luckiest man alive."

We arrived at Dev's office a little before eight. Dev briefed us on the report from the detectives who'd been tailing Hacking overnight, but there wasn't much to tell. Hacking had returned home after work and didn't leave until seven the next morning, when he walked back to his convenience store.

We left Homicide and drove the all-too-familiar route back to Sergei Pushtin's condo. He met us at the door in his black bathrobe again. "Shit, Sherlock! Back in Moscow in the olden days, the KGB didn't hassle me like you."

"Maybe they didn't care for you as deeply as I do." Dev walked into the condo as if he owned the place. Standing in the sprawling living room, he turned to Pushtin. "Tell me about Wayne Hacking."

Pushtin crossed his massive arms. "I don't know who the fuck you're talking about."

"Balding guy," Dev said. "With a smile that just won't quit."

Pushtin stared at him blankly.

"He filmed Anya getting beaten by Kolberg," I said.

"Oh, him," Pushtin grunted. "When I hear about the camera, we have conversation."

Dev swirled a finger in imaginary water. "You mean the kind of conversation that ends up with someone at the bottom of a river?"

"I forgot. Sergei kills everyone he talks to." Pushtin laughed then held up his huge paws. "Kolberg and I made a financial settlement. He paid for film rights. End of story."

"Another 'financial settlement,' huh?" Claire growled. "Did they film any other girls?"

"Couple girls. Sure. But Anya was the favorite." He sighed. "Can you blame them?"

"Did Hacking ever touch the women?"

"No, he just likes to take pictures. My girls tell me that when the beating starts, his smile gets even bigger."

Dev pointed at Pushtin. "Have you ever lost any girls?"

Dev didn't have to explain what he meant. Prostitutes go missing in Seattle every year. They run away from their pimps, die anonymously from overdose or disease, or get killed by their johns or pimps. "Only two." Pushtin grinned as if it was an achievement to be proud of. "One three years ago, from the needle. Another about six weeks ago. And no, Sherlock, Sergei didn't kill her."

"This latest girl," Claire said, "did she ever appear on film with Kolberg?"

"Olga?" Pushtin looked up at the ceiling and rubbed his chin. "A few times." Suddenly his blue eyes widened in recognition. "Wait a minute. You don't think that those losers did something to her?"

Dev ignored the question by turning for the door.

We left Pushtin's luxury building and headed back to Homicide. As soon as we arrived, Dev checked in with the surveillance team. They had nothing to report. While waiting on calls concerning the missing Olga, we sat around Dev's office and tossed out ideas. "So Hacking and Kolberg are thick as thieves," Dev said. "He films Stanley 'performing' all the time, but he never touches the girls."

"Fits his profile," I said. "Hacking likes the pain. He's not interested in the sex."

"Maybe Hacking decides to get into the act one day?" Dev suggested. "You heard what the Shoveler said about Hacking and the hookers and hitchhikers. Maybe Hacking takes his knife to poor old Olga right in front of Kolberg and Nichol. Would've spooked the old boys."

"A bit of a stretch, don't you think?" I said. "Besides, I can't see anything spooking Stanley."

"Never know, Doc," he said. "Either way, your ex-partners might've posed a risk Hacking didn't want to take. Hell, maybe they were just good target practice."

Claire shook her head. "We need to know what happened to Olga."

By the end of the day, we were no closer to that goal. Olga Fetisov had disappeared from the downtown streets without a trace. We still hadn't found Hacking's smoking gun or his motive for killing my colleagues. And according to the surveillance team, he stuck to his daily routine like it was a train schedule.

Once Claire and I returned to our hotel room, we had dinner and tumbled into bed. She fell asleep right after we made love, but I couldn't. The evening brought back all my anxiety from the night before. I didn't want to face the prospect of that miserable nightmare recurring. But in spite of myself, I nodded off around two in the morning.

I woke at 5:30 A.M. more resolved than ever. I crept out of bed and down the hallway to the spare bedroom. Flipping through the phone book, I found the number and dialed.

He answered on the second ring, sounding as cheery as if I was calling at noon rather than before dawn. "Hi, Dr. Ashman. What can I do for you?"

"You can tell me why, Wayne," I said evenly.

"Why what?" Hacking asked.

"Why you killed Cal Nichol."

"Wish I could help there, Dr. Ashman." His voice was as relaxed as ever. "But Yvonne and I were at the movies that night."

"We know you slipped out long enough to kill Nichol," I said.

I heard soft breathing on the line and then laughter. "Dr. Ashman, I appreciate what you must be going through with your partners' murders and all," he said, his voice dripping with empathy. "I want you to know that I take no offense at these groundless accusations—"

"I know you swung that knife at me, Wayne," I snapped. "You might've worn a mask, but I saw your eyes. I wouldn't forget them."

"Is that so?" Hacking laughed again. "Then how come we're having this discussion over the phone and not at Homicide?"

"Soon, Wayne," I promised. "I have a couple of loose ends to tie up before I identify you."

"Would those loose ends have anything to do with Stanley and Angela?" he asked pleasantly.

I felt the anger surge in me. *"You bastard!"* I hissed.

"Dr. Ashman, really, I am sorry," he said in his singsong tone. "All these murders, and I can't help you with any of them."

"You will," I said, swallowing the rest of my rage.

He chuckled again.

Remembering his childhood cross-dressing trauma, I left him with the line I'd rehearsed before the call. "When you go to trial, maybe they'll let you wear one of those frilly dresses, like you used to when you were a boy." I slammed down the receiver.

Staring at the phone, I had little doubt that a diligent sociopath like Hacking had caller identification on his home phone. And I'd made no attempt to hide my phone number.

I still wasn't certain why I had again chosen to be the

provocateur. It hadn't exactly worked wonders with Stanley in the days before his murder.

One week before Stanley's death, I launched my research into his other "patient-suicides." Of the names Bonnie had given me, I chose to start with the most recent, Mary Pierce. The only family I managed to track down was her father, Garth Pierce. He lived at Brock Derby, a nursing home in the center of the city that once had exclusively housed war veterans but now took all comers.

In my role with Cascade Mental Health, I often visited patients in nursing homes, where dementia is common and the rate of depression, understandably, runs sky-high. But as I walked down the hallway—smelling both the pungent cleaning agents and the urine they were supposed to cover—I experienced the same despondency that these homes always brought.

At the end of the hallway, Garth Pierce's door was ajar. I heard a hissing sound coming from within. I knocked twice. When I didn't get a response, I pushed the door open wider. Pierce lay on top of the bed covers, wearing pajamas over his long skinny frame. He had a withered face with sunken eyes, hollow cheeks, and a beak of a nose, under which ran oxygen tubing. With each labored breath, he let out a wheeze that overpowered the hiss from the oxygen tank. When he fixed his eyes on me, I could see through the ravages of emphysema and imagine what an intimidating presence he must have once been.

He pointed a bony finger at me. "What do you want?"

"To talk about your daughter, Mary," I said, stepping farther into the room.

His eyes narrowed to slits. "Who are you?" he wheezed.

"Dr. Joel Ashman. A psychiatrist."

"I told those stupid nurses: No more goddamn shrinks! I'm done talking."

"I used to work with Dr. Stanley Kolberg."

His face contorted into sheer hatred. "Get the hell out of my room!"

"I don't work with him anymore."

"So?" Pierce spat.

"I'm trying to find out if Kolberg had anything to do with your daughter's death."

The anger left his face, but not the suspicion. "The bastard had everything to do with it."

I took his statement as an invitation, and I walked closer to his bed. "What do you mean?"

He took a few deep breaths. "She didn't commit suicide. He killed her."

"How do you know?"

"Because she told me . . ." Pierce sputtered. "She was going to turn him in for molesting her and . . ." He made an awful retching noise in an attempt to clear his throat. "The son of a bitch knew my Mary was going to expose him." He stopped to catch his breath. "Next thing she's dead. You put it together!"

"So she wasn't acting depressed at the time of her death?"

Pierce scowled. "Garbage. She was fine." He gasped. "The whole business with Kolberg gave her a new focus. Distracted her from her worries . . . She was determined."

"Maybe she had a change of heart," I suggested.

"Garbage!" He wheezed so heavily that his color went dusky before clearing. "I spoke to her that morning. She was feeling fine. Besides, she would've never gone to the basement. Not that spot. No, sir."

"How come?"

He was slow to answer, but for a change, it wasn't due to a life-threatening shortage of breath. "Her mother died there when Mary was only seven," he said quietly.

"Your wife committed suicide?"

He nodded. "Mary's mom had problems in the head. And Mary was the one who found her. The poor thing." I wasn't sure whether Pierce referred to the mother or daughter, but I didn't interrupt. "Since then, Mary never went near the basement. . . ." *He took a couple of quick breaths.* "Not ever."

"Mr. Pierce, presumably you told someone about your suspicions?"

"Of course, I bloody well did!" *Another choking spell.* "They didn't listen. 'No evidence of foul play on the autopsy,' they told me. 'Suicide runs in families,' they said. . . . Why would they believe me? I was just a sick old man who didn't know any better. Hell, I've been dying forever." *He stopped for a few deep puffs.* "If I had just one ounce of my old strength left . . ." *He raised his veiny, emaciated limbs to show me.* "So help me God, I'd kill him with my own hands."

I started to move away from the bed. "Okay, Mr. Pierce, thank you for your time—"

"I might not have been the best father in the world . . ." *Pierce's panting words stopped me.* "Maybe I was too hard on Mary at times. That's how I was raised. . . . She was all the family I had. And Mary . . ." *He broke off his eye contact, and muttered with embarrassment:* "Well, she wouldn't have done that. Not in that same spot." *He shook his head vehemently.* "Kolberg strung her from that pipe. No question."

"Do you have any proof?"

"Proof! In the Service, I was in the Middle East for a while." *He was stopped by another paroxysm of wheezing.* "The locals had this expression: 'You don't have to see the scorpion to know you were bit.'"

I rested my hand on his cadaverous shoulder. "Know what, Mr. Pierce? I believe you."

"So what are you going to do about it?" *His eyes challenged me.*

"Try to trap the scorpion," *I said.*

After leaving the nursing home, I called the medical records department at the King County Medical Center and was pleased to learn that I knew the pathologist who had performed the autopsy on Mary Pierce.

The following noon I met Mitch Greene at Anthony's Pier 66, a trendy Seattle waterfront restaurant on Alaskan Way. I was already seated when, from halfway across the patio, I heard Greene bellow, "I can tell already, this is one of these 'haute cuisine' spots. That's French for 'miniature portions.' Maybe we should order in a pizza."

Cognizant of the other diners' attention, I waited until after he reached the table and had crushed my hand before I asked, "How are you, Mitch?"

"Look at me." He ran a hand over his chest and protuberant abdomen. "You think it's easy being this beautiful?"

"Must take a lot of work."

"Not really." He chuckled and patted his belly. "Secret is, I walk from the parking lot to the elevator twice a day, and I eat tons of beef jerky."

"And it shows." I laughed. "How's Trudy?"

"Good. Good. Mind you, she's elevated nagging to an art form. Now, she wants me to join her gym. Could you imagine?" Greene jutted his chin at me. "Ash-Man, how've you been since your patient's suicide?"

"Oh . . . fine."

"Then why did you drop out of the hospital and shut your practice right after?"

I'd forgotten how perceptive Greene was. "I needed a change."

He grinned mischievously. "Why don't you come work with me? Nothing so satisfying as working with the dead. They hardly ever complain. And no matter how much you screw up, they never spring to life on you."

After ordering lunch—and listening to Greene volunteer at the top of his lungs to go back into the kitchen and make the onion rings himself when he heard they weren't on the menu—I brought up the subject of Mary Pierce, the reason for our luncheon.

"I scanned her chart." Greene nodded. "What do you want to know?"

"Did you find anything unusual on her?" I asked.

"*Depends what you mean by unusual. Some people would consider a rope around the neck unusual.*"

"*Anything on toxicology, for example?*"

"*Her alcohol level was somewhere in the thirties.*" He stuck out his lower lip while he thought. "*She had a moderately high level of benzodiazepines. Not overdose-sized, but at least four or five tablets' worth of Valium.*"

"*Just like Angela Connor,*" I said.

"*That's common with suicides, though. People need a little something to get their nerve up before taking the final plunge, as it were.*"

I nodded. "*No other injuries or anything?*"

"*Just your standard circumferential neck contusions. Oh, and she had some abrasions and fibers trapped underneath her nails.*"

"*From?*"

"*In judicial hangings, the weight of the person dropping through the trap door usually snaps their neck at the second cervical vertebra, the so-called Hangman's Fracture. Most die in seconds. But the amateur home-variety isn't so humane. People are conscious for a period while they asphyxiate. I don't know if it's panic or change of heart, but people claw at the noose. It's normal.*"

"*Normal,*" I repeated. "*Nothing else, huh?*"

Greene tilted his basketball-shaped head and squinted at me. "*Ash-Man, you think someone might have murdered Mary Pierce?*"

"*Well, the timing of her suicide doesn't make much sense.*"

"*There was no other bruising to suggest her head was forced into that noose.*" Greene looked over his shoulder in search of our waitress. When he couldn't find her, he grumbled, "*You think she's out fishing for my salmon?*" He turned back to me. "*The autopsy isn't the be-all and end-all some people think. For example, I can tell you for one hundred percent certain whether or not someone shot themselves in the head. That's Mickey Mouse stuff. You can't fake it. And believe me, people have tried. But it's impossible to tell whether someone else persuaded that person—with, say, another gun pointed somewhere else—to pull the trigger. Same goes for your hanging. That's why we say the wounds are consistent with being self-inflicted. That doesn't always mean suicide."* He snapped his fingers. *"Sometimes it's even tougher. Take your gal who went off the bridge. If she were strangled before going over the railing, I'd have known. But if, say, someone tossed her over, I might be none the wiser based on the autopsy. Depends how much of a struggle was involved."*

"I see your point. Okay, did you find any pill fragments in Pierce's stomach?"

"No."

"Suppose someone was given an injection of Valium instead of taking it by mouth, could you tell the difference on autopsy?"

"We might see a bruise over the injected muscle, but if they died soon after . . ." He stuck out his lip again. *"Nah, we wouldn't be able to tell."* Greene tilted his head and raised an eyebrow. *"Ash-Man, what gives? Why are you so interested in a death that's basically ancient history?"*

"Remember, Mitch." I deflected his question with a smile. "I am a psychiatrist, which means I've got way too much time on my hands."

He laughed. *"Long as you're paying the lunch bill, I'm willing to go over the evidence in Cain versus Abel."* Which was his way of saying that he wasn't going to pry.

I left our lunch in a fog. Though I knew Mary Pierce hadn't voluntarily stuck her neck through a noose—just as Angela hadn't jumped off the Aurora Bridge—the idea that Stanley had murdered them in cold blood was still surreal to me.

Of more practical concern, the "evidence" I'd accumulated against him was, in legal terms, nothing more than coincidence and hearsay. So I turned my attention to his other patient-suicide, Kerry-Lynn Smith, hoping to stumble upon something more tangible.

Smith had overdosed on antidepressants, Valium, and

booze in June of 1996, the day before her twenty-second
birthday. After tracking down her autopsy records, I learned
that the pathologist who had performed the postmortem had
since died. So I huddled in an austere cubicle at King
County's medical records department and read his written
report.

By the end, I'd seen enough to reach a very different conclusion from the pathologist's verdict of "voluntary overdose of tricyclic antidepressants." To begin with, he'd found
only pink pill fragments consistent with the antidepressants
inside her stomach and intestine. There was no trace of blue
or yellow gunk that would've suggested Valium ingestion. Either Smith had taken the Valium first and waited at least two
hours before swallowing the antidepressants, or someone
had injected it. Then there were her assorted injuries to explain. The pathologist found the healing linear, whiplike striations and second-degree burns on her back to be consistent
with "masochistic sexual practices." He attributed the
"fresh, circumferential contusions" on her upper arms to the
same behavior, but I'd seen enough of these reports to know
such injuries were also typical of the marks left on victims
who had been grabbed and held during an assault.

Once home, I sat down in my home office, pulled out an
empty notebook, and began to write. Ten pages later, I'd finished documenting what I'd learned about Stanley's involvement in the deaths of three women—Kerry-Lynn Smith,
Mary Pierce, and Angela Connor—the oldest of whom was
only thirty-one. I reviewed my notes. Very damning. Very
convincing. And from a legal point of view, not worth the paper they were written on. Nothing pointed a finger directly at
him. If I was going to nail my ex-partner, the dead weren't
going to provide the proof.

Putting the notebook back in the desk's top drawer, my
hand brushed up against the textured sleeve of Angela's final
journal. I was halfway through reading it again when my
phone rang. Still reading, I grabbed for the receiver.

"Hello, Joel."

Five months had passed since I'd last heard his crisp ar-

ticulation, but it seemed as if we had just spoken that morning. I snapped Angela's journal shut. "What is it, Stanley?"

"Do you have a moment?"

"We have nothing to talk about," I said.

"On the contrary, Joel. We have much to discuss," he said pleasantly. "Let me at least try to clear some of the air between us."

"It's not clearable."

"I was an idiot for lying to you. But I didn't know how to tell you about . . ."

"Your hobbies," I snapped.

"My sickness," he said. "I've known for years that it would catch up to me. I'm not surprised you were the one who unmasked me. In fact, I'm relieved." He paused. When I didn't comment, he continued. "I suffer from a compulsion disorder," he said, as if it explained everything.

"A compulsion for sadomasochistic sex with your own patients?" I was incredulous. "I don't remember that from the textbooks."

"A miserable sexual compulsion that has ruined my life." Then he quietly added, "And others'." He took a deep breath. "I've tried, Joel. Honestly, I have. I've been on every horrid cocktail of antidepressants and antipsychotics. Nothing works. I've studied compulsive behavior in my anger-management patients for years. Compulsion . . . addiction . . . call it what you will, it's the least manageable beast in the human psyche."

"If you're expecting my forgiveness—"

"I'm not looking for forgiveness. Not even understanding. But I am concerned you might be laboring under some misconceptions about me."

I squeezed the receiver tighter in my hand. "Such as?"

"Bonnie said you were asking about the patients I've lost."

I said nothing.

"You're on the wrong track there. And I can prove it."

"How?"

"*I have tapes,*" he said. "*Audio and video.*"

"*Not interested. Bye.*"

"*Wait!*" he snapped, before I'd pulled the receiver from my ear. "*Don't you want to hear what Angela had to say? The words from her own mouth.*"

I hesitated.

"*One hour, Joel.*" He jumped on my indecision. "*That's all. After, you can do whatever you so choose with the information.*"

"*When?*"

"*How about tomorrow evening?*"

"*Doesn't work.*" I thought for a moment. "*Monday is my only free night.*"

"*Fine,*" Stanley said. "*I see my last patient at eight P.M. As you know, I tend to run late. Could you come by the office at ten?*"

"*Ten o'clock, Monday,*" I said, and hung up the phone.

Stanley's words had spawned an idea. I spent Saturday preparing for our meeting. I completed my first buy from an electronics superstore easily enough. The next purchase proved more complicated. It took me three hours to find the pawnshop that a Western State patient had told me about. After passing five hundred-dollar bills to the expressionless clerk, he handed me the paper bag. Though less than two pounds, I felt as if he'd given me a wrapped anvil. From the moment I held the gun, even concealed in a paper bag, I was gripped by foreboding.

The rest of my wait passed at a glacial pace. I jogged marathon-training distances, and wore poor Nelson out with walks, futilely trying to burn off my nervous energy. When the time finally rolled around, I threw on my nylon jacket and headed to my car.

Five minutes before ten, I passed by the front of my old office building. I circled back, and when I turned into the alley, my headlights hit Brent McCabe, though I didn't recognize him at the time, leaning against the wall of the building. I slowed the car and watched the accountant as he shakily lit *a cigarette. He didn't even look in my direction. Satisfied he had nothing to do with our meeting, I sped past him and down the ramp to the garage.*

Aside from Stanley's Mercedes and an old motorcycle, the garage was empty. Before getting out of my car, I turned on my new digital recorder, ran a quick and successful test recording, and then slipped it in my jacket's breast pocket. After ensuring that my chest wasn't aglow with the LED blue of the recorder, I climbed out of the car.

I unlocked the basement door then mounted the stairs to the third floor. I hesitated in front of the office's door, waiting for the wave of nausea to pass. I steadied my breathing, turned the handle, and stepped inside. The waiting room was dark, but a light came from the hallway that led to the inner offices. "Stanley?" I called.

No reply. As I was considering leaving, I heard footsteps and then Stanley walked out of the hallway and into my view. When he flicked on the waiting-room lights, I saw the bloodstains on his white shirt and tie. His lower lip was twice the size of the upper, and blood continued to ooze from the corner of his mouth and trickle onto his blood-encrusted beard. "Sorry, Joel," he said with a smile, and dabbed his lip with a bloody handkerchief. "I was just attending to this."

"Another 'seizure'?"

"Just straightforward clumsiness. Walked right into a shelf." It would be a couple of weeks before I would learn that the "shelf" was in fact Brent McCabe.

Stanley approached me with his hand extended, but I ignored it.

"Of course. Of course. You don't want blood on your hands," he said, and I wondered if he was trying to be ironic. He spun and walked toward the hallway, waving for me to follow him to his inner office.

On the desk sat a bottle of red and two wineglasses. "Do you want to take your jacket off?"

I shook my head.

He walked behind the desk, poured a glass, and held it out for me. I shook my head again. "Shame." He shrugged. "You don't mind if I do? I could certainly use it."

I sat down in the chair across from him. "You said you had tapes of Angela."

He opened the top drawer and pulled out a bulky antique of a cassette player, placing it on the desk beside the wine bottle. "I hear you can get these in a smaller size." He smiled. For a moment, I thought he might know about my recorder, but I dismissed the idea as paranoid. Stanley took a sip of his wine and then put the glass down, but continued to finger its stem. "Joel, I've made some terrible mistakes with you."

"I don't care about your mistakes with me."

"I do," he said. "The loss of our friendship has been tough."

"What about Angela's loss?"

Stanley shrugged.

"And Mary Pierce and Kerry-Lynn Smith?"

Stanley stared at his glass. "All very sad."

I decided not to push it. "The tape?" I prompted.

"In a minute." Stanley nodded absentmindedly. Then, apropos of nothing, he said, "Joel, I respect you as much as any other psychiatrist. That's why I need you to answer me a question. Do you honestly believe that we can modify human behavior?"

"I didn't come here for a philosophical chat."

"You're here nonetheless. It's relevant to our discussion."

I didn't see the point of this, but I replied, "Of course behavior is modifiable."

"I wish I shared your optimism." He laughed softly. "I'm at the end of my career. And I'm not sure that I've 'cured' a single patient in thirty-plus years."

"That's ridiculous. How many hundreds of depressed or psychotic patients have you seen through their illness?"

He waved the suggestion away with his free hand. "Depression and psychosis, those are simple chemical imbalances. We throw drugs at them like decongestants for a cold." He pointed his glass at me. "I'm talking about those inadequate personalities who lumber into our office week after week, no better for their effort."

"Where are you going with this?"

"We are glorified illusionists, you and I. Character is character. People don't change. Take you, for example."

"What about me?"

"You're a twenty-first-century Don Quixote." He chuckled. "Trying to save those damsels in distress. In fact, those beyond distress. All the while, tilting at your own windmills."

I folded my arms across my chest. "What are my windmills?"

He smiled sympathetically and wiped at his bleeding lip. "All the abusive men who have wronged you. Your father, your wife's uncle, Angela's father . . ." He paused. "And, of course, me."

Staring at Stanley, it dawned on me that I'd never known him at all.

"That's the fate you've chosen—to wallow among the dead, Joel," Stanley said definitively. "And we could spend the next ten years analyzing it without changing that."

"What's your fate, Stanley?" I asked.

He smiled sadly. "Not much better than yours."

"You don't sound as repentant as you did on the phone."

"I'm not repentant at all." He stroked his bloody beard. "It's not in my nature."

"And all those dead women?"

"What of them? At least they had the opportunity to experience the exquisite."

"Oh." I nodded. "Pain."

"Exactly, Joel." Stanley waved his finger at me. "The basest and most intense form of pleasure. To give and receive. You have no idea of the totality of the experience."

"Lucky women," I said evenly. "How come all of them wanted out so badly?"

He reached for his glass and emptied it again. "It takes a complex and clear mind to appreciate the experience for what it is. These women couldn't cope with an average day. How could they possibly understand the joy of agony?"

"So you killed them?"

"That sounds so callous, Joel." Stanley lifted the bottle to refill his glass. "You sure you won't join me?"

"Positive."

"I didn't want any of them to die." He poured himself a generous glass. "I tried every way possible to reach them, but nothing got through."

I took a deep breath. "Tell me about Angela."

"She was special, wasn't she?" He smiled nostalgically. "I understand your attachment to her. She was the best of the bunch. The only one who came close to touching the ecstasy."

I bit down, fighting to steady the muscles in my face and stem my welling anger.

He took a big gulp from his wineglass. "But when she stood on my doorstep and read me that inflammatory letter she planned to publish, she took away the last of my options. It became a matter of self-preservation."

It took every ounce of my concentration to remain in my seat.

"If it's any consolation, you meant the world to her," Stanley said. "She was devastated when you didn't believe her account of our relationship."

"Why are you telling me this, Stanley?" I dropped my right hand to my lap.

He took a long drink of the wine, finishing the glass and placing it softly on his desk. "I don't think I've ever needed wine as much as I do tonight. It's truly shaping up to be one of the worst nights of my life." He looked over my head and nodded, then he added: "Yours too, I'm afraid, Joel."

I slipped my hand under my jacket and gripped the cool handle of the gun. Then, slowly, I turned and looked over my shoulder.

There he stood, filling the doorway.

Dressed in black from his ski mask to his feet, the dark canvas provided the perfect backdrop for the glint from the massive blade in his hand.

17

A FTER DELIBERATELY PROVOKING Wayne Hacking, my vigilance peaked. Each time I caught Claire eyeing me, I wasn't sure whether she was appraising me or whether I was just more aware of her attention. Either way, it was getting to me. "What is it, Claire?" I asked, feeling her stare as I climbed into the passenger seat.

She rested her hands on the steering wheel without starting the engine. "I can't figure you out."

I forced a smile. "I'm an enigma wrapped in a mystery. That's what makes me so irresistible."

She turned to me, straight-faced. "Joel, I can't shake the feeling that I'm still being left out of the loop."

I decided to deflect her inquisitiveness with the truth. I reached for her hand and squeezed. "Claire, I'm falling in love with you."

Her eyes widened. "Where did that come from?"

"My heart."

"You know what I mean. Why . . . now?" she asked.

"Guess I could've picked a nicer setting." I pointed out the window at the oppressive gray concrete of the hotel's garage. "But I just wanted to tell you."

She hesitated. Then she cupped my face in her hands. "I feel the same way." She kissed me for a long time, before pulling her lips away. "But the last time I felt like this, I ended up having my heart broken." Her big green eyes pleaded and warned simultaneously. "Don't break my heart, Joel."

I flashed the most reassuring smile I could muster, but all I felt was guilt.

She kissed me again. "You really are hard to figure, you know that?"

Dev wasn't in as loving a mood when we stepped into his office. "This is bullshit! We know Hacking did it. He knows we know. And we're mincing around each other like a couple of pimply kids at a junior-high dance."

"What do you suggest?" Claire said, sinking into her seat.

"Maybe it's time to take the gloves off," Dev grumbled. "Throw him in a cell and let him sweat a while."

"His type doesn't sweat," I pointed out.

" 'His type,' " Dev said with a harumph. "Doc, I don't give a flying fuck about 'his type.' I want Hacking."

"But as you noted yesterday, what do we have on him?" Claire asked.

Dev looked from Claire to me, giving the impression that he felt outnumbered. Then he listed the points with his fingers. "We've got the car that nearly killed you. We've connected him to the kinky stuff with both victims. Maybe even a missing hooker. And we've deep-sixed his fake alibi. Besides which, he killed his only character witness."

"There's nothing to place him at either scene," I pointed out.

"And still no motive," Claire added. "Why don't we go back over the details one more time? Meantime, he might screw up under our watch."

"Or if he's as smart as Doc keeps telling us, he might just up and disappear."

"I have an idea," I said. "Could be a long shot, but I think it's worth another visit to Mitch Greene."

An hour later, we stood at Greene's open door. His was a large office, or would have been, if not for the mounds of journals, books, and papers piled all over the place. Greene sat at his desk. As soon as he noticed us, he dropped the journal he was reading. "Hey, it's the heat!" He pointed at me and laughed. "And the heat-wannabe."

After he ushered us in with a wave of his hairy arm, we joined him at his desk. "I see more of you guys than my own feet these days," Greene cracked.

"Mitch, did you have a chance to look at the files?" I asked.

Greene raised two files on the desk and dropped them back with a thud. "I didn't do the autopsy on either of those girls, but the pictures aren't bad."

"What pictures?" Dev asked.

Greene dug around in one of the files, pulled out two photos, and laid them on his desk. The first showed a woman's slim naked torso with multiple stab wounds covering her chest and abdomen. I wondered if we were looking at Hacking's ex-girlfriend or her sister, but I didn't ask. The next shot was a close-up of one of the wounds with a ruler lying beneath it, documenting the laceration's width.

Greene jabbed the second photo with a thick finger. "Look. This isn't graphology." He glanced at Dev with a mischievous grin. "For the benefit of our Arkansas guest, graphology is the science of handwriting analysis."

"Thanks," Dev said sarcastically. "Now remind me again what 'arrogant prick' means."

Greene howled a laugh and then turned back to the photograph. "My point is that this ain't no precision science. I can't look at a stab wound and say, 'Aha, that must be the handiwork of Jack Jones from Yakima.'"

Dev exhaled heavily. "So we're wasting our time?"

"Not entirely. I understand your job has a decent pension plan." Greene bellowed another laugh. He reached for a third file, pulled out another close-up of a stab wound, and rested it beside the others. "This is Calvin Nichol's chest wound. Compare it to the girl's." He rested an index finger at the base of both close-ups. "For starters, both victims were stabbed by almost the exact same blade. And it looks like the same depth of penetration, which has as much to do with force as it does with the weapon itself. But most relevant, in both cases, the knifeman knew how to wield his weapon. None of that amateur scraping or ragged edges. Just direct, clean blows. Right-handed, to boot."

"Sounds close to a match," Claire said.

"Detective Shepherd, you know what they say about close and horseshoes?" Greene grinned at her. "But I agree. To my eyes, they're as close to the same knifeman's signature as you're going to find. I just don't know whether it would count for anything in court."

Dev ran a finger over the last photo. "It can't hurt."

Greene turned to me. "Hey, on the murder of those two girls, didn't Hacking get off on some aliens-were-talking-to-me-through-my-dental-fillings defense?"

"Kolberg testified Hacking was suffering from a dissociative state at the time of the crime."

"Guess old Stanley didn't realize the guy kept a summer home in that particular state." Greene chuckled. "When you see Hacking next, ask him something for me."

"What's that?"

"Ask him why he threw everything at Stanley, including the kitchen sink, but killed Nichol with the efficiency of a bad heart surgeon?" He shook his head. "I still find that odd."

In the parking lot, Claire stood by the driver's door without climbing in. She was deep in thought. "Seems to me we have enough to pick up Hacking on probable cause now."

"Let's go get him," Dev said as he ducked into the passenger seat.

As soon as we pulled out of the lot, Dev's cell phone rang. He pulled it out of his jacket, answered it, and listened for a moment. Then he barked: "What? *When?!*" Another pause. "Just find him."

Dev slammed the phone on the dashboard and then turned to us, his cheeks red and eyes dark. "Hacking's gone!"

18

BY THE TIME WE ARRIVED AT HOMICIDE, the surveillance detectives had pieced together the details of Hacking's escape. He'd abandoned his job at the convenience store in the middle of his shift, ducking out back where, unbeknownst to the cops watching out front, he stored his motorcycle.

I hung around the department all afternoon, but there was nothing for me to do except watch Dev and Claire coordinate the manhunt for Hacking. By the time we called it a night, there was still no trace of him. And I had come to regret my taunting phone call. Freeing Hacking from his leash had seemed like a good idea when I knew where he was, but now that he was roaming unchecked, I felt acutely unsafe. I hoped his behavior wouldn't stray too far from my textbook-based prediction, but my doubts were growing.

Claire drove us back to the hotel. Ensuring that we didn't dawdle in the garage, I led Claire straight to the elevator. As soon as Claire opened the hotel room's door, I barged past her into the room. I was relieved to see Nelson lying half-asleep on the fabric sofa. At the sight of us, he hopped off the couch and trotted into the kitchen where he demanded his dinner by knocking his bowl around with his snout.

"I'm going to grab a shower before dinner, if that's okay," Claire said.

I walked her through the bedroom and into the adjacent bathroom. "I better get Nelson fed and out for a pee."

"Sure you don't want to join me?" Claire asked with a wink as she stepped out of her clothes and into the shower.

"Very tempting, but I answer to a higher calling—namely, Nelson." I forced a smile.

As soon as I heard the water running, I headed over to the room's wall safe. My injured arm ached even before I pulled out the gun. I held it in my right hand and pointed at the wall with a finger on the trigger. Though my wrist throbbed, I decided I could bear it if I had to fire the gun. Guts churning, I grabbed my nylon jacket off the bed and tucked the gun into the large inside pocket. I went to the kitchen and filled a bowl of dry food for Nelson. I emptied the rest of it into the garbage can and covered it with other trash.

Returning to the bedroom, I found Claire standing in front of the wall-mounted mirror. She had one towel wrapped around her midsection and dried her hair with another. A wave of guilt-tinged melancholy swept over me as I studied her sweet face in the mirror.

She cocked her head. "What's wrong?"

"Nelson has eaten us out of house and home," I said. "I'm just stepping out to pick up a bag of dog food."

She nodded. "You won't be long?"

"Hope not," I said, having trouble pulling my eyes from her. "Claire, in spite of all the crap around us . . ." I cleared my throat. "I want you to know how happy I am that I found you." I stepped forward and kissed her softly on the lips. I left her standing in front of the mirror looking perplexed but with a glow to her cheeks.

On the way out of the room, I tested the lock on the door before grabbing the elevator to the lobby. I loitered by the concierge desk, pretending to study tour pamphlets. When I saw the last of the taxis pull away from the front of the hotel, I ambled to the door and stepped outside.

Keeping under the lights of the hotel, I paced back and forth in front of the bellman's desk. Damp hands tucked in my pockets, I clutched the gun through the jacket's lining.

My training dictated that Hacking would be outside somewhere, biding his time. If he was nearby, I knew I would've made an easy shot for him. But that wasn't his style. Or so I hoped. I kept in constant motion not wanting to make it any easier than need be. Each squeal of a tire or screech of a brake was agony, as I fought the urge to dive under the bell desk.

After ten exposed minutes, a cab pulled up front to drop off another fare. I decided I'd given Hacking long enough. I climbed in the back and gave the driver my address. As the car eased out into the traffic, I had a furtive glance over both shoulders but I didn't see any suspicious lights turn to follow.

I kept my eyes glued to the rearview mirror during the whole trip, but I never spotted the solitary headlight of a motorbike on our tail. Approaching my house, I was gripped by a new and terrible thought. I'd always assumed Hacking would come after me, but suddenly I wasn't so certain. By phoning him and revealing our location, I'd exposed Claire, too. My mouth went dry. For the most part, Hacking killed women. What if he went after her?

In the minute I stood by the driver's-side window paying for the taxi, I didn't glimpse or hear another car or bike on my street. Walking up my pathway, I reached inside my jacket pocket, pulled out the gun, and slipped it into the more accessible outer pocket. I reached the front door and unlocked it with a shaky hand.

I walked to the stairs by the front door without turning the foyer light on. I climbed the stairs to my bedroom, reassured by the moan of the steps. I walked into my bedroom and sat down on the bed. Keeping an eye on the doorway, I reached for my cordless phone. I punched in the caller-ID blocking code and then dialed the number for the hotel. The operator patched me through, and Claire answered on the third ring. "Where are you?" she demanded.

"I can't explain now," I said.

"Where are you?" she repeated slowly, her tone a mix of anger and worry.

"Claire, Hacking knows where we're staying," I said softly. "I don't think he's looking for you, but you have to get out of there. It's not safe."

Her voice rose. "Joel, what the hell are you up to?"

I stared at the gun in my hand without answering.

"Joel, you said you loved me," she pleaded in a softer tone. "There's no love without trust. Tell me where you are—"

"Claire, I've got to go now. Please get out of the room!"

"Joel! Don't—"

Feeling like an absolute bastard, I pushed the phone's END button. The prophetic symbolism of the gesture wasn't lost on me.

Leaving the upstairs hallway light on, I walked into the bathroom, turned on the shower, and then headed back into my spare room whose mural-bearing walls never lived up to its billing as a nursery. I reshuffled a few boxes, switched off the room's light, and then sat down in the center of the room from where I had a clear view of the top flight of the stairs.

I rested my gun-bearing hand in my lap. I waited.

Minutes passed. Not a sound, except the soft hiss of the shower. And every moment my concern for Claire grew. I wondered if my call imploring her to leave the hotel room had had the opposite effect, serving only to keep her in the room while she worked the phones feverishly trying to track me down.

Half an hour later, nauseous with worry and regret, I decided I had to go back for her. I stood and crept into the hallway. Tiptoeing down the stairs—which were supposed to work in my favor, but now threatened to betray me—I managed to keep the creaks to a minimum. Until the second last step. The whine from the unstable board sent a shiver through me. I stopped and held my breath, but the silence seemed to forgive my misstep. I took one more step and reached the darkness of the main floor. I considered calling for another cab but opted, in the interest of time, to take my old car.

Halfway to the back door, I stumbled over something soft, barely catching myself before falling against the wall. Regaining my balance, I realized I'd been tripped by Nelson's cedar chip–filled bed. I continued until I got to the kitchen–family room where the skylights absorbed enough of the exterior light to vaguely illuminate the room. I had a quick glance around but saw nothing.

At the back door, I grabbed my car keys from the little wooden hanger, but a faint rustling stopped me. I dropped to my knees and extended the gun in front of me. I saw nothing, but the noise persisted. Rotating my head from side to side, I localized the sound as coming from my basement. I took a couple of slow breaths, rose, and walked to the top of the basement stairs. Squatting, I peered down but saw nothing in the darkness at the bottom of the staircase.

I inhaled a huge breath and then lowered a foot onto the top step. With each step down, I froze and listened intently. All I heard was the soft fluttering that had originally caught my ear. When I reached the bottom, a soft wind blew against my cheek.

Keeping one hand on the wall, I tiptoed along the concrete floor following the breeze. I crept through the laundry room and poked my head around the corner. At the end of the short hall, dim light from the back lane poured through the window inset in the basement door. It took a moment before I realized that the glass in the window was gone. A pile of shattered glass lay at the foot of the door. The ugly little curtain that once covered the window flapped back and forth in the breeze, producing the rustling noise.

I went cold, though not because of the wind or the basement's damp air. I knew who had broken the window. I just didn't know where he was now. I was overwhelmed by the need to get back to Claire.

I hurried along the concrete floor and up the stairs. I stopped a moment in the kitchen and glanced around but saw nothing in the weak light. I opened the back door and ran down the pathway to my garage. I pulled open the door to the garage and switched on the single sixty-watt light bulb. After a quick check, I darted over to my old Honda. I yanked open the door and hopped into the driver's seat. I rested the gun on the passenger's seat and reached in my jacket for the car keys.

I stuck the key in the ignition. Reaching for the garage door opener, I glimpsed a pair of opaque eyes in the rear-view mirror.

At the same moment, something cool and sharp touched my neck. I jerked away instinctively, nicking my neck on the blade.

In the mirror, I watched Wayne Hacking lean forward from the backseat. "Dr. Ashman, could I bum a ride?" he said through his black ski mask.

"I figured you'd be inside my house," I croaked, desperate to stall.

"Too predictable." Keeping the knife against my throat, he reached over with his other hand and grabbed my gun from the seat. "Mind if I hang on to this?"

My chest hammered. "Wayne, if you kill me here, don't you think the cops will know it was you?"

"Who said I was going to kill you here?" he asked as cheerily as ever, then pressed the blade harder against my neck. "Please drive."

I felt a trickle run down my neck. I didn't know if it was blood or sweat. "Where to?"

"Just drive, Dr. Ashman. I'll direct you."

I knew beyond a doubt that if I drove out of the garage, I was as good as dead. Deliberately leaving the gearshift in Park, I turned the key. As expected, the engine sputtered and coughed, but didn't catch. I tried a second time for effect, but of course the engine still didn't turn.

"Dr. Ashman, you can do better than that," Hacking said in a menacing whisper.

"You want to try?" I bluffed desperately.

Hacking didn't reply. The knife pressed harder into the skin of my neck. How did I screw this up so badly? I thought miserably.

Then the blade's pressure lightened. "Change of plans," Hacking finally said. "We're going back in the house. For your sake, please do what I say, Dr. Ashman."

The knife left my neck, but I barely had a chance to clear my throat before the cold metal of my own gun rested against the back of my head. "You stay in the car, until I say so." He pulled the gun away.

Hacking hopped out of the car with surprising agility. He tapped the gun on the window, indicating for me to get out. My intestines knotted and another cold chill swept me as I climbed out. Hacking waved the gun at the garage door. "Walk ahead of me to the house, please."

With the gun in my back, I followed the yard's path to the back door of my house. Once there, Hacking whispered, "Open it and wait inside."

Inside, I flicked on the dim pantry light, realizing it offered the least light.

"Upstairs, please," Hacking said quietly.

Feeling the gun against my spine, I shuffled slowly down the hall to the foyer. With each step, my foot explored the ground in front of me.

"Pick up the pace, Dr. Ashman," Hacking said.

I took two more exploratory steps before my foot brushed against Nelson's bed. I paused and then, in one motion, jumped over it. Distracted by my sudden lunge, Hacking stumbled and tripped over the bed.

I swung my right arm backhanded, slamming into Hacking's shoulder and throwing him into the wall. He lurched into the drywall elbow first, but he managed to stay upright and push himself off against the wall. I kicked wildly at his right arm, hitting him just above his hand. The gun flew from his grip and bounced down the hallway.

Hacking yelped in pain.

I lunged again, swinging my right hand at his face. He reacted with surprising speed. Throwing his arm out to block mine, he made contact directly on my surgical scar. Agony shot up my arm. Stunned, I didn't even see his foot fire out and hit me in the belly.

I groaned and stumbled back a few feet. Just as I straightened up, I saw him reach behind his back and pull the knife out of his belt. At the sight of the blade, I spun and ran for the staircase, flying up the noisy steps two at a time.

Diving into the spare bedroom, I rolled along the floor a couple of turns and then scrambled to my feet. I scurried through the darkness and crawled behind the boxes I'd earlier rearranged. I stuck my aching hand in a box, groping for anything that might pass for a weapon. All I found was an old kerosene camping lamp that I grabbed by the handle.

I dropped to a crouch behind the tallest box at the back of the room. My heart pounded in my ears. Sweat trickled down my forehead. Ages seemed to pass before I heard the slow heavy creaking from the staircase. Then the upstairs hallway light switched on. "Dr. Ashman?" Hacking called from nearby.

I sucked my chest in trying to make myself even narrower behind the box. Soon I heard him rummage through the master bedroom. I thought I caught the sound of a door opening, but I wasn't sure anymore what I was hearing over the sound of my own pulse. I considered running for the stairs but then I heard Hacking moving toward me.

"Dr. Ashman, you're making this so much harder than need be," he said.

His heavy footsteps approached the spare room. I tightened my grip on the lamp and held my breath.

"Dr. Ashman, really, this is just silly," Hacking said cheerfully. The room flooded with light. "There's nowhere left for you to go," he said sympathetically.

Slowly, I raised the lamp, readying to swing. Suddenly, one side of its handle snapped off and the lamp dangled for a moment, suspended by only one arm. I watched in breathless horror as the other arm slipped. Then the lamp fell to the ground with a dull thud and rolled out from behind the box.

"That's more like it, Dr. Ashman." I heard his approach at the same time as the staircase creaked. With a *whoosh,* the box in front of me flew sideways. Hacking stood less than three feet away, pointing my own gun at me.

"Dr. Ashman, just think of this as Stanley returning the favor from the other side of the grave."

Rage flooded over me, washing away the fear. *"Fuck Stanley, and fuck you, Wayne!"* I yelled.

Hacking laughed softly, then extended his arm, steadying the gun's barrel a foot from my forehead. I stared back defiantly.

Boom! The thunderous crack echoed in my ears. I was showered in blood. But I was still standing, which mystified me.

Then Hacking crumpled to his knees in front of me. He teetered for a long moment. Then he flopped forward and slammed headfirst onto the floor inches from my feet. He twitched once and then was still.

I looked up from his body and saw Claire standing a few steps from the top of the staircase. With both hands, she still clasped the gun that was now pointing at me. Slowly, she lowered the gun, never taking her wide eyes off of me.

19

IN A BLINK MY HOUSE was buzzing with cops and paramedics, none of whom had much to offer. Hacking was as
dead as they come. And once I'd scrubbed his blood off
me, I realized I'd survived our final standoff with just a
scratch on my neck and a couple of bruises.

Nate Schiff and his CSI team arrived on the heels of the
emergency-response teams. Even Mitch Greene showed up.
In jeans and a huge sweatshirt, he burst into the kitchen
where I sat at the table with Claire and Dev. "Ash-Man!"
Greene marched up and laid a thick hand on my shoulder.
"You okay?"

"Yeah, thanks, Mitch." I patted his hand. "What are you
doing here?"

"I'm the on-call medical examiner." He chuckled and
winked. "These days, that usually means mopping up the
mess at one psychiatrist's place or another's." His smile
withered, and a rare frown crossed his brow. "Is it over
now?"

"God, I hope so," I said.

"Me too, Joel. Me too." He freed his hand from my shoulder. "Better not keep my patient waiting," he said as he headed for the staircase.

Dev's eyes were set in the same suspicious glare he'd worn since walking in. "You were about to tell me what you were doing here."

"I came home to pick up more of Nelson's special-needs dog food," I said.

"Hmmm." The lines deepened around his eyes. "How do you think Hacking knew you were here?"

I shrugged. "Maybe he was waiting here all along?"

Dev dismissed my explanation with a grunt. He shifted his attention to Claire. "How did you know where to find the doctor?"

"Joel told me he was coming here," she lied. "But when I didn't hear from him for over an hour, I got worried and came looking."

"Lucky for you, Doc," Dev said.

My heart sank, realizing that I'd just forced Claire into the same deceitful quandary her ex-husband had. I reached for her hand and gave it a supportive squeeze, but it was limp in response.

Dev looked down at our interlocking hands and nodded. "Probably best all around if I didn't know all the details leading up to the hole in Hacking's head." When he looked up at me, his face was shrouded with mistrust. "Doc, you haven't been up-front with me since the moment you got involved."

When he turned to his partner with the same betrayed look, I spoke up. "Claire knew no more than you did, Dev."

"And yet she managed to find you." His tone was rife with doubt.

"Because of some brilliant detective work," I said with a faint smile. "Not because I was any more up-front with her."

Before Dev could respond, Greene stormed back into the room. "Detective Shepherd," he bellowed. "Do you cross-country ski?"

Claire rolled her eyes. "What's that got to do with anything, Mitch?"

"Well, if you ski anything like you shoot, you could bring home a gold medal in the biathlon." Greene held one hand like a pistol and closed an eye to sight his imaginary target. "In poor light from twenty-plus feet, you hit a moving target dead-center in the back of the skull." He dropped his hands to his sides. "Even though it means we're still stuck with the Ash-Man, I got to give you credit. It was one helluva shot!"

After Greene left, Claire and I walked Dev out to his van. Once inside, he rolled down the window. "Doc, one day long after we're retired, let's go for a drink and you can tell me what really happened today, huh?"

He drove off, leaving Claire and me alone in the cool evening breeze. I turned to face her. "You okay?"

She nodded blankly.

"Thank you." I leaned forward and hugged her tightly. But she was stiff and unresponsive in my arms. I let go. Suddenly, the brisk night air felt even cooler.

"I'm going to pick up my bags from the hotel," she said, and started for her car without waiting for a response.

She didn't seem to notice when I slipped into the passenger seat beside her. We drove the whole trip in silence.

Once in the hotel room, Claire pulled a beer out of the minibar. "Want one?" she asked without looking over her shoulder.

"No."

We sat across from each other. She sipped her beer and gazed at the ceiling. "How did you know where to find me?" I asked.

"After you phoned, I went and checked the hotel safe. When I saw your gun was missing, I called the telephone company and threatened, begged, and cajoled the supervisor until she agreed to trace your blocked call. Technically, she broke the law. Lucky for you, she was a very understanding lady."

"Claire, you have to know how sorry I am."

She took a long sip of her beer. "You told Hacking where we were staying, didn't you?"

I nodded.

"You wanted to set him up. To kill him." Her tone was matter-of-fact.

I sat still.

She put down the bottle. Her eyes shifted from the wall to me. "Joel, you killed Stanley Kolberg, didn't you?"

"What makes you say that?" I asked evenly.

Claire's eyes held mine, but her face was a mask. "Yesterday, when you were upstairs getting your gun—your *other* gun—I found the final volume of Angela's diary in your office. Then I came across your notes with all the details of Kolberg's three supposed patient-suicides."

I didn't reply.

"Hacking's final comment about 'returning the favor for Stanley' iced it for me," she said. "He knew you had killed Kolberg, too."

"Three innocent women." I locked eyes with her. "Three young women whom he sexually degraded and then murdered, leaving the families to wallow in the guilt of thinking they took their own lives." I took a deep breath to quell the aftershock of anger. "After all that's happened in my life . . . Suzie, Loren, Angela . . . I couldn't ignore that. I just couldn't sit back and watch while one more predator got away with it."

She pointed to her chest. "Why didn't you turn him over to us?"

"Stanley was too smart to leave a provable trail. Believe me, I looked. The worst he was facing was a damaged reputation."

"So you decided to take matters into your own hands."

"I went there to get the evidence I needed, but Hacking was waiting—"

"Evidence? Hacking?" Claire frowned. "You're losing me, Joel."

"It all got so screwed up."

"You owe me an explanation," she said flatly.

As soon as I started to explain, the words just poured out. I began with the day I first met Angela at Swedish Hospital and filled in the details up to the night Stanley died. "Stanley phoned me the Friday before, saying he wanted to meet to clear the air," I said. "From the moment I picked up the phone, I knew I'd pushed him too far. I was convinced he was up to something, so I went to our rendezvous armed." I paused. "But I didn't go planning to kill him."

"Why did you go at all?"

"To see if I could get him to confess. Catch him on tape. Which I did." I sighed heavily. "Then Hacking showed up with a knife and ski mask. Things went wrong in a big hurry."

"Did you know it was Hacking?" Claire asked.

"Not then." I shook my head. "Even later, the night he killed Nichol and took a swipe at me, I still wasn't sure. It wasn't until Anya told me about the grinning cameraman behind Calvin's twisted little video that it all clicked. I realized Hacking must have been Stanley's hatchet man for Angela and the others. The timing made perfect sense. None of Stanley's patients died while Hacking was serving his sentence at Western State."

"Why did Hacking kill Nichol?"

"I can only speculate. I think that once Nichol realized he was the prime suspect, he panicked. My guess is Cal wasn't involved in the patient murders but knew something. That might've explained his falling out with Stanley. I think Cal planned on spilling his guts, and that's why he wanted to meet me. Or maybe he was just setting me up. Either way, we were both liabilities for Hacking. He must've seen our meeting as a chance to kill two birds with one big knife."

Claire nodded. Curiosity had replaced the hurt on her face. "The night Kolberg died. What happened after Hacking showed up?"

I closed my eyes and shook my head. I could still see every detail of the tense standoff in Stanley's office. "It all went to hell in a handbasket . . ."

I took my eyes off the masked knifeman and swiveled my head back to Stanley, who was dabbing at his bleeding lip again.

I gripped the gun in my lap more tightly. "So I am to be your next suicide, huh?"

"Let's face it, Joel." He pulled the handkerchief away and ran his tongue over the welt on his lip. "You've been depressed ever since your wife died. And you went straight into the toilet after Angela's suicide."

"Her 'suicide,'" I grunted. "Have you completely lost it, Stanley?"

"I wish I had, Joel. This is anything but how I wanted it to end for us." He rose from his desk. "Still, I find myself out of options again." He pointed over my head. "I'm going to leave you with my associate—"

I shot up from my chair, spun, and leveled the gun straight at the masked man's head. "Drop the knife!"

He hesitated. His eyes looked past me to Stanley for guidance.

"Come on, Joel. You with a gun?" Stanley laughed behind me. "It's preposterous."

I pointed the gun and fired, flinching at the explosive roar. The plaster sprayed from above the masked man's head, and he dropped to the ground but clung to his weapon. "Drop the fucking knife!" I shouted.

He let the knife fall to the ground and stood up from his crouch.

"Kick it over here," I said.

He tapped the knife with a foot. It slid toward me, stopping inches from my feet. I bent down, picked it up, and stuck it in my belt, never taking my eyes or the gun away from him. I pointed the gun at Stanley. "Go stand by him!" I barked.

"Now what, Joel?" Stanley scoffed, but he walked out from behind his desk and joined the knifeman by the door. "We both know nothing will come of this. You're not going to shoot us. And let's face it, you've no proof for your outlandish allegations."

"That so?" I said through clenched teeth.

I reached my free hand into my pocket and pulled out the digital recorder. I rewound the unit and pressed PLAY. "'I didn't want any of them to die,'" Stanley said in a static-free voice. "'I tried every way possible to reach them, but nothing got through.'"

Stanley's eyes narrowed. "That's hardly a confession, Joel."

I fast-forwarded searching for his comments about Angela. As I was studying the LED display, I caught a blur of movement out of the corner of my eye. Startled, I fumbled and dropped the recorder. By the time my head snapped up, the masked man had bolted out the door. I tore after him into the corridor, but before I could even steady the gun, he'd rounded the corner into the waiting room. When I reached the waiting room, the office door was wide open and he was running down the hallway. "Don't!" I screamed and pointed the gun. In one motion, he shoved open the stairway door and dove into the stairwell.

Irate, I marched back to the inner office, where I found Stanley sitting at his desk with wineglass in one hand and my digital recorder in the other. "I really am a technological dinosaur." He beamed as he held up the device for me to see. "I think I might've really screwed up your recording by pressing this FORMAT button."

I stood in the doorway, my hand shaking as I leveled the gun at his head. "You . . . killed . . . Angela."

"So you say." He smiled.

"You're going to pick up that phone and tell the 911 operator what you did." I was dizzy from breathing so fast. "Now!"

Stanley put the glass and the recorder down and stood up from his desk. "Joel, we are such different people, you and I." He walked around his desk. "I'm a doer. You're a watcher. It's just how it is." He smiled helplessly. "You did nothing after you learned your father had had his way with your girlfriend, Suzie. And let's face it, you wouldn't have done anything about Loren's uncle if he were still around." He took a step toward me and extended his hand. "Give me the gun, Joel," he said with absolute calm.

"Don't take another step, Stanley," I growled, pointing the gun at his head.

"Oh, Joel." He walked toward me with a relaxed smile.

"Not another step!" I shook the gun at him.

But Stanley kept coming.

And I fired.

* * *

Expressionlessly, Claire studied me from across the room.

"I think I just meant to scare him—to shoot past his head like I'd done with Hacking. I don't know . . . I was so furious." I dropped my head and cleared my throat. "But it was no warning shot. The side of his neck exploded like a red geyser. The surprise on his face was indescribable. He stumbled backward a few steps, and then he swiveled as he collapsed to the floor, grabbing for his neck.

"When I got to him, he was staring up at me, looking very calm. He didn't say a word as the blood pumped out between the fingers he held against his neck. Without a word, he smiled at me and let go of his grip. The blood gushed from his neck, and then his eyes rolled back. He was dead in seconds."

Claire brought both hands to her face and rubbed. She spoke through her fingers. "Joel, it was self-defense."

"Was it? An old, unarmed man walking toward me with his hand extended, and I shot him in the neck." I shook my head. "I knew how it looked."

She pulled her hands from her face. Suddenly she looked very weary. "You don't know what we would've—"

I cut her off with a shake of my head. "I knew how it looked."

"Okay." She sighed. "Then what?"

"The rest was housekeeping. I found a garbage bag in the office's utility room. I tossed the bottle and glasses, the digital recorder, and even my shoes in the garbage bag. I checked his cassette player, but of course, the tape was blank." I chuckled grimly. "In the top drawer of his desk, I came across a loaded syringe—Valium, no doubt, and earmarked for me. I tossed all of it in the bag.

"Then I hit upon the idea of getting Nichol to the scene. After what he'd done to Angela, I thought he deserved to at least sweat a little. I called and left the urgent 'Meet me at the office!' message on his pager. I had a final look around, picked up my bag, and headed out."

Claire tilted her head. "And mutilating Kolberg's body? When did you do that?"

I shook my head. "I didn't."

"Oh?" She shook her head. "Who did?"

"I don't know for certain."

She pursed her lips and eyed me skeptically.

"Claire, it's true. It could've been Brent McCabe or maybe even Nichol—both had the opportunity—but I'm convinced Hacking did it. I bet he never even left the building after fleeing the office. I think he came back looking to surprise me and rescue his buddy."

"Why would Hacking mutilate Kolberg's body?" Claire grimaced. "It makes no sense."

"Might make more sense than you think," I said. "With Hacking's history and close association to the victim, he must've guessed the trail would lead back to him. Remember how quickly he did become a suspect? Besides, even if Kolberg's murder wasn't pinned on him, under scrutiny some of his other nastiness might have come to light. No. I think he was smart enough to frame someone else for the murder. To divert your attention with someone whose profile fit one of Stanley's anger-management patients."

Claire pointed at me. "Why not just turn you in?"

"Because he'd risk exposing himself. Remember, I didn't know who the guy in the mask was at the time. Making it look like one of Stanley's anger-management patients was the highest-percentage solution. What a job he did, too. The beating, the genital mutilation, the broken arms . . . textbook psychotic rage."

Claire nodded distantly. Her curiosity sated, she leaned back in her chair and lapsed into cool detachment. "Assuming what you just said is true, it means that you've been lying to me since the moment we met."

"What choice did I have?" I asked, knowing how weak it must have sounded. I lowered my gaze and spoke to the coffee table, unwilling to face her angry eyes. "I knew Dev would turn to me on this case, of all cases, for my input. I didn't know how to get out of it without looking suspicious.

And there was Tommy to protect. With his strong motive and lack of alibi, he was bound to become a suspect." Without looking up, I added: "Then I met you. . . ."

Claire didn't respond.

"I got caught up in a circle of lies of my own making," I said quietly. "Claire, there's no excuse for how I've treated you."

Without comment, she rose from her chair and walked into the bedroom.

I sat and stared at the floor. I wasn't sure whether she was going to arrest me or just walk out of my life. Both prospects struck me as equally miserable.

Ten long minutes passed before Claire returned. She held a tissue in her hand. Her eyes were red from crying. She approached slowly, stopping within an arm's length of me. "I believe that killing Kolberg was an act of self-defense. Period. Frankly, I'm glad he and Hacking are dead."

I kept my eyes on the floor.

"But I don't think I can get beyond your deceit," she said. I nodded.

"And besides, Joel." Her tone softened. "I'm not sure I can compete with all the tragic ghosts . . . Suzie and Angela and Loren . . ." She swallowed. "They still seem like such a huge part of your life."

I looked up at her. "Claire—"

She held up a hand to cut me off. "Joel, I need some time—alone—to sort everything out in my head."

She leaned forward and brushed her lips against my cheek. Then she stood and walked to the door. Before twisting the knob, she looked over her shoulder. "If you had it to do all over again?"

"I wouldn't do anything the same." I paused. "Except when it came to falling for you."

She nodded and opened the door. She stepped out, but before the door had a chance to close, she turned back to me. "You had no right to let me fall in love with you."

I thought her tone was resigned, not angry. At least I hoped. But before I could reply, she was gone.

Turn the page for a sneak peek at

DANIEL KALLA'S
BLOOD LIES

(0-7653-1832-6)

Available June 2007
in Hardcover from Forge Books

THE SIREN CHOKED off in midwail. Within seconds, the flashing red light swept through the frosted glass of the ER's sliding door like a disco ball on overdrive.

I heaved a self-pitying sigh. Ten minutes before the end of a long night shift, I'd counted on an uneventful and punctual exit. Any chance for either vanished when the ambulance stretcher and two paramedics burst through the main Emergency Room doors.

"Which room?" the tall scraggy paramedic yelled as they careened past the triage desk.

"Trauma Two," the triage nurse called back.

I ran alongside the paramedics, but our pace wasn't fast enough to outrun the acrid smells of urine and vomit wafting up from the stretcher. A woman of indeterminate age lay on her side, twitching and thrashing. Without the restraining hand of the female paramedic she might have bucked off the stretcher. Legs and arms jerked in violent rhythm. Her chin slammed into her chest. A mess of long brown hair covered her face. Her T-shirt was spattered with vomit. A chain of drool connected the corner of her mouth to the sheets. An image of Linda Blair from *The Exorcist* flashed to mind.

"What's the story?" I asked the baby-faced female paramedic running beside me.

"Seizing when we got to her. Found down at Cloud Nine." She glanced at me, deciding I was old enough to require clarification. "It's an after-hours club."

"Thanks," I grunted. "What's she got on board?"

"Her sister says she dropped two tabs of Ecstasy about an hour before we got to her. First-time user. Otherwise the kid is healthy."

"Kid?"

"Fourteen years." She wiped her flushed brow with a palm. "Name's Lara Maxwell."

"How long has she been seizing?"

"Twenty minutes, give or take."

Way too long. Within half an hour of a continuous seizure, or status epilepticus, irreversible brain damage can occur. "What have you given her?" I asked.

"Nothing. We scooped and ran. Impossible to get an IV in her in the back of our rig." She flailed her own arms, as if the wildly twitching patient wasn't explanation enough.

We wheeled into Trauma Two, one of St. Jude's three identical resuscitation rooms. Nothing architecturally unique about this or any resuscitation bay I've ever seen; all big bland rooms filled with medical supplies, lights, X-ray viewing boxes, and, at times like these, people. The place swarmed. Some moved with purpose, others—the usual array of wide-eyed students and ER lookie-loos (staff who find any excuse to turn up whenever something exciting rolls in)—just milled about.

Swaddling her in the ambulance stretcher's sheet, the two paramedics swung the patient over to the room's stretcher. Lara Maxwell was oblivious to her new surroundings; her arms and legs never missed a beat of their syncopated contraction.

Anne Bailey, arguably the poster girl for hardened frumpy

ER nurses the world over, was the nurse in charge. She had no time for the bustling crowd. "If you don't serve a purpose, get out!" Anne shouted and, on cue, the room thinned. She turned to the other nurses. "Lucy, two IVs. Jan, get an oral airway into her. Tommy, you record, okay? And where are my vital signs?" Anne turned to me, her lower jaw working side to side as if chewing a gobstopper. "What meds do you want us to give, Ben?" Despite her businesslike tone, her eyes clouded with urgency.

Relieved as I was to see Anne in charge, the rare show of concern on her face concerned me. "Lorazepam 4 mg IV push, now," I said, referring to the Valium-like drug we use for seizures. "Full lab panel including calcium, magnesium, and phosphate. ECG. Chest X-ray. Blood gas. Urine drug screen ASAP, and—"

The nurse cut in from bedside. "Pulse is 140, pressure 260 on 140, respiratory rate of 28, and temperature of 38.4." There was a pause as she fiddled with the oxygen saturation probe that kept slipping off Lara's jerking finger. "Oxygen saturation is sitting at 88 percent."

Not a normal vital sign in the bunch. "Sugar?" I asked.

"Glucometer was normal at the scene," the scrawny paramedic piped up.

Damn! Gone was the most rectifiable cause for a seizure: low blood sugar.

I edged closer to my patient. The mingled odors of vomit and urine assaulted me, forcing me to breathe through my mouth. Lara's hair had fallen back from her face, and I could see beyond the strands of drool and blood. The flickering eyelids and gnashing jaw belonged to the face of a child, someone who had no business near after-hours clubs and their inevitable cache of designer drugs. I felt familiar stirrings. *Fucking junk!* I wanted to shout.

I glanced at the clock. Five minutes since arrival, twenty-five minute since onset, and the seizure showed no sign of lessening. The drool at her mouth had begun to bubble, and became a rich froth like an exploding soda pop can. Reaching for my stethoscope, my worry meter crept higher.

"Another four of lorazepam. And hang a Dilantin drip. Run in a gram over fifteen minutes," I said, calling for the heavy artillery of anti-seizure drugs. Pulling the stethoscope off my shoulders, I leaned over Lara's jerking form and raced through a head-to-toe physical exam. Filled with fluid, her lungs were all gurgles and wheezes. A bluish tinge enveloped her fingers and lips. I glanced at the monitor. Her oxygen saturation had dipped into the seventies—respiratory failure territory—and her blood pressure had risen even higher. "We have to stop this seizure. *Now!*" That meant medically paralyzing the young girl. I recited the drugs and sequence I wanted them given.

"Dr. Dafoe, you better look at this . . ." Jan waved an ECG printout at me like it was a flag.

I studied the twelve squiggly lines, stunned by their implication. "A heart attack? *At fourteen?* She must have cocaine on board, too." I looked to the respiratory technician. "Everything ready?"

She nodded and pointed shakily to the tray beside me.

"Okay, Anne, give her 100 of sux."

Anne stuck a syringe into one of the four IV lines leading into Lara's arms. She pushed on the plunger. Within seconds of administering the succinylcholine—a fast-acting drug that paralyzes muscles and renders patients into rag dolls—the twitching began to subside. Soon Lara lay still on the bed. As expected, she stopped breathing. What I didn't foresee (but should have) was the fountain of foam spewing from her mouth, as her lungs passively expelled their fluid contents.

I grabbed for the scythe-shaped laryngoscope. The knuckles of my left hand ached, and I glanced down at the source: the healing jagged gash from my bike chain that ran across my knuckles like a jailhouse tattoo. Ignoring the pain, I clicked open the laryngoscope's blade and eased it into Lara's mouth pushing her tongue out of the way. To pass the endotracheal tube into her windpipe, I needed to see her vocal cords, but I couldn't visualize anything through the froth. I stuck a suction catheter in her mouth but it was as hopeless as trying to vacuum up water from a burst and still-spewing pipe. The monitor's alarm screamed, warning me what I already knew: Lara's oxygen level was dangerously low.

"Bag her!" I said to the respiratory technician who fumbled to cover Lara's mouth with the clear facemask and pump oxygen in with a balloon-shaped Ambu-bag.

I turned to Anne. "I have to do this retrograde."

Anne's eyes betrayed her skepticism as she reached for the retrograde intubation kit. Her doubt was well founded, too. It was a technically challenging procedure at the best of times, I was firmly perched on the 'wing and a prayer' side of the statistical success curve.

I took a long deep breath and willed my hands to steady. I reached for the open tray Anne held out for me. Setting it on the bedside, I scoured through it until I found the syringe with the long ominous attached needle. I slid an index finger along Lara's soft damp neck until I felt it dip into the groove of her cricothyroid membrane.

The alarm throbbed in my ears.

With a slight tremor, I aimed the needle, directing it slightly upward for the skin over the cricothyroid membrane. I held my own breath as the needle pierced the skin. I felt a pop, as I penetrated Lara's windpipe. Suddenly the tension on the syringe's plunger gave way, and air whooshed into its hub. I steadied the syringe and uncoupled it from the needle.

"Ben, her oxygen saturation is critical," Anne said calmly over the shrieking alarm.

"Noted," I grunted, as I reached for the soft metal guide-wire that looked like a loose coil of silver string. Steadying my hand, I threaded the guide-wire through the needle. "Stop bagging her," I said, needing a clearer view of her mouth.

Hesitantly, the respiratory tech pulled the mask off Lara's blue face.

I kept advancing the guide-wire through the needle until a glint of metal appeared through the froth of Lara's mouth. Then more wire poked out. My hand shot out to grab it. I nodded to Anne, and she handed me the clear endotracheal tube. I snaked the wire through the length of the tube. Then, using the wire as a guide, I threaded the tube into Lara's windpipe. Sighing with relief, I felt the welcome resistance of the cartilaginous tracheal rings as the tube bumped down the rest of her windpipe. The moment its tip reached her lungs, frothy white sputum erupted out of its end.

I grabbed the Ambu-bag, attached it to the tube, and squeezed the balloon-like pump, meeting fierce resistance. My forearms ached as I fought to squeeze breath after breath of oxygen into Lara's waterlogged lungs. For a while, the abysmal oxygen reading held constant on the monitor, but slowly, almost reluctantly, it began to climb as pinkness crept back into her blue complexion. I passed the bag over to the respiratory tech who pumped it feverishly. Lara's color steadily improved. Even the monitor took a much-needed break from its relentless screaming

Tasting the sweat drip into my mouth, I wiped my brow and turned to Anne. "What's a child doing with this crap in her blood?" Though, of course, I knew as well as anybody.

"She were my daughter? I'd kill her soon as she gets out of the ICU." Anne's lips cracked slightly at the corners in what passed for her version of a smile. She nodded once at me. High praise indeed, coming from Anne.

At nine A.M., three hours past the scheduled end of my shift, I still sat charting in Trauma Room Two. Though she awaited an ICU bed, Lara Maxwell was out of the woods. Her lungs had dried out, and the heart damage appeared to have reversed after the amphetamines and cocaine (their presence confirmed on the lab tests) had cleared from her system.

The nurse had stepped out to restock the carts, leaving me alone in the room with Lara. She lay peacefully on her back. Wires, IV lines, and tubes ran to and from her, but medical gadgetry aside, she now looked like a typical fourteen-year-old. Tall and gangly with budding breasts and a few scattered pimples, she teetered at that awkward stage between childhood and adulthood. But her high cheekbones and full lips guaranteed she was going to mature into a beauty, providing she survived adolescence.

Documenting Lara's rocky drug-induced ride along the brink of death, the frustration welled. Sleep deprived and adrenaline tanks empty, my temper control (shaky at the best of times) failed me. "Fourteen years old!" I snapped at the still-comatose teen. "What the hell were you doing at a rave, Lara?"

I dropped my pen and walked to her bedside. I glanced from the microwave-sized ventilator (that pumped oxygen in and out of her lungs) back to Lara. Staring at her naïve face, I suppressed the urge to shake her. "This the high you were looking for?" My voice rose. "*God damn it, Lara, what were you doing there*?!?"

I turned at the sound of the glass door sliding behind me. Anne stood at the doorway. She eyed me with an expression that questioned my sanity. Her left arm supported a waiflike girl, whose hair was dyed inhumanly red and whose legs swayed precariously.

"Lara?" the girl choked out before her voice dissolved into sobs. She scrambled to the opposite side of the bed, nearly yanking out two IVs and toppling the ventilator in the process. She grabbed Lara's flaccid hand and squeezed it with both of hers.

"Dr. Dafoe, this is Isabelle," Anne said. "Lara's older sister."

Isabelle gaped at me. With tears and mascara streaming down her cheeks, she could have passed for an underaged drag queen. "Doctor . . . ," her voice wavered. "Will my sister be all right?"

I ignored her question. "You're the one who took Lara to that club?"

"It wasn't like that," she sobbed. "Lara wanted to come. I had no idea that—"

"How old are you?"

"Eighteen, but—"

"Not even legal yourself! What possessed you to take your little sister there?"

Isabelle held up her hands, helplessly. "She kept pushing.

She was desperate to get to a rave. If I went with her, I thought it would be safer . . ." She dissolved into tears again.

"Safer? *Safer?!?* She's your own flesh and blood. She just about died because of you. Your own sister!"

Isabelle's head dropped. She buried her face in her sister's gown. "I am so sorry . . ." Her muffled whimper was barely audible.

"Siblings look out for each other, don't they?" I said, but I wasn't talking about Isabelle or Lara anymore. I was remembering my own brother.

Anne had heard enough. She folded her arms over her chest and took two steps farther into the room. "You've made your point, Doctor."

I looked from Anne to Isabelle and then nodded slowly. When I spoke again, my voice was calm. "Lara is going to pull through, Isabelle. But it will take time."

Isabelle looked up at me and sniffed her relief.

"Where are your mom and dad?" I asked.

"They're in New York for the week." She dropped her head in her sister's gown again, and added in a hush: "They left me in charge . . . I was supposed to look after Lara."

I didn't comment. My fury had dissipated. Replaced by guilt. *Who was I, of all people, to criticize anyone for endangering their sibling?* I reached across the bed and laid a hand on Isabelle's vibrating shoulder.

Tina, the young ditsy unit clerk, appeared behind Anne. "Phone call, Dr. D.," she chirped.

"I'm tied up, Tina," I said. "Can you take a message?"

"It's a policewoman. Made it sound kinda urgent."

Anne spoke up. "You go. I'll cover."

I walked over to the central nursing station. As soon as I picked up the receiver, Sergeant Helen Riddell boomed: "Benjamin! Hope I didn't catch you at a bad time? You weren't in the middle of pulling Christmas lights or a model airplane out of someone's rear end." She laughed heartily. "People sit on the darnedest things, huh?"

"No," I sighed. "Just finished screaming at a comatose girl."

"A coma, huh? Well, I'm sure she had it coming." She chuckled again. "Doctors. You're all a mystery to me."

"What's up, Helen?"

"Oh, yeah," she said as if she'd forgotten the purpose of her call. "We're at a murder scene. Wanted your help."

"A poisoning?"

"Who said anything about poisons?"

"Why else would you call me?" As the toxicology consultant to the Seattle Police Department, I only took calls on poisonings.

"You know at least one of the victims."

"What?"

"In the bedroom, where we found both bodies, there's a photo of the female victim standing with an arm around you and your brother."

I was overcome by a sense of déjà vu. My mind flashed to Helen's call of two years earlier. The one regarding my twin brother, Aaron. I sat down in the chair by the desk. "Who?" I asked, but of course, I already knew.

"Male victim not yet identified. His wallet is missing. But the woman? We're pretty sure her name is Emily Jane Kenmore."

I was quiet for a long time, and Helen respected my silence. I cleared my throat. "Why do you need me there?"

"For one, to confirm the woman's ID. Second, you might know our John Doe. And finally, to give us your medical opinion."

"My opinion?" I said in a monotone. "You'll get far more from the CSI team and the forensic pathologist."

"Ever since they got that hit TV series, those CSI guys are insufferable." Helen chuckled. "Besides, maybe you can add something. You see a lot of stabbings, don't you?"

"One or two."

"Can you drop by here on your way home? The address is—"

"I know the address."

After all, I had once lived there, too.